KILL ORDER

Center Point
Large Print

Also by Chris Mullen and available from
Center Point Large Print:

Dead Land

KILL ORDER

CASS CALLAHAN
BOOK TWO

CHRIS MULLEN

CENTER POINT LARGE PRINT
THORNDIKE, MAINE

This Center Point Large Print edition
is published in the year 2025 by arrangement with
Wolfpack Publishing.

Copyright © 2024 by Chris Mullen.

All rights reserved.

This book is a work of fiction.
Any references to historical events, real people or real places are used fictitiously. Other names, characters, places and events are products of the author's imagination, and any resemblance to actual events, places or persons, living or dead, is entirely coincidental.

The text of this Large Print edition is unabridged.
In other aspects, this book may vary
from the original edition.
Printed in the United States of America
on permanent paper sourced using
environmentally responsible foresting methods.
Set in 16-point Times New Roman type.

ISBN: 979-8-89164-636-0

The Library of Congress has cataloged this record
under Library of Congress Control Number: 2025936613

For the Raven in your life and those in mine

KILL ORDER

PROLOGUE

Camargo, Mexico
27.70799° N, 105.18971° W

Carlos Ruiz-Mata walked across the emblazoned courtyard of Casa de los Fuertes, passing through a cobblestone archway, stopping once to admire a statue of Jesús Malverde, a legendary figure in Mexican folklore often regarded as the patron saint of drug traffickers and outlaws. To Mata, he represented much more than that.

Under a sky absent from stars as if a black veil had been pulled taut to purposefully resist heaven's light, the bronze statue stood tall before him, almost lifelike in appearance. Torches illuminated the courtyard. Their flames danced in the subtle breezes and reflected off ancient tree trunks, the white stone masonry of the hacienda, and the luminous cast man before him. He reached out a hand and laid it upon the smooth, polished bronze shoulder of Jesús Malverde, rubbing it as a proud father might when admiring the good deeds of a son, though Mata had never felt the warming touch of such a figure in his lifetime. The frozen stare of Malverde's lifeless eyes and the cold feel of the sculpted metal caused him to react in a more visceral way.

Words rose from deep within him, but once

reaching his lips, fled without making a sound. He lowered his hand, then bowed his head before the bronzed legend. In silence, he stood motionless in reverence before this symbol of defiance and asked for his protection for he knew the risks of what would be asked of him. They were risks of which he was not afraid, but as with every task, there was never a guarantee that he would return alive. He kissed the palm of his hand, then pressed it to the solid chest of *El Santo de los Narcos*.

As quietly as Mata approached the statue, he moved on as if lifted by the warm breeze flowing through the courtyard making not a sound, even as he entered the office of his employer. It was his way and what made him a most sought-after assassin.

Señor de la Droga stood behind his desk. The orange pulse from a Cuban cigar and the squint of his eyes behind the fat roll of tobacco offered no welcome though the unspoken message resounded the importance of his summons. He lowered the cigar and stepped from under the cloud of smoke born of its trailing's, swirling the air as his movements commanded the very space that surrounded him. The sharp combination of earthy and leathery notes, and the herbal undertones wafting freely in the room filled Mata's nose with a rich aroma. His regard for the scent did not go unnoticed.

Señor de la Droga lifted the cigar as if offering a toast. "*Puro Habano.*" He returned it to his lips and puffed, drawing the flavors into his mouth to savor the complexity of such a fine indulgence.

Mata remained reticent, for speaking first would be considered an act of disrespect.

Smoke escaped Señor de la Droga's lips as he curled his face into a baleful smile.

"Carlos Ruiz-Mata, *El Despiadado*. You do not look so ruthless tonight. Come," he said, motioning to chairs set before his desk. "Let me tell you why you are here."

PART 1
Out of Sight

CHAPTER 1

Dust and stone flew from the knobby tires of my Polaris Ranger as the gas pedal pressed ever closer to the floor. I looked over my shoulder, the trailing path behind the UTV camouflaged by rising dust looked like a wave surging of sand and debris, rushing across the desolate terrain. Facing the front again, a lone standing mesquite bush long since dead, its dry, brittle limbs reaching out like skeletal fingers, raced to snatch the Ranger from its path. With a sudden heave of the wheel, life was spared, and limbs went undisturbed, though my heart pounded like the ancient thunderous beat of tribal drums.

"Yeah!"

The simple call of pure excitement when rising to the challenge of deadly consequences, then beating the odds to live and tell the tale, Spencer celebrated the near miss with a sudden skid to a stop.

"Butthole puckered on that one, Dad?" he asked, sporting a wide grin.

I looked at my son, the daredevil, and had not one complaint, save the truth of his statement, though one I would never admit. "So? What do you think?"

"What do I think? I think we've got a lot of ground to cover."

Without waiting for my reply, Spencer revved the engine, unleashing its raw power, and raced off in search of further dominance over whichever path beckoned him. I clung to the ride like a rollercoaster or a bumper car at the fairgrounds during rodeo time in Houston, relishing in my son's unbridled elation with each turn of the wheel and skid of the tires. He was home, and that made me very happy.

With Spencer in command, we raced over the rough acreage of the Callahan Ranch, widely known as the CR. We skirted along the south fence line where neighboring rancher Floyd Huckabee's cattle bearing the Flying H brand grazed, then double-backed and zoomed straight for the cottonwood grove. The sun showed no mercy, beating down on us with relentless intensity, though nothing could disrupt the high-octane adventure we were having. The anomalous outcropping of trees grew from a speck in the distance to a towering mass of inviting shade. I nudged Spencer on the shoulder, then circled one finger in the air and pointed to an opening between the twisting trunks ahead. He nodded, smiled, and poured on the speed.

Like a mockingbird soaring into the safety of its thorny, bush-laden nest, we shot into the heart of the grove. A familiar yank of the wheel and press of the brakes saw us skid safely to a stop under the canopy's embrace. Spencer looked at me and raised his palm in the air, offering a celebratory high-five. There truly is nothing better than that.

"Whew," Spencer yelled, hopping out of the Ranger. "That was intense!"

"You could say that," I agreed.

Spencer walked around to my side of the UTV as I climbed out.

"Glad you took the doors off this thing. Makes it look more suited for the ranch."

"Funny. Sheriff Gilbert said the same thing."

"He ain't wrong. Wonder how it would perform with a few engine mods? Maybe a Trinity Racing exhaust?"

"In your dreams, Spence."

He smiled, then walked around the UTV admiring its strength and performance, making his own secret plans to improve both aspects of what he felt was becoming *his* toy. He knelt to inspect the tires. Using his fingers, he unwedged stones stuck in the knobby crevasses of rubber.

"Here," I said, pulling two bottles of water from a small cooler I had secured in the bed of the Ranger.

He stood and caught the bottle mid-flight, reminding me that his reflexes were ten times better than mine ever were. Had he stayed active in the taekwondo scene, I had every reason to believe he would have been unbeatable. As it was, Spencer's interests fanned far and wide, and competitive training would have limited his ability to spread his proverbial wings. He slugged back the water and walked to the border of the trees, teasing the sun as he stayed hidden within the shade.

"That where you found those guys?"

I walked over and joined him as he gazed out toward the rocky crags and outcroppings that preceded the banks of the Rio Grande.

"Yeah, just over there."

"Can we check it out?"

To Spencer, finding the dead men on the CR was like finding Pecos Bill's buried treasure, more adventure and mystery than a pragmatic understanding of danger and loss of life. But, sometimes the best opportunity to teach is through guided exploration, and who better to lead him through the process than me?

"Sure, let's finish our drinks and drive the Ranger over."

Spencer stared at the rocks like they were the next challenge he was destined to overcome.

"Those mountains, bluffs, whatever you call 'em," he said, pointing. "Those over in Mexico or what?"

"Yep. Mexico," I said, trying to mimic his casual lingo.

Spencer turned and glared at me.

"Stop trying, Dad. You're way too old for that kind of talk?"

"What? That ain't right. I mean, I'm the man, bro!"

I swung my arms out to either side as if ready to grasp him in a giant hug, then froze in a stance better suited for Bill S. Preston, Esquire and Ted Theodore Logan.

Spencer stood, mouth slightly agape, then burst into laughter.

"Man! Do NOT do THAT in front of Mom. She'll disown you for sure?"

"Totally?" I said, stretching the joke further.

Spence smiled as he walked over and put a hand on my shoulder. He shook it gently as if to console me.

"Dad, you'll just never understand."

He walked on leaving me to ponder my age and my certain disconnection from the average Gen Z kid. I found it amusing, but a little sad at the same time. A double tap of the Ranger's horn snapped me out of my philosophical musings. A smile and wave from my boy sitting in wait of his next adventure reminded me that regardless of my age, as long as I was with Spencer, I was young at heart. Totally.

I joined him at the UTV and was preparing to load up, when a distant gunshot echoed across the CR. Since moving out west, I had trained myself to be less reactive to gunfire, but the direction of the sound caused me to stop and consider its precise location. Spencer got out of the Ranger and walked over to stand by me. I could sense his concern as he was not experienced with such things.

"Dad?"

He flinched as a second shot trailed across the CR.

"That sounds like it's . . ."

"Load up, Spence," I said, running around to the driver's side.

A third shot, followed by a fourth, sounded out. Spence jumped in and buckled up.

"Dad, is that coming from the house?"

CHAPTER 2

Raven's lip quivered and her ears rang after the first blast, her whole body in a fit of vibration, teetering within her desire to run and hide, or stand her ground. Her throat felt like sandpaper as she struggled to swallow. A mix of terror and exhilaration welled up from deep within her, spreading dull tingles from her chest to her cheeks as if her torso had fallen asleep. Her palms were sweaty, and her arms felt heavy under the weight of the Ruger EC9S 9mm in her grasp. Fighting through the initial shock of the jarring to her body and soul, she gritted her teeth and prepared for a second shot.

It had been more than three months since she had been the victim of a home invasion back in Houston. The ordeal had happened so fast and yet felt as if it were a long-playing silent movie, set in slow motion where each scene had been staged to draw her ever closer to the brink of danger, only to reveal a possible opportunity for escape. Each terrifying moment, she fought for her life. Each scream and plea, kick and punch only exacerbated her attacker's resolve to dominate her in every nightmarish way imaginable. In the end, it was her will to survive, to fight off the beast of a man that invaded her home. Was it blind luck or divine intervention that led her hand to the attacker's gun, nestled between the belt of his jeans and the warm, sweaty fat of his gut?

As the ringing in her ears began to subside, so did the surfacing terror she had fought so desperately to put behind her, for the last time she had pulled a trigger, she had taken a man's life.

Closing her left eye, she stared down the barrel of the gun she had bought in secret two days ago. While at first she had felt safe on the CR, Cass's new involvement with the South Brewster County Sheriff's Department had kept him away more than she liked, and it looked more like it was becoming a permanent assignment. He had promised to always protect her, but how could he live up to that promise if he were not around? Her latest trip to La Mariposa Mística gave her an idea she had never considered until now.

"Heeyyy!"

Raven smiled at the drawn-out welcome as she entered La Mariposa Mística.

Señora Cruzita Vásquez, owner of her favorite local hermetic boutique, was a new friend and someone Raven felt was a safe person in whom she could confide. Her therapist had helped her work out of a very dark space, but she never felt as sincere of a connection as she did with Señora Vásquez. Some people tell you to search yourself for answers. Others, like Cruzita, tell you *how* it is.

"How you doin' today, girl?"

"Same as always, I guess."

"Nah, you look better than ever. Especially with everything that's been goin' on around town. Your husband's been busssyyy." Cruzita leaned back and shook her head. "You findin' any time for . . ."

"What?" Raven said, surprised, embarrassed at the implication, but felt obliged to provide an update. "We might have, you know . . ."

"Girl, you better tell me," Cruzita said with a curious smile.

". . . found our rhythm."

Cruzita squealed, then embraced Raven in a tight hug.

"I'm sooo happy for you," she said, letting go. "Look here, I have the perfect thing to help keep things moving in the right direction."

She moved swiftly around a series of shelves, disappearing as she bent over to retrieve what she was looking for, then popped up like a cork escaping a fresh bottle of Cabernet Sauvignon. With short, stuttered steps, she raced over to Raven with a glass jar in her hands.

"Smell this."

She removed the lid and held it up to Raven. Raven took the jar and lifted it to her nose.

"Jasmine?"

"The smell of love, girl. It's irresistible. You light that and put on some Enrique Iglesias. Girl, he'll be *comer de la mano*."

Cruzita rubbed her palms together, then opened them and flexed her fingers as if she was squeezing an orange.

Raven grabbed Cuzita's hands and looked around the store. "You're bad."

"What? You think I only sell this stuff? Sometimes you gotta test things out to make sure they work." Cruzita bumped her hip against Raven's. "Come, let's get you squared away."

The store was empty except for the two women. Cruzita walked behind the counter while Raven glanced around. Other than music playing overhead, the store was still. A serene place, but the silence beneath the New Age rhythms made Raven feel uneasy.

"You looking for anything else, or just come by to see me?"

Raven walked to the counter, browsing the shelves of candles and trinkets, the lot of which she had seen a dozen times before.

"No, just wanted to come into town. The house was feeling a little empty today."

She approached the counter and placed both hands on the glass display. Silver charms and brass figures filled the shelves between them. Raven turned and looked around the empty store.

"You ever get creeped out being in here all by yourself?"

"Me, no way."

Raven turned around to see Cruzita reach below the counter and pull a .357 Smith and Wesson from a concealed spot beneath the register. Its polished stainless-steel frame reflected the ambient light, creating an aura of elegance and power.

"You see? Long as I have *mi burrito*, I'm never alone."

She kissed the barrel leaving red lips along its shiny shaft, then replaced the weapon in its hiding place.

Raven stood in awe, both frightened and excited about the subtle meaning of what Cruzita had said. A thought sparked within her, starting small like all flames do, but grew hotter as she stood across from her friend.

"You okay?"

Raven, having drifted into a new, burning idea, shook her head to clear her mind.

"Yup. I'm good," she said, lifting the candle. "I'll have to see how receptive Cass is to this."

Cruzita put the candle in a brown paper bag and leaned forward. "And when you do, I want to know everything."

Jerking the trigger, the Ruger recoiled behind the explosion of fire and projectile, jolting back with force to which Raven was unaccustomed. She rolled her neck and took a deep breath, doing what she felt were appropriate ways to shake away the emotional surge of flashback and stress that clawed at her core.

"You ain't never gonna hit nothin' jerkin' that the way ya are."

Surprised, Raven spun around, gun in hand, the barrel pointing directly at Flint.

"Whoa there, Annie Oakley," Flint said as he jumped out of the line of fire.

Realizing her carelessness with the firearm, she lowered it to her side and gave Flint an apologetic look.

"I'm sorry. I'm just . . . well, I'm . . ."

"In over yer head? Cass never show you how to shoot?"

Flint approached Raven, eyeing the gun the whole way. Inexperience far too often preceded injury when guns were involved.

"No, I'm mean, he did. But I was never really interested."

"Comin' out to the middle a nowhere change yer mind?"

"Something like that."

Flint walked next to Raven and held out his hand.

"Ya mind?"

Raven started to hand the gun to him. Flint braced her arms to keep them from rising, then pulled back. He pursed his lips, then let out a huff mixed of irritation and intrigue.

"Handle first. Never point a gun at someone when yer handin' it over."

Raven froze, then twisted the gun around and handed it grip first, to Flint. He held it in his palm, looking at it as one might a child's toy.

"Cute. Guessin' ya like the color purple?"

"So?" she said, feeling a little embarrassed. "Maybe I do."

Flint laughed and then firmly gripped what he considered a girly weapon in his hand.

"Hell. All right then. It'll stop ya just as any other, I reckon."

He turned and spotted the target Raven had set up. Three bottles stood untouched by her first two attempts, set upon adjacent fence posts that ran from the back edge of the house to open terrain.

"First thing to know, if ya miss yer target, yer likely ta kill a cow or horse an' not even know it. A bullet flies a long way out here so be mindful of what yer shootin'."

Flint gestured at the bottles, then walked a few paces away from Raven, changing the angle of fire.

"Step over here an' you'll see a slight rise of ground in the distance. If'n ya stand an' aim from here, the worst ya can do is lop the head of a prairie dog if ya miss again."

Raven cringed at the thought, forcing a look

of appreciation as she walked toward him.

"You mean *when* I miss again?"

"Ain't no one should be handlin' a gun with a piss poor attitude. Here," he said, returning the gun to her. "Take aim and blow the head off one of them bottles."

Flint stepped aside and watched as Raven held the gun in her hands and raised it before her.

"Hold up. Yer grip is good, but yer stance is way off balance. One wiggle an' ya can kiss yer target goodbye."

"Okay," she said. "Show me."

Flint paused, then looked to the horizon and shook his head.

"Should be Cass ta show ya the rest."

"Cass doesn't know I have the gun. At least not yet, so show me, or get outta the way."

Raven's temper flared a bit more than she would have liked. She saw Flint out of her peripheral vision and regretted speaking in such a way, regardless of the person for which it was intended. Flint, on the other hand, enjoying the bruteness in her voice, raised his opinion of her a notch or two. She had fight in her. He liked that.

"Fine. Face the target."

Flint stepped behind Raven and waited while she positioned herself.

"The first thing ta remember is ta stand with yer feet shoulder-width apart, then square your shoulders toward the target."

Raven moved her feet apart, aligning them with her shoulders as instructed.

"Now, hold the gun like before. Yer grip was good. Just remember ta use both hands. One on the grip, one cupped underneath fer support. When yer ready, extend yer arms in front of ya, bending yer elbows just a bit."

Raven wobbled back and forth as if digging her shoes into the dirt for added measure, then slowly raised the pistol.

"Only way yer ever gonna hit anythin' is to take careful aim. See the sight at the end of the barrel?"

Raven nodded.

"Good. Focus on the sight while centering it with the target. Yer right-handed so use yer right eye."

Flint waited as Raven took aim. Her arms swayed, causing a ripple in her stance. Instinctively, Flint put his right hand on her shoulder and his left hand on her waist to help stabilize her. Raven flinched at first but allowed him to help her in this manner. He stood close. His words filled her ear with warm, gentle tones, and he spoke more softly than she had heard before.

"Take a deep breath, let it out halfway, and hold just before pulling the trigger. When yer ready, gradually press the trigger with your finger. Don't jerk it like before. After the shot is fired, try to keep steady if ya can. That'll help with yer accuracy."

Flint let go of Raven and stepped back to observe. Taking her time, Raven ran through the steps in her mind, found that she was ready, and fired.

The blast echoed, and the shot cut through the air, splintering glass in one harmonious crack, disintegrating the bottle in Raven's deadly sight. Without stopping to contemplate her actions, Raven twisted, and in one fluid motion, took aim and pulled the trigger a second time. Call it what you will, beginner's luck, fate, blind skill, Raven took out another bottle. Glass exploded as the bullet penetrated the ill-fated bottle, sending shards of green glass and the leftover remnants of an unfinished beer spraying into the air.

Raven lowered the gun, thumbed the safety, and turned to face Flint. His face wore a look she could not remember seeing before. A smile.

"Well, goddamn. Blew the shit outta those, didn't ya?"

"Guess I did."

Raven lowered the weapon, inadvertently touching the hot barrel to her thigh, burning her skin through the fabric of her shorts.

"Shit!"

Flint walked over and took the gun from her hands as she hopped around.

"Come on. Got some salve over in the barn. That'll stop the burn an' fix ya right up."

Though Raven had an abundance of balms and creams from La Mariposa Mística, each that had its own healing properties, she did not put up an argument and followed Flint to the barn.

"Here," he said, tossing her a curled-up, well-used tube of lube that looked to be at least fifty years old.

"*VerduraViva*. Um, what's this?"

"Mexican goop. Has Aloe Vera and other stuff in it. Works like a charm. Yer welcome ta finish it off."

Raven glanced back at the tube. She forced a smile, then removed the cap and dabbed a nickel-sized helping onto her palm. Turning away from Flint, she lifted her shorts just enough to uncover her right thigh halfway to her hip. The skin looked raw and was fire engine red where the barrel had burned her. The salve felt slimy, heavy even, in her hand.

Here we go, she thought, and pressed her goopy palm to her leg. The application stung for a moment, then turned cool, tingling like a gentle caress from a summer breeze, leaving a trail of goose bumps in its wake.

"Wow, this stuff really works. I'll have to buy you a new tube."

"Nah, don't think they make it any longer. Somethin' about it the FDA don't like."

Raven glared at Flint, aghast at what he had just said. She lifted her hand to her face wondering if she should race to the house to wipe off what was still clinging to her palm, or freak out because it was too late and the damage was done.

"Don't worry. Ya ain't gonna grow more fingers er get hairy palms," he said, smiling again. "I been usin' it fer years. Ain't nothin' wrong with me."

Raven smirked.

"Oh, I see. Ya think there is somethin' wrong with me?"

Flint stood, his face turning to stone as he looked at Raven.

"No, no, Levi. Er, Mr. Flint. Just Flint. Fuck."

Hearing her ramble sent Flint into a flurry of rumbling laughter loud enough to catch the attention of Tucker, Cass's horse, and earning the displeased hiss of a barn owl perched in a dark spot up in the rafters of the barn. Flint's laughter was contagious, catching Raven off guard, then sending her into a fit of her own. With sore stomachs and dry mouths, and all laughed out, the two came together in the middle of the barn.

"Thank you, Flint."

"Ain't nothin', miss."

She held her hand out to shake. Flint looked at her palm. It was the same hand that she used to lather in the salve and had not yet been wiped clean. He grunted, his lips curling to one side as he took her hand in his grasp. Their friendly gesture was interrupted when the barn door opened.

CHAPTER 3

Tuned into *KINT-FM 93.9*, the cab of the two-door Toyota Hilux hummed with voices as Ana Moreno sang along with the radio as she waited for her turn to cross into El Paso, Texas. Keeping in rhythm with the music, she tapped her fingers on the steering wheel and looked around. A long line of vehicles stretched ahead of her, a colorful tapestry carrying diverse faces and stories, each with their own hopes and dreams, or so she thought. The building warmth and lack of a functional air conditioner might try anyone's patience, but Ana smiled. With the windows down, she felt the caress of a gentle breeze. Mixed within the folds of its cooling spirit, it carried a symphony of languages, blending English and Spanish in a harmonious melody that resonated through the air. This had not been her first jaunt across the border though each time brought about new sights and sounds and possibilities.

Her gaze drifted to the towering Paso del Norte International Bridge, its proud arches spanning the Rio Grande, marking the physical and cultural divide between two nations. The bridge stood as a symbol of connection, uniting people from different backgrounds in pursuit of new opportunities and a better future.

Time seemed to halt as the minutes passed. As traffic became more condensed funneling into the overflowing lanes that preceded the border checkpoint, idling engines from neighboring vehicles added to the heat of the day causing sweat to form across Ana's brow and in the slits of her armpits. Her heart fluttered as she approached the border agents. The car in front of her had license plates that read Minnesota and was waved ahead without even so much as a welcome home.

That was easy, she thought.

Two border agents waited stoically as Ana crept her small truck forward. Her brakes squeaked as she pulled to a stop. One agent walked behind her vehicle while the other approached the open window.

"*Buenos dias*, passport and travel documents please."

She held her breath, presenting her passport with trembling hands, hoping for a smooth passage.

"Name?"

Ana hesitated.

"*Como se llama?*"

"Ana. My name is Ana Moreno."

"Oh, you speak English. Good. State your purpose of travel."

"Um, I'm going to visit my aunt in Lubbock."

Through the dark lenses of his aviator sunglasses, the agent studied her passport, glancing at her time and again. He noticed her black tank top, the long slinky strings that tied it securely in place at both shoulders and the sweat that glistened from her exposed skin. He took his time observing her figure while pretending to verify her legal papers.

"How long do you plan to stay?"

"Only a few days."

The second border agent circled the truck once, then waved over an additional agent and his canine partner, a German Shepherd. At the direction of his partner, the four-legged agent inspected the perimeter of the truck. Ana watched their reflections in the side mirrors as the dog and its handler made their way around one side and then the other.

"Everything okay, Ms. Moreno?"

Ana looked away from the mirror. The agent holding her passport leaned over, coming uncomfortably close to her window, so much so that she could smell the odor emanating from his uniform.

"I do not like dogs."

The canine finished making his rounds and was led into a shaded area of the checkpoint. The border agent occupying her window flashed a disingenuous grin.

"This dog likes you."

Ana knew what he meant but was in no position to challenge his unwanted attempt at distasteful charm. The agent's repulsive demeanor only solidified her disdain for him.

"Miguel."

The agent at Ana's window looked back over his shoulder. He nodded to the voice that called out to him, then turned back to Ana. With reluctance, he pulled his head away from the window. He handed her passport and papers back, but his gaze lingered. Ana looked up at the border agent and saw her reflection in the black of his glasses. She looked small. Vulnerable.

"The truck is clear. Is there a problem with her papers?" the voice sounded out again.

Border Agent Miguel's gaze held an unmistakable tinge of desire. With a huff, he tore his eyes away from Ana.

"No problem."

He glanced toward her again, sliding his glasses down the bridge of his nose to reveal his dark brown eyes, eyes with a message no girl traveling alone would want to hear. Looking upon her, he reluctantly waved his hand before him, signaling she was free to go. As she drove away, relief poured over her, for the longer she remained at the checkpoint, the more opportunity for her and her truck to be unwillingly detained.

The highway through El Paso was just as filled as the roads leading to the border at Ciudad Juárez, but here, she felt free. The wind blew her hair, warming her face and drying the sweat from her skin. As the blacktop rolled on, her purported route took a southerly turn. She bypassed the eastbound exit for US 62, a winding road that crosses the southern corner of New Mexico before reentering the Texas panhandle, eventually running through Lubbock. Now, mileage signs for Sierra Blanca, Van Horn, and distant San Antonio appeared along the shoulder of Interstate 10.

As the miles wore on, the traffic became sparse. With an 85 mph speed limit teasing her adventurous nature, Ana rolled down the highway with the radio on, filling the cab with music from both sides of the border. She brushed away thoughts of why she was headed in this direction, choosing to simply enjoy the solace and anonymity of the open road.

CHAPTER 4

"Mom?"

Flint and Raven turned to see me and Spencer walk in. I looked at the two of them, watched their hands fall between them, and gave Raven a curious gaze.

"We're not interrupting anything, are we?"

"Cass Callahan! No, you are not interrupting anything." Raven crossed her arms over her chest and glared at me. Flint stood next to her, his eyes tightening. The air seemed to be sucked out of the barn leaving a stale scent to linger in the space between us.

"Awkward," Spencer said, smiling.

Raven walked over and gave him a hug. She pulled away but kept an arm wrapped around her son's waist.

"No," she said. "Your dad is just a dumbass."

"Okay. Okay," I said, raising my hands in surrender. "We heard shooting. Sounded close to the house, so we hurried back to see what was up."

I paused, hoping Raven would fill in the blanks, but her silent stare let me know right away that I would have to work for this one. I turned to Flint. His face was still crinkled behind his squinted eyes.

"You shoot some coyotes or something, Flint?"

Flint glanced at Raven, then glanced at the ground before speaking.

"This ain't got nothin' ta do with me."

Perplexed by his response, I turned back to Raven.

"Well, is everything all right?"

Raven sighed, still irritated by my implied assumption about her and Flint.

"Come on, Spencer, run into town with me. Maybe by the time we're back, your dad will come to his senses."

Spencer looked at me and seemed as confused as I was. He shrugged his shoulders, then followed Raven out of the barn, leaving me and Flint by ourselves.

"Mighty fine detective work. Teach you that in police school?"

I swallowed what felt like a mouthful of glass to keep my temper in check. I mustered what calm I could spare, walked past Flint, and leaned on the workbench behind him.

"Ain't yer first day on the CR, but running in here like ya did kinda reminds me of when ya first arrived."

"What's that supposed to mean?"

"It means things ain't always what they seem. Raven burned her leg, and I was givin' her some salve I had out here in the barn."

More questions filled my head.

"Burned? How did that happen?"

"Mishandlin' a gun. Girly little piece if'n ya ask me. But it'll do the trick if ya get in its way."

I stood wondering what gun he was talking about and why Raven would be holding one in the first place. Flint watched as confusion scrambled my thoughts. He grunted, then leaned against the workbench and folded his arms. His face softened as his lips curled back with pleasure-filled satisfaction.

"She ain't told ya she had a gun yet? Maybe before you go off half-cocked, put aside that police thinkin' of yers, and ask her why?"

As much as I wanted to shove Flint's suggestion back in his face, he was right.

"An' the shootin' . . . that was her too. Set up some bottles on the other side of the house. I was in here when the first shot sounded out. Startled the shit outta me. She'd already pulled the trigger a second time before I come up to her."

"She was shooting bottles?"

"An' whatever cattle may have been grazing over in the south plots. Had her change position before firing off the last two."

"She look like she knew what she was doing?"

"Nope."

"You just stood by and watched?"

"Nope. She asked me to show her a few things. Told'er it wasn't my place, but that woman . . ." Flint paused, realizing he might have stepped out of line with the beginning of his last remark. "Er,

Miss Raven, well, she was gonna shoot anyway. She's kinda stubborn if ya ask me. I told her how ta stand and where ta aim. She got so excited about hittin' the targets, she let the barrel brush by her leg. Burned the hell outta her."

I nodded while Flint finished his story.

"That's what led us in here. Offered her some salve I use fer burns an' such. She was shakin' my hand to thank me when you came in. You know the rest."

"Yeah."

Flint turned and began organizing tools for a job he was planning to start, then stopped and looked at me.

"Come to think of it, she left one bottle untouched. Seems like any rancher, or city-beat detective for the matter, oughta be able to take it out in one shot."

I caught Flint's gaze, his challenge poised for my reply. Though I was still frustrated with the way things were, maybe shooting something was just what I needed to regain a bit of focus. And, if I could best Flint in the process, that would be a double win in my book.

"Lead the way," I said, spreading my arms in the direction of the barn door. "Gotta swing by the house and grab my firearm though."

"Nah, get the rifle from the cabinet. You've used it before, so ya can't complain about not bein' familiar with it when I beat ya."

"It's like that?" I asked.

"Yep."

I went to the cabinet and retrieved the Winchester .308. Its weight felt comfortable in my grasp, and I already knew its accuracy, but I still wondered if this rifle was used for more than shooting coyotes out on the CR.

Flint opened the barn door allowing fresh air to swirl inside. It swooped the staleness from the room in a fluster of dancing breezes. The wind was warm, but it smelled refreshing.

As we rounded the corner of the barn, Raven was sitting shotgun in Spencer's Jeep. She gave us both a look of interest and disgust.

"If you're gonna shoot him, Flint, aim for his legs will ya?"

Without missing a beat, Flint nodded.

"Will do, Miss Raven."

I locked eyes with her as Spence backed away from the house. I tried to convey my apologies with a smile, but it came across more like I was confused and needed to take a shit. Flint, witnessing our exchange, looked amused.

"Hold on ta that one. She's got fire in 'er."

"Yes, she does," I agreed. "You ready to be handed your hat?"

Flint gave me a side-eye and grunted. Without reply, he walked to the makeshift gun range Raven had set up. As much as I wanted to blow off some steam, beating him and seeing how good a shot he was weighed on my mind.

We both agreed that the bottle remaining on the fence post was much too close, and a beginner level shot at best to test who was king of the mountain, so we found our targets elsewhere.

"Ya see the rise in terrain beyond the fence? Aim fer the mesquite brush. Call yer limb, and we'll see what ya got."

I raised my palm over my eyes to shield them from the lowering sun and located the doomed bramble.

"Thought you said it was dangerous to shoot out here like this. May hit something unintentionally if you miss."

"I don't miss," Flint replied as he lined up for the first shot.

I bet you don't, I thought.

CHAPTER 5

The bright luster of midday turned to an ever rushing forth of purple and black waves rolling in from the eastern horizon as evening advanced. The flicker of light from distant buildings looked like stars fighting for their spot in the sky. Blue road signs with advertisements for gas, food, and lodging tugged at Ana's desire to get off the road. It had been a long day already, and she was ready to pack it in for the night.

She exited the first chance she got and looked for a convenient, and hopefully inexpensive, place to stay. Not far off the highway, Ana saw what she was looking for. The Van Horn Inn displayed a neon sign that read *vacancy* and was just on the outskirts of town. She pulled in and parked under the overhanging archways just outside the motel office door.

As she got out of the truck, she looked around and noticed that the neon sign's flashing vacancy must have been an understatement. There were only a few cars parked outside the elongated building, but it was still early, and this was not what most travelers would consider a first-choice place to stay.

When Ana walked through the doors of The Van Horn Inn, the stench of old cigarettes filled her nose. A platter of cookie crumbs stood on a display table to the right of the counter while an oscillating fan did its best to send what crumbs remained soaring into the breeze with each pass of the blades. The clerk, a disheveled figure with tired eyes, appeared from a back room and took a seat on a stool behind the counter.

"Looking for a place to stay just the night, miss?"

"Yes, only tonight."

"Traveling by yourself, or are there more of ya outside?"

"It's just me."

The clerk shifted on the stool, looking at her with a curiosity that made Ana want to walk out the door and find a different place to stay. She started to back away from the counter.

"That'll be sixty-five dollars," the man said. "There's breakfast pastries and coffee in the morning."

As uncomfortable as the clerk made her feel, she would not find another place with such a low-priced room. She reached into her pocket and counted out what cash she had on her until she had the correct amount. She pocketed the remainder and placed the sixty-five dollars cash on the counter. The clerk eyed the money, then pocketed the payment instead of depositing it in the register. His gaze continued to linger on Ana.

"You got number eighteen. Bottom floor. Drive

around to the back. You'll see it's on the end facing the highway."

"Thanks," Ana said.

He handed her a key, the touch of his fingers brushing against her palm.

"Check out is 11:00."

As Ana retreated from the counter, she couldn't help but notice the unsettling transformation that overcame the clerk's worn face. His lips stretched into a distorted smile, contorting his features in an unnerving manner. The tiredness etched into his cheeks and the sagging skin beneath his eyes only amplified the sinister impression he emanated. It was as if a glimpse of something dark and unsettling had seeped into his thoughts, leaving an uncomfortable residue. This was the second time today she felt uneasy.

Despite the discomfort that stirred within her, Ana maintained her smile, a facade to mask her true feelings. The clerk's unsettling demeanor served as a stark reminder that appearances could be deceiving, and that danger often lurked in the most unexpected places.

She drove around and parked in front of door number 18 at the edge of the building. The dome light illuminated the interior of the old truck. Ana unloaded her bags and walked to the room. Before unlocking the door, she glanced back toward the motel office and noticed a figure standing just within the shadows of the building.

"What a creep," she muttered to herself.

Without further hesitation, Ana unlocked the door and went inside her room. She found a switch next to the door and flipped it up. The lights on the nightstand turned on. The room had one full-sized bed, an easy chair with a stain running down its middle that looked like a bony spine and an old relic of a TV left over from the 1980s dangerously sitting on a dresser that bowed in the middle under its weight. The walls were bare except for the dark trails of previous water damage, and upon looking in the bathroom, she decided on the spot that taking a shower may cause her to come out dirtier than she already was.

She walked to the middle of the room and placed one of her bags on the bed. She lifted the other onto the chair and slipped off her shoes when there was a knock on the door. She moved slowly to the door and pressed her eye against the peephole. Standing outside was the clerk holding a stack of towels in both hands.

"Brought you some fresh towels and a shampoo. Sorry, I forgot to give them to you when you checked in."

She could see him tilt his head, wondering if he had gotten her attention.

"That's okay," she said through the door. "I don't really need any tonight. Thank you."

Ana continued to look through the peephole, watching the clerk grow agitated.

"They just came out of the dryer. Ain't no extra charge for fresh towels, miss."

This time, Ana remained quiet and listened.

"I could set them on your counter in case you change your mind."

Stepping back from the door, she began to realize that the only way to get rid of him was to let him in to make his delivery. Reluctantly, she walked back toward the door.

"Hold on."

With a click of the lock and a twist of the knob, Ana opened the door just a crack and peered outside. Light from an overhead streetlamp showed a wicked stream of white around the clerk's body, casting darkness across his face as if he were bleeding shadows. The clerk lifted the towels just a bit, acknowledging her, and mustered the same disturbing smile as before.

"I'll just put these on the counter if it pleases you."

Ana did not answer. Instead, she opened the door and stepped to the side allowing the clerk to pass into her room. She followed him halfway to the bathroom when she heard the door close behind her. Whirling around she saw a second man standing in front of the door.

"It would be best if you don't scream," the man said with a deep rattle in his voice.

Ana turned to the clerk who had set the towels down and was staring at her from behind with eyes that looked as if the devil himself was about to cash in on another soul.

"You don't want to do this," she said.

"Oh," he said, almost with a touch of surprise in his voice. "But I do."

Ana lowered her head, then glared at the clerk as she felt the presence of the second man draw near.

Muffled grunts and thuds could be heard just outside room 18, but not one scream found its way past the threshold of the door. A pale moon rose above Interstate 10, its dull glow casting a veritable sheen off the aged paint and metal of Ana's truck and the brass numbers that clung to the merciless motel room door.

CHAPTER 6

Spencer chauffeured Raven on errands around Brewster while she asked him about college and classes, and of course girls, then told him how life on the CR was so different from that back in Houston, but that she was adjusting. He was a good son and truly enjoyed spending time with his mother, even if some of her questions were a little too nosy.

As with every trip into town, a visit to La Mariposa Mística was an essential ritual for Raven. This trip gave her a chance to boast about her son to her friend and shop-owner, Cruzita.

"Oh my god. Look at this man," Cruzita said when Raven introduced them. "I bet the girls are all over this one, huh?"

Cruzita winked at Raven, and the two friends shared a harmless laugh. Spencer endured while Raven told Cruzita all about his college studies and the fun things she had planned for his visit. When Raven saw that she had embarrassed him enough, she gave Cruzita a hug and said they had about a "million things to do" still.

Spencer offered Cruzita his hand.

"It was very nice to meet you."

Cruzita squinted her eyes and pulled her lips to one side. "Oh, nice. He's a gentleman, too,

Raven, my girl. And why didn't you tell me he was so handsome."

Cruzita disregarded his hand.

"We hug around here, Spencer. Bring it in."

Cruzita gave Spencer an uncomfortable squeeze. Raven saw Spencer blush, then swooped in for the rescue.

"Don't get any ideas, Cruzita. He's going back to college in a few days."

Cruzita let go, then hip-bumped Spencer. "Well, he is welcome anytime."

They made two more stops before heading to the Food-Mart, where Raven indulged Spencer with snacks and gorp, ensuring he would have plenty to enjoy during his stay. Spencer insisted that he did not need all the things she placed in their shopping cart, but his protests fell on deaf ears. Raven bought what she pleased, knowing fair well that Spencer would indulge himself once they were home. She relished in the fact that he was not yet old enough to understand that once a woman has her mind set there was very little anyone could do to change it.

Spencer joked that they looked like doomsday preppers as they loaded all the bags into the Jeep before heading for home. Raven chuckled at the thought.

When they were on the road, Spencer asked, "So, you still mad at Dad or what?"

"Nah, but he doesn't have to know that. I'll let

him squirm a little while longer. Sometimes he says things before his brain tells him not to."

"It's a guy thing, Mom."

"I know, and you'll never grow out of it. Just make sure you know the five magic words that will help to begin making things better when you screw up."

"What can I buy you?" Spencer said with a smile.

"No goofball! Two phrases. The first is *I'm sorry*. The second is . . ."

"I love you?"

"Close, but not quite. It's a simple phrase and always true."

Spencer slowed to a stop waiting for a red light. He glanced at his mother as she had yet to finish what she was saying.

"Well?"

"You were right."

"About what?"

"No. That's the second phrase. *You. Were. Right.*"

Spencer laughed, not entirely convinced.

"I don't know about that one."

"You will," Raven replied. "You will."

Raven took his hand and squeezed, proud of the young man next to her and thankful he was home for a visit. This was his second year in college, and she missed him every day, especially now that he was so much farther away.

"How about some ice cream before we get home?"

"I'm not a kid anymore, Mom."

"Alright, that's fine," Raven replied, pretending to be put off.

"But," Spencer added, adopting the tone of a needy eight-year-old, "I mean, if you want some, where should we go?"

The sun was setting as they pulled into the parking lot of Spencer's all-time favorite, Dairy Queen, where the soft serve cones were gigantic and the chocolate dipping so rich it was like eating ice cream and a candy bar at the same time.

"Let's go in," Raven suggested.

Spencer parked the Jeep, and they both hopped out. He followed Raven to the door, holding it open for her as she passed through. Walking to the counter, Spencer discovered a new reason to come by the local DQ for treats while he was in town.

"Howdy y'all. Do ya know what ya want?"

Raven glanced at Spencer when he failed to order, then smiled when she saw he had fallen into the trap she had laid out weeks ago.

Standing opposite them in her DQ uniform with rolling locks of blonde hair brushing the tops of her shoulders and eyes bluer than the waters off the coast of Grand Cayman was the most beautiful girl Spencer had ever seen. He gazed upon the young lady waiting to take their order.

"What would ya like?" she asked, her voice melodically calling to him with a distinctive yet subtle, West Texas drawl.

Raven nudged Spencer in the ribs, breaking him from the spell under which he had fallen. He knew what he wanted, but something so sweet was not on the menu.

"Uh, Dip cone and, uh, a tea sweet, please?"

The girl behind the counter giggled.

"Tea sweet?"

Spencer could feel his knees weaken as a rush of blood surged to his face, engulfing him in a sea of embarrassment. In that fleeting moment, he gathered his courage and owned up to his slip of the lip.

"Yep, one tea sweet," he said, glancing at her nametag. "Thank you, Charlotte."

Charlotte's cheeks rose, revealing two delicately placed dimples at the corners of her smile.

"Alrighty. And for you, ma'am?"

"I'll take a plain vanilla cone."

Charlotte rang up their orders. As Raven pulled her wallet from her purse, Spencer caught her arm.

"My treat, Mom," he said, still swirling in an endearing gaze.

Charlotte's smile melted into an empathetic mix of affection and tenderness.

"Aren't you the sweetest?"

55

Wisely choosing not to answer, Spencer smiled and took the receipt Charlotte held before him. Raven turned, biting her lip to keep her from throwing what could be seen as ice water on the small fire building right before her eyes, and slowly walked to a table by the window. She took a seat and saw that Spencer was still standing at the counter like a puppy in a pet shop display. Charlotte smiled courteously, though Raven could see through her just like she could Spencer, and that, for the moment, made her happy.

Charlotte broke the tension by handing an empty cup to Spencer and pointed out where the self-serve drinks were located. Parting as if they might not ever see one another again, he kept eyes on her as he backed away and stumbled into a chair behind him. The screech of its legs across the tile floor was worse than fingernails on a chalkboard, but it made Charlotte laugh. She quickly turned, forcing herself back to work while doing her best to regain some composure.

Spencer's cheeks flushed, and he bobbled the empty cup in the air when he lost his balance. Raven enjoyed the sideshow as Spencer fought to keep the cup from landing on the floor. After four juggling attempts, he snatched it out of the air, locked eyes with Raven, then raised both hands high as if he had just scored a winning touchdown. In a cool, no-frills transition from hero to regular Joe, Spencer spun on one foot and headed over to fill his cup.

He joined Raven at their table and caught her wearing a mischievous grin.

"What?"

"Oh, nothing. Looks to me like you might be in for something sweeter than ice cream if you play your cards right."

"Mom!" Spencer said, his voice a forceful whisper that carried a mix of embarrassment and amusement.

"I'm just sayin'. She's cute, and you're available, and . . ."

"And what happens if she's not available?"

Raven pursed her lips and did not answer. Instead, she kicked Spencer's shin under the table, causing him to jump in his seat. Luckily for him, it was a perfectly timed distraction.

"Here ya go," Charlotte said as she delivered their treats to the table.

She handed Raven her cone first, then she turned her attention to Spencer. "If ya see anything else ya want, I'll just be over there." She handed him his dipped cone and pointed to the counter.

Spencer's mouth gaped open but was too captured in her gaze to respond. Raven spoke up when Spencer failed to answer.

"Thank you, sweetheart."

Charlotte shared a smile with Raven. "Y'all enjoy."

Spencer watched as Charlotte walked away until she disappeared behind the counter.

"Close your mouth before your tongue falls out," Raven said. She reached over and tapped him on the head.

"Hey."

Spencer faced his mother, who was quick to lick her cone before adding to his embarrassment with any further commentary. Spencer squinted at her and took a large bite of chocolate.

They enjoyed their cones uninterrupted, though Spencer ate too quickly and suffered through two bouts of brain freeze in the process.

"You are your father's son." Raven laughed.

When their cones were consumed and Raven was ready to return home, she glanced at her phone and saw that she had two missed calls.

"Your dad is probably wondering where we are. Throw out our trash, and I'll meet you at the Jeep?"

"Sure."

Spencer cleared the table, then walked to the drink station and refilled his sweet tea. Charlotte stood at the counter and waved at Raven, then turned to see Spencer walking toward her. Nervous tingles in her stomach surprised her. She did not even know this boy, but something deep inside urged her to learn more. Spencer had similar feelings, though his were more confused and excited than rational at this point. He placed his palms on the counter and looked Charlotte in the eyes.

The front door closed leaving the two kids alone inside while Raven called home. Leaning on the Jeep, she held the phone to her ear with anticipation, eager to share what was happening.

"*Hell-o.*"

"Cass, you're not going to believe what is going on inside Dairy Queen right now," Raven said as excited as a teenager dishing the goods on her best friend.

She stood and talked, oblivious to the rusted Camaro that had pulled in the last parking spot in front of the glass windows. Music blared from the radio, but even that did not distract her from explaining the details of their Dairy Queen experience.

A boy dressed in Black Sabbath T-shirt, blue jeans with oil smudges along both thighs, and well-worn work boots stepped out of the car and stepped up to the glass windows that looked into the restaurant. He placed one hand over his eyebrows to deflect the glare from the final rays of the setting sun, feeling the heat from the day's final moments warm the back of his neck while a hot surge of jealousy welled up inside of him.

"Who the hell is she talking to?"

CHAPTER 7

A single candle flickered, casting shadows on the walls that embodied malevolent spirits eager to ensnare unsuspecting souls in eternal darkness. In the center of the small room, Carlos Ruiz-Mata, known as El Despiadado, sat with closed eyes, his hands resting on his knees. His breaths were shallow, steady, purposeful, as if he probed the depths of his soul. The air around him felt cool yet beads of sweat glistened on his shirtless form.

Tattoos adorned each of his arms, a testament to his tumultuous journey through life. Skulls with blades emerging from lifeless sockets surrounded his right shoulder, a constant reminder of the violence that trailed him like a shadow. A black scorpion with dagger-like claws clung to his wrist, its body coiling up his forearm, transforming into a woman's torso with flowing hair concealing her breasts behind a menacing Toledana sword. Behind the topless demon, small gravestones littered the background, bearing the haunting inscription "a menos que"—unless. Tiny crosses etched within the scales on the underside of the scorpion symbolized the lives he had taken.

Baring his chest, one striking image of the

Virgin Mary, forever scarred over his heart, evoked a sense of remorse and longing for redemption. From her eyes, she wept, mirroring the tears he had shed for his sins. Each inked masterpiece etched into his skin held the weight of his past, a past that shadowed his every step, never allowing him to escape.

Carlos Ruiz-Mata kept vigil into the night, his silence an act of reverence and penance. Tomorrow, with the rising sun, his journey would reach its pivotal moment. But before facing his external demons, he had to confront the one question that gnawed at his conscience, a question kept secret from the world—can he be forgiven?

CHAPTER 8

The sun dared to kiss the horizon, bumping into the rising peaks on its descent as it lowered itself closer to its perpetual dance with twilight. I watched, mesmerized with the transformation. Its fiery embrace with the distant mountains painted the sky in hues of crimson and gold. The world seemed to hold its breath, caught in the fleeting moment of transition between day and night. A sense of mystery hung in the air, as if the sun's descent held a secret it was reluctant to reveal. A secret much like that which Raven had been keeping.

   In the waning light, I knelt to remove the shattered pieces of glass strewn across the ground that surrounded Raven's not-so-secret target practice from earlier in the day. One by one, I collected fragments of broken bottles as if I were working a crime scene, noting the size and shape of each piece before placing it into a brown paper bag in wait of further analysis. As I removed the remains of Raven's victims, I contemplated the only question that seemed to matter: why? Why did she feel the need to hide this from me? Why did I fail to recognize her rising discomfort? Her sensitivity and tolerance of weapons had always been at arm's length. She knew they were a part of my job, so why the sudden change of heart?

I removed the last piece I could find and stood up, returning my gaze toward the outstretched lands of the CR. The Gateway to Paradise, aptly named for its beauty, and, in the same breath, signified its open embrace of opportunity, set out before me, slowly succumbing to growing shadows of night. Turning back toward the house, I noticed a disturbance along the road leading to the entrance of the CR.

Dust swirled in the air, leaving a brilliant trail, reflecting the last light of day like a spinning kaleidoscope, signaling a coming visitor or perhaps the return of Raven and Spencer from their jaunt into town. I watched until I saw the familiar red of Spencer's Jeep come into view. A hint of calm washed away the wonder of who else it might have been. As I walked to meet them, I prepared my apology speech for Raven. However, I was interrupted by a rugged vibration coming from my front pocket. I slipped my fingers in and pulled out my cell phone. Expecting it to be Raven calling to tell me they were home, I answered the call and pressed the phone to my ear.

"Little Bird, I am so sorry for . . ."

"Hey, amigo. What have you done this time?"

"Shit! Chance? I . . . never mind. What's up?"

"Remember how you always say, 'guys like us are never off duty?'"

I glanced to the drive and watched as Spencer's Jeep drove under the archway at the entrance to the ranch. "Yeah."

"I could use you now. Got a situation developing near Panther Creek."

Spencer's Jeep slowed to a stop in front of the house. I could see Raven through the passenger window. She was looking at Spencer, her head bobbing as if she were excited about something. During her call earlier, she had mentioned that Spencer had met a girl, but my mind had been elsewhere. *Another thing I'll have to answer for later,* I thought.

I picked up the pace, bypassing meeting up with them, and leaped to the porch. I darted into the house and was out again before the door had fully closed. With keys to the Explorer in one hand and my badge and gun in the other, I left the door ajar for Raven and Spencer. I hopped off the porch in time to see Raven stepping out of the Jeep.

"Gotta run, Rave. I'll be back soon."

"Where you headed, Dad?" Spencer said, his head popping above the Jeep as he stood on the driver's side running board.

"Helpin' out Chance. That's all."

"Can I come?"

"Not this time."

Raven looked at me. I could tell she was worried, but it was more than that. She seemed agitated, like I was doing something wrong or without her blessing. I stopped before entering the Explorer to look into her eyes.

"I love you, Little Bird."

"You, too," she replied, her lips pressing together as if the words had been forced.

I pressed the ignition button, and the Explorer roared to life. As I pulled away from the house, the headlights sent a stream of artificial light across the dwindling ambiance of twilight that was setting in over the CR. Before driving away, I saw Raven and Spencer unloading bags from the back of his Jeep and wondered if I was making a mistake. Truth be told, I was. Time was precious, and Spencer would only be here for a few days. Why was it that I felt so compelled to be a part of something else when I knew my leaving would take time away from what mattered most to me? Family. I had every right to stop and pull back to the house, but Chance had become family, too.

I set aside the tug-of-war in my head and pressed the accelerator. The gravel crunched under my wheels, and the cattle guard sent momentary harsh vibrations throughout the car as I left the CR en route to back up Chance.

As I pulled onto the blacktop of RR170, I flipped a switch on the police lights I had suctioned to the front window, activating the strobe, and raced south toward Panther Creek. As I sped along, the rise and fall of landscape and roadway, and the red and blue lights illuminating the dark around me helped suppress my feelings about being at home. Tonight would be but a tiny blip in the grand scheme of things. Although I felt that I never took time for granted, this was a necessary obligation to serve South Brewster County and answer the call of a friend when my help was needed.

I reached for my cell and secured it against the magnetic phone mount affixed to the dash, then placed a call to Chance. The phone automatically connected to the car via Bluetooth. A buzz sounded out over the car speakers, followed by Chance's voice.

"Sheriff Gilbert."

"It's Cass. I'm five minutes from the scene. What do we have?"

"Got a semi-truck tryin' to do a Michael Phelps into the creek. Trouble is, someone is still in the cab an' is refusing to come out."

"ID the truck yet?"

"In the works. We'll know soon enough. If yer runnin' lights, cut 'em. You'll see the spotlights as ya approach the north end of the bridge at the creek."

"Ten-four."

When the line disconnected, my thoughts exploded with the possibilities of what the situation held. The numbers on the Explorer's speedometer clicked higher as my focus homed in on the darkening road that led to Panther Creek.

The road wound itself around, hugging the path of the Rio Grande and the border between Texas and Mexico, rising to one final crest before revealing my destination.

With twilight blending into the black inky cloak of night, the bridge over Panther Creek was illuminated like a high school football stadium on Friday night. Beams from three county vehicles converged on the semi. Red and blue strobes flashed atop another car a hundred yards south of the bridge to stop oncoming traffic, though I was unsure if it was ours, DPS, or Border Patrol. This stretch of road was lightly traveled after dark, but the roadblock was necessary to keep our investigation safe and any potential cars at a distance until we could establish a controlled perimeter.

As I approached from the north, I had an unobstructed view of the scene. It looked as if the driver had missed the bridge altogether, running off the road, then swerving to the right before taking the plunge. The semi's front wheels and most of the hood were submerged in the creek. Water rose over the driver's side door but did not reach the window.

The trailer was still attached to its couplings behind the cab. By some miracle, it had not rolled into the water, though it leaned as if it was considering its options. It was plain white, except where a vandal had tagged it with bubble letters that read, R-O-W-D-Y, and had an old rust stain that began near a dip in the center of the roof that cut a diagonal streak to the rear corner of the cargo hold. This was a derelict of an eighteen-wheeler if I ever saw one, which caused my suspicions to rise.

I doubt you're haulin' furniture, and you sure aren't an Amazon truck, I thought. *Where were you headed, and what ya got holed up back there, buddy?*

I slowed down and pulled into the oncoming lane, then farther to the shoulder, and parked behind Sheriff Gilbert's Bronco. I sat a moment before stepping into the warm night air. The A/C cooled the interior of the Explorer in a furious attempt to combat the outside temperatures. Even now, with fall not too far off, West Texas felt like a sauna.

I looked out the window but felt a compulsion to close my eyes. It was a resurging feeling I had not experienced since my rookie days as a detective in Houston, and just as similar when I was first deployed in Iraq during the war. Back then, each new case or mission was a maelstrom of chaos and uncertainty. The rules were different, the stakes impossibly high.

Now, as I looked at the half-submerged eighteen-wheeler, those old instincts kicked in, sharpened by years of experience and survival. This was a different battlefield, but the game was the same: a puzzle to be solved, a hidden danger lurking just out of sight. The sense of anticipation was familiar, but it was tempered by wisdom, by lessons hard-earned. In that moment, the past and present converged.

A dry, burning odor lingered in the air as if the hairs on my forearms had been scorched by fire and the smell had become trapped in my nose. Dull glows pulsed at different points across the horizon, the sky drawn pitch black by smoke rising from flames in the distant oil fields in Iraq. Above me, a foreign cluster of stars brought about the one beauty from this place that I chose to set before all others. Though strange to my eyes, it brought with it a familiarity in which I felt connected to home, to family, even though I was half a world away.

I was part of a joint operation team working with Iraqi security, targeting insurgent strongholds and seeking to dismantle the underground networks that were wreaking havoc. The mission that night was a routine one, at least on the surface. Intelligence had flagged a pair of houses in the Al-Doura district, close to

Camp Victory, the US Army base. Recent satellite imagery had shown movement, a flicker of life in an area that was supposed to be vacant. The houses were suspected of being used as a staging area for insurgents, possibly even a cache for weapons or bomb-making materials.

The night air was thick with tension as we approached our target. My heart pounded in my chest. My hands were slick with sweat. I was part of Lieutenant Tucker's squad, and we were led by the experienced and battle-scarred Sergeant Murphy.

"Callahan!" Sergeant Murphy's voice cut through the darkness, a commanding whisper that sent a chill down my spine. "You've got instincts. I need you on point with me."

I nodded, feeling a weight settle on my shoulders. "The briefing was clear, Sarge. This is more than just a routine check."

Lieutenant Tucker's eyes met mine, intense and probing. "Those houses are hiding something, Private, and we need to find out what. We have specific orders to investigate, neutralize if necessary, and secure any intelligence. Stay frosty."

We moved forward like phantoms, the moonless night swallowing us whole. I could feel the eyes of my fellow soldiers on me, trust and expectation mingling with a shared sense of foreboding.

"Callahan, if anything feels off, you sing out. Understand?"

"Understood, Sarge," I whispered back, a knot of unease growing in my stomach.

The first house loomed in front of us, a dark silhouette against the even darker sky. We breached the entrance with flawless precision. The building was empty, but the lingering scent of food and the stacks of recently fired Kalashnikov rounds told a tale of recent occupation.

I felt a chill down my spine, my instincts on high alert. "Sarge, something's not right here."

Murphy's eyes narrowed, his voice barely above a whisper. "I feel it, too."

We moved on to the second house, the sense of enigma hanging in the air, following my every footstep. My instincts were screaming that something was lurking just out of sight.

CHAPTER 9

Out of sight!

As certain as a painful jolt of electricity running through skin and bone when crossed wires yields hard lessons learned, I knew, or at least thought I knew, what we were facing.

I stepped out of the Explorer and saw Sheriff Gilbert standing at a perimeter set up at the north corner of the bridge overlooking the rig. He stood with Deputy Javier Santos and Deputy Diego Leo. Deputy Leo noticed me first.

"Special Investigator Callahan. Come to join our fishing party?"

"Something like that."

I stopped next to Sheriff Gilbert and acknowledged the men with a nod.

"Any sign of the driver?"

"Not yet," Deputy Santos said. "We've seen some movement, but that's about it."

"What about the truck? We get any intel back on it yet?"

Sheriff Gilbert pulled a notepad from his shirt pocket and handed it to me. I read his notes aloud.

"Plates originate in Monterrey, Mexico. Truck belongs to a transport company named Transportes Estrella del Sur Manuel Jiménez.

Operations Manager claims the truck was headed to San Antonio with half a load of mechanical supplies shipped by Mecánica Velázquez S.A. de C.V.; Solo driver: Eduardo Velasquez."

I handed the notepad back to Chance.

"You have a plan to see if it's Eduardo moving around in the cab?"

Chance looked at me, smiled wide enough to show teeth, and placed a hand on my shoulder.

"Why do you think I called? I'm sendin' you over for a look, amigo."

Some days, the best defense to being the butt of another person's joke is to fire back with an answer they may not have been expecting.

"Okay," I said. "Santos, you're with me."

Santos straightened, then looked at Sheriff Gilbert as if he were hoping to be rescued from the assignment. I stepped two paces away before Chance called me back.

"Come on, Cass. Can't head over there blind. Until we know who we're dealing with, the plan is to wait him out."

"That sounds good and all, but what if he needs medical treatment? What if there are others?"

"Others?" Deputy Leo asked, his voice rising with a questioning look.

"I'm sure that it doesn't take an East Texan to assume there might be more than cargo in the back of that truck?"

"True," Sheriff Gilbert said. "But ain't much

to assume as the doors broke their hinges and swung open before it came to rest where ya see it. We got a clear view from the south side of the bridge into the trailer. It's empty."

I looked at the rig, at the cab, then traced my eyes along the edges of the trailer.

"Still, waiting this guy out may take longer than any of us likes. If you'll allow it, I'll head over for a closer look."

Chance looked me dead in the eye.

"You didn't call me out here for the fun of it. Let's get to the bottom of this," I said.

"You ain't got nothin' to prove out here, Cass."

"No, but my gut is telling me to go."

Without another word, Chance nodded his approval. I knew he understood the feeling, the unspoken instinct that something was amiss. I had earned his trust in the past. He was man enough to accept that just because he felt one way, didn't mean it was the right way.

"Be careful, Cass," he warned, his voice low and serious.

"I will. Plus, my volunteer here will cover my back." I slapped Deputy Leo on the shoulder. "You're on me."

I stepped past Deputy Leo and headed for the sloping embankment that led down to the banks of the creek at the base of the bridge.

"Hey, don't you want to cross the bridge first?" Leo asked before following.

I continued down the slope, sliding with the small stones and sand, letting my answer rise with one resounding word. "Nope."

I waited for Deputy Leo at the base of the bridge. He stumbled down the slope like a goose slipping along the top of a frozen pond. For his sake, the element of surprise was not a top priority. When he made it to the bottom, I headed along the water's edge on the opposite bank in relation to the truck.

Steam continued to filter out from under the hood though the engine had been cut off for some time. The driver's side front tire was shredded as was one of the rear tires. The two main tires on the rear of the trailer were flat but did not undergo the same carnage as the others. One headlight shot its beam into the water, but all the semi's running lights were out. The windows were rolled up, which by assumption, meant it was getting hot inside the cab.

Proceeding ahead with Deputy Leo three steps behind, covering me, I angled my position to get a direct view of the driver's side window.

"See anything?" Leo whispered.

"Not yet. Wait."

A hint of a shadow moved from front to back as if waving in long drawn-out strokes.

"Stay here. I'm heading over."

Before Leo could object, I was knee-deep in the water, on my way toward the large truck. As

I waded through the warm, playful current, the truck seemed to grow right before my eyes. The soft ripple of the creek mixed with the hissing sound of the dying engine to form the oddest melody of sounds I had ever heard, and yet, there was a melodic harmony between the two. I focused on the mixed arrangement, absorbing it fully. This heightened my awareness of changes within the mechanical and natural blend, which in turn would reveal the precise direction of any new sounds I might chance to hear.

Water rose to my waist as I came close to the front of the rig. Beyond the gentle tinkle of water and hiss of steam, a muffled groan sounded out from inside the cab. I looked back to Leo and flashed a series of hand signals. By the looks on his face, he understood.

"Hello in the rig," I called out.

No answer.

"This is Special Investigator Cass Callahan of the South Brewster County Sheriff's Office. If you're injured and need assistance, please respond, or make a noise. Help is here."

With eyes glued to the window, I watched and listened for anything that might be a signal for help. Seconds passed. I looked back at Deputy Leo. He shrugged his shoulders, then jumped as I did when a single thud sounded out as if a blunt object had unsuccessfully tried to break through the window.

I whirled around, water splashing up to my waist from my quick motion. In the distance, I heard the faint whistle of a siren and wondered if that was the ambulance from Brewster Regional on its way out. A low, guttural groan grumbled from inside. It was the moan of an injured human but sounded similar to that of a distressed and dying cow.

"I'm coming up to help you. Are there any weapons in the vehicle?"

No answer.

Laying my hands on the side of the truck for balance, I turned to Deputy Leo once again.

"When this door opens, make sure you're ready."

Deputy Leo positioned himself and raised his firearm to cover me when I opened the driver's side door. I glanced up at Chance. He watched with intent while Deputy Santos ran across the bridge and advanced on the rear of the trailer.

Another, more deliberate groan rattled out of the cab. I faced the door, reached for the handle, and pulled. As gentle as the trickling water in Panther Creek was, it defied my efforts when I tried to open the partially submerged door. The weight and flow of the creek, though limited, was strong enough to make my actions slower than I had intended, throwing off my timing to peer into the cab of the truck. That slight delay saved my life.

With a savage cry, the driver thrust his arm forward to where my head would have been holding a semi-automatic pistol and opened fire. I threw myself back toward the front of the truck, plunging into the creek to escape the flurry of aimless bullets. Water rushed into my nostrils, forcing me to swallow that which drained into my throat. I quickly emerged from the water, coughing and spitting, and scampered to shore to hide behind the stump of a fallen willow tree. More shots were fired, but now, instead of trickling water and the dying hiss from the engine, a distinctive plink of metal and crack of glass rocked the truck as it absorbed its own barrage of bullets.

I pulled my weapon but did not have a chance to return fire. There was no need. The gunman's body slumped into view, his dead weight falling through the narrow opening of the door. The creek caught the body with a dull splash.

"Hold!" I yelled. "Hold your fire!"

I looked at Deputy Leo, still crouched and aiming at the truck. His face was a mask of concentration, but a slight tremor in his hands betrayed his nerves, manifesting in the wavering of his gun.

"You good?" I yelled at Leo.

He stood without answering, keeping his aim on the truck.

"Leo!"

"I'm good," he replied, a mix of adrenaline and fear adding to the tension in his voice.

"On your left," Santos announced.

I turned to see him appear next to the front right corner of the truck's bumper.

"See anything from there?" I called out.

Santos disappeared, but his voice let out a resounding, "All clear!"

I stepped into the water and sloshed over to the bobbing body. Amid the spotlights' white illumination, a chilling red filled the warm water around the man's torso. Strings of blood drifted downstream as if they had been freed from captivity and were left to dance and play and glide as they saw fit. The macabre beauty of the sight struck me, a vivid contrast to the violence that had just occurred.

I reached down and rolled him over in the water. His eyes glared at me with a terrorizing, eternal confusion, a haunting mix of frightened realization and disregard for the consequences earned.

"Damn," I whispered.

I reached down and grabbed his collar, then dragged him through the shallow waters to shore near the blown rear tires of the semi. The moist slopes of the creek bank made it easy to slide him to shore. I let go of him and leaned against the exterior wall of the sleeper cabin. Deputy Santos joined me.

"You okay?" he asked.

"Yeah. Just a little wet." I reached into my pocket and let an exasperated sigh escape as I pulled out my cell phone. A rainbow of color already showed across the screen, and water dripped like a leaky faucet from the base. "Shit!"

CHAPTER 10

"Dad's phone keeps going to voicemail. When do you think he'll be back?"

"No telling," Raven said. "Why the urgency to know?"

"Well . . ." Spencer set down his phone on the kitchen table and fingered a few pretzels from a bowl in front of him. "I was thinking about running into town for a bit. You know, just drive around."

Raven sat across from him and helped herself to a handful of pretzels as well. A sly smile crept from the edge of her mouth. "You sure you only want to *drive* around? Maybe, by chance, roll by a certain Texas favorite restaurant to see if a certain young lady is . . ."

"Mom!" Spencer tried to cover his embarrassed smile by acting tough, a tactic Cass had used many times early in his relationship with Raven, but she was not fooled. It would take more than a sour face and a furrowed brow to pull one over on her.

"I'm just sayin'." Raven paused, allowing her smile to grow. "She is cute, except."

"Except, what?"

"Well, there was that boy that huffed in right after you came out. He looked kinda like he might have had his eye on her already."

"I didn't see that."

"How could you? You were all starry eyes and puppy-like when you finally came out. Kinda like how you look at some of those Aggie girls in their boots and short skirts."

"Oh, god!"

Spencer scooted his chair away from the table and stood up.

"Don't be angry, Spence. Or embarrassed. She was cute. And . . ." Raven paused again, this time for dramatic effect. She rolled her eyes away from Spencer as if she had something to hide, leaving him hanging on without further explanation.

"Well? Mom?"

Raven calmly stood up and walked to the sink, ignoring his impatience and loving it at the same time. She began to fiddle with items around the sink—twisting the soap dispenser just so, nudging the cleaning brush in its holder, moving dirty dishes from one side of the sink to the other.

"You're killin' me, Smalls!" he yelled out, showing his true colors as a sheepish grin surged across his face.

Raven turned around and leaned against the sink. She looked at the young man in front of her with visions of the little boy she wished she could travel back in time to see, if only for a moment. Pride swelled within her, for even if she were able to turn back time, she would not, for the last thing Raven was, was selfish. Spencer had grown up, albeit too fast, but that's life.

With a sigh, Raven walked over to Spencer and brushed the hair away from his forehead. Spencer took his mother's hands in his as if they were eggshells and he wore padded gloves.

"I think you may have lit a spark in her, too." Raven pulled her hands free of his and wrapped them around his wide shoulders. "Don't be out too late, okay?"

Love, or even the prospect of love, has a way of making even the manliest man act like a goof once the notion changes from dream to possibility. Spencer was no different. He squeezed Raven once, then bolted for the front door, grabbing his keys along the way and yelling over his shoulder, "I won't. Love ya, Mom."

As the door clacked behind him, Raven mouthed the words, *Love you, too, kiddo*. Her eyes filling with emotion only a mother could know.

CHAPTER 11

The wail of the ambulance siren chirped off as it pulled across the bridge, its red and blue strobes swirling from the thick of night across the white palette of spotlights aimed at the semi. Its endless revolution pulsed as if we were at a rave, yet there were no reckless celebrations here. Sheriff Gilbert made his way across the bridge and down the slope. His shoulder-mounted radio announced the play-by-play between dispatch and the ambulance driver, static squelching once after each transmission. I sensed the irritation in Chance as I watched him swat at the radio like he was chasing a pesky fly. We met at the rear of the trailer.

"Didn't expect things to go down like that," I said.

Chance, more Sheriff Gilbert now than solid friend and drinking buddy, placed his hands on his hips and pinched his lips to one side of his face. He leaned to look past me, nodding at Deputy Leo who was leaning over the dead driver and would-be assailant taking notes. He straightened his stance and dropped his arms to his side before speaking.

"What am I supposed to tell Raven when you go and get yer head blown off, Cass?" He turned to look at the EMTs struggling with a gurney down the incline from the road to the base of the bridge. "Coulda been you they are comin' for."

"What do you want me to say, Chance?"

"Nothin'. But your gut feeling affected more than just the man in the driver's seat tonight. He won't own up to it, but Diego Leo never fired his gun on anyone before."

I turned, catching a glance from Deputy Leo. Whether he was contemplating what to write next in his notes or watching Chance and I converse I did not know, but the look in his eyes painted a picture of a man who had been handed a weight greater than any he had been made to carry until now. He raised his chin, a subtle nod acknowledging me, but his face was absent of emotion. I returned the gesture.

"Think I was wrong? Think we should have waited him out like you were planning?" I said, still looking at Leo.

"Doesn't matter now. What matters is we've got to wrap things up and move forward."

"All right," I said, turning back to face Chance. "You said the trailer was empty, but we have a driver who would rather die in a suicide-by-cop situation than be hauled in and questioned. He's got to be hiding something."

Without waiting for a reply, I walked past Chance to the rear of the trailer. The left cargo door hung open, dangling on bent hinges toward the creek. The other remained closed. I pulled the locking pin from its latch and pulled the right door open until it rested against the side of the trailer, then affixed the locking mechanism on the hinge so it would not close unexpectedly. Chance ambled over and watched as I climbed in. It smelled, but not like I expected. If this were the type of truck to transport mechanical supplies and equipment, why did it smell more like a cattle car?

"See?" Chance said behind me. "Empty."

I walked to the front of the trailer, the wood floorboards jostling under my footsteps. I looked back along the cargo hold. Only a lone tarp and a few dead cockroaches were between me and the rear opening of the trailer.

"Damn it!" I yelled as I kicked the side of the trailer.

A loud metallic thud reverberated throughout the enclosure. Frustrated, I took one step toward the back of the trailer when I heard a low, muffled sound as if someone were speaking to me underwater. I froze, closed my eyes and centered my senses around this mysterious noise.

"¿*Qué pasa*?"

"You have a flashlight?"

"Yeah."

"Give it to me."

Chance pulled a small Maglite from his belt. I walked over and took it from him, then began walking back into the heart of the trailer. I turned it on and concentrated the beam along the floor.

"Cass?"

I ignored Chance and stopped when I reached the spot where I had kicked the trailer wall.

"Listen," I said, then kicked the metal wall again.

This time, more than one sound revealed itself. Low, frightened sounding whimpers rose from the floor. With a long, sweeping motion, I searched the interior until I saw a knothole in the wood. Sticking out of that small opening was the tip of a finger.

"Chance! Get in here!"

I stepped over to the knothole and shone the light to where I had seen the finger. It disappeared into the small hole like a frightened groundhog. Chance scrambled into the trailer and hurried to join me. Under our feet, hidden beneath the floor, desperate words reached out to us.

"*Por favor.*"

"Someone's under the floor," Chance said. "Quick, let's see if we can pry it up."

I ran the flashlight's beam along the floor of the trailer, carefully examining the gaps between the pressed boards. Each was nailed securely in place. I knelt and tried digging my fingers into between the boards, but they would not budge.

"We're gonna need a crowbar, screwdriver, something to wedge between the slats to help dislodge the nails. We get one up, the rest will be easier to remove."

Chance jogged to the trailer opening just as the EMTs were passing by with the gurney.

"Hey! Emilo, right? You have a crowbar in the rig?" I heard him ask.

"Sure. Bring it to you after we handle the . . ."

"The body can wait. We have a more serious situation inside here. If you have two, bring 'em both."

A new voice spoke out. "What's the trouble?"

"Just grab the damn tools and get back here as quick as ya can."

Chance turned his back on the EMTs and rejoined me over the knothole. More muffled sounds rose from beneath the dusty wood-slatted floor. Most filtered through in a deep, sad tone, but one called out to me above all others.

"Papá!"

As shrill and clear as a child's voice could sound, a young wail cut through the floor with enough fright to make my teeth hurt. Chance and I froze, then shared a horrified glance. Determined to find the child first, I dropped to my knees and crawled across the floor, stopping over where I thought the child was hidden, and spoke.

"It's okay. You're okay. We're gonna get you out."

Chance went to check on the EMTs and their

progress with the tools. Keeping his frustrations in check, he reached for his shoulder-mounted radio and pressed the PTT (Push-to-Talk) button.

"Santos, Leo, meet at the semi's trailer doors. ASAP."

The urgency in Chance's voice resonated through the radio, the order carrying a weight that left no room for questions. Moments later, Santos and Leo appeared at the rear of the trailer.

"We need blankets, water, everything. Move!" Chance barked orders, and the men set into action.

Still on the floor, I continued to comfort the hidden child, my voice gentle but strained. "Hang on. Help is on the way. Can you tell me your name?"

A whimper was the only response, followed by a hushed murmur in Spanish. I cursed my limited language skills but continued my soothing reassurances.

The EMTs arrived, crowbars in hand, their faces ashen with anticipation. Chance grabbed one of the tools and tossed the other to me.

"Let's make this quick."

With determination and grim resolve, we wedged the crowbars between the tight wooden slats, the tools biting into the compressed fibers. Our combined strength and the leverage of the crowbars caused the boards to groan and creak, the nails screeching as they were forced from their moorings.

One board sprang free, then another. The child's cries grew more frantic, and I could hear other voices, now sounding less muffled as the flooring was pulled away—men and women, their tones fearful and pleading.

"It's okay," I said, more to myself than to them. "We're almost there."

Working together, we were able to peel back a small section of the flooring. The dank, stifling space beneath was filled with frightened eyes, all looking up at us with a mixture of hope and terror. Men and women were lying flat on their backs, smashed together like sardines in a can, and the child whose cry was so gut-wrenching, was pressed tightly against a mother's bosom.

"*Papá!*" the child cried again, this time reaching for me. The heartbreak in that single word nearly buckled my knees.

I extended my hand, my heart aching. "I've got you."

Chance was already radioing for additional support, his voice steady but tinged with anger. "We need more units out here. Notify DPS and Border Patrol. We've got multiple individuals concealed in the trailer. Possible human trafficking situation. Relay request for additional medical assistance from Brewster Regional."

I continued to work on prying up the floorboards, each one revealing more terrified faces. The smell of sweat, fear, and human waste was overwhelming, but there was no stopping. Not now. Not with those desperate eyes looking up at us. Santos, Leo, and the EMTs set up a staging area at the rear of the truck and began assisting the overwhelmed victims.

As we worked, the sound of sirens grew closer, and soon other officers and emergency personnel were on the scene. They arrived with tools, blankets, and medical equipment, initiating a coordinated effort to provide care for the freed individuals and those still trapped inside.

One by one, we pulled them from the cramped spaces fabricated beneath the false flooring of the trailer, each face telling a story of hardship and desperation. Some were too weak to walk and had to be carried. Others clung to each other, tears streaming down their faces.

The gravity of the discovery hidden within the underbelly of the truck settled over all of us like a dark cloud. The driver's desperate actions, the empty trailer, the smell all made sickening sense.

When the last of the floorboards were removed and the final person was helped out of their hiding place, I walked to the edge of the trailer and looked out. The scene before me was a cluster of flashing lights, officers, and emergency personnel working with individuals in all matters of recovery.

Sheriff Gilbert was everywhere, his face etched with concern and determination. He ensured that the victims were treated with dignity, taking care to liaise with Immigration and Customs Enforcement (ICE) and human trafficking units. He was on his phone, securing additional resources and speaking with other jurisdictions. Amid the chaos, he took time to talk with the victims, offering reassurance and directing them to available support services.

With the last of the hidden victims brought to safety, a strange quiet settled over me. The urgency of the rescue had been replaced by a numb realization of what we had uncovered. I turned away from the scene and found myself drawn to the lifeless body of the driver—a bitter taste building in my mouth.

I hopped out of the trailer and inhaled a deep breath of fresh air. Warm as it was, it smelled better than the stifling confines I had been working in since the discovery. My muscles ached, and my mind was still reeling from what we had found.

I walked to where the truck driver lay covered by a black medical tarp. Kneeling next to his body, I pulled the tarp away, uncovering only his face. His caramel color had drained and his skin sloughed over his cheeks. A portion of his left ear was missing, not because of the gun battle earlier, but from a past accident or perhaps a punishment.

The black hairs on his chin were crusted in a mix of dirt and spattered blood.

"You son of a bitch, you got off easy. Rot in hell, Eduardo."

CHAPTER 12

"This is Heavy Eyes," country music by Luke Bryan, filled the interior of Spencer's Jeep and sailed out his open windows as if inviting the evening air to dance with the tunes as he drove to town. The off-road tire treads hummed along as they sped over the pavement, the rhythmic vibrations adding a visceral feeling throughout Spencer's body. Anticipation grew in his stomach like a herd of angry butterflies as he sang along with the radio, "When I'm old, I will recall all the nights we spent outlaws." His smile grew and his foot pushed heavier on the accelerator. He had one thing on his mind, and it was sweeter than any dairy treat on the menu at the local DQ.

The lights from Brewster that littered the horizon with an ambient glow turned crisper the closer he came to town. To Spencer, the brilliance of business signage and streetlights standing guard overnight were all a blur except the one with a bright red ellipse and white lettering.

Opting first for a casual drive-by, a reconnaissance of sorts, Spencer slowed his Jeep and lowered the volume of his radio. He pulled into the parking lot of the Drop and Pick Thrift Store, performed a tight U-turn and stopped at the entrance to gaze across the street.

Except for an old Camaro and a beat-up Ford truck, the Dairy Queen parking lot was empty. Lights flickered around the perimeter, causing shadows to appear and disappear like tricksters playing late-night hide-and-seek.

"Come on, Spence," he said to himself. "Now is not the time to puss out."

Swallowing once, Spencer pulled across the street and parked in a spot to the left of the main door to the restaurant. The large pane-glass windows offered an unobstructed view of everything going on inside. With the time nearing eleven o'clock, closing time, Spencer could see Charlotte wiping down the countertops as her lone coworker mopped the floor outside the entrance to the restrooms. One booth along the outer wall was occupied, but Spencer was too consumed with Charlotte to care about anyone else.

He turned off the ignition, glanced in the rearview mirror long enough to check his hair and his teeth, and stepped out of the Jeep. His suave stride brought him to the door with a casual urgency. He pulled the door open and walked directly to the counter.

"We're closing soon," Charlotte said without looking up.

"I know," Spencer replied. "I was hoping you'd still be here."

Charlotte stopped wiping the counter and

looked up. Her cheeks flushing with pink as she looked at Spencer.

"I'm sorry. I was in here earlier today, and . . ."

"With your mom, right?"

It was Spencer's turn to feel the rise of heat in the room.

"Yeah, well. I came by to see if . . ."

"You came back to see if you could find some tail for the weekend, ain't that about right?"

Charlotte's eyes bulged. Spencer turned around to see a young man who looked about his age. He stood next to his booth and sipped on a large drink, a devious smile forming around the straw.

"Lane!" Charlotte said in a voice mixed with embarrassment and anger.

Spencer's gaze at Lane lasted only a moment. He turned away to face Charlotte again and smiled. "Look. I know it's late, and you don't know me, but I was hoping that you might be open to chat for a bit once you're done with work?"

"Chat? That what you city boys like to do back at the country club by the pool? Chat?" Lane tossed his drink cup at a corner trash can, missing the shot, then walked toward the counter. The container fell to the floor and leaked the remnants of cola he had been drinking over the freshly mopped floor. He stopped at the nearest table and rested one leg across the top. Leaning forward, he looked past Spencer. "Thought you might like to go for a drive with me, Charlotte. Old time sake? You know."

"Hard pass," Charlotte replied.

"Come on. Ain't nothing to do in this town except work and sleep and take a shit."

Spencer's eyes caught Charlotte's gaze, pulling her to him. In the same moment, the muscles around Spencer's jaw flexed and his teeth began to grind in his mouth. The butterflies that had been fluttering about inside of him scattered, making immediate room for another side of Spencer to fill the void. It was a piece of his father—inherited, engrained, learned—regardless of its origins, the Callahan Pitbull mentality tugged at the leash that held Spencer's temper under control. In one fluid motion, he spun around and took a step away from the counter, eyes ablaze and muscles on high alert.

"Oh, I bet there is more to do out here than that."

Lane stood up, fingers flexing like he was in a standoff at high noon. By the look on his face, he chewed the interior of his mouth, a subtle nervous tick, but one Spencer picked up on right away.

"There might be. But nothing no chickenshit city boy would have the balls enough to try."

"Lane!" Charlotte yelled again from behind the counter. "Enough!"

"What?" he said, his voice changing to a

guiltless squeal. "We're just havin' a chat."

Lane's face was a blend of false innocence and hidden jealousy. The rage within Spencer was a living thing, clawing and biting at his restraint. He knew he had to keep it caged, or Lane would bear the brunt of its fury.

"Go on home, Lane," Charlotte said, her voice settling but still agitated.

Lane kept eyes on Spencer, then smirked. "Come on, Charlotte. Me and the new guy are just gettin' ta know one another. But . . . you know I'd do anything for my girl." His eyes grew stormy, his glare ever fixed on Spencer.

Charlotte walked around the counter, stopping between Spencer and Lane. "I ain't *your girl* anymore, Lane. Get that through your thick-headed skull. We've been done for a long time."

Lane straightened his posture. Then, tilting his head to one side, he parted his lips as if he were going to reply but stopped mid-thought. His teeth gleamed through the sour slit on his face. He ran a hand over his head, pulling back his hair until it flopped free over his forehead.

"Done," he muttered, bitterness and anger mingling in his voice. He looked at her, his eyes aflame, and spoke with an insistent tone. "Done? Let me tell you one thing, Charlotte. We ain't never gonna be done."

Spencer shifted forward, but stopped when he felt the press of Charlotte's hand on his chest. Her touch sent chills through him, spreading from her palm in all directions, calming his immediate desire to put Lane in his place. The dogs were growling, and he too had teeth he could show, but Charlotte's intervention was enough to tame the beast within him.

"I think it's time you all leave," Charlotte's coworker announced, clutching a mop like a mobster ready for a rumble. An older woman with dangling cheeks and flopping waddles, whose hair grew in salt-and-pepper strands, stepped in with an attitude demanding of attention. Her Dairy Queen uniform made her defiance almost comical, but the look in her eyes and the way she squeezed her fingers around the mop were proof enough that she meant business.

"Darla . . ."

"Don't you worry, hon. I've handled bigger than these two." With a delicate grace that belied her bulky body, Darla twisted the mop handle like it was a baton and aimed the rounded end at Lane's crotch. Standing no taller than five-foot-three, her pear-shaped figure moved with the improbable agility of a bumblebee. Despite her size, she seemed to defy the laws of physics, her movements like a dance that championed over her form with uncanny speed.

"Whoa, Darla!" Lane said, flinching backward.

"Whoa nothin', Lane Jespers. March your hind end out the front door right now, or I'll be draggin' ya out by yer hair while yer cuppin' yer balls like a sling."

Charlotte and Spencer watched Darla take control.

"What about him?" Lane argued.

"He'll be right behind ya, don't you worry 'bout that."

Lane grimaced. He walked to the door but stopped before exiting. "I'll see you around. Both of you."

With a harsh shove of the door, he pushed his way outside. Firing up the engine of his Camaro, he revved the engine and peeled out of the parking lot in a squealing cloud of dust and smoke.

With her weapon-clad mop in hand, Darla turned to focus on Spencer.

"What's yer name, fella?"

"Spencer Callahan."

Darla lowered the mop to the floor, returning it to the duty for which it was made.

"Callahan? You related to the Callahans out at the CR?"

"Yes, ma'am. My parents moved out here a short time ago after my great-uncle Stewart passed away. My dad works for the county."

"That's it," Darla said, her eyes lighting up. "Thought I recognized the name." Her eyes shifted to Charlotte. "I need to run him off, too?"

Charlotte paused long enough for Darla to

tighten her grip on the mop. Her noticeable movement caught both Charlotte and Spencer's attention.

"No. No, Darla. I'll take it from here."

"Okay, darlin'. But if he so much as . . ."

"I won't," Spencer interrupted.

"Good. This one may not be a troublemaker after all," Darla said, giving Charlotte a wink before returning to work.

Charlotte turned and faced Spencer. "But you are a troublemaker, aren't you?"

"Who? Me?" Spencer said, his sarcastic tone followed by a like smile.

"What did you want, anyway?" Charlotte asked.

"It's like I said, I was hoping that you'd like to . . ."

"Chat?" Charlotte said, interrupting him. She smiled wide, her natural beauty beaming from the curve of her cheeks to the sparkle in her eyes.

Spencer smiled back, caught by her interruption, captivated by her playfulness. "Yeah."

"I'll be off in a bit. You can drive me home if you like."

"You betcha," Spencer said.

Charlotte giggled at his reply, then turned and disappeared behind into the kitchen. Spencer felt a surge of heat swarm over him as the angry butterflies returned to violently flutter in his stomach.

You betcha? he mouthed. He shook his head, cursing and laughing at himself as he took a seat at the closest table to the counter he could find, and waited for Charlotte.

CHAPTER 13

The time on the Explorer's digital dashboard clock read 3:30, but it might as well have said, "Cass, it's fucking late." The bright white numbers pulsed with every blink of the colon that separated the hours from the minutes, and I needed a drink. Raven would correct me by suggesting that I "wanted" a drink, but tonight, after everything, it was a necessity.

I was both physically and mentally exhausted, and had it not been for Chance sending me home, I would have remained on the scene with him for the duration. He was just as spent as I, but his capacity to oversee everything kept him working on very little rest. I objected to my leaving, but Chance made it clear that he did not need my help with what he had left to do. "Go home to your family. Go spend time with Spencer, amigo," he had said.

Family. Had I lost focus? Since joining the South Brewster County Sheriff's Department, I had thrown myself into work beyond investigating the murders on the CR. It did not matter the size of the investigations, being on the job felt good. It felt . . . right. I was able to find myself, my place way out in West Texas much like Raven had rediscovered hers. Still, I wondered if I was making a mistake as I made my way back to the CR.

Turning onto the CR highway as Spencer had dubbed the final road that led home, I felt the distinctive rumble of dirt and loose stones under the wheels. My mind drifted in thought, lulled by the familiar churn. By now, everyone would be sound asleep. Everyone except Flint, who seemed to keep the hours of a barn owl.

Halfway down the bumpy road, I noticed a glare appear in my rearview mirror. I glanced at the clock again.

3:47

Who could that be at this hour? I wondered.

I kept an eye on the headlights behind me. When I reached the entrance to the CR, I pulled in, still curious about who else was up at this hour. The clang of the metal cattle guard bars always sounded loud enough to wake the dead, but in the still of night, rang out with the ferocity of ancient swords clashing in battle as the Explorer crossed over them. I slowed my speed and observed the approaching lights, then watched as they turned into the CR.

I pulled to one side of the gravel drive and waited for the vehicle to draw near. With my right hand resting on the butt of my Glock 17, safely housed in a car holster mounted next to my right leg, I rolled down the driver's side window. I felt a jolt of adrenaline surge through me as the headlights disrupted my night vision. With a crunching halt, the car pulled next to the Explorer and stopped.

"Hey, Dad! What are you doing out so late?"

A wave of relief washed over me, and though I could relax, the anticipation had squashed my exhaustion for the moment, further exacerbating my longing for a swig of whiskey or ice-cold long neck. Spencer turned on the dome light in his Jeep so I could see his face. He looked tired, but an overwhelming smile suggested he had a story to tell.

"I should be asking the same of you."

"Oh, man! Let me tell you. I drove into town . . ."

"Hang on. Pull over to the house, and we can talk on the porch. We'll have to keep it down so we don't wake your mother."

Spencer gave me a thumbs up, then turned off the interior light before driving the rest of the way to the house. I followed behind and parked to the right of his Jeep. My body had grown stiff from sitting in the Explorer, and my bones ached as much as my soul for what I had experienced earlier, but there was no better road to recovery than spending time talking with my son, even if it was in the middle of the night.

Spencer plopped into one of the two chairs sitting at the end of the porch. During daylight hours, the view from that spot was endless. Now, in the pitch black of night, the barn just across the yard looked like a bulging shadow, and the land beyond an inky pit waiting to swallow its next victim. I sat down next to Spencer and waited for him to speak.

His chair creaked as he rocked back on its hind feet. I gazed into the nothing, listening to noises carried across the CR on the drifts of breezes that seemed to flow in mindless twirls and gentle bursts. The most distinctive sound of all did not glide across the wilds of the CR but came from Spencer. The front legs of his chair clacked on the ground as he leaned forward and let a satisfying sigh escape his lips.

"Dad, you ever meet someone and think to yourself, 'There's nothing I wouldn't do for them?' "

I turned my head to see Spencer gazing off the porch. I could tell his mind was reeling, and I could almost see the cartoon hearts swirling around his head.

"Yes, I have, Spence. In fact, if you listen carefully, you might hear her snoring away inside."

Spencer bowed his head and laughed.

"Shhh. Let's not wake her."

"Okay. Sorry. It's just . . ."

Spencer paused, his words caught in a vision or wrapped up in trying to think of the best words to describe his experience. Distraction and attraction have a way of muddying the thoughts of even the most celebrated linguist, but I knew what he was trying to say.

"This is the girl mom was telling me about over the phone. The Dairy Queen girl?"

"Yup. Dad, you've been to campus with me before, and you've seen what I've seen, but tonight, it was like nothing I ever could have imagined. This girl is smart and funny and has just a hint of drawl that makes the hairs on my neck stand up when she talks. And she is beautiful, even in her Dairy Queen uniform."

"Does this girl have a name?"

"Charlotte. Charlotte Huckabee."

Thanks to Spencer's love-struck gaze and the limited porch light, he did not see my eyes bulge, though I swallowed a bit of air that caused me to cough aloud.

"You okay?" Spencer asked.

Still coughing, I laid a hand on his shoulder as I fought for a clear flow of air. "Swallowed a bug."

"Gross."

When I gained control, I leaned forward and looked at my son.

"You gonna live?" he asked.

"Yeah. I'm good. So, I'm guessing you've been with her this evening?"

"Mostly. I drove into town to see her, and

we kinda just hit it off. She asked me to drive her home, but we ended up at some overlook. El Lobo Vista? Something like that."

My heart pounded in my chest and the coughing returned. It was my turn to have distracting visions, but not for the same reasons as Spencer. My visions were filled with blood and sharp flashes of light and smelled of terrified sweat and gunpowder. El Lobo Vista was closed off since Ramón had been shot during our meeting there and should still be inaccessible. The investigation into the identity of his shooter was ongoing, and we still had no leads. El Lobo Vista was a crime scene, and my son had no idea.

"Dad?" Spencer poked my arm. "Dad. You keep eating bugs, everyone will want one."

I forced one last cough to clear my throat. "El Lobo Vista is not somewhere you want to be going this late at night. It's a trashy shithole frequented by drifters and who knows who else."

"Well, we were the only ones there. We sat looking at the stars for the longest time and talked. Did you hear me? We *talked*. If I'd have been there with any number of the college girls I've seen, there would not have been as much talking, get me?"

"Oh, I get you, Spence."

Instant memories from my youth washed away the anxiousness I was developing for his being up there, and with a Huckabee. As dangerous a place as El Lobo Vista was, Raven and I had spent our fair share of time hopping fences and trespassing on properties to find some privacy from the world. And we talked much less than Spencer was admitting to having done.

"Just be careful, wherever you go, especially when a girl is with you."

"I always am. It was her idea. At first, it kinda felt like one of those cult movies where one person brings the other to a secluded location, then tries to chop off their head or something."

"But you went anyway?"

Spencer tilted his head and furrowed his brow just enough to show a degree of judgment. "Dad, if you were me and that was Mom, would you have said no?"

When he has a point, he knows how to make it stick.

"How'd you get to be such a smartass?"

"Learned from the best, I guess."

"Planning on seeing her again?"

"Tomorrow afternoon, if that's okay?"

The underlying guilt I felt from leaving the family earlier to join Chance changed to jealousy about Spencer's plans with a girl he just met. As hard as it was to admit, and as proud as I was to think it, he was his father's son.

"Of course. You are a man in charge of his own destiny, Spencer. Do with it what you will but keep in mind that there will be many people you will meet along the way, and the road is a long one to be traveled."

The gleam of white in Spencer's eyes swirled as he rolled them around in his head.

"That's pretty corny advice, Dad."

"But it's true."

Across the yard, a light flicked on inside Flint's tiny house.

"What's he doin' up so late?" Spencer asked.

"Don't you mean early? Flint's about to get to work. Wanna head over and see if he needs a hand?"

"No, I'm good."

"Then let's call it a night. The sun'll be rising in about an hour anyway."

We stood up at the same time. Though brief, it felt like our talk had lasted for hours. Before opening the door, Spencer turned around and wrapped his strong arms around me.

"It's good to be home, Dad."

I absorbed his squeeze and returned one just as tight.

"Love you, son."

We let go and Spencer punched me lightly on the shoulder.

"Love you, too, old man."

"Old man?" I said, sliding one foot back to take a stance we both knew well.

Spencer glanced at my feet, then slid his right

foot back to mirror mine. "Think you can take me?"

"Guess we're about to find out. But if we wake your mother, she'll hand us both our asses."

We remained in our playful standoff a moment longer before erupting in quiet laughter. Wrapping an arm around Spencer's neck, I reached for the door with the other and swung it open.

"Get some rest, Spence."

I let go and followed him inside. The value of a father/son relationship is greater than anything I could have ever imagined. It is the sum of all time, that which is spent together and time wishing the other was near. It is the bumps and bruises, the hard lessons and the a-ha moments, the skinned knees and the damaged egos all wrapped into one wonderful feeling. It is a tough job, watching my son mature and grow, knowing that one day he will be on his own without the need of my protection. I always hoped that when the time came, our relationship would take on a whole new level, and tonight, I think we have started that transition. I was so glad he was here, and that he had called it home, for that was what the CR had become.

PART 2
Canyon Jumpers

CHAPTER 14

An unseasonal chill accompanied the Saturday morning sunrise that cracked the horizon with blazing yellow beams shooting across West Texas. Dry air set in, and though the cool would only last a short while, it gave Ana Moreno the breath of freshness she so desired after such a long and horrible night at The Van Horn Inn.

She sat on the opened tailgate of her pickup, lost in thought. *Maid service won't arrive until after noon; two hundred miles will take around three and a half hours; need to eat and gas the truck; bags are packed and the room is taken care of.* She hopped off the tailgate and closed it with a gentle bang of metal latches interlocking. Running her hand along the old, beat-up exterior, she smiled at the memories she had made with this truck.

As Ana approached the door, regret entered her mind, though a woman like her could not afford such feelings. She twisted the knob, pushed the door open, and stepped inside.

The smell of decay was beginning to overpower the candles she had lit last night. She walked with deliberate steps, avoiding the moist sections of carpet where blood had been spilled. Like a child playing hopscotch, she moved through the room to the sink and mirror that ran along the back wall. In the reflection, Ana saw the pale, outstretched fingers of the motel clerk poking past the sheet at the end of the bed.

Talking to the image in the mirror, Ana frowned and said, "You know it's not polite to point." She turned around and tiptoed over to the bed. The top sheet was soaked in red and wet with death. In one tug of the sheets, she uncovered the clerk, revealing a man who looked to have died from a thousand cuts. Each incision was made with surgical precision and with a blade sharp enough to slice through cloth and skin and muscle beneath. The cuts were deep enough to cause significant damage, but not so that he would have bled out right away. Looking down on him, she continued her postmortem chastising. "And it is a crime to pocket other people's money, but you knew that, too, didn't you?" She leaned over the pale corpse and dug into the front pocket of his pants, pulling out a wad of cash. Being careful to avoid any leftover bodily fluid or bloody puddles pooling on the mattress, she sat down next to him and laid the crumpled bills out before her. "Looks like somebody was keeping more than his fair share." In all, she counted one hundred and ninety-five dollars equaling three rooms worth of the nightly rate. She gathered the money and stood up to slide it into her pocket. "Such a bad boy." She said, giving the clerk's face a gentle slap, before pulling the sheets taut over him far enough to cover the end of his rigid fingers.

Stepping to one side, Ana glanced at a bloody lump, stuffed on the floor between the bed frame and the wall. "You were nothing but an asshole," she said to the mangled body of the second man. She had not bothered to conceal him after their soirée. If she had, what covers would she have used to sleep with through the night? His forehead had been cut to resemble a second mouth, grinning right down to the white of its teeth, except with this smile, it was skull that gave it that freshly brushed look. Both of his eyes had been gouged and shreds of cheek sloughed to one side of his face like freshly sliced flour tortillas. His torso was saturated in blood and innards that had forced their way out of the openings Ana had carved into his stomach.

As she stood over the corpses of her doomed attackers, Ana scoffed. She then looked into the mirror once again and nodded as if acknowledging someone across the room. *These men had brought this upon themselves,* she thought. The reflection mirrored her sentiment, then invited her to come closer.

She returned to the sink, turned on the faucet, and washed her face. When she opened her eyes, she saw herself again. Water dripped from her nose onto the countertop. She had used the last of the towels to clean up and wipe down most of the surfaces in the room and to dry herself after a mediocre but cleansing shower. She had learned from experience that when her knives slice through flesh, blood tended to spray in a variety of directions. The speed with which she dodged and cut, moved and sliced, caused her to feel the warmth of fresh blood on her skin more so now than any other kill she had previously performed.

The regret that she felt upon entering the room was not that life was ripped violently from these men, but that it had happened so fast that she did not have an opportunity to savor the taste and smell and feel of it. Killing, to Ana, was like preparing a gourmet meal, each course offering more than the last, culminating with a fine, sweet dessert and possibly an after-dinner glass of wine. This had been more like hitting the drive-thru at a Taco Bueno—quick service, fast food, and post-consumption guilt. She had no intention of working until she reached her final destination, but the clerk had insisted, even after her warning, that she clock in early.

Wiping her hands on her pant legs, Ana retraced her steps to the door. She picked up her bags that she had repacked and placed on a table by the front window, and without a second thought, walked out of the room and closed the door behind her.

The sun was scaling the sky, brightening the

blue above. At the truck, she opened the passenger door and placed her bags on the seat. With a gentle touch, she closed the door again and walked around to the driver's side door. Before getting in, she threw the keys to the room as far as she could into a bramble of cactus and overgrown grass near the parking lot.

"Mornin'," a voice blurted out.

Startled by the unexpected voice, Ana's heart jumped, and her hand instinctively dropped to her belt, fingertips grazing the hidden spring that concealed her knife. Two locks of black hair dangled before her eyes before she brushed them back behind her ears.

"Oh, darlin'. I didn't mean to frighten you." A plump, older woman dressed in a bright red sundress walked toward her from two doors down. "You walking over for breakfast?"

Straightening her posture, Ana shook her head and twiddled her fingers together, pretending not to understand. She was ready to go but did not want to give the woman any cause to remember her.

"Esta tu gonna eat?" she said, bringing her hands to her mouth to help convey the message.

Ana cringed but smiled politely and shook her head again.

"Well, suit yourself. More for me, I guess. I always make a point to get up early and eat before all the good stuff is taken. You never know what they're serving at places like this, but if it is part of the room cost, I'm eating first."

The woman wobbled away through the parking lot to the main lobby where breakfast was being offered. Ana watched for a moment. Once the woman had disappeared inside, she loaded up and started the truck. Music sounded out in scratchy bursts through the old speakers of the truck. Ana turned the volume down before searching for a station. The first thing she wanted to do was leave this place behind without being noticed.

She drove slowly to the exit, turned on her blinker, and pulled onto the feeder road. In no time, Ana and her tiny truck were on their way, heading south along Highway 90 toward Marfa, Texas. Taped to her dashboard was a torn strip of paper with the coordinates, 29.493664° N, 104.220629° W. Below the numbers was the name of a town, written and circled in black ink. Brewster.

CHAPTER 15

Hot coffee steamed from a pot in the kitchen, beckoning me to refill my cup a third time. My late night turned early morning left me with only a few hours of shut-eye before life on the CR woke up. Raven was kind enough to give me until nine o'clock, but I could tell who she loved more because Spencer was still sound asleep with no signs of even being alive.

Sitting at the kitchen table, Raven eyed me over the brim of her cup as she sipped. I watched her, wondering when the questioning would start. She placed her drink on the table and leaned back in her chair.

"Thought your position with the sheriff's office was temporary."

There it was. No beating around the bush or sugar coating. I knew more than just coffee was brewing this morning.

"Was, except . . ."

"Except you're liking it. Feels like old times, right?"

She had me from the get-go, and she knew it.

"What do you want me to say?"

"It's not what I want you to say, Cass. It's what I want you to remember."

I shifted in my chair, uncomfortable about where our conversation was headed.

"Look." I paused while Raven folded her arms across her chest. She was out for blood this morning. "We came out here for a fresh start. To get away from the city and all the crap we had to go through."

"And look where that got us."

"It gave us a fighting chance. You think I wanted to go back to that life behind a badge? You think I looked for an opening and did what I could to wiggle in? Chance was after me for weeks to join the county." I could feel the tension building behind my eyes. My chest felt warm. I took a deep breath, followed by a sip of coffee. Raven held her mouth crooked as she fixated on me. "Raven, my answer was always no."

"Not always," she replied curtly.

"I made you a promise that I would always protect you. I did what I had to for us. For the CR. Now, you want me to give it all up?"

"Chance is your friend. I'm sure he'll understand."

"I don't understand, Raven. Why the sudden change of heart? What's the real reason? What aren't you telling me?"

That struck a chord. Her eyes welled up. Her cheeks flushed red. I could tell she had things to say, but the emotion of admitting something she might not be able to take back prevented her from blurting it out. Large, beaded tears rolled down her cheeks.

I sat back in my chair, slumping like an ego-damaged teenager, and looked at what remained of my coffee. Brown swirls moved around the rim like tiny thunderstorms building in my hand. Even my morning pick-me-up seemed to sense the pressure building in the room.

I glanced at Raven, my heart aching for upsetting her but feeling just as frustrated that she would ask me to quit.

"I can't walk away. Not right now."

Raven stood up and pounded her hands on the table.

"You're hardly here, Cass. You know what it feels like to be all alone, in the middle of fucking nowhere?"

Her bottom lip quivered, and the tears continued to fall. As we stared at each other, the recent events with Flint and the gun and the shooting range began to make sense. My heart sank.

"That's why you bought the gun, isn't it?"

Raven brought a hand to her mouth, then wiped her nose. I stood up and walked around the table to her. She bowed her head, giving in to her rising emotion. Gentle convulsions began to ripple through her body. I placed my hand on her shoulder, hoping she would not pull away. Instead, she leaned into my chest and wrapped her arms around me.

We stood in the kitchen, embracing one another.

I rested my chin on the top of her head. The warmth of her body mixed with mine, sending a wave of calm through me.

"I'm sorry, Raven."

I felt her chest rise and fall in one lengthy exhale.

"After what you found, you know, the bodies, I haven't felt safe when you aren't here. That's when I got the idea of buying the gun." Raven pulled back and looked into my eyes. Her cheeks streaked with tear trails, her eyes bloodshot red. "I am trying to be tough, but sometimes it gets so overwhelming."

I raised my hands and squeezed her arms just below her shoulders. "You are tough. Always have been." A flicker returned to her eyes and her lips curled just enough for me to feel like she was coming around. "And I saw the remains of those bottles you blew away. None of them stood a chance."

"I was kinda like Dirty Harry," she said, finding her way back to me.

"Yup, just another of a long line of badass Callahans."

"Oh yeah, that's right," she said, enjoying the realization.

"What's right?"

With hair stuck up in all directions and a dried line of drool yet to be washed from his face, Spencer walked into the kitchen right at the end of our scene. Raven had many sides to her. Some she let flow like Niagara Falls, others that she could turn off at a moment's notice, but her most talented trait was becoming that fun-loving mom to Spencer even when she was not at her best. We would revisit this talk another time, but for now, her focus exploded onto her son, both with love and in jest.

"Are ya feeling hungry, punk?"

CHAPTER 16

The sun beat down on Carlos Ruiz-Mata's Range Rover causing wavy visions of heat to rise from its hood that mimicked the same temperature inversion distorting the horizon as he drove across the barren regions of Mexico just south of Highway 257. The SUV's GPS pinged his location, though his destination had yet to appear on the map.

Crossing into the United States through back-channels ensured his anonymity, which was how he preferred to operate: remain in the shadows, then blend in like a chameleon until the operation was complete, be memorable and forgettable at the same time, and when circumstances demanded action, leave no one alive.

The Range Rover growled along the rugged path, its engine a steady hum that merged with the natural sounds of the wilderness. Mata drove with a clear purpose but allowed his mind to drift, taking in the beauty of the desert, a stark contrast to the violence that marked his life. The cacti stood like silent sentinels, the wildlife like fearful targets fleeing, the distant mountains a reminder of the challenges ahead.

As the day wore on, the sun climbed higher, casting a harsh, unrelenting heat that mirrored his own internal fire. Mata's thoughts were a tangle of memories and reflections, a mixture of regret and determination. He knew that he was a product of his choices, a man shaped by circumstance and necessity.

Stopping briefly to eat, he savored the simple meal, each bite a grounding sensation that connected him to the present. The taste of the food, the texture of the bread, the refreshing sip of water—all were reminders of his humanity, fleeting moments that anchored him in a world that often seemed surreal.

Back on the road, the sun's glare was relentless. Mata squinted against the brightness, his eyes ever watchful for signs of danger or unexpected obstacles.

As the afternoon waned, the landscape began to change, the flat desert giving way to more rugged terrain. After miles of silent thought, processing the path ahead, a new pin appeared on the GPS, marking his destination.

Miles from the nearest semblance of civilization, Mata's Range Rover eased to a stop in a secluded ravine. Hidden from prying eyes, this was his designated cover point. He stepped out, the world around him bathed in the warm glow of the sun. The air was thick with the scent of arid earth and a distant tang of blooming desert flowers. To the east, the mountain range where he would make his crossing, loomed before him.

Opening the rear hatch, he retrieved a backpack filled with essentials for the journey ahead. Food, water, a change of clothes, tools for survival. He pulled a second, larger canvas bag from the rear of the Range Rover and unzipped the zipper. Leaning further into the SUV, he lifted a section of flooring to reveal a series of hidden compartments, each holding his most vital tools of trade—a carefully chosen assortment of weapons, each with a specific purpose.

He first unpacked his sniper rifle, a silent witness to his skill, a weapon that allowed him to reach out and touch someone from a distance. It was sleek and precise, an extension of his will.

A second compartment held his handguns, each tucked into custom-fitted holsters. They were reliable and deadly, and his companions in close quarters offered a balance of power and control.

But it was what lay securely hidden in the third compartment that he anticipated unpacking most of all. His knives. They were intimate weapons, each one chosen for its unique characteristics. There was the combat knife, its blade honed to a razor's edge, perfect for quick, decisive strikes. And there was the smaller, concealable blade, designed for stealth and subtlety, spring-loaded for instant attack. Its small figure was a beautiful, but deadly, piece of craftsmanship.

One by one, Mata placed each weapon into the canvas bag but stopped packing when he picked up the combat knife. He removed it from its sheath, admiring its feel. Holding the hilt, he twisted his wrist, catching the sunlight with each rotation. It gleamed, seeming to smile at him, thankful that it had yet again been trusted to fulfill its deadly duties by his side. With great satisfaction, he returned it to the leather sheath, undid his belt, and added the combat weapon to his waist. With a final zip of the canvas bag, his arsenal was packed and ready.

He hefted the weight onto his shoulders and looked to the mountains, their peaks like jagged teeth against the sky. There, he would wait before crossing into the United States under the cloak of night.

As he began his trek, his mind wandered to his past. Once a man of ideals and dreams, he had become a part of a harsh world, a shadow within shadows. The mountain path was a maze of rocks and crags, thorns and venomous creatures poised to strike should he lose focus. It was a landscape as unforgiving as his own soul.

Hours passed in a rhythm of exertion and introspection. Sweat stained his clothes, his breath came in ragged bursts, but his mind remained sharp, alert to every sound and movement.

The terrain grew more challenging, each step an obstacle to overcome. Sharp rocks cut at his hands as he scrambled up steep inclines while loose stones threatened his footing as he navigated narrow ledges, but his skill and resolve endured.

When he reached the crest of a ridge, he paused, looking back at Mexico, his home, a place of contradictions and complexities. Ahead lay the United States, a land of promises and lies. Finding a spot in the shade, he stayed put and sipped water from a canteen, reflecting on where he had come from and where he was headed. Most of all, he waited for night to swallow him before making his descent.

CHAPTER 17

Time with Spencer was a gift these days, but there was no corralling a mustang when it was meant to run free. I stood on the porch with Raven and watched him drive off to meet up with Charlotte. He had been chattering non-stop about her during our late breakfast, and by the look in his eye, he had no intention of hanging around the CR much longer. It was past noon already, and he seemed to have been counting the minutes until he left.

"You remember what it was like when we first met?" I asked, reaching my arm around her shoulders.

"How could I forget? You wouldn't leave me alone." Raven bumped her hip against mine, then twirled out of my grasp to face me head-on. "And . . . I'm glad you didn't."

Rising to her toes, she wrapped her hands around the back of my neck and kissed me once on the cheek. Then, with a caressing trail of her tongue, she moved her mouth over mine and lit an inextinguishable fire in me. I pulled her closer, our bodies pressed together in a passionate smash of love and forgiveness. I could feel the heightened rhythm of her heart beating as we remained locked in our embrace. It was as if we were young again, exploring each other's limits, hoping that neither would stop.

Sensing my arousal, Raven pulled back slightly, then, brushing her cheek against mine, brought her lips to my ear, and whispered something that made more than my eyes bulge. I squeezed her tighter, answering her secret words with the pulse of my body. With a lover's grace, she leaned back and stared deep into my eyes. Hers were like endless pools while mine seemed like the cartoon wolf who had just fallen for the lounge singer in any number of cartoons. Her lips parted, forming a seductive smile. She ran her hands down my chest, stopping at my waist, then tortured my interest further with a subtle, yet powerful raise of her right eyebrow. Hooking her thumb into one of my belt loops, she tugged at me to follow. Without objection from me, I let her lead me into the house.

"Lock the door," she whispered over her shoulder.

The hairs on my arms stood at attention as she released her grasp on my waist. I felt like a dog having his collar removed, a freeing feeling filled with anticipation for what was to happen next. Merging passion and reality was a skill I had never mastered, causing me to fumble with the simple lock.

Raven giggled at my futile attempts to follow

her instructions. "You're better with your hands than that, Cass."

I felt my breath shoot from my lungs, her words heightening the pressure and fueling the fire within me. I glared at the door, shaking the handle and pressing the thumb turn as if I were beating a confession out of it, when at last, the latch gave in and slipped into place with a satisfying *click*.

Feeling a ridiculous sense of winning pleasure, I turned to find Raven standing over a rumple of clothing in the entrance of the hallway. Her smooth, bare skin was more beautiful than ever. With only a sly scrunching of her nose, she turned and walked away, one finger trailing in the air, beckoning me to follow.

CHAPTER 18

Spencer's Jeep slid over the gravel parking lot as he pulled to a stop, heat swelling inside his chest when he saw who was sitting on the benches outside the entrance of the Dairy Queen. He stepped out of the vehicle and was immediately greeted.

"What the fuck are you doing here, East Texas?"

Lane Jespers stood up and walked over to Spencer, his head cocked and jaw locked like he was looking for a fight. Spencer pocketed his keys and walked up to Lane.

"Question you should be asking, is why are you here?"

"Charlotte ain't for you, East Texas."

"Don't you think that's for her to decide, although it was pretty clear what she said last night."

"Last night," Lane huffed, spitting a stream of tobacco juice aside. "We shoulda figured this out then."

"Oh, I'm sorry. You misunderstood me. What I meant to say was when Charlotte and I were out last night, alone. Seems to me it's figured out."

Lane glared at Spencer, his eyes filling with a jealous rage. "I should kick your ass, right here!"

Spencer focused his attention on how Lane was standing, the tone with which he spoke, and the mannerisms that crawled over his face. He could tell two things right away: should Lane throw a punch, it would be a right-handed strike that Spencer could dodge or block without much effort, resulting in a defensive take-down in two skilled moves, but, and this was the more likely of the two, Lane was a fake using a tough guy persona to intimidate others into getting what he wanted. Either way, Spencer knew Lane was not up for the challenge.

"I'm not gonna fight you, Lane."

Lane smiled, his gritty teeth poking through an unshaven lip. "I knew you were a chickenshit."

Spencer had Charlotte on his mind, which was the main cause for his maintaining self-control, but like it or not, those few words began to rile the beast within him.

"That's the second time you've called me that, and you couldn't be further from the truth."

"Well, if it ain't true, prove it."

A small, pale blue Toyota Corolla pulled into the parking lot. Spencer noticed the car approaching over Lane's shoulder and saw Charlotte behind the wheel, a nervous look on her face. "I told you already. I won't fight you."

"I ain't talkin' about fightin'. I know another way, but you ain't gonna wanna do it."

Charlotte pulled to a stop and hopped out

of the car. "I'm ready to go," she called out.

Both boys turned to look at her. Spencer began to walk over when Lane stepped into his path.

"I knew you were a chickenshit."

Spencer glanced at Charlotte. She was so naturally beautiful. The way her blonde hair dangled in places gave both an unkempt, yet desirable look about her. Even as she stood, her discomfort was outlined with a hint of vulnerability that made her even more attractive to Spencer. The problem was not that Lane had called him out, but that he did so in front of her. Spencer pursed his lips at Charlotte, then turned and stepped into Lane so that only the thinnest amount of space separated the two.

"You name your game, and I won't back down. You draw me into a fight, though, I promise you'll be looking for excuses to cover the fact that a guy from East Texas kicked your ass."

"I guess we'll see about that."

Charlotte hurried over and tried to squeeze between them.

"Slow down, darlin'. Me an' East Texas are just becomin' friendly."

She pushed harder, forcing first her arms, followed by the rest of her body between them. With her back to Spencer, she faced Lane, despising him more now than when she broke up with him after high school graduation. The three pressed together like passengers on an overcrowded city bus, two of them uncomfortable with their close proximity, one relishing it. With gentle hands, Charlotte pushed Spencer's stomach, coaxing him to back away.

"Friendly? That what your callin' this?"

Lane smiled, leaning in closer to Charlotte's face.

"Ask him. We're headin' over to *Cañón del Águila Perdida*. Wanna come along? Probably see him cry like a baby though, seein' I'm the only one here who . . ."

"You're crazy, Lost Eagle Canyon is in Mexico," Charlotte interrupted. She pushed harder on Spencer. When the three had separated enough for her to turn around, she faced Spencer, her eyes full of warning.

"Don't do this. What he's suggesting isn't only dangerous, but illegal."

"It ain't illegal," Lane blurted out behind her.

As if her head were on a swivel, she glared back at Lane. "Crossing over the river into Mexico is *illegal,* Lane."

"Mexicans do it. Except we'll be the wetbacks this time."

Disgust boiled in Charlotte. Spencer grabbed her hand and pulled her away. The feel of his fingers wrapping around hers felt as natural as it had when they touched for the first time last night. Her heart fluttered with concern and elation, a confused emotion she had never experienced before. She did not know what it meant, but that was not the issue. She knew if Spencer went with Lane, he would be putting himself at risk, as Lane could not be trusted.

Looking into her eyes, Spencer spoke in a calming voice. "It'll be okay."

"No, it won't. You don't know him."

"I know that if I don't go, he'll never let us hear the end of it."

"Don't give in to him, Spencer."

"I'm not giving in, I'm standing up. For both of us."

Charlotte squinted at Spencer, her demeanor changing its tune right before him. "I don't need you to fight my battles. You go, and you're just as bad as him."

"No, you don't," Spencer said, falling deeper for Charlotte by the moment. "And there's no way I'm like him, but I won't be walked over."

Looking at her, Spencer knew he had won this round, though it was not something he felt proud of doing. He could see the disappointment in her eyes.

"We goin', or what?" Lane spouted with impatience.

Spencer glanced at Lane, then refocused on Charlotte. "I'll call you when I get back."

Charlotte's heart sank. She looked over her shoulder at Lane and had a burning desire to walk right up to him and kick him in the balls.

Nothing would make her feel better. Nothing, except Spencer driving away with her right now. With a defeated sigh, she pulled her hands free of Spencer's and folded her arms across her chest.

"Don't bother," she said, then marched to her car and revved the engine. Her Corolla's front wheels spun and squealed as if they were just as angry at the boys for their foolishness.

Lane walked over to Spencer as Charlotte drove out of sight. "Looks like it's just you and me. We goin' or what?"

"We're goin'."

"Good. I'll drive."

Spencer followed Lane to his beat-up Camaro, beginning to second guess his decision to go. Why on earth did he decide to spend what limited time he had with an asshole when he could have been with someone much more desirable? Regardless of how he felt now, the cards had been dealt, and he had a hand to play.

"Let's get whatever *this* is over with," Spencer said, rolling down the window.

"Oh, we will," Lane said with a devious smile.

With a muscular peel of the tires, the Camaro raced out of the parking lot, leaving Spencer's Jeep to eat its dust.

CHAPTER 19

The ceiling fan over the bed spun at low speed, moving the air around the room just enough to chill the droplets of sweat that had formed a thin sheen of moisture over my body. I watched the blades circle around and around as I savored the afternoon high Raven and I had reached together.

Next to me, her bare body lay on top of the sheets, covered in the same lust-provoked sweat as I. Her skin glistened. Her back rose and fell in gentle movements as she slept on her stomach. The small, blue bird tattoo nestled beneath her tan line fluttered as the muscles in her hips and legs spasmed in gentle, calming ripples. She lay with her cheek on her pillow, facing me, her mouth curled in a dreamy, satisfied smile. She draped one arm over my chest while the other dangled over the edge of the bed.

The house was quiet as was everything else on the CR. It had been a day of revolving emotions and forgiving ecstasy, but I allowed one troubling thought to remain in my mind. Had I become so focused on my new role with the sheriff's office that I lost sight of why we were here in the first place?

I leaned over and kissed Raven's forehead,

lingering long enough to taste the sweat on her brow and feel her warmth radiate over my lips. A rousing moan vibrated within her. With eyes still engaged in sleep, she slid her body closer to mine, curling her left leg over me. The feel of her thigh and the natural scent emanating from her acted like fresh kindling teasing hot coals. I rested my hand just above her knee, stroking her skin with my thumb. Raven moaned again, then nuzzled her face into my shoulder.

"Cass," she whispered, though her words seemed far away as if she were caught in the hazy comfort between sleep and wakefulness. "I love you."

"I love you, too, Little Bird."

Her arm that rested on my chest tensed as she pawed her fingers over me, her nails electrifying my skin with sensual scratches. Anticipating another round of afternoon delight, I shifted my weight toward her. She moved with me, her eyes opening just enough to capture me in her light. It was like dawn breaking the moment the sun crests the horizon.

As I moved in closer, her arms pulled tight around me, and the buzz of my cell phone rattled on the bedside table.

Like any man would do, I ignored the buzz and leaned over Raven. Her eyes popped open, a seeming mix of wonder and frustration. Continuing to ignore both the buzz and her curious look, I closed my eyes and attempted to seal the deal, again.

"You going to answer that?" she whispered just as my lips met hers.

"Nope." I kissed her cheek, moving slowly toward her ear lobe.

"What if it's Spencer?"

"He's a big kid, he'll . . ."

Raven sunk the back of her head into the pillow, interrupting my advances and misplaced reasoning. "What if he needs something? He's only just come out here. What if . . ."

"All right. Okay."

I rolled off Raven and reached blindly for my cell phone. The buzz continued until I pressed the send button and answered the call.

"What's up, Spence?"

"It's not Spence, amigo."

"Chance?"

"Yeah. I've got something you're gonna want to hear."

I looked at Raven. She slid back and sat up, her curiosity turning to concern. I had left her once already this weekend, and I was not about to make the same mistake twice.

"Is it about Spencer?"

"No, nothing like that. I just heard . . ."

"Whatever it is, it can wait. I've got my hands full and am officially pulling myself off duty until Spencer goes back to school."

Hearing my words brought a smile to Raven's face. Turning my attention away from her right now would squash everything we had worked at rebuilding between us this afternoon. And, on top of that, it just felt good to say. "I love you," I mouthed to her. With my cell phone in hand, I leaned forward to give her a kiss.

"Joe Sinclair was stabbed to death this afternoon."

I froze, the words chilling me like a bucket of ice water had been poured over my head. I straightened up and kicked my legs off the side of the bed. "Say again?"

"I just got off the line with the jail administrator. Joe was attacked by an inmate during cell block transfers just after lunch. I'm heading over to talk to them now. Figured you'd want to tag along, but if you're . . ."

"No," I interrupted. "Give me a second." I turned around to face Raven and muted the phone.

"What is it?"

"There's been a murder at the jail."

"What does that have to do with you?"

"It was Joe Sinclair. One of the inmates stabbed him to death. Chance is . . ."

"Go." Raven looked at me with eyes no longer filled with want and desire but understanding. Pulling the sheets over her, she nodded. "You should go. I'll be here when you get back."

"You sure?"

"I'm sure. As much as I hate to admit it, Chance needs you more than I do on this one."

I unmuted the phone and lifted it to my ear.

"I'm on the way. See you in half an hour."

I ended the call and sat with my hands on my knees staring out into the room. It did not make any sense. What reason would anyone have to kill Joe?

The room was silent, except for the wobble of the rotating blades overhead. My life, it seemed, was like that damn ceiling fan, a ceaseless pattern from which there was no escape. It did not matter that Raven and I left Houston to start fresh and rebuild our lives on the CR. We fell into the same revolution of trouble coming around to find us again, only now in a different location. This whole Sinclair mess was supposed to be behind us, but here we were, another dead body on our hands.

I stood up and began to get dressed. Raven wrapped herself in the top sheet and walked around the bed to me.

"I don't have to say it, but I will. Be careful."

"Always, Little Bird."

CHAPTER 20

Waiting for me on the steps of the South Brewster County Jail, shaded by his Stetson and blackened aviators, Chance's body language communicated one thing; he was pissed.

"Sheriff Gilbert," I greeted, noting the tension in his jawline as I approached.

"Cass," he said, lifting his sunglasses to meet my eyes. "Come on, let's get to the bottom of this."

I followed him through the heavy metal doors at the jail's entrance, bypassing the metal detector and into the dimly lit reception area. The space smelled of antiseptic and stale coffee. A correctional officer behind the tempered glass barrier gave me a curt nod, then buzzed us through a secure door, her hand never leaving the computer mouse as she clicked through some report on her screen.

Chance led me down a corridor framed with chipped paint and flickering fluorescent lights. We stopped at a door marked Control Room.

"After you." He gestured.

The room was bathed in the soft glow of monitors displaying real-time footage of the jail. We were greeted by a tall man in a gray suit.

"Afternoon, Sheriff Gilbert."

Chance shook hands and then introduced me.

"Cass Callahan, meet Deputy Warden Mitch James."

We acknowledged each other with a shake, then turned our attention to the wall of screens. A correctional officer sat at the controls watching a feed projected onto a larger screen that was centered among the rest.

"Do we have footage of the incident?" Chance inquired.

"Right here, Sheriff," the officer replied, clicking on a video file.

On the main screen, a group of inmates loitered in a common area. Standing alone to the side was Joe Sinclair, as unassuming as ever. The inmates looked to be interacting calmly with one another. Some played cards while others stood and talked. Without warning, one inmate surged out of the crowd and lunged at Joe. He first punched him in the face, then jabbed at his chest in quick, violent thrusts. It looked like he was holding a pike or a shiv. Inmates near the scene scattered as the commotion ensued. In a matter of moments, Joe's body crumpled to the floor, blood spilling out of his chest from multiple punctures. Guards flooded the scene in seconds. The attacker slipped among the onlooking inmates before being detained and hauled away.

"Play it again," Chance instructed the officer. We watched the clip a second time. "Looks unprovoked."

"That's putting it mildly," I added. "Joe was an asshole, but among these guys, he'd be way over his head to start something with any one of them. What could have set this off?"

"No idea," Deputy Warden James said. "And I wouldn't have pegged López as a killer either."

"Luis López, busted for B&E, aggravated assault, and evading arrest if memory serves me right," Chance said. "Murder would be a big step up for him. Were you able to recover the weapon?"

Deputy Warden James's face soured. "We did not, and no one is talking."

"Let me guess, no one saw anything, right?" My sarcasm was met with an equally sour glance. "Put me in a room with him. He knows the two of you. As for me, I could be anyone."

"We'll go in together, Cass," Chance said. He turned to face the Deputy Warden James. "Where are you holding him?"

"He's in solitary, cell block AA-23. I'll have him brought to interrogation room seven."

We navigated a labyrinth of hallways to the high-security area, a place where the air grew denser, and the sense of freedom became a distant dream. Chance knocked on a metal door, and a voice came over an intercom.

"Hold your IDs up to the camera."

We showed our badges and the door buzzed open. Sitting alone in the sterile confines of the interrogation room was Luis López, his eyes a blend of confusion and defiance. One at a time, we took a seat across from the man who had just killed Joe Sinclair. The fluorescent lights hummed overhead, the walls seemed to close in, and the stainless-steel table between us was cold and unforgiving.

"Why Sinclair?" Chance asked, eyes unyielding.

López smirked, his disconcerting expression chilled the room even further. "I don't need to tell you anything."

"Right now, you're in a world of trouble, Luis. You're not doing yourself any favors by not cooperating," I replied, leaning forward.

López's gaze met mine. He seemed to weigh his options, then chose silence.

"Silence won't help you here," Chance said.

"Ain't my problem no more."

I leaned in further, trying another angle. "Maybe not, but it could help you. If you had a reason, let's hear it."

López locked eyes with me. "And why would that help me?"

"Because you're on the ass end of a murder charge, and Texas has no problem tossing you a life sentence on top of what you are already looking at," Chance said.

"Or a death sentence," I added. "That's not out of the question either."

A flicker of something crossed López's face.

Uncertainty? Doubt? He stared at his handcuffed hands, contemplating. Then, he looked up and shook his head. "I've got nothing to say."

"Isn't there someone out there that's waiting on you? Waiting for you to serve your time and come home? Keep silent, and you'll die in jail, Luis."

"I'm dead either way," López grumbled.

Chance and I shared a look, then he waved at the camera signaling the guard to come in and remove López from the room. As he was escorted to the door, I said one more thing that seemed to rattle him. "If someone put you up to this, is it worth trading your life for theirs?"

Luis López, small-time thug and everyday low-life turned stone-cold killer, flashed a surprised glance at me over his shoulder. His eyes had changed their tune. They looked hollow as if his secret had been discovered, yet he did not say a word. And he did not have to.

"We need to see the visitation logs. If he had contact with someone on the outside, maybe they can shed light on what happened," I said.

Back in the Control Room, we watched footage of the man's recent visits and reviewed logbooks with records of every visitor in the prison for the past month. According to the sign-in sheet, López had three visitors in all for a total of six visits. Every Tuesday, López was visited by the same woman, Esmeralda Garcia-López, presumably his mother. She spent the entire allotted time speaking on the phone with him, and each time left in tears. The two visits he had from a man wearing a suit turned out to be local attorney Danny Guzmán. Those occurred on consecutive Thursdays—the first on September 7, 2023, and the second on September 14, 2023. The footage from today revealed something different. A much younger woman appeared in the video.

"Pause the tape," I said, pointing at the screen. "Who's that?"

"Log reads, Marta Jiménez," Chance replied. "She spent two minutes and thirty-six seconds speaking with López before leaving."

"That's it? Run it back again. See if there is a clean shot of her."

We replayed the footage and discovered that there were no clips that could be pulled for use in a visual identification scan. Puzzled, I replayed the clip a third time. "How is it that we can't find an angle that shows us her face? It's like she knows where the cameras are."

"That's a little Hollywood, don't you think, Cass?"

"Look again, Chance." I followed her movements with my finger along the screen. "See? Each time a new camera angle was shot, she looks down or to the side as if to conceal her identity."

Chance grunted. It was his way of parsing out his thoughts.

"She's as ordinary as anyone, but she is definitely up to something," I said, flipping back to today's logbook entries. "She was here just after two o'clock."

"And long gone by now," Chance added. "Let's talk with Luis again and see if he has had any second thoughts."

We stepped out of the Control Room and were heading for interrogation again when an alarm sounded throughout the jail. A Quick Response Team (QRT) comprised of four guards and one administrator rushed past us closely followed by Deputy Warden James. We joined the pursuit, moving step for step behind them. We passed through the same common area where Joe had been killed to a high-security wing located up one flight of stairs and down a long, windowless hallway. We were buzzed through two checkpoints, the second of which was located at the head of a string of high-security cells. We came to an abrupt halt in front of detention cell 2187. Guards stood in the doorway, a mix of disturbing chatter filtering through the group.

"Step aside," Chance ordered.

The guards moved out of our way, revealing a sight that punched me in the gut. I looked at the floor of the isolation cell. "Son of a bitch."

Luis López's body twitched in sporadic convulsions, a halo of crimson seeping across the cold tile floor from a single, brutal puncture wound in his eye. His mouth hung open in a final, silent scream. The shiv, still lodged in his eye socket, marked the deadly, sudden end to his life's story. With López dead, our last hope of identifying his latest visitor evaporated into the thick air of the South Brewster County Jail.

CHAPTER 21

"This was a mistake," Spencer said to himself. "But there is no going back now."

"Come on, East Texas, afraid of gettin' wet?" In water up to his knees, Lane shuffled his feet away from shore, away from the safety of the United States of America. "We ain't got far ta go. Then we'll know if yer a chickenshit er not."

Spencer looked at the barren terrain across the river: steep cliffs, ragged bluffs, red and brown boulders, and very little vegetation worthy of creating shade. *Cañón del Águila Perdida*, Lost Eagle Canyon, was in Mexico, but other than that, he had no idea where he was being taken. His head told him to turn around, but his pride said, "Fuck Lane Jespers."

He pulled his cell phone from his pocket, noted an eighty-six percent charge, but had no reception bars. The time read, 3:17. Looking forward, he saw Lane closing in on the shore across the Rio Grande. "Let's do this," he said, his voice rising as was his adrenaline.

Walking to the water's edge, Spencer looked up and down the river. The current seemed light. It was murky and the possibility of a run-in with a water moccasin was not out of the question, but if Lane had done it, so could he. He paused a moment longer to remove his shoes and socks. He slid his cell phone into one sock, then wrapped the other around it for added protection. He then placed his bundled cell phone inside one of his shoes and stepped into the water.

A warm sludge spread between his toes, covering his feet in a rapid suction of river water and mud. Step over sloshy step, Spencer maneuvered into deeper water. His wet pants felt heavy. The current pulled at him as if the river itself disapproved of this illegal dare.

Holding his shoes above his head, he pushed forward. Water rose as high as his waist, but that was it. At one point, something under the water brushed past his leg, sending an uncomfortable chill up his spine. He moved ahead at a quicker pace, not waiting around to see if whatever was under the water returned.

Under the hot sun, the warm river water offered a deceptive relief, cooling his body. But as he trudged forward, the weight of his soaked clothing clung to him like a second skin. It was as if the river itself was playing a cruel joke, giving with one hand and taking with the other. For a moment, the duality of his situation struck him; much like this foolhardy dare, every choice had its price.

By the time he reached the shallows on the Mexican side of the river, Lane had already pulled off his boots and was dumping the water out of them. He sat on a large rock, unimpressed with Spencer's forethought to keep his shoes dry.

"Took ya long enough," he said.

"I'm here now," Spencer replied, shooting Lane a glare.

Spencer sat down and wiped each foot with his bare hands. He brushed away most of the dirt and sand, then removed his shirt to dry his feet completely before putting on his socks.

"Fucksake! Need me ta tie yer shoes, or what?"

Spencer ignored Lane. He pulled the bundle of socks and cell phone from his shoe, enjoying the feel of dry cotton in his hands. Taking care not to place his clean sock on the dirt before slipping on his shoe, he dressed one foot before starting on the other. When he finished, he stood up feeling the comfort of soft soles and dry feet beneath him. He slipped his cell phone into his pocket and walked over to Lane.

When Lane stood up, his boots made a sloshing sound.

"That's gonna come back to bite you before long. Bet you wished you'd done like me, huh?" Spencer tapped his dry shoes together. He rarely acted like an ass, but Lane was deserving.

Lane glanced at Spencer's feet. "Whatever. Let's get goin'." He turned and stomped ahead.

Before following Lane, Spencer glanced back at the Rio Grande. All markers of their point of entry were hidden by the landscape, replaced by a sense of unfamiliarity. His thoughts momentarily drifted to the consequences of his actions and the risks he had disregarded. Yet, against his better judgment, he pressed forward.

While the physical crossing had been straightforward, the mental toll was accumulating. What would his parents say if they knew he had willingly ventured into such risky territory? Why had he compromised his principles for a dare? He had always been the voice of reason among his friends, the one they looked up to for making sound decisions.

His rationality screamed caution, arguing for safety and prudence. Yet, in the face of reason, an untamed part of him roared louder. It was as if he had a point to prove, not just to Lane but to himself. And when all of this was over, he hoped that Charlotte would understand.

Moving south along the river's edge, the cliffs began to cast shadows long enough to reach Texas. Lane walked ahead of Spencer; his stride determined to profess dominance. As the river bent into Mexico, Lane stopped and looked up.

"This way, East Texas."

Using his hands like an animal, Lane started up a slope that led to the rocky base of a treacherous-looking cliff, complete with jagged outcroppings, and a sheer drop from the top. Spencer followed, finding better footing than his challenger. Lane saw the ease with which Spencer was following.

For his next few steps, he twisted his feet sending displaced stones sliding down toward Spencer.

"That was a dick move," Spencer said, shuffling his feet and clawing at the slope so he would not get caught in the current of sliding rocks. A shrill laugh fell down on him as Lane twisted his foot one more time.

The slope ended at the base of the cliff. Lane stood upright, then looked at Spencer as he found his way to the top to join him. A crafty smile split Lane's face. "Now we'll see what yer made of," he said.

He stumbled along the wall, slipping once before catching his balance. A sea of loose, chipped stones littered the ground, making it a dangerous path to negotiate. The wall wound its way like the river until, at one point, it folded back on itself creating a gouge in the rock that ran from the base of the cliff to its highest point. Lane slipped into the fold, disappearing.

Spencer followed. The gouge was dark, shaded by its curling formation. It was like the world was slanted and the wave rolled along the face of the cliff. Inside the tube, Spencer looked up to see Lane above him hanging on the edge of the cliff wall. Iron rungs had been pounded into the rock creating a hidden ladder that ran to the top of the cliff.

"It's easy. Even Charlotte climbed this. We used to come here all the time to . . ."

"Shut it, Lane. Get moving or get out of the way."

Lane laughed again, his crafty cackle attempting to chip away at Spencer's resolve. "We can turn back. Alls ya have to do is say, 'I'm a chicken-shit,' though I think we already know that it's true."

Fury roiled inside Spencer. He felt heat radiate from his neck and behind his ears. He had kept his cool this far, so falling into Lane's mental trap would only make things worse. Raising his right hand, he gripped the first rung and pulled himself up. Like linemen climbing an electrical tower, the two rivals ascended the dangerous ladder.

His palms felt the rusted rot of the metal rungs. As each grip led him higher, Spencer found himself plunging deeper and deeper into the worst decision of his life, but he was too stubborn to stop. His heart pounded. His muscles ached from exertion, and his mouth wrought with thirst. As many times as he had been on extreme adventures, he had always been ready for anything. He had known others to suffer severe consequences due to inexperience or lack of planning, but never for a second thought he would find himself unprepared and on the ass end of a dumb idea.

When Lane reached the top, he howled like a wolf. He pulled himself over the edge, and once again, disappeared. Spencer reached the top rung of the ladder and found his face in line with Lane's boots.

"Kiss my feet?" Lane joked.

"Kiss my ass," Spencer replied, climbing to safety on the rocky ridge of the cliff. He stood up and dusted himself off. His palms were sore from blisters that had formed during the climb. "Where are we going from here?"

"You'll see, East Texas."

Lane turned to walk off, but Spencer had had enough of his follow-the-leader games. He reached out and grabbed Lane's arm, spinning him around. Lane thrust his arms to shove back, but Spencer was too quick, stepping out of the way.

"Where are we going, Lane?"

Lane glared at Spencer. His exertion from the climb and rising temper caused his breaths to churn in heavy puffs. His chest swelled and deflated. Sweat dripped over his temples past eyes that seemed to burn with growing rage.

"Put yer hands on me again an' we're gonna see if you can fly."

Eyes locked, the boys stood motionless. When Spencer would not back down, Lane flinched. "The canyon is just over there. Ten-minute walk. Maybe twenty if ya need some beauty rest."

"I feel fine. You're the one sucking wind."

Lane forced himself to breathe slower. Flashing Spencer a scowl, he turned and huffed away.

Spencer could tell that Lane was at his physical breaking point. There was no way for Spencer to know the last time he had made the climb, or the trek to this canyon, but from the way he was slumping his body, and the deep breaths he was taking, Lane was out of shape.

"Come on, East Texas. I'ma put ya in yer place in just a few more minutes."

Spencer felt the burn in his legs but was disciplined enough to overcome the little aches and pains that went along with strenuous activities. He caught up, stopping next to Lane.

The sun was lower in the sky, but the heat still scorched everything it touched. In the distance, a small cluster of storm clouds built upon one another, but it would take a sharp, steady wind pointed in their direction to give them any relief.

Just as Lane had said, they stood looking over a small canyon nestled among the towering cliffs and mountains on which they hiked.

"There," Lane said, pointing. "Lost Eagle Canyon."

Hidden from view, except when looking over the rim of the surrounding terrain, Spencer thought it to be a beautiful sight. Desolate, but full of mystery, which to an explorer/adventurer like him was pure gold.

It looked like a giant animal had scratched the earth, leaving jagged claw marks behind. A darkness filled each. Set within the cliffs and mountains, the sun had little chance of filling every crag and cut in the rock. Spencer could not tell how deep these shadowed areas sank into the canyon, but he wanted to find out.

"How do we get down there?" Spencer asked.

"There's a path that winds its way, but only to the edge of the canyon. But . . ." Lane paused, the crafty look returning to his face. "We ain't going to the base, we're jumping the cliffs."

CHAPTER 22

It was late afternoon, and Raven found herself walking through her makeshift gun range, head to the ground admiring the reflective colors the late afternoon sun made on the splinters of glass leftover from her shooting spree. Her leg ached where she had burned herself, but it was more bothersome than painful. Finding herself alone yet again on the CR, Raven let her mind wander. Though she had told Cass to go, that Chance had needed him more, she would be the first to admit that she had lied point blank to her husband's face.

"But," a voice from inside her said, "It was the right thing to do."

"Right or not, I'm still alone out here," she answered aloud.

"So, what if ya are?" a deeper voice called out behind her. "Just gonna pussyfoot around?"

Raven whirled around to see Flint standing between the house and the barn with his hands on his hips.

"You judging me, Flint?"

"Hell no." Flint dropped his hands and walked toward Raven. "Wanted ta give this back." Reaching into his jeans pocket, Flint produced her Ruger. Holding it in his palm, he smirked.

"What's funny?"

"Oh, nothin'. It's purty, that's all," Flint said, with a rare hint of sarcasm.

It was Raven's turn to place her hands on her hips, a gesture that looked and worked better coming from her. Flint stopped in his tracks. He raised his free hand in front of him in surrender.

"If looks could kill. Maybe we oughtta call this the Purple Demon."

"That's more like it," Raven replied, taking her gun from him.

"I gave it a good cleanin'. All fun aside, that's a good weapon. Can't go wrong with a 9mm."

"A what?" Raven said, looking confused.

Flint leaned his head back and looked to the sky. "Lord, protect me should I ever walk these lands when this poor woman is armed an' alone."

"Stop it," Raven said. Balling her empty hand into a fist, she raised it as a warning for Flint to stop. "The man at the gun store said the same thing. 'Can't go wrong with a nine-something-or-other.' I wasn't sure if he was just trying to make a sale, or what." She gripped the gun in her palm, then turned and aimed it toward the rise Flint had pointed out yesterday. "Obviously, it worked."

"Mind if I give you a piece of advice?"

"Sure."

"You probably already know this, but . . ." Flint paused.

To Raven, it looked like he had lost his train

of thought. The look on his face, while usually rough and demanding, seemed softer behind the stubble.

"But, what?"

Shaking his head as if he were unscrambling his words, he looked at Raven and, in a quieter, more serious voice said, "Don't pull that on anyone unless yer willing ta pull the trigger."

The two stood across from one another, silence and understanding filling the void between them. Flint's words resonated with Raven.

The CR had become her refuge from a life and time that she would much rather leave in the past. She kept her scars hidden, but Raven knew better than anyone how powerful the truth was behind what Flint had said.

"Understood."

Flint gave a brief nod, his expression unreadable. Before turning to walk back toward the barn he asked, "Ya goin' to town today?"

Raven shrugged her shoulders. "No wheels."

"Take mine."

"I couldn't."

"Why? It's just sittin' there. Needs ta run around every once in a while. You'd be doin' me a favor."

"Well," Raven said. "I guess. Otherwise, I'm stuck out here with you."

Her answer caused him to shake his head and laugh once out loud. "I'll bring it around, Ms. Raven."

Flint was a hard ass, set in his ways, and was short tempered when it came to Cass. To Raven, though, there was a connection between them. Not a romantic feeling or taboo urge, but an unspoken acceptance and respect which allowed both of them to lower their defenses when around one another.

Without another word, Flint turned and headed to the garage behind the barn. Before he had taken three steps, Raven called out to him.

"Levi."

He stopped and looked over his shoulder. His eyes squinted in the sun's forceful rays and listened.

"Thank you," Raven said.

"Anytime, Ms. Raven."

A smile emerged from her lips. Flint answered with a nod before walking the rest of the way to the garage.

Raven looked at the gun in her hands, then focused her aim once again on the distant terrain. Beyond the ranch and the borders of the Rio Grande, she noticed darkening clouds rising in the sky. Although she did not hear any thunder, a rumble inside of her made her shudder. She lowered the weapon and walked back to the house feeling more alone now than ever.

Raven took Flint's truck and drove to town, his words echoing in her head, *Don't pull that on anyone unless yer willing ta pull the trigger . . .*

pull the trigger . . . pull the trigger. She wondered why his words held such sway. Did Flint know that she was attacked? Did he know what she had done to save herself? Perhaps it was as simple as him catching a glimpse of emotions she kept locked away.

Her fingers tightened around the steering wheel as the gravel road turned into asphalt, marking her exit from the rustic solitude of the CR. The road unfurled before Raven like an endless reel of uncertainties, each bend and turn prompting a flurry of thoughts that seemed impossible to quiet. Recent events blended with past horrors, and since Cass had returned to work, being alone had caused distant feelings to resurface.

At first, life on the CR had helped her make huge strides with her recovery, though some images and feelings would never truly go away. Neither would the look she saw Gordo make as the bullets ripped through him. Today, with everything that had been going on, she found herself in a lull.

Driving had always calmed her, and she knew a visit to see Cruzita would do her some good. At the very least, she would not be alone.

As she entered the outskirts of Brewster, the Dairy Queen sign came into view, its fluorescent glow a stark contrast against the dimming light of the afternoon. Her eyes zeroed in on Spencer's Jeep, parked near the edge of the building.

"The girl has no idea," she murmured, and for a moment considered pulling in for a closer peek. With the entrance to the parking lot in sight, she dismissed the idea. "I'm turning into my mother," she said to the reflection in the rearview mirror. As she drove on, the thought of Spencer and Charlotte together brought a moment of peace to her restless mind. It was as though that fleeting thought served as an island of normalcy in the stormy sea of her rising emotions.

As she continued driving, her mind returned to her impending visit to La Mariposa Mística. Cruzita had a way of steering lost souls through the mist of their own mysteries, and Raven felt that today, of all days, she needed that guidance more than ever.

Turning the corner, she pulled up in front of the little shop, its windows adorned with symbols and artifacts that beckoned the curious and the troubled alike. Parking the truck, she took a deep breath, her hands lingering on the keys before pulling them out of the ignition. Her finger touched the small feather charm hanging from its keychain, and she felt a slight, almost imperceptible, lift in her spirits.

She exited the truck and walked to the entrance of the shop. She pushed open the door to the sound of tinkling wind chimes announcing her arrival.

"Cruzita, you here?" Raven called out as she

walked inside. The immediate scent of incense and candles filled her nose.

"Raven! Girl, come in, come in," Cruzita welcomed her with a hug. As she pulled back, she held onto Raven. "¿*Que pasa*?"

"What do you mean?"

"You may not be showin' it, but I can sense something is off with you."

"I'm fine. I just . . ." Raven looked up and noticed a young woman standing close by. "I'm sorry. I just barged right in here, didn't I?"

"Don't even think about it," Cruzita said, locking her arm around Raven's. "Let me introduce you two."

Smiling at the woman, she continued. "Raven, I'd like you to meet Alma, she's new to town. Alma, Raven is one of my favorite chicas. She's new in town, too. Sort of. Her husband works for the sheriff's office. He's some kind of . . ." Cruzita looked to Raven for help.

"Busy," Raven said, her emotions beginning to show through. "Always busy these days."

Alma extended a hand, her eyes meeting Raven's for just a moment too long.

"Pleased to meet you," she said.

"You, too," Raven replied, an awkward sense of unease coming over her. Her gut told her that there was more to Alma, but what, she could not pin down.

Cruzita smiled, interjecting her boisterous

personality between them. "Now that you're here, let's get you feeling better."

"What do you have in mind, Cruzita?"

"I have just the thing. Follow me." Cruzita walked down one of the aisles toward the back of the store. "You, too, Alma."

Raven and Alma shared a glance and smile, then moved to see what Cruzita was up to.

"I've set up a new spread of tarot cards," she began. "Maybe they'll give you some guidance."

Raven bit her bottom lip, not wanting to participate, but not wanting to be impolite either. "I don't know," she said.

"It'll be fun. The cards are like our private messengers from the universe. Listen to them or not, it's your choice, but they have helped me a time or two," Cruzita said, sitting down at the table.

Raven and Alma sat down and Cruzita began shuffling. After a moment, she motioned for Raven to cut the deck. One by one, she laid out the reading.

"The Hermit," Cruzita said, pointing to the first card.

Alma leaned in with interest. "Solitude can be a healing balm, can't it?"

"Indeed," Cruzita replied, her eyes moving quickly between the card and Alma. "The Hermit seeks wisdom through isolation but also cautions us about becoming too secluded."

Thinking of the CR, Raven felt a resonance with the interpretation.

Next, Cruzita unveiled the second card. "The Wheel of Fortune," she declared. "This represents the ups and downs of life, the cycles we all go through."

Alma smirked. "The wheel spins, and we're all just hanging on for the ride, aren't we?"

Cruzita looked at Alma with a puzzled expression but continued, "Exactly. Life is full of surprises, both good and bad."

Pulling the last card, Cruzita hesitated before revealing it to everyone.

Anticipating another symbol of advice, Raven said, "Well? Has my luck changed? Will riches be heading my way?" She smiled, finding the reading not so bad after all.

"Death," Cruzita said, her voice tinged with a surprise she had not displayed before.

Alma's eyes lingered on the card, then shifted to Raven. "Death, what an intense card to pull."

Raven's heart thumped against her rib cage. "I don't think I want to know what that means," she said, losing all interest in their fun and games.

"Don't worry," Cruzita quickly added, catching Raven's eye. "It's not literal. Death represents transformation, the end of one cycle and the beginning of another."

Alma leaned in closer to study the card. "Death

means letting go, making room for something new. It can be liberating if you allow it."

Raven felt a chill crawl up her spine. Transformation she could understand, but letting go? Letting go of what, or who? Was the card suggesting she was hanging on to something, or someone, that was holding her back?

"Does this speak with you?" Cruzita asked.

"It does," Raven said softly, "more than you could know."

Alma leaned back in her chair, eyeing Raven intently. "The universe doesn't play cards just for amusement. There's a message here for you."

Raven met Alma's glance, holding the gaze this time. "I'm beginning to realize that, but it's a little scary."

Alma smiled gently. "Fear is part of the journey, Raven. Maybe the cards, and our fears, are just signposts along the way, guiding us to where we need to go."

As she spoke, something in the atmosphere shifted. Raven found herself torn between feeling comfortable with Alma and wishing they had never met.

Cruzita sighed and collected the cards. "It's true. The universe has its ways of bringing people together, often when they most need each other. Pay attention to the signs, both of you."

Raven stood up, her knees feeling wobbly.

"Leaving already?"

"Yes," Raven said, sharing looks between each woman. "Spencer should be getting home soon."

"And Cass better be, too, right?" Cruzita added playfully.

"Yeah. Anyway, it was nice to meet you, Alma. Maybe we'll run into each other again."

Alma smiled at Raven. "I'd like that."

Cruzita stood and gave Raven a hug that lasted longer than usual before letting go. "Call you later, girl."

When Raven left La Mariposa Mística, she did not feel that same relief or good sensation as she had on previous visits. She felt better, but still, she had hoped for a revitalization and found only confusion. Alma seemed nice, and though she had tried to be comforting toward the end, something just did not feel right. Cruzita had said, "Pay attention to the signs." Was that one in itself?

The keys slipped into the ignition, and Raven backed her car out of its parking space. She pulled out of the parking lot, away from her friend, her favorite store, and a small, white pickup truck that had seen better days.

CHAPTER 23

"All you have to do is jump."

Lane's voice crackled, his dangerous dare lingering as he stood looking over the edge. Spencer looked ahead, plotted his lift-off point, and ran full steam. With a heave, he leaped into the air, soaring over the edge of the cliff to safety on the other side. Lane jumped next, yelling like an Apache warrior in the height of battle. He landed with a theatrical forward roll before popping to his feet.

"You're a regular Jackie Chan," Spencer said.

"And yer a funny guy, East Texas. We're just gettin' warmed up."

The Mexican sun lay on them like the weight of a stone *molcajete*, grinding them under its relentless pressure. Each felt the burn of late afternoon. Each was drenched with sweat. And each was unwilling to recognize that their desire for drink teetered on necessity.

The next challenge posed a vicious threat. Though the depth was barely twenty feet, still an ample height to cause significant injury, the opposing cliff fell at a steep gradient instead of a straight drop. Should a jumper miscalculate the distance, they could still scramble to the edge and make it, but luck would have to be on their side.

"I'm going first," Lane announced.

Without waiting for objection, Lane stepped back three steps like a field goal kicker measuring his try, and sprinted for the edge. His effort propelled him higher into the sky than the previous jump, but when he landed, his foot slipped at the edge, causing him to face-plant on the ground.

Gravel and dust scattered on impact, and Lane let out a grunt, a painful contrast to his warrior call after the first jump.

Spencer did not hesitate. As Lane dragged himself to his feet, Spencer flew over the opening, landing with the skill of a seasoned Olympian.

"Looks like that one almost had your number," Spencer said, his voice rising and falling with false concern. "Wanna turn back?"

Lane stood up without brushing himself off and squared up to Spencer. "Do you?"

The sun sank lower, catching the sky on fire with deep hues of orange and red, each swirling around a canary yellow flair that extended from horizon to horizon. It would soon be twilight and what brightness that was left would succumb to the clutches of night. Spencer looked in all directions, taking in the beauty of his surroundings, and at the same time, feeling the danger grow stronger each minute they remained across the border.

"No, but it's getting late."

"Ha! You're afraid of the dark. What a chicken..."

Stepping forward, Spencer moved into Lane's space, his jaw firm and serious. "Where's the next jump?"

In that moment, Lane saw something awaken inside of Spencer. It was a noticeable change in demeanor that made Lane realize that he was not going to win this challenge, let alone any fight he tried to stir up. Spencer noticed a change in Lane, too, except what he saw was uncertainty.

Their muscles tensed. Hot breath swirled between them. Neither budged nor spoke for what seemed like minutes. The sun continued to sink. Had there been an audience present to witness this duel, their silhouettes in front of the setting sky would have marked the beginning of a grand finale.

When backed into a corner, a person has but two choices that are innately wound and primed for action when survival is at stake. Do they stand and fight, or flee with reckless abandon? Both often result from irrational thinking, but doing anything at all was better than giving up. Spencer had Lane on the ropes, and the bell for round fourteen was about to ring.

Scare tactics were all Lane had in his arsenal. Digging deep, in both his resolve to kick Spencer's ass and prove him a chickenshit once and for all, he realized the only way to accomplish that was to skip to what he considered the final, most daring canyon jump of all. Adding considerable danger to the perilous challenge, a jump after dark would add a fear factor he had not had to face before today.

"Fuck it," Lane spouted. "Let's finish this." Ramming his shoulder against Spencer's, he pushed by. "All this piddly crap we've been doin' is fer sissies. You make this last jump, an' I'll believe you ain't a chickenshit after all."

Lane stormed off, walking farther from the rim of the canyon fingers that they had been poised to leap. Spencer let out a breath of mixed relief and pent-up aggravation. He pulled his phone from his pocket as he followed Lane. The time read 7:03. The phone's charge displayed forty-five percent remaining. But it was the words NO SERVICE that stood out most of all.

Looking back in the direction of home, Spencer saw a purple band take over the horizon. Where there was once light, darkness dwelled. And it was growing.

The boys trekked on for the better part of twenty minutes, all the while keeping to themselves. An early moon peeked over the horizon and began to rise, glowing like an incandescent bulb at the end of a tunnel.

"Almost there," Lane said, breaking the silence.

Looking ahead, Spencer could see a growing gap of darkness spread out between the ledges, but something else caught his eye. A small, orange glow next to the adjacent rock wall flickered like the tail of a lightning bug.

"What's that?" Spencer asked.

"What?"

"Hang on, Lane." Spencer reached out his hand and touched Lane's shoulder. Lane whirled around and pushed Spencer in the chest. This time Spencer was so engaged with the strange light that he was caught off guard by the shove and stumbled back.

"Get yer hands off me, East Texas."

As Spencer regained his balance, he continued to look past Lane. Squinting his eyes, he fought to see through the waning light.

Using a low voice, Spencer spoke. "I think there is someone over there."

"You were funny before, but I ain't fallin' for it."

"No, I see someone. I think they're smoking a cigarette or a cigar. Can't you smell it?"

Amused by Spencer's concern, Lane played into what he considered a charade. "Oh! Just our luck. Maybe they're smokin' pot and are just waitin' to share with a couple white boys. Let's check it out."

"Keep your voice down."

"Or what?" Lane had a resurgence of bravado, fueling his bully mentality while clouding his limited judgment.

"I think we should turn back. I don't want any trouble."

"And there it is, ladies and gentlemen. He just confirmed it. He is a chickenshit."

"Come on, Lane. Don't be stupid. We have no idea who that could be. What if they're dangerous?"

"I'm dangerous," Lane said, puffing his chest. "Stay here if ya want. I'ma check it out."

Lane turned to go. Spencer laid a firm grip on Lane's shoulder, trying to restrain him, but Lane pulled free and walked ahead.

"Don't be a dumbass."

"Don't be a chickenshit."

CHAPTER 24

As night fell, the world transformed. The once-vibrant landscape became a monochrome puzzle of shades and shadows, illuminated by the cold, indifferent glow of the moon. The chill of the early evening air seeped through his clothes, but Carlos Ruiz-Mata, El Despiadado, welcomed it.

A cigarillo dangled from his lips. The aroma wafted through the air, a potent mixture of rich, smoky tobacco tinged with undertones of cedar and leather. It was a smell that spoke of complex rituals and clandestine meetings, lingering in the atmosphere long after the smoke itself had dispersed. He pressed his lips around the elegant spiral, its velvety leaf a textured roadmap of flavor, and puffed a long, slow stream of smoke into his mouth. Savoring its delicacies, El Despiadado let the taste linger before cracking the corner of his mouth to expel his draw.

He leaned against the rock, still warm from absorbing the heat throughout the day, and stared at the canyon before him. He had been here many times before, but each time felt new. The solitude felt like a rebirth of purpose, or perhaps an opportunity to escape a life that had ensnared him since childhood. Regardless of the feeling, he dismissed it like any other victim of his cruelty. He knew he was stuck in an endless cycle, no matter what he hoped his life could become. He had accepted that evil had a tight grip around him, and rather than fight the urge to flee, he embraced the darkness.

The shadows of the mountains seemed to whisper to him, their voices mingling with the call of distant coyotes. It was a familiar sound, yet tonight, something else tickled his ears. This was desolate terrain, far from civilization, but it was not a secret place by any means. He had encountered others a time or two in the past, most of the time at a distance. Now, the crackle of sharp voices was close. He dropped his cigarillo to the ground. The orange glow petered out, like the last breath of a dying man.

El Despiadado watched and listened as he homed in on the voices, one of which grew louder than the other.

"You comin' er what?" one voice called out. Silence followed until the same voice muttered another word. "Chickenshit."

That brought a smile to El Despiadado's face, though he had already made up his mind about what he would do if he were to cross paths with someone along his way. He unclipped the strap of his combat knife and pulled it free of the sheath. In the moments that passed, El Despiadado yanked away the veil that sheltered his thoughts of why and how and what if and became the man he was molded to be.

The ground crackled beneath approaching feet. In the night, his shadow cast by an early moon upon the rock behind him, a killer waited to strike.

CHAPTER 25

"Well, what do we have here? *¿Hablas inglés, amigo*?" Lane smirked, his swagger that of a cage fighter before a match. Led by curiosity and what he considered American privilege, he stepped closer to a lone man standing near the base of a rock wall that towered more than fifty feet above them. Lost Eagle Canyon stretched out to the East, its jagged claws now looking like pits of tar in the absence of pure light. "I said . . . do . . . you . . . speako . . . English . . . amigo?"

Spencer followed five paces behind. With each step, he felt the tug of reason fight to overcome his poor judgment.

"But, of course," the man answered, sounding as educated as any university graduate would sound. The distinction in his voice caused Lane to crack up but resonated with Spencer in a much different way.

"Oh, yer a fancy talker. We saw ya from over there," Lane said, thumbing over his shoulder. "Got any smokes ta share with us, amigo?"

The man stepped forward, his face becoming a clear, white sight in the moonlight. "But, of course."

Lane moved closer, his mouth curled, his thoughts prejudiced. "That all ya can say?" He moved his hands in front of his body, waving them around as he spoke in a voice that mocked the stranger's. "But, of course?"

The man smiled. He pulled a pack of cigarillos from his rear pocket with his right hand and extended it out to Lane. Lane reached forward. The man jiggled the pack, helping one to wiggle free for the taking.

Spencer stopped moving forward, and instead, took one cautious step to the side so that he could have a clear view of both Lane and the man. The man regarded him with a nod, followed by a smile more fit for a crocodile, then refocused his attention on Lane. The hairs on Spencer's neck and arms began to stand. He tried to swallow, but his mouth had grown dry. He licked his lips and tried again. Only a slight moisture covered his tongue. It was like he had licked the fur of a house cat and tried to swallow the hairball that formed in his mouth.

"Got a light?" Lane said, his tone demanding attention.

The man began to answer, "But . . ."

"Of course?" Lane interrupted. He turned around to look at Spencer. "Do you believe this guy?"

"Lane, we should go. I'll buy you a pack back in town."

"Your friend over there has a head on his shoulders," the man said, looking at Spencer once again. "Maybe you should listen to him?"

Lane faced the man and gave him an oversized look of surprise. "What? I ain't listenin' to nobody. Especially, a chickenshit like him. Now, you got a light, or what?"

Spencer flexed his fingers. The air was cool, but at that moment became still, like a fog settling over a pasture.

The man sighed. "But, of course . . . amigo."

Lane reached his hand forward, glancing at Spence over his shoulder with a face that rivaled the ugliest of looks. *I told you so,* it seemed to say. Without hesitation, without flinching, his look melted away, becoming almost transparent. Moonlight illuminated his face, but the whiteness that covered his cheeks and filled his eyes was not a reaction to the heavenly beams, but from a terror that caused shock and confusion to roil over him.

Lane looked back at the man in time to see him holding a large, bloodied knife before him, and his hand, still holding the cigarillo, twirl away and land on the shadowed ground. In disbelief, he raised a bony stump in front of him, gripping it with his other trembling fist. Blood spurted in pulses, staining his shirt. It ran over his fingers as if he had squeezed a tomato, forcing its juices to drip and ooze from its mangled skin. Blood painted his face with warm streaks of red. Once screaming like an Apache warrior, Lane opened his mouth but only a high-pitched gargle escaped.

With three quick motions, the man swiped and jabbed his knife again. Lane's remaining hand was severed from his wrist, though it clung to the stump which it had held just before its end. The second jab entered his chest. The third slashing his throat above his collarbone.

Lane crumpled to his knees, gasping and wheezing. Tears ran down his cheeks, mixing with the blood that was already there, forming a smear of red over a horrified, white face.

The man stood and watched Lane fall face-first onto the ground. His body thumped on the dirt like a single beat of a leather drum. Leaning over, the man wiped his blade on Lane's back, then turned his attention to Spencer.

Frozen with fear and refusing to believe what he had just seen, Spencer did not know what to do. The shock of seeing Lane slashed to death held him prisoner. His muscles were capable of flight, but they lacked the signal to move.

"Such a shame," the man said. "For his sake, he should have listened to you."

Tears filled Spencer's eyes. They burned and stung him, yet he did not try to wipe them away. He locked eyes with the man.

"You are smart. And, I think brave, too. Not like him. Like I said, it's such a shame."

The man's eyes narrowed, and Spencer saw

his fingers tighten their grip around the hilt of his knife. That was enough. The horror of it was, that was what Spencer needed to see. The shock of witnessing a murder held him captive, but becoming a target lit enough fire within him to react.

Years of taekwondo training kept him quick on his feet. With lightning speed, he reverse-stepped and pivoted into an all-out sprint. He ran for his life, not daring to look back. He only knew which direction to go, but in the dark, was unsure how close he was to running off a cliff.

The claws of the canyon lay quiet. A predator waiting for unsuspecting prey to wander too close and then, certain death.

Seconds felt like minutes. Spencer's experience in the ring had taught him to use each moment with skill and precision to overcome his opponent. He kept a mental clock running in his head as he ran close to the rising rock on his left. Each pound of the foot meant he was still alive, but he must keep moving.

A shot blasted from behind him, followed by an immediate zing from the rock and spray of chipped shards that cut at his hands and face. Spencer yelled out in pain and from fright. It felt like the sting of a thousand bees. He slowed for a moment. In that sudden pause, he heard the man's footsteps closing in.

Where the hell am I going? His mind screamed.

He ran again, sweat filling the scratches on his face. His legs ached, but he had no choice but to push harder. Five seconds more, then ten.

Another shot rang out, this one passing so close to his head, he felt the warmth of the bullet as it singed the air.

With nowhere to hide, Spence made a choice only a survivalist would chance to make. He changed his path, running closer to the canyon's jagged rim. With no time to change his mind, he leaped over each small opening, soaring over the blackness beneath him. Forcing himself to focus, he began to recognize some of the landscape. With only the moon to guide him, Spencer hurdled the openings Lane had led him past on the walk-in. He jumped two more openings, both nearly five feet in width, and felt he was gaining ground.

Closing in on the jump where Lane had fallen, Spencer pounded his steps harder, ready to make a determined flight. He remembered it to be a challenging leap, but that depended on where his take-off point was located. This brief contemplation distracted him enough that he lost sight of the smaller obstacles in his path. With one wrong step, Spencer rolled his left ankle on a disproportionate chunk of ground near the canyon rim and fell reeling with pain. He rolled once, clutching his leg, and found himself staring face-first into the black abyss of the canyon below. With a quick turn of the head, he searched for the man.

"Unbelievable," he said to himself as he saw the man leap over the openings in *Cañón del Águila Perdida* just as easily as if he were playing leapfrog in the park.

With no time to think, and nowhere to go, Spencer did the one thing he hoped the man would not attempt.

"This is gonna hurt."

The steep incline that Lane had stumbled to recover from following his second jump, now acted as Spencer's only means of escape. With a sudden scooch, he covered his face with his arms and rolled himself off the edge of the cliff.

The man slid to a stop at the canyon's edge and looked down. He stood for a moment and listened. When he did not hear anything, he smiled.

"Brave, indeed," he whispered.

The darkness swallowed Spencer, and the canyon bit down hard, but only silence followed.

PART 3
Dark and Deep

CHAPTER 26

"That has got to be one of the strangest goddamn things I've ever seen."

I sat across from Chance in his office. He leaned back in his weathered leather chair, and by the look of him, his mind was racing. The door was closed, and the blinds were lowered to cover the windows. Stacks of papers littered one side of his desk. On top of the papers sat the jump drive I had recovered from the murder scene on the CR.

"I know we've both seen some pretty nasty shit, but have you ever known anyone to stab themselves in the eye as an act of suicide?"

Chance bit his lower lip. His mustache twitched. With an exasperated sigh, he leaned forward and reached below his desk, pulling open one of the drawers.

"*Amigo*," he said, pulling a bottle of 1800 Silver Tequila into view. "I'm already trying to forget it." He placed the bottle on the table and produced two small copita glasses. He poured a generous amount in each, then slid one over to me. He picked his glass up and raised it in front of him. "*Salud.*"

The tulip-shaped glass felt comfortable in my hand. I raised mine as well, mirroring Chance's gesture, then brought the rim to my lips. The earthy, and slightly sweet, aroma of agave funneled out the opening, filling my nose. Hints of citrus added a zesty appeal. My first sip ignited a trailing warmth from the back of my tongue to the center of my chest. Each subsequent sip flowed with less burn, but the pulse of each swallow added to the fire building within me.

We sat and drank in silence until our glasses were emptied. This was not a celebration. It was a momentary escape. The past twenty-four hours had been hell on earth.

"Want me to head back over to the jail?" I asked. "Have another look at the tapes?"

"It's late, Cass. We talked to everyone we could have already and still haven't been able to discover a motive or ID López's last visitor. Not much more we can do over there right now." Chance collected the glasses and placed them, along with the tequila bottle, back in his desk drawer. "Raven is probably wondering when yer coming home."

I looked at the old-school-style clock mounted on the wall behind Chance. Its red second hand moved in perpetuity. The black hands of the antique timepiece held firm, yet I was certain as I read the time, that they were giving me the finger. "Yeah, I should probably give her a call."

Chance motioned to the door, and I excused myself from the room. Using the phone at Deputy

Leo's desk, I called Raven. The phone rang only once before it was answered.

"Hello?"

"Hey Little Bird, it's me."

"Thank god. When are you coming home?"

"Soon."

"Have you heard from Spencer?"

"No. Wasn't he out with his Dairy Queen today?"

"Yes, but he hasn't come home and hasn't called either."

"Rave, Spencer is an adult, like it or not. Remember when we were that age? Since he hasn't come back, I'm guessing he's getting lucky."

"Cass! It's after eleven. I'm worried."

"Hang on." I pulled the receiver from my mouth and yawned. It had been a long day, and from the tone in this phone call, would not be ending how I had hoped. Placing the phone on my shoulder, I cocked my head to one side to hold it in place while I reached for a cup and the coffee pot on a counter next to Deputy Leo's desk. "Listen, I'll head out now and give him a call from the car."

Raven paused before making a reply. I could tell she was upset.

"Okay," she said, her voice wavering. *"Hurry home?"*

"I will."

I set the coffee cup down and relaxed my neck

grip on the phone. I caught it as it fell from my shoulder, then placed it back on its cradle. It was no secret that Raven had been missing Spencer, and his visit had only reignited her maternal instincts. To Raven, he was still her little boy. I suppose he always will be, regardless of age. I saw him as a man, thriving in life, continuing to mature and grow responsibly. I also saw him as any other college-age kid—ready for adventure and as horny as the stray dog that wanders the street along sorority row. Two perspectives, neither of them wrong, both honest.

I ducked my head back into Chance's office. "Gonna head out."

"*¿Todo bien en casa?*"

I gave him a confused look. "What about my house?"

"*¡Ay, Dios*! For a man who lives as close to Mexico as anyone, you would think your Spanish was better. But don't worry, *amigo*. Let me say it for your English-speaking ears." He grinned as he spoke. "Home? Is everything all right at home?"

"Pretty much. Raven's concerned about Spencer. He met a girl yesterday and has been with her all day today."

Chance smiled. "What I wouldn't give to be young again, *amigo*."

"Really?"

"No," Chance said, stretching his smile into a

laugh. I joined in, understanding the dream of relieving my younger years but not wanting to go through most of what it had comprised. "I am sure he is just fine. He's a Callahan. Let's just hope he takes after his uncle Stewart."

"What's that supposed to mean?"

Chance stood up and walked around his desk, meeting me at the door. "It means, if he is anything like you, maybe I should put an APB out right now, amigo."

"*Pendejo*."

Chance slapped me on the shoulder and held on. "Now you're getting the hang of it."

"Call you tomorrow," I said, walking away from the door.

"No, you won't," he replied. "Did you already forget? You pulled yourself off duty. I'll see you when Spencer goes back to school. Give Raven my love."

I pointed at him, confirming what he had said as truth, then left Chance alone in the sheriff's office operating a skeleton crew. It was late and would hopefully be a quiet night, for once.

CHAPTER 27

Carlos Ruiz-Mata adjusted the rearview mirror, the dome light illuminating the interior of the Camaro enough for him to see his own cold eyes staring back at him. Before discarding Lane's mutilated body, Mata found the keys to his car in the front pocket of his bloody jeans. He took his wallet as well, noting the four one-dollar bills inside, an expired driver's license, and a faded picture of Lane standing next to an attractive looking young girl.

He reached into the passenger seat, retrieving a sleek black device about the size of a smartphone from the backpack he had carried. Matte-black lettering running along the top read: Artemis OmniLocator. Mata looked at a small, handheld GPS tracker, regarded the high-tech power in his hands, and pressed a button on the side of the device. It powered on in silence, emitting a soft, dull green glow from its screen.

With swift precision, he connected the Artemis to his own encrypted satellite phone via a USB-C cable. As the two devices talked to one another, Mata reflected on the mission which Señor de la Droga had entrusted him to carry out. His objective was to retrieve the stolen USB drive and eliminate anyone he deemed to have been in contact with it as well as anyone standing in his way.

With the Artemis powered on, Mata input the coding on its touchscreen interface and began the trace. Only a few moments had passed when a message box appeared on the screen: DEVICE OFFLINE.

"You will have to do better than that," he said to Artemis. "Let's run *Thin Air*."

He closed the message box, then opened a drop-down menu and selected the protocol. It was fascinating technology, enabling the user to interface with a ghost signal, or established nano beacon, even in the absence of an internet connection or a functioning power supply.

Servicios Financieros Cortez y Asociados, the accounting firm where the information had been stolen, operates a proprietary, and comprehensive security software program that has the capability to trace data movements, even to external devices, anywhere in the world. This cutting-edge technology employs a specialized nano-file beacon that acts as a powerful tracking mechanism, enabling precise location of the device to specific coordinates on a map, with a margin of error of fewer than five hundred feet. Each nano-file beacon embedded in the firm's software was programmed to send out periodic, encrypted ping signals. The Artemis, equipped with an RF sniffing module, could detect these pings, thus pulling a location out of thin air.

Tapping a series of commands into the touchscreen interface, Mata activated the device's RF module. Within seconds of inputting the beacon ID associated with the stolen jump drive, Artemis began scanning for the encrypted ping signals. Moments later, a map materialized on the screen with a red dot indicating an approximate location of the missing drive.

"So, you have moved from your original location, my little friend."

It was the initial activation of this very nanofile beacon that had tipped Mata off to its general location when making preparations for this mission.

"It seems you are no longer in a residence near the border. Why have you ventured into Brewster, Texas, of all places?" Mata ran his thumb over the screen, caressing the map as if comforting a lost soul. "Do not worry, little one. You will be safe soon enough."

He glanced at his watch.

11:16.

Leaning his head back, Mata closed his eyes. It had been a long day of preparation and travel. The unexpected encounter with the two boys added a degree of fatigue, both physically and mentally. On one hand, he had taken unfortunate but necessary action to ensure his identity remained a mystery, while on the other, he thought the boy he killed was a complete asshole. The other boy got away, earning a degree of Mata's respect, and yet leaving him to die in the middle of the desert at the bottom of the canyon did not bother El Despiadado.

Finding no comfort in the old Camaro, Mata slipped the keys into the ignition. Struggling to turn over and making sounds under the hood much like that of a life-long chain smoker, the engine finally spit and kicked itself to life. It ignited with a growl, reminiscent of an old guard dog, long in the tooth but not lacking in spirit. The sound reverberated through the rust-speckled frame, causing the entire vehicle to quiver and rumble.

Not dissuaded by the condition of the vehicle, Mata shifted into D, turned on the headlights, and eased away. He felt rather lucky to have wheels so close to the river. It saved him the hike to a vehicle he knew was hidden in a deserted barn further south near RR170.

The Camaro crept along, tossing stones and crunching gravel and earth beneath its tires. Mata was in no hurry. He drove along the worn path that led to the highway like he was out for a Sunday drive with his family. The a/c blasted inside the car, but he drove with the window down, his left arm hanging limp against the door's exterior. It was warm outside, but the wind against his skin soothed him.

The primitive gravel road came to a dead end at RR170, thirty miles south of Brewster, Texas. To his right, he knew that Lajitas was only a short drive. He could head south and pay a surprise visit to an old flame. A hot meal and sharing a soft bed with a beautiful woman were enticing. Shaking the thought away, he turned onto RR170 and headed north.

As the Camaro's engine rumbled along the desolate road, its sharp headlights cut through the night. The patterned reflection of white lane lines painted atop black pavement flashed into view like artillery tracers embedded in live ammunition, each one missing its intended target as Mata drove on.

The sky above held a blanket of stars. If it was not for the pollution of the Camaro's headlights, the endless black would have swallowed Mata, scrubbing him with salted stars and distant, vibrant colors. Keeping his speed in tune with posted limits, he focused on what he must do next, instead of falling victim to the beauty and solitude lathered above him.

RR170 rose and fell, winding with the terrain that followed the flow of the Rio Grande and the US/Mexico border to the west. At one point, the rise in the road was so extreme it looked as if he might jump off the end of the world. Cresting the asphalt summit, Mata coasted over the pavement as he made his descent to a long, straight stretch of roadway that lingered well beyond the reach of his headlights.

When the road leveled out, he glanced in the rearview mirror. The glint of flashing red and blue lights approaching behind him caught his eye. He felt a pang of irritation. He slowed the Camaro and pulled to the side, straddling the main road and the shoulder to allow the emergency vehicle enough room to pass by safely. The strobes grew brighter as they drew nearer. With a chirp of the siren, the patrol car fell in line with the Camaro.

Annoyance surged through Mata. With a resigned sigh, he applied gentle pressure to the brake, steering the Camaro onto the roadside where the gravel crunched like brittle bones beneath the tires.

Behind him, the patrol car aligned perfectly. Its spotlight switched on, bathing the Camaro in an intrusive wash of white light. Long shadows cast upon the dashboard seemed to dance in the swath of white light and strobing red and blue. Mata looked in the driver's side mirror, watching and waiting.

For a law enforcement officer, every detail mattered—the spotlight was not just illumination; it was psychological warfare, a tactic Mata knew well.

The patrol car door opened. A man stepped out of the car, his flashlight beam joining the spotlight, further piercing the darkness as he approached. Mata could hear the sound of his boots crisply breaking the quiet night air as he walked over. With his arm still resting out the open window, El Despiadado remained calm, like a serpent before it strikes.

"Evening, sir. Do you know why I pulled you over?"

Fighting past the glare of the flashlight's beam being shone in his face, Mata saw that he had been pulled over by a South Brewster County Deputy. Squinting, he read his nameplate.

"Deputy Santos? I am sorry, sir, but I do not," Mata replied, doing his best to feign innocence.

"You have a taillight out," Deputy Santos informed him, taking a moment to shine his flashlight into the Camaro's interior. The deputy's gaze lingered on the car's upholstery before meeting Mata's eyes. "You know, this car looks awfully familiar. Isn't this Lane Jespers's vehicle?"

Mata felt his pulse quicken but kept his face expressionless. "I bought it from a man named Lane, yes. Is that a problem?"

Something in Santos's eyes shifted, a tightening, a microscopic squint that could almost go unnoticed. "Would you kindly step out of the vehicle, sir?"

Mata felt his annoyance grow. This was more than an inconvenience. Now, it was a complication. But he had no choice; he needed to play this carefully. He complied, opening the door, and stepping out onto the gravel.

As Mata rose to his full height, he surveyed Deputy Santos: late twenties, well-built, emanating an aura of seasoned experience, and holding an automatic pistol at his side. This was not a rookie. This was someone who had seen things, someone who trusted his gut. His eyes narrowed just a fraction more as Mata stepped into the patrol car's spotlight.

Facing Deputy Santos, Mata felt the weight of the situation. He did not know this deputy, but he did know that a single wrong move could unravel everything he had worked for. His fingers twitched, itching for the comfort of the weapon he kept concealed.

Santos's eyes homed in on him, narrowing just a fraction more as he spoke. "How did you come to acquire this car, exactly? I know Lane Jespers. Never figured him on selling it to anyone."

Mata stared back, calculating his options. This was a pivotal moment, a fulcrum point on which the entire night could tip. "So, are we going to have a problem here, Deputy?"

The tension between them became palpable, a charged field of unspoken challenges and implicit threats. Both men recognized the magnitude of this seemingly mundane interaction, knowing it could either escalate into a catastrophic showdown or dissolve into an awkward memory. They were locked in a psychological dance, and each man's next step would drastically influence the rhythm and flow of their encounter.

"Turn around and put your hands on the car," Deputy Santos ordered. He pointed to the hood with the flashlight, his hand tightening its grip on his service weapon. Keeping calm and asserting his authority, Deputy Santos remained on highest alert for any resistance from Mata. "Slowly. Do it now."

Mata smiled, then raised his hands even with his shoulders and began to turn. Facing the hood, he saw the beam of the flashlight wobble across the Camaro.

"Spread your legs apart."

Without looking back, Mata knew the deputy would be reaching for handcuffs. In the split moment when Deputy Santos returned his weapon to his belt holster before removing the handcuffs, El Despiadado took over.

"But, of course."

One swift pivot and swipe of El Despiadado's left hand onto Santos's right arm was enough to surprise and overpower the deputy, causing him to drop the handcuffs and flashlight. Years of training made this an easy exercise for the experienced killer. As he turned to grasp Deputy Santos's arm, he brought his right hand to his waist, pulling his concealed blade with expert timing. In one motion, he depressed the locking mechanism that sprang the blade into service and slashed Deputy Santos across the neck. It was an exquisite movement, fluid in its destructive qualities and precise with his lethal follow-through.

Deputy Santos staggered back, both hands clinging to his throat. His eyes bulged in disbelief while his fingers flexed in unsuccessful contractions meant to stop the bleeding. Blood flowed in steady pulses from the gash in his neck. It slid through his fingers and down the inside of his uniform. He tried to speak, but all that was discernible were terrified gargles.

The radio mount on his shoulder crackled, but the call was not for him. Losing his strength, Deputy Santos fell to one knee, still grasping his throat. The spotlight from his patrol car illuminated his body, casting a silhouette on the highway as if he were a rock star leaning over to grant an overzealous fan their one wish of simply touching hands with their idol.

El Despiadado knelt beside him and spoke with a soft, soothing tone. "Relax, my friend. Do not try to fight it. Things will end quickly if you just let go."

Deputy Santos released one hand from his neck, scrambling to pull his weapon. El Despiadado watched the deputy's valiant effort. Deputy Santos tried to lift it, but the blood on his hands acted like oil, causing him to drop the weapon on the ground between them. El Despiadado reached down and picked it up as if he had found a quarter on the street. Holding the automatic pistol in his right hand, he gazed into Deputy Santos's dying eyes.

"You are a hero, my friend. A true, blue hero."

El Despiadado stood. In one merciless act, he aimed and pulled the trigger, shooting Deputy Santos once on the head.

In a bloody crumple, Deputy Santos fell away from El Despiadado, his throat seeping, his eyes frozen open in a stare filled with fear and desperation.

"*Qué desperdicio de vida.* What a waste of life," Mata said, taking a long slow breath.

He looked in both directions along RR170. To the north, the road was as black as death. To the south, a flicker of lightning flashed but was too far away to hear its thunderous call. In silence, Mata turned and hurled the deputy's weapon into the brush, then walked to the patrol car. He leaned in and disengaged the strobes and turned off the spotlight. With a flick of the keys, the car became as quiet as its driver. Before exiting the vehicle, he ejected a small SD video card from the dashcam and slipped it into his pocket.

Mata closed the door and returned to Deputy Santos, avoiding his life's spillage on the asphalt. He grabbed each of his ankles and dragged him to the passenger side of the patrol car, rolling him so his body leaned against the frame.

Static from the patrol car's radio sounded out, followed by a female's voice, this time addressing Santos.

"Javier, we have a ten-sixteen in progress. Cooter Malloy is at it again. 717 Valley Road. You know the place. Code three, please acknowledge."

Mata reached through the open window and pulled the radio from its cradle. Taking note of the vehicle identification number on the dash and mimicking what he could remember of Deputy Santos's voice, he responded.

"Unit eleven, en route, copy, Code three."

"Unit eleven, copy, Code three. Be careful, Javier."

The radio squelched once, then rested. Mata tossed it onto the driver's seat and walked back to the Camaro. Before getting in, he picked up Deputy Santos's handcuffs and flashlight from the ground and tossed them into the passenger seat.

Closing the door behind him, he leaned his head back on the seat. He closed his eyes so tight, the pressure caused him pain. Before driving away, he whispered something to himself. He spoke low, his tone intimate, reverent.

"Dios Todopoderoso, we commend to you the souls of our loved ones who have departed.

Grant them eternal rest and let perpetual light shine upon them," he began, his voice barely a murmur against the hush of the night.

"For those of us who are here, we ask for your blessing. Grant us the strength to overcome sadness and the wisdom to follow your path. May the living find comfort and the dead find peace."

He paused, contemplating the weight of his own words. "*En el nombre del Padre, del Hijo y del Espíritu Santo. Amén.*"

Opening his eyes, Mata felt a quiet calm wash over him. It was as if, for a brief second, the boundary between the living and the dead blurred, offering a fragile, unspoken reconciliation.

He turned the key, and the Camaro roared to life, breaking the fragile silence. As he pulled back onto the road, he could not help but wonder if the prayer had been for them, for him, or for both.

CHAPTER 28

The canyon floor was a brutal bed of jagged stones and fragmented rock, but in a cruel twist of fate, this punishing terrain had saved Spencer's life. Lying on his back, he peered up at the towering rim of the canyon, praying with every fiber of his being that the killer would not return. Above him, the stars winked like a heavenly mobile, a cosmic lullaby in sharp contrast to the danger he had just narrowly escaped.

He was covered in small cuts and bruises, but it was his ankle that gave him the most concern. It throbbed like a bass drum banging in rhythm to his heartbeat. His mouth felt like sandpaper, and his lips were beginning to crack.

Wincing, he fumbled in his front pocket for his cell phone. Though its screen had cracked in the harrowing tumble down the twenty-foot, sixty-degree slope, Spencer's phone powered on like a warrior ready for the next fight. As he looked at the screen, his hand and cell phone dropped to his stomach.

"Shit!"

His voice echoed through the canyon. A chilling fear iced his veins, making his fingers tingle when he realized he may have just told the killer he was alive and where to find him. He froze, listening intently for any sign of movement. Minutes passed, but all remained quiet. When it was apparent that he was alone, he tipped his phone up to view the screen again.

"No service. Battery at twenty-nine percent. Eleven fifty-one. No one even knows I'm in trouble yet. What have I done?" he scolded himself. Squeezing his fists, he punched the ground.

Spencer, at twenty years old, had a roster of adrenaline-filled adventures to his name, but this was no ordinary challenge. Blindly following Lane, unprepared, and into the wilderness of Mexico no less, was the biggest mistake of his life. It was a dick-measuring, bone-headed, dumbass thing to do, and Spencer knew it. He cursed himself for his recklessness, already imagining the words his father would say once he made it out of this hellish situation. "You know what your grandfather would tell me? A man acts like one because he has to. A boy acts like one when he wants to. What are you?"

With those words echoing in his mind, Spencer closed his eyes and wept.

CHAPTER 29

I drove the Explorer across the cattle guard at the entrance of the CR, its rustic tubular rumblings welcoming me home. The hours between midnight and four a.m. were the most peaceful on the ranch. Most nights the air was still. Like clockwork, the calls of distant coyotes added a western ambiance to the open terrain, their barks and howls fading like ghostly echoes. A barn owl that roosted in the loft would perch on the railings overlooking the corral and make clicking sounds before soaring into the dark to hunt. It reminded me of pilot radio chatter requesting take-off clearance. The endless sky overhead marked a glorious path of spectacular lights that seemed to follow our very own Gateway to Paradise. And yet, it was the stillness that spoke to me most of all. The solitude of this magnificent region had a way of wrapping its arms around me with a comfort I had never experienced in Houston. Regardless of the time, the hustle of the big city never stopped. When darkness fell on the CR, so did a welcoming semblance of calm.

As I pulled up to the house, the glow of the dashboard clock seemed to reprimand me for being out so late. The time was 12:34. I smiled at the sequential numbering, feeling that supertitious childhood connection that Spencer would enjoy, and cut off the engine. As I stepped out of the Explorer, all that was peaceful and good was shattered.

"He's still not home!"

Raven met me as I closed the car door. The concern and volume in her voice propelled me from the mental serenity I was enjoying to a rapid response of questioning and confusion.

"Look for yourself. His Jeep isn't here, and he hasn't called."

"Raven, take a breath."

"It's not like him at all, Cass." Her voice crackled as her chin quivered from micro convulsions. "I'm worried."

I pulled Raven into me and felt the convulsions explode into sobs.

"Rave . . . Raven . . . it's gonna be all right." I hugged her tight, then with gentle hands, moved her back to look into her eyes. "I'll call him now, okay?"

Raven nodded. She let go of me, wiping the tears from her face and waited while I pulled my cell phone from my pocket. I placed the call, switching the audio to speaker so we could both hear. Instead of ringing, the call went straight to voicemail.

"This is Spencer's cell, and ya missed me. Leave a message, and I'll call ya back . . . maybe."

"Spencer. This is Dad. Call me ASAP, buddy."

I ended the call and looked at Raven. "It's like I said before, he's probably out having the night of his life with this girl."

"But he should have called to . . ."

"I agree. And I will remind him of that when we see him. Right now, let's not jump to any conclusions."

Raven looked defeated. She leaned her cheek against my chest. I wrapped my arm around her and coaxed her inside. Together, we sat on the couch and waited for Spencer to walk through the door, or at the very least, return my call.

The lights in the living room filled the front of the house, spilling through the windows, and onto the porch. Raven had nuzzled into my chest, then pulled her legs onto the couch in the fetal position. Her left arm wrapped around her legs, hugging, and hanging on to them. It was not long before she drifted into a restless sleep. Her hands and shoulders twitched as if she were playing a role within an uncomfortable dream.

Time passed, and still no sign of Spencer. I caught myself staring at the lamp that stood on a pinewood table next to the couch. Its porcelain base had been artistically formed into a cowboy riding a bucking bronco. The horse's lips were curled back in a snarl making its teeth visible. Its back was arched, and its hind legs kicked up behind its body. The cowboy riding the horse had a similar expression that I interpreted as, *Ain't nothin' ya kin do ta throw me.* He gripped a rope with one hand while throwing his opposite hand back in a display of balance and control. Both fought to overpower the other. Both frozen in time, forever stuck in their struggle.

A glance at my phone told me the same thing it had a dozen times already. No missed calls. No incoming texts. And the time kept getting later and later without any news of Spence. It was after two in the morning, and it was my turn to become worried.

I tried slipping out from beneath Raven without disturbing her, but like any mother waiting on the edge of her seat for good news, she woke with a start.

"Did he call? Is he home?"

Her anxiousness abounded.

"No, Raven. I'm going to take a drive and see if I can find him."

"I'm coming, too."

"Why don't you wait here so that the house isn't empty if he beats me home."

"No way. If you think for one minute I'm going to hang around here by myself while both of my guys are out and about . . ." Running out of breath, she gasped for air. When she caught up with the speed of her flying words, she stood looking like she was ready to take on anyone who tried to stop her. Her eyes looked like they were on fire, and the way she clenched her teeth told me right then that nobody could. "I'll meet you in the car."

Raven stormed to the bedroom, then shuffled back down the hall while trying to walk and slip on a pair of shoes at the same time and was out the front door without another word. I followed her out, leaving the door to the house unlocked. Beating me to the car, she lifted the door handle. It was locked.

"Goddamn it!" she yelled, her worry and frustration boiling over.

I clicked the key fob to unlock the doors and walked to the driver's side of the Explorer. She yanked the door open and sat down. I slid behind the wheel and fired up the engine. Backing away from the house, I turned the steering wheel to aim the Explorer at the entrance to the ranch. The headlights cut through the night, but I saw that the archway was not the only thing illuminated by the lights.

I pressed the gas and rolled down my window. Walking toward us, still fully dressed and rifle in hand, was Flint. I pulled up and stopped next to him.

"Everything okay?" he asked.

"Spencer hasn't come home. Raven and I are headed out to look for him."

Flint leaned forward. He looked at Raven, then back at me.

"You headin' ta town, then?"

"Yeah. Gonna swing by the station first and see if I can get the number of the girl he's with. His phone keeps going straight to voicemail."

Flint glanced at Raven again, then stood up and looked over his shoulder.

"Shit."

"We gotta run, Flint."

"You start in town. I'll head the other way and see if I can track 'em down. I've lived here a long time an' know a couple spots the kids around here like to disappear to."

Flint's statement caught me off guard. I looked at him, both questioning and grateful, and yet, I did not respond.

"Go on," he said. "I'll call ya if I come across 'em."

Before I could reply, Flint jogged away, disappearing behind the garage.

"Is Flint going to help?" Raven asked.

"Yeah." It was all I could think to say.

The rumble of the cattle guard felt different this time as we exited the ranch. It hurt, like each metal post drove itself into my gut. Turning onto the gravel road, I sped away from the CR, the rising dust catching the lights of Flint's truck as he followed behind.

The smooth glide of the Explorer over RR170 added a touch of calm to an anxious drive. The ambient light from Brewster sat like a heavy fog on the blackened horizon.

"Should we call Chance?" Raven said, her voice barely above a whisper as she stared out the window.

"No. We aren't to that point yet."

"Yet?"

Damn, I thought. Raven was one to hang on to every word when she was nervous and had a way of misinterpreting whatever message I was trying to convey. "Not, yet. What I mean is, I'm not calling Chance for help only to find Spencer and Charlotte curled up together asleep somewhere. He's a responsible kid, but even the most responsible kid makes mistakes from time to time."

"That's what worries me, Cass."

Again, *damn!* I shifted our conversation so that Raven felt in charge. "Where should we look first?"

Raven turned her head to face me, her eyes opened wide with wonder.

"I . . . I . . ." She paused, then jolted her body as if she had been hit by a surge of electricity. "DQ . . . Dairy Quee . . . shit! I saw his Jeep there earlier today." She smacked herself on the forehead. "I almost poked my nose in to see how they were doing. Maybe I . . ."

"Maybe you should have acted like your mother?" I said, trying to lighten the mood.

"Not funny. That's why I *didn't* stop in the first place."

Raven sat forward like a child looking for a lost puppy. Every shadow caught her attention, every car sparked and doused hope, but she did not give in to despair. She teetered on the edge, but I could tell she was fighting it off.

As we approached Dairy Queen, Raven rolled down her window and stuck her head outside the car. I slowed the Explorer to a roll as we pulled off the main road. All the restaurant lights were out, including the sign and the surrounding streetlamps. The DQ sign looked like a blurry UFO hovering over the darkened parking lot.

"There!" Raven pointed out the window as if she had been stranded at sea and had just discovered land. "His Jeep is still here." Pulling her head inside the car, she sat back and let a long, slow breath escape her lips. I did not have the heart to tell her that although the Jeep was here, Spencer more than likely, was not.

I pulled to a stop so that the Explorer's headlights lit up the rear of his Jeep and the front of the restaurant. We both stepped out of the car. Raven rushed to look inside the Jeep, calling out Spencer's name while I scanned the parking lot and the building. We were the only ones here.

I heard a series of thuds and saw that Raven was banging on the passenger window, a helpless reaction to finding the Jeep empty. I walked to the driver's side and peered through the glass. Nothing looked out of place.

"Ugh! Where are you?" Raven said.

"Get back in the car. We'll head over to the sheriff's office and see if we can get Charlotte's number."

With a final bang of her fist on the window, Raven turned and walked to the Explorer. She swung the door open, then slammed it behind her like she was the one who had been out late and was feeling the consequences of her actions.

I turned to head back to the car when my cell phone rang. I pulled it from my pocket and saw that the call was from Flint. I felt a premature swell of relief, though I had not yet heard what he had to say. Raven opened the car and stood looking over the door.

"Is it him? Is it Spence?"

"It's Flint."

"Oh, thank god. He found them."

Ignoring Raven, I answered the phone.

"Flint, tell me you have good news."

The line was silent.

"Flint?"

"Damn, Cass. I hate to be the one to tell you this."

The blood in my head rushed to my legs, causing my head to spin. Tiny prickles lined the back of my neck as the hairs felt more like tiny shards of glass rubbing my skin raw.

"Fuck, Flint. Tell me what! Is it Spencer?"

"No, it's not him. Or the girl neither."

The news should have brought some relief, but the tone in Flint's voice told me there was much more I needed to hear.

"I'm on RR170, just past Panther Creek."

Raven waved to get my attention. I turned away from her and stood facing the building. Time seemed to slow to a crawl as I waited to hear what Flint had to say. With the cell phone held to my ear, I looked straight ahead at the windows of the empty restaurant. Staring back at me were the lifeless, cartoon eyes of a creepy looking clown in a ridiculous polka dot outfit with a name badge that read Curly the Clown. He held an ice cream cone in one hand. From the center of a horrific smile, he stuck his tongue out to lick the dairy treat. This was a place for fun and happy times, where kids could enjoy the cool sensations of dessert food and tasty treats, but all I could envision was a nightmarish story from my childhood. The clown seemed to take his eyes off the treat to glare at me, and all I could think of was red balloons and floating.

"Cass. It's Javier Santos. I just found his cruiser parked along the road." Flint paused as if trying to find the right words to say when none would be welcomed by any ear.

"What about Santos?"

I turned to see that Raven had walked up behind me. Her eyes filled with worry, her face withdrawn and losing color.

"He's dead. Somebody killed him."

CHAPTER 30

Mata stretched his legs across the full-sized motel bed, laced his fingers behind his head, and stared at an oil painting hung on the wall over a small floor lamp he had yet to turn off. With a sword poised to strike in one hand, El Matador taunted a bull with a red *muleta* that he held in the other, daring it to charge. The bull's fierce horns jutted ahead. Its eyes glowed red as if the devil himself sought to kill the honored bullfighter. Blood dripped from the bull's shoulders where colorful banderillas had been stuck by eager *banderilleros*. Frozen in time, the bull and El Matador were locked in an eternal dance of death.

After a time of consideration, placing himself both as El Matador and the bull, Mata swung his legs off the bed. He walked over to the painting and stood close enough to smell the moldy undertones of the paint. With eyes fixed on El Matador, he reached for the dangling chain of the floor lamp and pulled down.

Light raced from the room with a sudden flash. In that moment when the last strand of light was extinguished and darkness filled the room, an afterimage burned into Mata's mind. The shrillness of the blackened image caused him to take a cautious step back. Though it disappeared as fast as it had materialized, the mental burn remained, for it was his face that he saw, dark and empty, like a forsaken demon lurking before his very eyes.

Sliding his feet backward, he bumped into the end of the bed and sat down. He placed his elbows on his knees and covered his eyes with his palms, but he could not escape the tormenting image.

"Corre, Carlos! Run for your life!" the older boys teased.

Carlos's small feet kicked up dust on the narrow path, his heart pounding in his chest as he tried to outrun the older boys' taunts. "Lechuza is coming for you!" The laughter of the boys felt like a swarm of hornets, relentless and stinging, buzzing in his ears. Carlos looked for an escape, his eyes darting from tree to tree, desperately seeking a hiding spot. Filled with fear, he had broken the one rule set forth by his papá; do not go out after dark.

Spotting a narrow clearing veiled by a curtain of vines, he ducked behind it and crouched low, praying that the shadows would hide him. He clamped a hand over his mouth, his rapid breathing misting up the cool night air.

"There it is," one of the older boys screamed. "It's coming!" Sarcastic laughter echoed through the night.

Carlos felt a surge of panic. Just as he dared to breathe, a rustling echoed from the treetops, and a shadow seemed to swoop low—so real, so close. His blood ran cold. Could it be Lechuza?

The breeze picked up, sending a swirl of dust and dried leaves soaring into his hiding space. The displaced air sent shivers down his spine. His imagination succumbed to his fear, manifesting a large, feathered beast, eyes aglow and beak dripping of blood. Landing on talons that clawed into the earth, his wakeful nightmare blocked the only path of escape.

From deep within the dark, he heard his name. HIS NAME. "Caaa . . . rrr . . . lo . . . ssss . . ."

"Stop it!" he yelled. "Go away!"

Carlos squeezed his eyes shut so tight it hurt. Colors popped behind his eyelids and his head pounded. He pressed his palms over his ears, but nothing he did could muffle the voices or the sounds around him. Not knowing what else to do, he prayed. One line was all he said, but he repeated himself over and over again.

"Señor, protégeme de todo mal . . . Lord, protect me from all evil . . . Señor, protégeme de todo mal . . ."

These words helped to calm him, but all was shattered when he felt something touch his arm. Carlos screamed, the terror in his voice unimaginable, yet so very real. Eyes jammed shut, he ran from his hiding spot. Laughter surrounded him. It cheered him on. It tormented his soul. He fell once but did not open his eyes. Tripping a second time caused his chin to hit the ground and his bottom teeth to bite into his upper lip. Warmth filled his mouth as his lip bled with violent ambition. Forcing his eyes open, he ran toward a stacked rock wall that ran behind his church, past the cemetery, ending near the open field across from his casita.

Out of breath, but still alive, he reached the rock wall. Doubling over, a pain stabbed his side, and he felt dizzy. His heart thumped his chest and throbbed in his cut lip. Daring to look over his shoulder, he saw that he had not been followed. He stood a little straighter, feeling a tiny bit better, and exhaled long slow breaths.

Lamplight glowed in the church windows. The warm pulse looked inviting as it pierced the night, yet it seemed to stop at the cemetery's border as if forbidden from entering. Taking a final huff of air, Mata walked slowly along the rock wall as he headed for home. His vision had vanished, and the boys who teased him were nowhere to be seen or heard.

As he approached the field where the rock wall ended, a dark figure jumped into view, howling like a banshee. Carlos screamed out, then losing control of himself, dropped to his knees and wet himself. Crouching on the ground, he felt the hard, thick form of a mighty stone beneath his palm. In one frantic, thoughtless motion, he picked up the rock, jumped to his feet, and threw it as hard as he could at the terrible beast.

"Get away from me!"

Hearing a sickening thud followed by a painful grunt forced Carlos to open his eyes. Terror filled him yet again.

"What the hell? Carlos!"

Instead of hitting a nightmarish Lechuza, the rock hit one of the older boys in the head. It was a perfect shot. The boy dropped to the ground, lifeless, his face a mask of shocked finality. Blood pooled around his head, dark and thick.

The rest of the boys appeared, creating

a semi-circle around their friend, their laughter replaced by gasps of horror.

"I . . . I . . . think he's dead!" one boy stuttered.

For a split second, their eyes met Carlos's, and he saw something he had never seen before: fear. Not of Lechuza, but of him.

Without another word, Carlos pivoted and sprinted all the way home, bursting through the door. His papá looked up, concern filling his eyes at the sight of his distraught son.

"Carlos, what happened? You look terrified."

He opened his mouth to speak but found no words. Instead, he collapsed into his father's arms, a sob escaping his lips.

His papá held him close, knowing without being told that something had irrevocably changed. They both felt it—the birth of a shadow that would follow Carlos, darken his days, and haunt his nights.

"Sit down, hijo," his father murmured, dread settling over him like a dark cloud. "We needn't speak of it now. But always remember, the darkness is not just out there; it is within us, too. I have a feeling that tonight you've met yours."

Alone, in the dark, Carlos Ruiz-Mata let El Despiadado fill the void in his thoughts and suffer the pain of what deeds he had done, for once the light returned, there would be more to do. So much more to do.

CHAPTER 31

"What is going on, Cass?"

The words, "somebody killed him," rang in my head as if I stood inside the bell on the church tower at high noon.

"Cass!" she pleaded. "Is it about Spencer?" her voice quivered, her nerves losing control.

I turned to hurry to the Explorer, but Raven blocked my path.

"Shit! Raven . . . get in the car."

She grabbed both of my arms and squeezed. "What is it?"

My concern for Spencer and the shock of the news made me snap. "Goddamn it! Move!"

The words were out before I could take them back. Maybe it was the way the headlights shone on her, maybe it was shadow, but Raven's whole demeanor changed before my eyes. Her jaw sagged open, a high-pitched chirp emanating from deep in her throat. Her eyes grew hollow, and what hope she had left disappeared, leaving a stark, gray look about her. She let go of my arms and stepped back.

"I can't . . . I . . . where is my son!"

The depth of her anguish surpassed mine. I tried to reach out, but she recoiled. "Raven."

Tears streamed down her cheeks.

"It's not about Spencer. We'll find him. But . . ."

I looked for a sign that I was getting through to her, but she did not budge. "Javier Santos was killed. That's what Flint was telling me."

"Oh god!" Raven fell forward into my arms. "I thought . . ."

"I have to call Chance, and I have to take you home."

Raven pulled away; her cheeks flushed beneath streams of falling tears.

"What about Spencer?"

"He is a smart kid. I have to believe that he is okay. Right now, I must respond to this." I looked at her hoping she would understand, needing her to understand, but I knew that there was no reason in the world that would pull her focus away from finding our son. "Come on. We gotta go."

I stepped around her and opened the passenger side door. Raven stayed still, her shoulders shaking with each quiet sob.

"Rave."

Turning with the speed of a three-toed sloth, Raven inched her way toward the Explorer. She walked with her head bowed and got in without looking at me. I closed the door behind her and walked around to the driver's side.

How much worse could this night get?

I sat down behind the wheel and fired up the engine. Holding my cell phone where I could read my list of contacts, I scrolled until I found

Chance's number. A quick tap of my thumb and his line began to ring. With an aggressive stomp of my foot on the gas, we peeled out of the parking lot. I was not waiting around for Chance to pick up.

The tires bounced onto RR170, screeching when the rubber met the road. Chance's phone rang three times before he picked up. His voice sounded gravelly.

"This is Chance."

"It's Cass. Get dressed. We have a ten-thirteen, I repeat, officer down. Javier Santos has been killed."

I could hear Chance shuffling around on the other end of the line.

"Come again, Cass. Who did you say?"

"Levi Flint found Santos's patrol car near Panther Creek. It's a long story, and I don't have much more info to share than that at the moment, but I'm headed out there now."

"You notify dispatch?"

"That's my next call."

"Hang on." I heard Chance set his phone down. In the background, radio static squelched to life. Though garbled and sounding far off, I heard Chance relay the information. A moment later, he was back on the phone with me. *"Where are you, Cass?"*

"Heading south on RR170, just past the DQ."

"Dispatch has been notified. All available

units responding." Aside from Chance's deep breathing, the line fell silent.

"Chance?"

With a surge of authority, Chance's voice responded with a resounding boom over the phone. *"Get out there immediately and take charge of the scene until I arrive."*

The line disconnected and silence returned to the cockpit. I activated the strobes on the dashboard and pressed the gas pedal to the floor. With a mix of urgency and worry gnawing at my gut, we raced down the dark road toward Flint and our fallen friend.

I had known police officers who had lost their lives in the line of duty, but this was the first time since the Gulf War that someone close to me had been killed. Now was not the time to let emotion dictate action, though it was hard to separate personal from professional feelings.

Raven sat with her fingers clenched in her lap. I could see the reflection of her face in the side window. Her eyes looked despondent as she stared out into the night. I felt torn by my duty to take charge of the crime scene and find Spencer. How could I put aside one for the other?

The dull swirl of red and blue strobes and the wail of multiple sirens rose out of the blackness, seeming to surface on all sides of us. South Brewster County had awakened to a hometown nightmare.

"Listen," I said, glancing at Raven. "Change of plans. We're gonna drive straight to the crime scene. Stay in the car. I'll have Flint drive you home."

"So, you're giving up?"

Heat radiated from my chest to my neck. "No. I'm not. Finding Spencer is just as important to me as it is to you."

"But . . . there's always a *but* these days."

"No but. Absolutely no but. Raven, Javier Santos was just killed. The kid was like family to us."

"Spencer *is* family, Cass." Raven crossed her arms, her stare shifting to me. "You can have Flint take me home, but I'm not giving up. I'm going to find our boy. Tonight!"

The Explorer gripped the pavement like a NASCAR truck speeding down the track. The world around me became a blur. My vision tapered to a tunnel of blacktop highway and shooting white painted lines. Minutes passed and miles raced by, but Raven and I did not speak again.

When the Explorer crested the final hill before Panther Creek, the pulsating glow of hazard lights caught my attention from the northbound shoulder of RR170. Drawing closer, the intense illumination from Flint's roof-mounted light bar enveloped Santos's patrol car in a stark white sheen.

As we drew nearer, the scene seemed to magnify, and the sobering gravity of the situation weighed heavier and heavier. Driving across the center lines, I pulled behind Flint's truck and shifted the Explorer into P.

"Please. Stay in the car, Raven."

Raven did not answer.

I left the Explorer running. The red and blue strobes swirled across the highway and over the scene before shooting into the darkness beyond the desolate West Texas road, the endless fluidity of the lights signaling ground zero of our tragedy.

Stepping out, I saw Flint leaning against his truck, his typically stern face betraying just a hint of vulnerability. When I approached, he looked up, his eyes carrying the faintest shadow of sorrow, but the steel in them unmistakable.

"Cass," he grunted, nodding at me.

"Flint," I acknowledged. "Where is he?"

Flint glanced over his shoulder. "Other side, against the car. I didn't touch a thing after I saw 'im. Goddamn it, Cass, of all the things to find tonight."

I looked at Santos's patrol car, then over to Raven still in the Explorer. Flint must have spotted her, too.

"You didn't find Spencer yet, did ya?"

"No. Raven's pretty shaken. Now that this happened, I can't be in two places at once. For all we know, Spence is having the time of his life."

"But . . ." Flint said, waiting for me to fill in the blank.

"But . . ." I paused. "It's not like him."

I stepped away from Flint and walked toward the patrol car. Before I had a chance to see Santos, Flint called out to me.

"Want me to take her home?"

"Yeah. Thanks," I said, stopping to look back.

Flint nodded, and I watched him walk over to the Explorer. He rapped a knuckle on the window, gaining Raven's attention. I continued around the patrol car, breathing into my nose and out of my mouth. I was no stranger to dead bodies, but circumstances were very different in this case.

Lying on his side, face-first against the rear door, I could have mistaken Santos for trying to reach for something underneath the car had I not already known the truth.

My stomach twisted in angry knots. Using my phone's flashlight, I began a careful examination of Javier. Starting from his boots, I trailed the light upward, taking in every detail. A large hole protruded out of the back of his head. Blood spatter and brain matter matted his hair. Skull fragments littered the exit wound like dead pine needles under the tree at Christmas. I could see the beginning of a cut along the edge of his neck, but it disappeared under his body. Blood stained his uniform, its tan color looking as if it were caked with mud.

Surprised and enraged, I stood up, looking around for no other reason than to clear the palette in my mind. The gruesome nature of this scene was more difficult to process than I had expected.

Sirens grew louder, and the horizon pulsed red and blue. I walked around to the clean side of the patrol car and waited for backup to arrive. I noticed Raven standing outside of the Explorer talking with Flint. The approaching vehicles must have caught their attention because they both looked in the direction of noise, then turned their heads and looked at me. Raven stepped away and headed over to me. I met her next to Flint's truck.

"Flint offered to take you home."

"I know."

"Maybe Spencer is already there."

"Maybe."

"The last thing I want to do is leave you alone right now, but I have to handle this."

"I know."

She was not putting up much of a fight. I suspected she was angrier with me than she was leading on, but doing her best to cover it up.

"I'll be back as soon as I can. Call me if . . ."

"Cass," she interrupted. "I know this is terrible. It's the most horrible thing in the world, and you are in it up to your neck. This job, this place, it was good to us at the beginning, but now it feels like it is dragging us down more than helping us heal."

"Raven," I said, with a soft undertone of empathy and hurt.

"The only thing worse, Cass, is the regret you will feel if Spencer really is in trouble. Do what you have to do. I'm going to do the same."

Without another word, Raven opened the truck door and climbed inside. Flint stood by the driver's door. We shared a glance.

"Thank you, Flint."

He nodded, then loaded up. The engine growled as if it protested having to leave. As the first of many county vehicles arrived, Flint headed for the CR with Raven. Even as the sirens' wail filled the night, I could hear the rumble of the diesel engine as it drove away. I listened until I could no longer hear it and thought, *how much worse can things get?*

CHAPTER 32

The cab of Flint's pickup was as quiet as prayer time at a funeral. It remained somber until Flint took his foot off the accelerator. The engine revved down, but Raven spoke up.

"You're not taking me home."

"Ms. Raven?"

"You heard me. You're taking me to find my son."

Flint opened his mouth to speak, but one look from Raven and he knew there was no winning this battle. Instead, he pressed the accelerator, reawakening the beast under the hood. Thick exhaust filled the air, swirling in the dark behind the truck.

With hands on the wheel and eyes on the road, an agreeable Flint asked, "Where to?"

CHAPTER 33

The air grew thick as the crime scene came alive with activity. Deputy Leo was the first to arrive, his cruiser skidding slightly on the gravel.

"What the hell happened?" he said, jumping out of the car.

"I don't know yet, I just arrived myself."

Deputy Leo looked past me at the familiar patrol car, his expression one of dawning realization. His eyes, red-rimmed and weary, showed a depth of emotion. "Where is Javier?"

My heart sank. From what I knew, Leo and Santos were friends long before they became deputies.

"He's on the other side of the car." I placed a hand on his shoulder. "There's a lot to do, Diego. The best way to help him now is stay focused and do our jobs. We'll find out who did this, and I'll make sure you're with me when we do."

As we talked, two patrol cars pulled onto the far shoulder. "Coordinate with those two. We need to secure a perimeter around the scene."

Deputy Leo nodded, his jaw clenched tight as he turned and sprang into action.

RR170 transformed rapidly, the darkened highway filling with a flurry of headlights and swirling red and blue strobes. It was not long before the crime scene took on a life of its own.

The road became a beacon in the dead of night, flares placed at hundred-yard intervals to the north and south, their fiery glow casting elongated shadows that danced on the pavement. Manned patrol cars barricaded the road in both directions. The cold, steel glint of floodlights set up by arriving deputies gave the crime scene an eerie, detached ambiance.

When Chance arrived on the scene, I walked him over to see Deputy Santos before I brought him up to speed with the investigation. Leaning over, I pulled back a blanket that had been used to cover his body.

"*Dios mío.*" Chance rubbed his jaw as he looked at the deceased deputy. "Cover him up again, Cass."

I laid the blanket down, covering Santos again. When I rose to my feet, Chance and I locked eyes. The pain was real, as was our understanding that this was not the time to mourn the loss of our friend, but it was time to catch the son of a bitch who killed him.

"Give me a sitrep."

"Looks like a typical traffic stop at first glance. The placement of Santos's unit is by the book; the tread impressions in the gravel indicate the assailant's vehicle decelerated gradually before coming to a full stop. It appears that whoever he pulled over initially seemed cooperative. That's where things heat up."

I led Chance to where the subject vehicle had stopped, maneuvering around evidence cones and markers so as not to contaminate the scene.

"As you can see, Santos approached the vehicle on foot. The distance between the front and rear tires places him at the driver's side door. At some point, the driver exited the vehicle and stood in front of Santos. Partial footprints on the gravel suggest Santos had the driver turn around, probably to place restraints on him." Squatting, I pointed to a swept area of gravel and dirt. "It seems the driver made a quick motion to overtake Santos prior to being cuffed. Blood spatters indicate he was cut or stabbed. The amount of blood around the scene suggests he suffered a traumatic arterial wound. The final, lethal attack resulted in a single gunshot to the head."

Chance surveyed the scene once more, echoing my words to himself as he assessed the situation. I gave him a moment to process it all.

"Have we found any projectiles or casings?"

"Not yet, but we are canvassing the area. Chance, there is one more thing. Deputy Santos's service weapon is missing."

Chance placed his hands on his hips and bowed his head. "This is a goddamn nightmare. You contact the medical examiner?"

"Yes. Dr. Frannie Lopez-Tasker is on her way with her team."

"Good. I'll get on the horn with DPS out of Lajitas. They can have a CSI crew up here in no time to help process the mess."

We stood together assessing the scene, hurting and angry, trying to piece together what had happened. A seasoned detective excels not just in procedure but in the art of observation. While glaring irregularities might capture their attention, it is often the subtle incongruities that intrigue them. An out-of-place pebble or an inexplicable metal shard amid a crime scene might be overlooked, but to the professionally trained eye, it would stick out like a fart in a library. I could sense more questions were coming from Chance, and I was right.

"You told me Levi Flint found Santos? Should we bring him in for questioning?"

"No, he was out helping look for Spencer."

"Spencer? What's going on, Cass?"

"It's a long story, Chance, but I'll make it brief. After being out all day with a girl he met in town, Spencer didn't come home tonight. He hasn't called, which is out of character for him. Each time I tried to reach him, the call went directly to voicemail. It's like his phone battery is dead, or he is beyond cell service range. Maybe his phone is turned off, I don't know. Not knowing is eating Raven up. I share her concerns, but I think we both know what it was like at his age; he's a guy out with a girl and may have other things on his mind."

"Gotta be hard waiting at home."

"That's just it. She refused to stay at home, so we went out to look for him. That's how Flint got involved. He saw us leaving and offered to help. Flint said he knew a few places to look, so Raven and I took the road to town, and Flint headed south. We had just located Spencer's Jeep parked in front of Dairy Queen when he called me about Santos. My thought is that he rode off with the girl, but it's only a guess."

Chance took a deep breath, rubbing his temples. "This is the night that never ends. Once we get things squared away, and if your boy doesn't show up by daybreak, we'll put the full weight of the county behind you to help find him."

The distant hum of an engine grew louder. We both heard the approaching vehicle and saw that it was a medical examiner's van rolling past the north barricade. As it pulled up, the side door rolled open, and Dr. Frannie Lopez-Tasker hopped out.

Dr. Frannie was in plain clothes, a distinct contrast to her usual flair for fashion, even when on the job. Our eyes met, and I nodded. Her face was a mask of professionalism, but her eyes betrayed a hint of sadness. "Cass, Chance, hate to say it's good to see you under these circumstances."

"Thank you for coming so quickly, Frannie," Chance replied.

I had only known Dr. Frannie a short time, but she had become good friends with Raven during a previous investigation on the CR and during time spent with her doting over Chance as he recovered from injuries obtained during a raid at the Double S ranch. Chance had known Dr. Frannie for years, and while he was at least ten years her elder, he harbored some affection for her. She knew it, and liked it, but they were good friends, and that was all.

"Can you take me to him? I'd like to get started right away," Dr. Frannie asked.

Leading her to Deputy Santos's covered body, we watched as she examined him, her experienced hands moving with a mix of precision and reverence.

"This is bad," she murmured.

During the examination, she repositioned Deputy Santos, revealing the gruesome aftermath of the attack.

"Any preliminary observations, Frannie?" Chance asked.

She stood up, removing her gloves. "Too early to say, but the wound to his neck is consistent with a knife or sharp object. The amount of blood loss is consistent with a severed artery, but that's not what killed him."

She moved her hand over Deputy Santos's

forehead, circling her finger around the blackened and bruised bullet hole. "There is stippling around the gunshot wound. It's faint, but present, indicating that the gun was fired at close range. I see no other obvious trauma to the body. I'll need to conduct a full autopsy back at the lab to give you more."

Chance nodded, his gaze never leaving Santos. "Thanks, Frannie. Do what you have to do."

Time seemed to meld into oblivion. Word had spread about the officer-involved shooting, drawing a news crew eager to edge past the northern barricade. The deputy on duty held his ground, skillfully keeping them at bay. For them, it might have been another story, another headline, but for us, it was a heart-wrenching loss of one of our own. The thought of his final moments becoming breakfast TV was unbearable.

A swift response to Chance's call to DPS brought their elite CSI team to our aid. I briefed them when they arrived, and they went straight to work processing the scene. Once they finished their preliminary work, Dr. Frannie was cleared to move Javier Santos's remains. The slam of the rear van door infused a finality like the sound of the last nail being hammered into a coffin.

I stood by Chance as the van drove off. The scene around us continued to buzz with activity, yet in the midst of the chaos, a deep silence settled between Chance and me, a shared grief over the loss of our friend.

"Sheriff Gilbert!" Deputy Leo's voice called out. "We found something!"

Chance and I rushed over.

"What is it, Deputy?"

"Found a casing," he said, holding up a clear evidence pouch. "Looks like what we are issued by the county, Sheriff."

Chance took the bag and inspected the casing. "We located Santos's weapon yet?"

"No, sir. But we did learn who he pulled over. Dispatch asserts that he stopped an old model Camaro, Texas license plate L5W-2940, for a rear taillight being out. The car is registered to a Bruce Jespers."

Chance nodded. "Let's track down Mr. Jespers and see what we can find out from him."

"Sir, I know that Camaro," Deputy Leo said. "It may be in Bruce Jespers's name, but it's not his car. It's his son's. Lane Jespers."

Chance inhaled a deep breath, letting it whistle through his nose as he let it out again. He looked at me, his mustache twitching. "Cass, let's go have a chat with that little son of a bitch."

CHAPTER 34

The reception area at the South Brewster County Sheriff's Office was eerily quiet, its ambiance more reminiscent of a funeral parlor than a beacon of law and order. Raven hesitated as she entered, taking in the dimmed lights overhead. The silence inside the office was punctuated by the occasional murmur of a distant police radio. The indistinct chatter crackled through the air. Raven's thoughts drifted to Cass, imagining those distant voices were coordinating with him at the chilling scene on the side of RR170.

A blast of air from an air conditioning vent washed over her, making her skin feel cool and clammy. Her footsteps echoed louder than she would have liked, announcing her arrival as she moved toward the reception window.

On the window, Raven noticed a removable nameplate—Deputy Manuela Mendoza. The woman sitting behind it seemed like she was worlds away, her eyes bloodshot and distant, signs of a long shift or a tough night. But what caught Raven's attention was the subtle stain on the deputy's cheeks, the trails of recent tears.

Raven cleared her throat. "Excuse me, Deputy Mendoza? I . . . I need help."

Taking a second to process Raven's question,

Deputy Mendoza maintained her professionalism despite her exhausted look.

"How can I assist you, ma'am?"

"Yes. My name is Raven Callahan, and I want to report a missing person."

Deputy Mendoza's eyes sharpened with focus before they dulled back to their tired state. "Missing person? Who's missing?" she asked, her voice conveying the routine nature of her question but with an undertone of concern.

Raven's voice trembled. "It's my son, Spencer. He hasn't been in touch for the past twelve hours."

Deputy Mendoza shifted in her chair. "I understand your worry, Mrs. Callahan, especially concerning a family member. But generally, for adults, we wait for a twenty-four-hour window before we can officially record them as missing."

Raven felt a chilling tingle at the base of her neck. Her fingers fidgeted on the countertop. Noting Raven's distress, Deputy Mendoza sat up in her chair and leaned forward.

"Was Spencer with friends? Was he out by himself? Did he say where he was going?"

"He only came home from college for a few days. He was supposed to be with Charlotte Huckabee, but I found his Jeep parked over at Dairy Queen, and he wasn't there."

"Is it possible that she drove him somewhere, and they just left the car behind? Have you tried reaching the young lady?"

"I don't know. They only just met, and I don't know how to get in touch with her. Spencer isn't the type to just go off the grid. This isn't like him. He always checks in."

Deputy Mendoza jotted notes onto a notepad, then turned her attention to the computer screen in front of her. Her fingers raced over the keyboard, each click of the keys feeling like tiny prickles in Raven's ears.

The whir of the air conditioning fell silent, but the sound of the sheriff's office front door closing filled the void. Raven turned around to see Flint standing near the entrance. He nodded but did not join her at the window. Raven gave a halfhearted smile, then turned around to face the deputy. She put her hands on the counter, wrestling her nerves as she waited.

Deputy Mendoz studied the monitor. After a brief moment, she scribbled something down and peeled a fresh Post-it from its pad. "Here we go." She slid the note across the counter to Raven. "This is bending protocol, but it may give you a head start." With edgy eyes sweeping side to side, Deputy Mendoza confided in Raven. "I have a son, too. If he were missing, I'd do anything to make sure he was safe. If he still doesn't turn up, come back, and I'll refer you to a case officer."

"Thank you."

Raven picked up the small, yellow square. After reading the note, she offered an appreciative smile. Deputy Mendoza nodded, then returned to clicking keys on the keyboard and staring at the computer screen. Raven turned away and walked toward the exit. Flint held the door open, then followed her outside.

With swift steps, Raven walked down to the parking lot and got into the truck. By the time Flint was behind the wheel, she had her phone out and was entering the numbers written on the paper. She pressed send and held the phone up to her ear.

Raven lost track of how many times the line rang before voicemail picked up. She hung up and redialed the number. On the unsuccessful third try, she waited for voicemail to answer, but did not hang up. After the automated recording played, and the beep sounded, Raven left a message.

"Charlotte. This is Raven Callahan, Spencer's mother. Please call me back as soon as you get this message. We are worried about you and Spencer. He hasn't come home. Please call. My number is 319-555-2024."

Raven disconnected the call and dropped the phone in her lap. She covered her eyes with the palms of her hands and fell into a flood of emotion. Her imagination ran rampant, conjuring up the worst possible scenarios her subconscious dared to create. Her breath and tears moistened her hands and face. She was unable to comfort herself. She needed Cass. She needed to know what was going on with Spencer.

As she drifted into depths of despair deeper than she had ventured in the past, two things happened. First, she felt the warm touch of a hand on her shoulder. It helped steady her nerves just knowing someone was nearby.

The second surprised her, although it would not have been much of a surprise to anyone who knew Raven. The tears stopped rolling from her eyes as if someone had closed the floodgates. A warmth radiated in the pit of her stomach and a numb sensation fanned out across her hands and into her fingers. At that moment, when rock bottom stared Raven in the face, she fought back.

An angry voice in her head screamed like a drill Sergeant at morning PT, "Stop this sniveling crap! It won't help one damn bit! Pull it together and find a way to find your son!"

As if having an epiphany about what she must do, she sat straight up, wiped her face with her hands, and fastened her seat belt.

Pulling his hand away from her, Flint asked, "You . . . okay, Ms. Raven?"

"I will be." Crumpling the yellow Post-it in her hand, she let out a long, assertive sigh. "Take me to the Flying H."

CHAPTER 35

Exhausted, in pain, and facing extreme dehydration, Spencer thought to himself, *I'm in serious trouble.*

Trapped on the canyon floor, he leaned against a large rock wall that towered into the darkness so high he could not tell where earth ended and sky began. The coarse ground beneath him felt cold, and every pebble and grit seemed to press into his already bruised body. He had brushed aside as many small stones as he could, attempting to create a smooth surface to sit on, yet, as if mocking his efforts, for each stone he set aside, another obstinate rock emerged.

His ankle throbbed with a ferocity that made his whole leg sore. He did not know if it was broken or badly sprained, but it hurt like hell, and that was real enough. Tiny cuts and scrapes on his arms and face burned, feeling like hot razors slicing into his skin. Each time he tried to swallow, it felt like shards of glass digging into his throat. His escape from Lane's killer took its toll on Spencer's body, but he was alive.

The air grew cooler causing him to shiver. The breeze carried a fresh scent—a clean, sweet smell found before summer rainstorms—though from the bottom of the canyon, all Spencer could see above were bright, twinkling stars in the clear Mexican sky.

Fatigue teased him. Unable to sleep, he closed his eyes and imagined that he was on another of his extreme adventures. Rock climbing and rappelling Enchanted Rock in the Texas Hill Country, skydiving over Wharton, four-wheeling it along the barren sands of Padre Island; Spencer had a love for adventure. The visions brought him some comfort, but that good feeling vanished every time he opened his eyes to his current reality. He only wished for one thing to come from this mistake—*to survive.*

It was pitch black, and even though his eyes had adjusted, visibility was limited to a mere arm's length, save for the distant twinkling stars. He intended to reevaluate his predicament come daylight and then act. The plan, while riddled with uncertainties, seemed like the only viable option. The unfortunate truth was that even the best-laid plans do not always unfold as expected.

This grim reality hit Spencer hard. A chill ran down his spine and his heart pounded against his chest, causing his ankle to thump harder with each beat. An unmistakable growl, low and rumbling permeated the darkness. And it was getting closer.

CHAPTER 36

"Special Investigator Callahan, Deputy Leo, you're on me. Roll out, Code two."

The formality of our situation demanded we act accordingly. This was not a good-ol'-boy operation where only those who drank and hunted together rode off in search of glory. This was a manhunt, a search for answers, and we all needed to focus in order to do our best for our deceased friend.

"Cass, grab a radio from unit three, and follow me."

Sheriff Gilbert marched to his unit, his stride purposeful, his jaw clenched and determined. As I headed for the Explorer, I noticed Deputy Leo held back, head turned and eyes locked on Deputy Santos's patrol car. I stopped and spoke to him.

"Hey. Diego. Leaving now doesn't mean you're turning your back on Santos. There's nothing more for you to do here. Come on, we gotta go."

Santos maintained his stare but nodded his head. Behind us, Chance pulled onto the highway and chirped his siren once. In reverence of his friend, Deputy Leo touched his fingertips to his forehead, dragged them down to his chest, and then reached out to each shoulder, marking the sign of the cross. He made a fist and kissed his fingers, then turned and jogged to his patrol car without saying a word to me.

Like a train of roller coaster cars, we followed behind Chance's Bronco as he led the way, racing up and down, over and around the elevated, windy northbound road to Brewster. We knew exactly where we were headed and tensions ran high. A house call at this hour would give anyone cause for alarm, so our tactics had to be professional and direct while wielding extreme caution. I knew very little about Bruce Jespers or his son, Lane, but experience has taught me that trouble usually runs in the family. And at this hour, anything could happen.

In record time, we crossed into the city limits. Streetlights lined the main road into Brewster at staggered intervals. The old sodium bulbs gave off a pale, yellow hue. Some cycled off and on, flickering as if drowning in an electrical current too strong for the bulb to survive.

We sped past houses and businesses, and at one point, Dairy Queen. I glanced at the parking lot and saw that Spencer's Jeep was still there. *Where are you, kid?*

Gripping the steering wheel tighter, I forced myself to suppress my worry, though it festered like a cancer in the pit of my stomach.

"Roll on. Code one. We're two minutes from the Jesperses' residence."

Chance's voice crackled on the radio, then fell silent. Depuy Leo responded first.

"Ten-four."

"Copy that," I said.

We turned left off RR170 onto Mercado Drive and crossed three intersections before turning right onto 5th Street. Chance's Bronco slowed the pace of our pack as we approached our destination, 1847 5th Street.

We stopped in front of an old, one-story house. Our headlights centered on the front door. Light stretched out to illuminate the full face of the house. A filthy picture window to the right of the door glared back at us. Tattered boards with flecked paint wrapped themselves around the structure like old wounds left uncovered to heal on their own. An old gas lamp burned in the yard between the front walk and the gravel driveway. Brown vines entangling the base of the lamppost looked brittle yet clung to the metal pole like a sticky spider's web. A covered carport ran the length of the left side house. An old Chevrolet pickup was the only vehicle I could see parked beneath, though there was a junker set atop blocks between the truck and the chain-link fence that divided the Jesperses' property from the neighbors. There was no sign of Lane's Camaro.

We each stepped out of our vehicles and convened on the cracked walkway that led to the front door.

"Mr. Jespers won't be too happy about us being here so early. Fact is, I don't give a shit. Back me up, an' keep yer eyes peeled."

Chance nodded to each of us, his orders clear, his temperament grounded and professional. We nodded back and followed him to the front door in a stack formation. With Deputy Leo flanking Chance's left, I took position on his right. I scanned every detail from the front door to the window, then to the house's edge before sweeping back over the scene.

Chance paused when we reached the front door. His eyes sharpened, his look a blend of caution and determination. The intensity of his gaze silently communicated the weight of our next move. With a subtle nod, he signaled it was time. He raised his hand and balled his fingers into a fist.

The dull wood thumped as Chance knocked three times on the door. When no one answered, he knocked again, then called out, "This is Sheriff Chance Gilbert, South Brewster County Sheriff's Office. Open the door, Mr. Jespers."

From deep inside the house, as if we had awoken a bear in its cave, a loud, disgruntled murmur grew. With an angry heave, the door swung open.

Commanding the entirety of the doorway, Bruce Jespers stood before us, face scrunched and wrinkled, his eyes bleary yet pulled wide and seemed to burn with a fire from an interrupted sleep.

"What the hell are you doin' comin' out here at this time a night, Sheriff? You got that no-good boy-a-mine with ya?"

A rank smell of body odor and spilled whiskey invaded my nose. He stepped forward one step and glared at each of us. Chance did not budge. My hand, however, found that resting on the grip of my Glock 17 felt quite natural, though I held back my urge to draw for now.

"Mr. Jespers, we need to speak with Lane."

With a disgusted, questioning look, far from what a concerned father might make, Bruce barreled his way outside and looked around. His quick steps found him surrounded, though he did not show any signs of intimidation. His mix of weariness and the apparent leftover alcohol in his system made his ornery attitude less than desirable.

"Move outta my way," he said, brushing past Deputy Leo. He cocked his head to one side as if straining to see around the corner of the house. He stopped after only a couple of steps, then straightened his stance. Dressed in boxer shorts and a stained white undershirt, Bruce scratched the top of his head, then swiped his arm down and slapped his right leg. "Car ain't here. Middle of the fuckin' night! Where are you, you little bastard!"

Deputy Leo moved as if he were going to approach Bruce, but Chance caught his arm and held him back. Trading glances, Chance shook his head, then lifted his chin in Bruce's direction.

"He has no idea where Lane is."

Bruce whirled around with his hands out to his side. His shirt lifted with his arms revealing his white gut and hair-choked belly button. "Son of a bitch ain't here." He lowered his arms, then walked back toward us, cursing once again when his bare feet stepped on a rock in the yard. He hopped three times, then hobbled the rest of the way over to us. "What do ya want with Lane, anyway?"

"Do you know where he might be?" Chance asked, answering Bruce's question with one of his own.

"Hell, if I know. You try lookin' in Mexico?"

"Mr. Jespers," I said. "It's important that we locate him as soon as possible."

Bruce shifted his frustrated glare onto me. His lips curled around under his nose, and he sneered when he spoke. "Oh, well. If it's important, let me go inside and check his rolodex. Maybe that'll help." His sarcasm was palpable. "The boy's probably off smokin' with them wetbacks he calls friends, er probably tryin' ta get back inta Charlotte Huckabee's pants again."

A surge of adrenaline coursed through my veins. "Say that again."

"The part where he's off smokin', or off fuckin'?"

"Mr. Jespers . . ." I paused, forcing the father's worry inside of me to remain subdued behind the Special Investigator badge on my hip. "What was the name of the girl you said?"

"Charlotte Huckabee. Lives over at the Rio Vista somethin' er other."

"Terrace. Rio Vista Terrace," Deputy Leo said.

"Yeah. You know the place. It's a real dump. She should be livin' out on the ranch with her uncle, but he's an ass. Everyone knows it."

I could not have agreed more.

"Mr. Jespers," Chance said, handing him a business card. "When Lane gets in, call me right away."

Bruce took the card, squinted his eyes as he looked it over, then saluted with an erect middle finger. Chance stepped forward, but this time did not stop until he was nose to nose with Bruce.

"You forget, I know you, Mr. Jespers. Lane ain't the only prick in town I've had to deal with before. You call me as soon as you see him, or the next time we meet you'll be bangin' yer hand on the gang side of a cell door, begging for my attention."

Chance was a boulder, a solid jamming force which Bruce had no way of avoiding. His glare began to falter now that his junkyard dog persona had been gagged by the true alpha in Brewster.

"Okay, okay," he whispered, overwhelmed in submission.

"Good." Chance turned to us. "Deputy Leo, head over to Charlotte's. Get her address from dispatch. See if she is home and ask her to come down to the office for questioning."

"Yes, sir."

Deputy Leo headed out while Chance and I waited behind. Bruce lingered in the yard, looking like a wounded mutt at the county pound.

"I think it's time you fill me in about Spencer."

Looking Chance in the eye, I took a deep breath and told him everything.

CHAPTER 37

The knobby tires on Flint's truck chewed the gravel road, spitting out the larger stones while devouring those that caught beneath its rubber jaws. The digital clock on the dashboard read, 4:37. Raven laid her head against the window, her fatigue marred by adrenaline-filled concern. When the truck began to slow, Raven glanced ahead and saw an archway appear in the truck's headlights similar in design to the one at the entrance of the CR. This one was twice the size and had a large "H" mounted in the center. The word "FLYING" was inscribed where the cross stroke of the "H" would typically be.

"Just about here, Ms. Raven."

Raven shifted around in her seat. Flint steered the truck under the archway. The cab shook as they rumbled over a cattle guard at the entrance to the ranch. The vibrations ended as fast as they began, but a residual fuzzy feeling toyed with Raven's nerves.

Flint noticed.

"Sure you wanna do this? We can always come back with Cass another time."

"We are not waiting for Cass. I'm not waiting for anyone. If you don't want to go, stop the truck, and I'll walk the rest of the way."

"Whoa, now. I ain't goin' nowhere, but you oughtta consider gettin' that outta yer system before we go an' wake up the whole ranch. The moment we arrive, we'll be in the sights of any number of rifles seein' how we're arriving so early, and uninvited at that."

"You trying to handle me, Levi?"

Flint looked at Raven and laughed.

"Ha! No, ma'am. I am not. If I may say so, I don't think there's a man that could."

Floyd Huckabee's ranch house looked like a misplaced Mexican-style mansion more apt for the hills of Southern California or the streets of Polanco, Mexico City. Blackened windows poked through the house's smooth, milky, star-washed facade. Positioned on the east edge, they gave the appearance of a large skull, staring down those who might dare approach at night.

As Flint and Raven pulled into the courtyard, the full face of the house revealed a stunning transformation that Raven could not believe given her previous, ghastly impression of the ranch.

Its terracotta walls shimmered under the caress of the moonlight, while decorative arches and intricate ironwork balconies hinted at the artistry of a time long past. A series of impressive chimneys lent it an air of regality.

Raven's eyes were drawn to the grand wooden entrance door, its very grain pulsing with history.

It seemed to be both an invitation to step back into time and a barrier meant to keep the unwelcome away. Flanking it were large pots of desert cacti and yuccas, their prickles glinting in the flames from candelabras that adorned each side of the massive entrance.

The mansion's windows, tall and slender and framed by thick wooden shutters, were closed tight, but the faintest glow of light seeped through the cracks, suggesting some rooms had already awakened to face the coming day. A faint ripple of water from a fountain standing before the house shimmered and danced in a mix of flame and ambient light.

Aside from the trickle of the fountain, there was no noise, no movement. The mansion appeared to be asleep, save the thin glow from between the shutters, but some appearances were meant to be deceiving.

The palatial house loomed ahead, an anomaly in the Texan landscape but a testament to the influence and affluence of Floyd Huckabee. Flint's truck came to a gentle stop, its engine humming low. With a twist of the key, he cut the power and silence swallowed the last grumble of noise like a barn owl snatching a mouse from an open field.

Raven took a breath, absorbing the surroundings. Her eyes scanned every detail, every shadow. The play of moonlight on the terracotta walls gave the mansion an ethereal glow.

Determined to find Spencer, or answers that led to his whereabouts, Raven stepped out of the truck, her footsteps assured and purposeful. The mansion's entrance seemed to grow with each step as she approached.

Flint followed closely, casting a wary glance around. "I'd reckon they've got eyes on us already," he muttered.

Raven shrugged. "Good. Let them look. The sooner they notice us, the closer I am to finding Spencer."

Reaching the door, Raven did not hesitate. She rapped the large iron knocker hanging on the door three times, each clack of the wooden door announcing her uninvited arrival. Stepping back, she waited for the door to open. After moments of waiting, and her knocking still not answered, Raven tried again. She raised her hand to grasp the knocker but stopped short. A new sound, disturbingly familiar, caused her to turn around with slow, non-threatening movements.

Flint stood facing Raven, head bowed and hands raised at his sides. Looking past him, she saw the figure of a man step out of the shadows, rifle in hand and poised to fire.

"Hands where I can see 'em, darlin.'"

Refusing to lift her arms, defiance and impatience began an assault all of its own.

"That you, Mr. Huckabee?" she called out. "I'm looking for . . ."

"I don't care what you are looking for, miss. Ya ain't gonna find it here."

Flint raised his head and turned to face the man holding the gun.

"Floyd, yer talkin' to Raven Callahan. Maybe you could point yer weapon away from her?"

"Well, if it ain't Levi Flint. I've been meanin' ta talk with ya, but ya never seem ta be around when I come lookin'. Some might think yer avoidin' me."

"This ain't the time, Floyd."

"Let's make it the time, Levi."

Floyd Huckabee stepped forward, eyes smoldering, gun unwavering. Behind Raven, the front door swung open. A man stepped out holding a steel-plated semi-automatic pistol in his left hand. His right arm was fully wrapped in a cast that extended his pointer and middle fingers straight ahead.

"How we lookin', Mr. Huckabee?" the man asked.

"We're doin' just fine, Harv. Looks like an old friend of yers decided to pay a visit."

Harvey Oglethorp, Harv to most who knew him, cast his eyes onto Flint, rekindling a rage within him. "Look here, you remember what ya did to my finger? I think maybe it's time I collect my due from you."

Harvey stepped forward, but Raven blocked his path.

"Kindly step aside and let the men talk, miss."

"Men? That what you're calling yourselves? Looks more like a bunch of boys seeing who can piss the furthest."

"Beggin' yer pardon, but I don't think . . ."

"That's right," Raven continued. "Don't think. As a matter of fact, keep on *don't thinkin'* until I've had my say. Then, if yer still up for it, do what you like, but until I get someone's attention and start finding some answers, y'all ain't gonna do so much as spit!"

Raven became more enraged as she spoke, her words slurring into the local drawl of which she meant to mimic, but the naturality of it flowed off her lips as if she was meant to play the role of authoritative ranch boss her entire life.

Floyd Huckabee looked at Harv, then over to Flint.

"What the hell's got inta her?"

"Why don't ya hear her out, Floyd?" Flint said.

Floyd lowered his rifle and motioned for Harv to holster his pistol. Walking over to Raven, he wore a look of utter confusion and modest respect. When he stopped before her, he tipped his hat back and gazed into Raven's deepened eyes. She had his attention.

"Mr. Huckabee."

"Call me Floyd, Mrs. Callahan."

She nodded. "Okay . . . Floyd. I am sorry to barge in here in the middle of the night, but I don't know where else to turn. I'm looking for Charlotte. She and my son, Spencer, well . . . they became friends today, if that's what you want to call it. Anyway, he was supposed to have been with her this afternoon. Problem is, I haven't heard from Spence, and I can't get Charlotte on the phone. It's been so long, and I am worried something has happened to them."

Even in her strongest moment, tears welled up in her eyes. Floyd Huckabee's face softened. He glanced over her shoulder at Harv.

"Head inside. Rustle up some coffee." He locked eyes with Raven. "Ma'am, why don't we step inside." Laying a hand before him, Huckabee motioned toward the door.

"What about Flint?"

Huckabee's eyes dropped. He turned around and looked at Flint, huffing once.

"Fine," he said, glaring at Flint. Their feud was far from over, but a line in the sand had been drawn. Floyd Huckabee was a proud man, set in his beliefs and one who considered his way the only way. He was also someone who knew compassion even when it was not his best trait. "He can come if he likes."

"Well, I like," Raven said.

Floyd Huckabee walked to the door and opened

it wide, extending a polite nod to Raven and an olive branch to Flint.

Entering the house was like walking through the foyer at a lavish Mexican restaurant. Fanciful artwork hung on the walls, most depicting scenery from Mexico or Spain. Some portrayed the rough life of a *caballero*. Hard riding and herding cattle, distant dust storms framed by gilded light, daring landscapes placed to evoke comfort or instill fear, and scenes within a scene meant to immerse any art admirer that should gaze upon the piece. Pewter statues of horses rearing, running, and grazing lined a series of shelves in an off-set office. Travertine floors paved their way as Huckabee closed the door to the house before leading them further inside.

Like a tour guide weaving his group from exhibit to exhibit, Huckabee pointed out a few of his favorite pieces. He gloated about its rich history and made sure to add the ridiculous cost of each. Upon entering the kitchen area, Harv had coffee brewing. Its aroma filled the air.

"It's Colombian," Huckabee offered. "Only the best."

Raven enjoyed the smell, and under different circumstances might have let herself become impressed with the art collections and high-end décor, but this morning she could not have cared less.

"Please, have a seat."

Huckabee pulled a chair from beneath a large, round table and motioned to Raven. She sat down, and Harv placed a cup of coffee in front of her. Huckabee took the chair on her left. Steam rose from the coffee cup as Raven lifted it to her lips. Her hands trembled, causing her drink to ripple. She blew away the steam and took a sip, then set the cup down on the table.

"Now, what's this about Charlotte and your son?"

Raven turned to Huckabee.

"It's like I said. Spencer headed into town to pick her up, hang out, do whatever there is to do around here with her for the afternoon, but he never came home. I got Charlotte's number from . . ." Raven paused, remembering the implied discretion of Deputy Mendoza. "I called Charlotte, and she didn't pick up. I know you two are related, but forgive me, I don't know how. I hoped maybe she had spoken with you today. I am so worried. This is not like Spencer at all. Have you heard from her? Do you know where she is?"

Floyd Huckabee took a cup of coffee from Harv. He sipped before answering, his eyes seeming to consider both Raven and Flint. Beginning to believe Huckabee was playing games with her again, Raven stood up, tipping her chair over in one frustrated motion.

"Mr. Huckabee, please. If you know something, tell me."

"Hot damn, Flint. Mrs. Callahan's got about as much fire as you. Come ta think of it, where is Mr. Callahan? Why are you two gallivanting around together? Still hoping to get yer piece of the CR, Flint?"

Flint's eyes narrowed. "Watch yer mouth, Floyd."

Huckabee stood up and pointed at him. "No one tells me how to act in my house, especially a no-good son of a bitch like you."

With tensions exploding like dueling volcanoes, the kitchen turned into a hot mess of finger-pointing and raised voices. The immediate escalation forced Raven between Flint and Huckabee, to keep them from trading blows, and saw Harv reaching for his gun.

Like thunder clapping above their confrontation, the loud knocking of iron on wood echoed through the halls from the front door.

Exasperated, Huckabee stormed out of the kitchen. The door took three more impatient beatings before Huckabee could reach the handle. Raven and Flint filed behind ready to push by but slid to a stop as the door opened.

"What is this? Grand Central Station?" Huckabee said as if he had already had enough of the day.

"Mr. Huckabee, we'd like a word with . . ."

Sheriff Gilbert stopped short of finishing his statement when his eyes locked onto Raven's.

"Chance? What are you doing here?"

The mental wear and tear of the past few hours was apparent on Chance's face. He looked at Raven, his eyes suggesting that he too had a question, but that he already knew the answer.

"Maybe I should be asking the same thing about you."

CHAPTER 38

If the low growl emanating in the dark was not enough to cause Spencer genuine concern, a higher pitch yowl echoed off the canyon walls marking the presence of a second predator on the prowl.

Mountain lions, Spencer thought.

Unable to see the creatures, Spencer closed his eyes and took deep, silent breaths to calm his nerves. Straining his ears in a desperate attempt to gauge their position, he focused on each noise, each guttural warning, but the acoustics within the canyon made it impossible to pinpoint their location. The growling and hissing escalated. Growing louder, the warnings and threats reverberating off the tall rock walls screamed at Spencer to act. But what could he do? His ankle was useless. It was too dark to see. Weighing his options, he made the quick decision that to remain where he was and hope they would grow uninterested and go away was unrealistic. Chances were, they had already locked onto his scent, which meant they were hungry and out for blood.

Looking up, all Spencer could see was clusters of stars among an inky blackness. What light there was did not aid him in any way, except to allow him to see mere feet in front of him. An idea crossed his mind as he sat and contemplated his plan of escape.

"You'll kill yourself," Spencer whispered as he located the spot where the canyon wall met the sky.

As fast as he could sort through scenarios and past experiences that could help him, he came to one realization, and that was he had to climb.

He remembered the slope of the canyon walls were steep, riddled with stoney outcroppings and handholds, but he also remembered that in some areas the angle of inclination might make for an easier ascent. With slow, quiet movements, he gritted his teeth to swallow the pain in his legs as he began to stand.

Come on, Spence, don't puss out. You got this.

Channeling his focus from years of exhaustive taekwondo team training, he focused his mind on the end goal of climbing to safety while ignoring the pain in his ankle and the danger that lurked just out of sight. Master Martinez would have expected nothing less from him.

"If you want it, fucking do it," he would say. "Don't think for one minute your opponent will back down in a fight because you got injured, Spencer. No. If he's any good, that's when he'll strike the hardest. You must be mentally capable of pushing past the pain—withstand exhaustion and tell yourself, 'I'm not fucking tired,' process in your mind what you want and how you'll achieve it, and push your body harder as each second ticks by. Do that and you've got an edge over any opponent you'll ever face."

Spencer recalled the exhaustion, the burning muscles, and the sweat dripping into his eyes during those sessions. Now, this was the ultimate test of mental fortitude in the face of substantial danger and difficult odds. He knew that as long as he remained focused, he would have a fighting chance. The pain he felt would be temporary, an insignificant obstacle to overcome when his life was on the line.

Using the wall as a guide, he ran his fingers along the dusty edge. The coarse rock felt like sandpaper on his skin. Being careful not to make any noise, he crept along in search of the slope he had rolled down during his escape from Lane's killer. He took long breaths into his nose, then let them out in slow, silent bursts. This repetitive action calmed him. His thoughts remained sharp, but his mind slowed to a crawl as he took each painful, determined step.

Sweat caked his brow, dripping over his skin. He took that as a good sign. Though severely dehydrated, his body had not reached a point where it began to shut itself down. The wind picked up, blowing in gentle gusts. It carried a sense of freshness as if picking up the fragrances of yucca and agave blossoms and desert marigolds, swirling their smell like a natural mix of potpourri. An undertone of rain joined the blustery recipe, but the skies overhead spoke nothing of it.

As the two beasts continued to channel their ferocity at each other, Spencer put some distance between him and the spot where he had heard the first growl. Though frightening, the mountain lions' assertion for dominance over each other was the distraction Spencer needed to try and get to safety.

He forced his feet to move in slow, purposeful motions. *"Step . . . slide . . . step . . . slide . . . don't drag your foot!"* he whispered to himself. The wall began to angle away from him, hinting he was closing in on the base of the cliff he had hoped to reach. *"A little further . . . step . . . slide . . ."* Sliding his palms over the deteriorating rock, he felt the slope had shifted to an angle that would be, in his experience, manageable.

A sheer drop in the daylight was not an unrealistic challenge for Spencer. He had done it many times before, always using the proper gear: climbing harness, helmet, proper shoes, rope, carabiners, quickdraws, nuts, cams, and hexes. Safety was always a top priority when rock climbing, and Spencer was meticulous in planning each grip, each foothold, and the pathway he intended to take during his ascent.

He likened this location to slab climbing.

Unlike walls that shoot up at ninety degrees, slab routes lean away from the climber. Though they might seem less daunting, the potential danger is very real. A single misstep or loss of traction could send the climber hurtling downward. And in the absence of any safety gear, every meter ascended only amplified the risk, making each climb a more tangible dance with death.

Climbing blind was the riskiest thing he had ever attempted. He had no harness, and could barely see through the darkness, but Spencer had no choice. Reaching as high as he could, he felt for his first and second handholds. Gripping each, he found both were solid. He found a lower spot for his foot and wasted no time pulling himself onto the wall.

Satisfied with his balance and position, Spencer let go with his right hand and scoured the surface in search of his next hold.

"There you are," he said as his fingers and palm wrapped around a knobby rock sticking out at just the right level. "That's the kind of chicken head I like." He pulled and repeated the process of searching for holds in the dark like a blind man reading braille.

After two more successful holds and repositions on the slab, he took a breath. He had climbed only ten feet, but his fingers and arms were already beginning to ache. He needed water. Food. Medical care. Before reaching up, he took a moment to look down. The calm of the canyon would have made this climb on any other day peaceful. It was then he realized everything had gone silent.

"Shit!"

The growls and hisses had stopped. That could mean any number of things, but Spencer feared the worst. He knew that when animals fight over territory or mates or food, the dominant animal would return its attention to what it was defending. In this case, what it had been hunting, and silence would be its ally.

Becoming more constant, the fresh breeze swirled around Spencer, chilling the sweat on his face. As the cold sensation trickled down his cheeks, he wondered, *was this genuine fear creeping back, or just the trick of the wind playing with his already frayed nerves?*

While Spencer had gained some distance on his climb, he was still dangerously within reach of the mountain lion. He needed to climb at least twice as high to reach a safe height to be out of the creature's leaping range.

Spencer reached and swiped his palm along the rock. Finding a pinch, he latched his finger onto the hold and pulled up. As he moved his foot to a previous handhold, Spencer heard another ominous sound.

Like a bowling ball rolling over an old, splintered lane, the rumble of thunder barreled into the canyon. It grew louder as it bounced off the rock walls. The rumble became more like a frustrated yell as if it became angry for being trapped in such a low, secluded place.

Rising another five feet, Spencer took a moment to rest his forehead against the wall again. His body hurt. The skin on his fingers was raw. A burning sensation radiated from his wrists to his shoulders. His injured ankle felt like it was encased in a cement boot as it dangled freely beneath him.

Becoming more frequent, the lightning and thunder transformed the canyon into a battlefield. Bolts of charged energy spread out, cracking the sky in brilliant threads. Each clap of thunder struck like a mortar shell, exploding with growing intensity. The swirling winds, once gentle and soothing, now blew at Spencer as they funneled around the canyon like shock waves following each traumatic rumble and boom. His hair blew and his loose clothing flapped.

Lifting his head, he glanced up and caught a glimpse of the cliff's edge illuminated by a quick flash of lightning. Thunder followed. Rising just beneath the fading boom, a sharp, airy hiss sounded out. The mountain lion was back.

He looked down. Another flash from above lit the canyon floor long enough for him to lock eyes with a large mountain lion pacing back and forth below him. With its head raised and its mouth pulled tight and showing teeth, it seemed to be calculating its next move.

Spencer tried to swallow, but the lump that had grown in his throat and lack of spit in his mouth made it impossible. He thought he had made good progress on his climb, but seeing the mountain lion so close now, Spencer knew he was not out of the dangerous animal's reach.

"Hey!" Spencer yelled out. "Get outta here!"

The mountain lion flattened its ears but did not go anywhere. Instead, it bared its teeth and crouched, looking as if it were ready to spring.

Climb! he thought, gazing upon the beast. *Don't look back. Just climb.*

Spencer knew mountain lions were athletic creatures built for running fast, jumping, and worst of all, climbing. The one thought he could not escape was, could this wild cat find a way to reach him, or at least find a perch where one swipe of its paw or lunge of its body would be enough to bring him down?

As if the animal knew Spencer's thoughts, it hissed again and raised itself onto its rear haunches, placing its front paws against the rock. It swiped twice with its right paw, then recoiled to pace in impatient circles at the base of the slab.

Spencer's mind raced. He was caught facing two obstacles, both of which could result in a painful death. If he could not find handholds to pull him higher, it would be only a matter of time before his strength subsided and he fell, or the mountain lion figured out that one leap would knock him off the slab. The other issue was, the higher he climbed, the further he could fall, and even from this height, he risked substantial injury.

This whole stupid escapade was one big clusterfuck, and it kept getting worse for Spencer each moment he was out here. Promising himself to never act this irresponsible again, and wishing more than anything to see his family, he made a difficult choice: *ignore the creature and climb.* He had nowhere to go but up.

Taking a determined breath, he looked along the slab. Sporadic lightning helped him see how far he had yet to climb. It also cast dark shadows where crimps and jugs, pockets and knobs were located. Each a possible handhold. Each with their own difficulty.

Hand over hand, he reached up and out, pulling and straining to raise himself higher. On any other climb, this rate of ascent would be laughable. But this was not any other climb. Reaching the top would not mean breaking a record or receiving a medal. It meant he would live to climb another day.

The hisses and growls continued below him. At one point, he heard the scraping of rock near his feet, followed by a screech and a thud as the cat landed after an unsuccessful leap.

As the lightning and thunder persisted, a new, steady hum joined the mix of clap and boom. It started out low but grew rapidly as the canyon caught wind of it, too, amplifying its approach like a distant train roaring closer from down the track.

Spencer reached higher and found a crimp. Using only his fingertips as leverage, this tiny malformation in the rock would have to be a sufficient hold. He clawed at the rock, releasing pressure from one hand and slowly pulling with the other.

Another jolt of lightning, this one more explosive, trailed from the clouds to the ground in an instant heart-wrenching blast. The simultaneous crack of thunder boomed in Spencer's ears, setting every hair on his body on edge. The violent surprise made Spencer's finger jerk on the crimp, unbalancing his precarious hold.

The nail of his left middle finger snagged on the rock, peeling back in an excruciating rip from flesh. The searing sensation was immediate, almost blinding. Its torturous pull sent a rapid sting down his finger and across his palm.

His nerve endings screamed for relief as did Spencer from the pain.

"Ahhh! Shit!"

His left hand lost its hold entirely, and for a heart-stopping moment, it seemed he would fall. Experience and physical strength were the only two things that saved Spencer. His foot position held firm, and in one swift motion, he regained a grasp with his right hand, anchoring himself to the slab. Adrenaline surged through him, chilling him while also lighting a fire beneath his waning resolve.

His chest tightened. Each breath he took burned. Looking up, he had no choice but to regain a grip on the crimp. He placed three fingertips on the hold, pointing his middle finger straight up as if to give the building storm a silent *fuck you,* and pulled.

The storm answered, gesturing back at Spencer with its own violent reply. Large, cold drops of rain began to pound the canyon, the walls, and anything in its path. The surging wind blew and the thunder echoed in Spencer's ears, but the storm brought about a far worse danger to him. His clothes grew heavy as they soaked up the rain. The slab became a spillway for every drop of water that fell, drenching the surface of the rock. And his fingers that held firm to the safety of their holds began to slip.

CHAPTER 39

"Raven? What are you doing here?"

I stepped from behind Chance to see a small mob standing in the foyer of the Huckabee compound. Each face wore a different look. Huckabee was pissed. Raven appeared weary and flustered. I recognized a man squaring off with Flint as the one he had argued with a few weeks ago in town, and it did not look like their animosity toward one another had changed. Had we not arrived when we did, Flint may be wiping the floor with him right now. Chance turned to me, his face a tapestry of questions.

"Raven? I thought Flint was taking you home."

"That's where you said he was taking me. I never intended on going home just to sit around. I wanted to find Spencer, and that's what I'm going to do." Without allowing anyone else to chime in, she stepped forward and addressed the lot of us. "I know there are things going on tonight and that some may think they are bigger than this or that there are more important issues at hand. But not to me. Spencer is my only concern."

Raven glanced at Chance.

"I am sorry about Javier, but nothing any of us can do can bring him back. Spencer is missing. And I have a real feeling that he needs our help."

"Javier?" Huckabee asked. "Will someone tell me what the hell is going on?"

Too many voices spoke up at once. The noise filled the house and echoed into the courtyard.

"Enough!" Chance bellowed.

Huckabee squinted his eyes and opened his mouth to speak when a small voice rained down from the banister that overlooked our emotional mob.

"Spencer hasn't come back?"

We all looked up and saw Charlotte holding the railing, eyes puffy, and hair disheveled, wearing a look of genuine concern, but also that of tremendous guilt.

"What about Lane?"

Chance stepped forward and looked up at her.

"Charlotte?"

"Yes."

"Would you mind coming down here, so we can speak with you?"

This time Huckabee found the words he meant to say and spout them out before Charlotte could answer Chance.

"Unless you have a warrant of some kind, you need to get out of my house or I'll . . ."

I stepped in front of him and looked down. The top of his head barely reached my shoulder, so when he turned to face me, his nose was front and center with the middle of my chest.

"Floyd, there are things going on here bigger

than you, bigger than warrants, bigger than all of us." A quick glance at Chance as I spoke saw him return a quick nod. It was his way of letting me know I had permission to share some of what had happened earlier.

"I don't see how that's any problem of mine," Huckabee grumbled.

He glared up at me, and we locked eyes again.

"Floyd, you've lived here a long time. It's no secret. I bet you knew the sheriff before Chance, and probably the one before him. Hell, you know most of the deputies that work for South Brewster County. Deputies Leo, Bostwick, and Santos to name a few."

"Yeah," Huckabee fired off. "I know 'em all. And I ain't never had a problem with any of 'em. I told ya before, we got a way of doin' things out here that a city cop like you wouldn't understand. Comin' to my house in the middle of the night. And for what?" He looked at Deputy Leo standing just outside the open front door. "You, Diego Leo. You and Javier Santos used to ride horses with some of my workers when you were kids."

Deputy Leo nodded his head but remained silent. I spoke up before Huckabee could continue.

"You keep that memory locked up inside, Floyd. Javier Santos was murdered a few hours ago." I pulled the attention back on me with that one statement, and the whole house fell silent when I spoke. Lowering my tone, I continued, "That's why we are here. And before you ask, no, we have no reason to believe anyone here is a suspect. What we have learned is that the last person who may have seen him alive was Lane Jespers, but we can't find him anywhere."

I looked up at Charlotte. She had moved from her spot on the landing to take a seat on the stairs. The oversized Taylor Swift concert T-shirt she wore was pulled over her knees. Her arms wrapped around her legs as she sat in an upright fetal position. She looked like a younger, blonde version of Raven trying to overcome emotional distress when in the midst of her darkest days following her attack in Houston.

"We know that Charlotte knows Lane. We were hoping she might tell us where to find him."

What had been a heated exchange turned sullen in a matter of moments.

"Javier's dead?" Huckabee said, looking at me.

I nodded. Chance stepped over and placed his palm on Huckabee's shoulder.

"We could use your help, amigo. Charlotte's help."

All eyes turned to the stairs. It became clear that Charlotte felt the weight of this entire evening fall on her. She buried her face in her hands and cried.

"I told them not to go."

Raven climbed the stairs and sat down next to Charlotte. She wrapped an arm around her, and pulled her into a caring hug.

"Who did you tell, Charlotte?" she whispered.

Pulling away from Raven to look her in the eyes, Charlotte trembled. "Lane and . . . Spencer. They went off to do stupid boy things this afternoon. We met at Dairy Queen, but Lane was there, too, and started causing problems, as usual. I was mad at Lane for . . . for being Lane and disappointed that Spencer got wrapped up in Lane's tricks. Spencer shouldn't have gone with him. I should have stopped them. But . . . but . . . I didn't. I thought Spencer would call me or try to see me after they finished their dumb games, so when he didn't, I came out here to hide. I was hurt and didn't want to talk to anyone. I didn't know Spencer hadn't come back. Please, is he all right?"

Chance walked to the bottom of the stairs. "Charlotte. When was the last time you saw either Lane or Spencer?"

Charlotte kept her eyes on Raven, sniffing and huffing.

"Umm . . . like one or two o'clock. Maybe a little later. It was this afternoon."

Chance placed a foot on the bottom step and leaned forward. "And do you know where they were headed?"

Charlotte turned to look down the stairwell at Chance. She seemed frightened.

"Charlotte, tell us where they went. The sooner we locate the boys, the sooner we will know that they are safe. Maybe they know something that will help us solve this case we are working on."

Charlotte gulped. "They . . . Lane, I mean . . ."

Raven took her hand. "It'll be okay. You're helping them. Anything you can say will only help." Raven glanced at me, seeming to look for assurance in what she had just said, but I was unable to give her the agreeable look she wanted.

Charlotte took a deep breath. "They went to Lost Eagle Canyon."

The room fell just as silent as it had before. Chance turned around. A grave look plastered his face. He walked over to me.

"Let's step outside, Cass."

I followed him out the door until we reached the Explorer.

"If what she said is true, the boys are in Mexico, Cass. Lost Eagle Canyon, *Cañón del Águila Perdida*, is a desolate place, only reachable on foot. If that's where they went and did not come back . . ." he paused.

The anxious feeling I had set aside earlier returned with a vengeance.

"What are you saying, Chance?"

"That's some bad country, Cass. Not only because of the terrain, but cartels have been known to use the remote canyon for one reason or another. Reasons of which I will not elaborate, but you can probably imagine."

"Where is this canyon?"

I could tell by the look on Chance's face he already knew what I was planning to do.

"You can't cross over like they did. You are a government employee. You poke your nose across the border without going through proper channels, and you're liable to spark an international incident."

"It's Mexico, for Christ's sake!"

"Yes. It is. A foreign country, Cass."

I walked away from him thinking of all my next possible moves to find the boys. To think that Spencer was wrapped up in this was ridiculous, but I had to face the facts. I did not know Lane Jespers. If he was as bad as Charlotte was making him out to be, they both might be in serious trouble.

"Look," Chance said. "We will figure this out, but I need to be clear about one thing. You are not to cross that border unless we have clearance from the State Department. Do you understand?" He spoke with a soft voice, but the firm nature of his words rang clear.

Deputy Leo approached the two of us.

"Sheriff Gilbert, Mr. Huckabee would like a word with you."

"Thank you, Diego. We'll be right in."

Deputy Leo walked back to the house. Chance shook his head. I knew his mind was racing. He hurt just like the rest of us, but unlike everyone else, he had the final say on how we went about investigating the murder, which now seemed to coincide with the disappearance of both Lane and Spencer. The onus was on him to bring a killer to justice, and to bring the boys safely home.

"Cass. Take Raven home. Grab a shower and something to eat. I'd tell you to rest, but we both know you won't. Meet me back at the office at seven, and we'll pick up where we left off."

"Chance, I . . ."

"I'm not asking, amigo."

Huckabee stepped into view, but to my surprise, did not interrupt our conversation. Flint followed behind, but there was no sign of Raven. Chance and Flint passed ways, regarding each other with a nod. As Chance spoke with Huckabee, Flint walked up to me.

"Ms. Raven made it very clear she had no intention of sittin' and waitin' for you or Spencer at the CR. Figured it better to watch her back than let her go it alone."

"No. I get it, Flint. Thanks."

Flint nodded, then began to walk to his truck.

"Flint."

"Yeah."

"We'll be heading home in a minute. When we get there, I'd like to talk with you a bit more."

Flint chewed on his bottom lip, seeming to contemplate what it was I wanted to speak with him about, then nodded once and walked the rest of the way to his truck. He fired it up and pulled away. The red glow of his truck's taillights and the rumble of his engine seemed to convey displeasure with everything that had transpired tonight.

"I couldn't agree with you more," I said aloud.

When I reached the front door, Raven was walking alone down the stairs. She met me in the doorway and wrapped her arms around my waist.

"What is going on?" she whispered.

It was a question that had many answers, but she was not seeking a particular explanation. It was her frustration and confusion and concern that had asked. She pulled back, and looking at me did ask one thing she wanted to know. It was something I had been thinking too but did not yet have the answer myself.

"What are we going to do?"

CHAPTER 40

Within the tumultuous storm, the night became even more black and dreary than Spencer could have imagined, save the bright flashes crackling overhead that blinded him with each electrifying spike. The rain poured in sheets. The only sound he heard now was water pelting the rock and the thunderous report in the clouds. There was no sign of the mountain lion since the deluge began, but the thought of it lurking nearby was still unsettling.

Spencer held onto the slab for dear life but took a moment to laugh at the irony of his predicament. The one thing that could save his life, or at least give him a fighting chance, could also be the source of his demise. Water.

He tried adjusting his hold on the crimp but the rock and the runoff were not cooperating. He estimated that he was twenty feet above the canyon floor and that a controlled fall would be better than a mishandled slip. Realizing he had little choice in the matter, Spencer took a deep breath, released his fingertip grip on the rock slab, and looked down.

"This is gonna hurt."

Spencer closed his eyes, imagining he was at Typhoon Texas on his favorite water slide where colorful tubes lead the way down and around a maze of rushing water, then for a moment, as speed picked up and the ride neared its end, blackness fell all around causing screams of delight to echo through the tubes, back to the top of the ride.

With one quick motion, and before he could change his mind, he twisted his body and slid down the slab of rock. Gravity and the rush of water guided him downward. His hands dragged along the wall. His shirt pulled up above his waist, giving the skin on his back a taste of the coarse rock. This ride gave him the same fuzzy feeling in the pit of his stomach as the one back home, but it lacked the familiar splash and comforting embrace of a gorgeous lifeguard at the end.

Forcing his eyes to stay open, and anticipating impact, Spencer let out a war cry as he fell. In the seconds it took to fall, Spencer angled his body so that his right foot would hit the ground first. He aimed to roll away from the impact like a paratrooper making a PLF (Parachute Landing Fall). It was a technique he had learned from stories his dad shared about military training. If timing and luck worked together for once, he could hobble away from this without adding additional injuries to himself.

As planned, his right foot touched down first, absorbing the initial shock. In an almost fluid motion, the impact's force traveled to the side of his calf, then his thigh, and finally his torso. The practiced roll saw him momentarily on his side, then his shoulder, dispersing the landing's energy across his body.

He grunted as his injured ankle jostled as he gained control. He rolled two more times across the ground before coming to rest on his back. His muscles were spent. Adrenaline had used up what reserves there were, leaving Spencer to drift into an exhaustive state.

The rain continued to pour, pooling in puddles on the canyon floor. Now that Spencer was on solid ground, he relished the cool touch of raindrops against his skin. He opened his mouth and let the drops run in. It coated his lips and tongue, extinguishing the fire in his tender throat. At first, it was hard to swallow, but drip by drip, water found a way past the swollen, fleshy barricade and into his stomach. Each drink felt better than the last. It was unlike any bottled water he had ever had, with a freshness only nature could provide.

Feeling the water begin to slosh in his stomach, he stopped swallowing and simply let it shower over him. Moving slowly, he sat upright. Water trickled down his back in a mix of chill and sting as the beads ran over the scrapes and cuts from the rock. Reaching down to his right foot, he removed his shoe and then his sock. He let the water soak into the cotton, then with a twist of his wrist, he squeezed it out again. He repeated the soaking and wringing until he felt the sock was as clean as it would get. Satisfied, he rolled the sock into a ball and stuffed it inside his shoe. He placed his shoe on the ground next to him.

"Soak it up. We may need something to drink later."

With nowhere to go and no shelter to speak of, Spencer laid back down where he was. Rain continued to fall. Lightning flashed in sporadic dances between clouds. Thunder rumbled. Spencer closed his eyes and drifted into a deep sleep that would carry him beyond the storm and into the first light of day.

CHAPTER 41

The road was dark and deep, and silence traveled with us as we returned to the CR without our son. In the distance, presumably over Mexican soil, flashes of lightning illuminated the sky. Ahead of us, caught in the glint of the Explorer's headlights, the entrance to our home drew near. Beyond the land and to the East, past Brewster and as far as the eye could see, a sliver of gold appeared across the vast horizon. Reminiscent of the jagged teeth of a jack-o-lantern, the first light of dawn looked more like a warning of what was to come as the sun slowly began to rise behind the peaks along Oso Mountain.

We rumbled onto the property and pulled up to the house. The lights were still on as if we had never left. Flint's truck was parked at an angle in front of his tiny house. A pulse of orange light inside the cab led me to believe he was still sitting behind the wheel. I had known Flint to enjoy a smoke when work was done, but this time it was different. There were no celebratory cigars to pass out or contests to see who could puff the most brilliant smoke ring. I imagined Flint sat in his truck wondering how the hell he allowed himself to get wrapped up in all this. I looked over at Raven as the Explorer came to a stop and had my answer.

I cut off the engine, but neither Raven nor I moved. We sat for what seemed like minutes in silence. Raven's question lingered in my head all the way home. "What are we going to do?" We had a lead to his whereabouts, but the complications that accompanied the information made it hard to know what to do. Chance had given explicit instructions not to cross the border on my own. As much as I respected him as a law enforcement official, and as a friend, I could not help but consider ignoring his order. There was nothing I would not do for my family, but the potential consequences that accompanied a poor decision could be life altering for more than just me.

The dome light came on when Raven opened her door. I reached over and laid my hand on her shoulder. Surprisingly, after all we had been through today, she allowed it to stay. Without looking at me, she spoke, and her words hit me like a bullet through the heart.

"I'll never forgive myself if . . ."

Her words seemed to fall out of the car.

"Raven, I'll find him."

She turned to face me. Her quick motions forced me to recoil my hand.

"You heard Chance. I heard Chance. Everybody heard Chance! If you go into Mexico, you risk everything."

"I risk everything if I don't."

Raven's eyes, bloodshot and puffy, widened in wonder.

"Before we worked under an assumption. That's why I didn't act. I gave Spencer the benefit of the doubt. I still find it hard to believe, but this time, I was wrong about him. Now, we have an idea about what he was up to and with whom."

Raven's eyes flickered as if a glimmer of hope still burned within her.

"I've got a lot to do." I paused, then rephrased my words. "*We* have a lot to do. First, I need to talk with Flint. Head inside and freshen up, and I'll be in shortly."

I leaned over to kiss Raven. She made it difficult to reach her but accepted my token of love.

"We'll get him back. I promise."

Raven smiled, though I could tell it was forced, and exited the car. I watched her walk to the porch and into the house and wondered, *how could a woman like her stand to be with a guy like me?* I've been tough all my life. My identity always gravitated toward the extreme. Fighter. Soldier. Police Officer. Detective. Special Investigator. All those titles and none of them compared to the steely backbone and raw determination of her love, a mother's love, for her child. She would cut off her own arm, then use it as a weapon against anyone threatening Spence. And as if that were not enough, she would have the wherewithal to sew it back on and use both arms to carry him to safety. She may have been through the wringer this past year—the attack in Houston, the house fire, relocating, the bodies on the CR—so, I ask myself again, how could she stand to be with a guy like me? Fact was, I was lucky she stuck around all these years. But that's Raven. Stubborn. Faithful. Loving. And tougher than I'll ever be. I knew what I had to do. I did not like it, but I had no choice.

I exited the Explorer and walked across the yard to Flint's truck. He rolled the passenger window down when he saw me approach.

"Flint."

"Yeah."

"I want to ask you . . ."

Flint raised a hand, palm facing me, as firm and steady as a sniper before pulling the trigger.

"I know what yer gonna say, so let me go ahead and answer it now. Lost Eagle Canyon, right? I know where it is, and I can be there within the hour."

"Thanks Flint. Let me grab a few things and . . ."

"Uh-uh. You ain't goin'."

My heart began to pound, and I could feel my ears start to heat up.

"Like hell, I'm not."

Flint exited the truck and walked around to me. His gait was aggressive and his breathing powerful. He stopped closer than I liked, but I did not budge.

"You ever stop to ask yerself why I stick around? Why I do what I do? Well, Cass, Mr. Special Investigator? This may be your place on paper, but to me, the land, the animals, the houses, the people, everything that the CR stands for means something to me, too. Always has. Always will. If that means you stayin' behind while I go out to look for your son, that's what I'm gonna do."

"I can't ask you to do that alone, Flint."

"Ya ain't have ta. I heard what Sheriff Gilbert told ya, but don't think I'm doin' this just fer you."

At that moment, Raven appeared behind us holding three cups of coffee. Her hands trembled and coffee spilled out of each cup as she walked up. Flint did not finish what he was saying. His whole demeanor changed in Raven's presence. A fleeting thought struck my mind, *did he have feelings for Raven?* I glanced at both of them.

"Cass. Flint." She handed each of us a cup, knowing fair well what we had been talking about without hearing a word of what was said. There was no need to wonder about it. She was a Callahan. It's what she expected.

"Thank you, Ms. Raven."

"You're welcome, Levi." Raven smiled at him, then looked at me. She stepped close and kissed me on the cheek. "You two work things out. Just don't leave me out of it."

The three of us stood together and sipped fresh coffee as morning continued to reveal itself to the CR. Light cascaded across the sky, bathing the distant bluffs in radiant orange, but it was the storm clouds that caught my attention. The puffs of ragged air remained as black and gray as a bruise in the sky, but the rain and the ground beneath glowed a sinister red. I squinted my eyes, but there was no doubt in my mind, the sky, dark and dangerous, seemed to bleed, and the earth looked soaked with blood.

CHAPTER 42

Carlos Ruiz-Mata walked the two blocks from his motel room to the Stripes gas station in search of a fresh cup of coffee. The sun had just crested the horizon, and he needed something that felt warm in his hands with a smell that was just as satisfying. It was too early to find that comfort in the storied grip and smoking barrel of his handguns, so coffee would have to do.

He walked with his hands in his pockets, enjoying the crispness of the morning air. A storm to the west offered a bit of scented breeze. He thought as he walked, mainly about what life was like on this side of the border. Glancing at the stoops and porches of the few houses he passed, he wondered how it would feel to wake up on a morning such as this in a home, with a family, where no one was waiting to kill you, and no one expected you to kill for them. He smiled at the thought. It was like looking at toys behind a glass window when he was young. How he wanted to reach in and play with each one. They were tools of imagination that could transport him away from a life that he knew was not for him but was one that he would live anyway. The touch of something new in his hands, and that it could be his forever, brought a smile to the young boy, but to Mata, it brought about regret.

As he walked along, he heard laughter, though it was not for anyone else to hear. It was in his head. It was El Despiadado, and he was saying, "This is not for you. It will never be for you. You are not a man, but a killer. It's all you've known, and all you'll ever be."

Removing his hands from his pockets, he used both palms to brush back his hair. He stopped and looked back at the houses. The voice inside him faded, recoiling to the solitude of its lerkim. Mata smiled. For an instant, he imagined his father sitting on one of the porches. Drawn further into the mirage, his *papá* noticed him as he stood on the corner by the road. His bushy mustache curled upward beneath his nose. His teeth gleamed, and there seemed to be a sparkle in his eye. He stood, and called out, "*Hijo, estoy orgulloso de ti.*" He stood and waved, then slowly disappeared as the words echoed in Mata's ears, reverberating like a curse to the hollows of his soul.

"Proud," he whispered. "How could he ever be proud of me?"

Mata turned to the street and crossed over to the convenience store. Posters for special prices on bags of ice, hot tamales, and thirty-two-ounce drinks were taped to the glass windows. A metal propane gas cart stood near the entrance with a scratched and faded picture on the front cabinet door of a blue rhino with a flame for a horn. Two pumps stood in wait for their next customer. An ATM sign blinked in a far corner of the window, and Texas Lotto paraphernalia filled the gaps on the glass between advertisements. There was so much to read on the front windows, it was difficult to see inside the building.

One car, a black Ford Explorer, was parked in a space near the front door. Mata reached the entrance and pulled on the cool metal handle. A mix of aromas swirled about, teasing and testing his nose as he entered the store. Just as the signs had promised, fresh tamales wrapped in aluminum foil sat in a warmer on a counter with a sign that read, $9.99/doz. or 3 for $3.99. Next to the tamales were breakfast tacos with choices of bacon, sausage, chorizo, potato, or beans, all mixed with a blend of eggs and cheese. They looked tempting, but what Mata desired most was a caffeine-filled cup of black coffee.

He stepped to the self-service bar and waited behind a man who was busy fixing two cups. He noticed the man opted for the large, Styrofoam option. As the man was finishing up, Mata commented, "Two large. That's one way to start the day."

The man turned around and looked at Mata. His eyes looked bloodshot. He nodded, then smirked. "You said it, mister."

"You are tired, my friend. It is Sunday. The

Lord's Day. A day of rest. Maybe you should rest, too?"

The man chuckled. "I wish it were that simple."

Mata stepped forward and filled a small cup with black coffee. Steam rose as he covered it with a plastic lid. Turning, he walked to the counter as the man fumbled for his wallet while holding both coffees.

"Here," Mata said, placing a ten-dollar bill on the counter. He addressed the clerk. "For all three, please."

The man turned and gave Mata a surprised look.

"That's not necessary," he said.

Mata smiled at the man. "When is kindness ever necessary?"

The clerk took the money and handed Mata his change. Walking to the exit, the man with the coffee leaned his back against the crossbar and pushed the door open so Mata could pass through.

"Thank you, my friend."

"No. I should be thanking you. It's been a hell of a night." The man placed both cups of coffee on the hood of the Explorer and offered a hand to Mata. "I'm Cass."

Mata took his hand, and the men shook.

"Carlos."

"You have a good day, Carlos."

Mata smiled at the man as they released hands.

"But, of course."

CHAPTER 43

Once again, Raven found herself alone on the CR. She sat on the porch looking out at the tire marks in the gravel where Cass's Explorer had been parked, then over to Flint's house. His truck was gone, too. Cass and Flint had come up with a plan to find Spencer that circumvented Chance's orders but kept Cass in the clear. To the surprise of both Cass and Raven, it was Flint's idea.

"I know the territory. I know the risks. Ain't nobody gonna say a word about me if I get caught, but the whole world will come down on both yer heads if'n it's you."

They worked fast to collect and stow gear and were set to head off just as the sun began to flood the CR. Before Cass and Flint left, Raven put up a fight, reminding them of her one demand, *don't leave her out*. They listened to her argument. She was adamant about going with Flint to find Spencer, but the dangers that lay ahead and the speed at which he intended to travel were the deciding factors. Getting to Lost Eagle Canyon was no easy task. Though the boys may have been oblivious to the danger, Flint knew what to expect and was well prepared. Raven, as strong willed and driven as she was, would only slow him down, and as much as it hurt to hear, she would be a liability. With a growing lump in her throat, Raven agreed to stay behind and wait for Flint to call.

"I've got the SAT phone, Ms. Raven. I'll call you as soon as I locate Spencer," he had said.

The sun had begun its daily climb while Raven sat alone. She gripped her cell phone, anxiously awaiting Flint's call.

CHAPTER 44

"It's going to take a lot more than coffee to get me through today, amigo."

"Tell me about it."

Chance sat behind his desk and cocked his head. "Is there something you would like to tell me, Cass?"

I gave him the most innocent look I could muster and shook my head. "No."

"Very well. We have things to discuss." He motioned to the seat across from him. "Let's start with what happened at the jail."

"Okay." I took a sip of my drink and glanced at the wall clock behind his desk. The long, black arms pointed out the time. It was seven minutes after seven, and the red second hand raced infinitely on. "We still have no information on Marta Jiménez or what took her only two minutes and thirty-six seconds to say to Luis López. But I think we are both leaning toward the same theory."

"Which is?"

"That she gave him a kill order to take out Joe Sinclair."

"Why Joe?"

"He said it himself when you first asked him to take a ride the day we solved the CR murders.

Before he pulled a gun and shot you. 'I'm dead if I do.' I think Joe may have gotten in deeper than he could handle with the Camargo Cartel, and now they're cleaning up his mess. What I can't figure out is how could Luis kill himself the way he did. And why?"

"That's been bothering me, too. A man would have to be extremely desperate to attempt suicide by jabbing a shiv into his own eye."

"Maybe, and I hate to consider this, but maybe there was someone on the inside that knew to take out Joe's killer. Make it look like suicide?"

The two of us sat and considered the idea for a long time. Steam no longer rose from either of our cups, but we drank anyway.

"Let's get a list of every guard who interacted with Luis from that morning until after his body was found. Let's also make a list of every guard who was in contact with Marta Jiménez." Chance folded his hands atop his desk. "¡Ay, Dios! If we have someone working for us that has ties to the cartel, so help me . . ."

I leaned back in my chair. My muscles were stiff. I closed my eyes for a moment, then opened them again to catch the tiniest of items in my view. I sat up and reached across Chance's desk to a stack of paperwork waiting to be filed. Laying on top of the stack was the USB drive I had found on the CR. It was the very USB drive that held all sorts of information about the Camargo Cartel, including undercover FBI informant Blade Ramos's video outlining the contents as well as his final plea for help and the name of his contact . . . Sinclair.

I picked up the USB drive and held it in front of me. "I wonder if there is anything else on this that we might have missed."

"We have been over every file on that drive, Cass."

"Right, but we were focusing on information related to Joe Sinclair and the victims he tried to bury on the CR. I think we ought to run through it again."

"That will take a long time, amigo."

"For us, yes. But for Special Agent Zuñiga and his FBI goons, not so much. They have tech that can shred this apart and glue it back together ten times over. Plus, he's been wanting me to send it to him for a while now."

"That brings up the topic of why you haven't sent it already?"

I sat back in my chair. "There was something Agent Zuñiga had to do first."

"This is evidence, Cass. You're playing with fire by withholding it from them."

"Technically. But it's our evidence, too. Look, let's get on the horn and see if they can help us out."

"Maybe that request should come from me," Chance said, sounding skeptical.

"Took the words right out of my mouth. In the meantime, I'll head back to the jail and start compiling a list."

"Okay, Cass. Now . . ."

A knock on the door interrupted our conversation.

"Come in," Chance called out.

Deputy Joey Figgs opened the door and stepped into the office.

"Sir, we've located Lane Jespers's Camaro. It's parked behind Chavez Wrecker Service."

Chance and I stood up at the same time.

"Let's go see what ol' Hector can tell us about it," Chance said. "Deputy Figgs, yer on watch detail. Load up and follow us out."

"Yes, sir."

Deputy Figgs about-faced, immediately following orders. I put the USB drive back on the stack of papers.

"Don't you go anywhere," I said to it, then followed Chance out the office door.

CHAPTER 45

"Ring, damn it, ring!"

Raven stared at her cell phone. A picture of Cass and Spencer saved as her home screen image stared back. She raised it high and swiped it from left to right, checking to make sure it was receiving a full spectrum of 5G connectivity, though three bars were the best she could hope for at the ranch. She pressed a button on the side of the phone ensuring that the volume was at maximum. It was nearing eight o'clock. It had not been an hour since Cass and Flint left the CR, but her impatience fueled her worry.

Standing up, she walked around the house and looked out across the CR. Mexico was within eyesight, though she had no idea where to cast her gaze. Following the horizon from north to south, she took it all in.

"Where are you, Spencer?"

The morning breezes answered her with a brush of cool, tantalizing West Texas aromas. The storm clouds to the west and south had begun to dissipate, though a haze beneath them showed that it was still raining.

Lifting her phone, she looked at the screen again. Nothing. Alone and afraid, she began a mindful argument with herself. Each voice in her head took a stance against the other, and though each point was valid, it did not make her feel any better.

"The CR was supposed to be a place to start over. A place of calm."

"It has been those things. You know as well as anybody that life happens, no matter where you are."

"But it's been a shitshow since we arrived."

"Not all of it."

"Most of it. I mean, what good have we gained out here anyway?"

"You found yourself again, didn't you?"

"Seems like all we found were dead bodies. When will it all just go away?"

"What about Chance? Flint? Cruzita? Those are all people who brought a newness to your life. Where would you be without them?"

"I feel so alone."

"You don't have to be."

Looking down at her cell phone, Raven pressed the Contacts icon. She scrolled down to the name she was looking for and pressed the number, activating a call. The line rang twice before it was answered.

"Hello? Cruzita? I know it's early, but I need to talk with you. Is there any way you can come out to the house? So much has happened overnight, and I'm so afraid."

CHAPTER 46

The 1979 Camaro is a vintage muscle car whose performance and style has made it a favorite among classic car enthusiasts. The idea of finding Lane's Camaro brought back memories from my childhood when my father and Uncle Stewart would take me to monster truck rallies near San Antonio and Seguin in the late eighties. I was only seven or eight years old, but I'll never forget where I was the first time I sat in the driver's seat of a fully restored, classic sports car.

There were all sorts of oversized, mean-looking trucks with tires bigger than my dad. Each one was painted to look like a beast or demon. I was fascinated by their power and strength, especially when crushing the junker cars on the course, but there was also a classic car meet that accompanied each monster truck event. That was Dad's favorite part. He would talk with each owner, and I could tell, even back then, that Dad dreamed of cruising down the road with the top down in an old 1965 Mustang or 1967 C2 Corvette Stingray.

"Come here, Cass," he would say after discussing the restoration of his latest object of admiration.

Taking me by the shoulders, he would guide me to look under the hood, pointing out the carefully rebuilt and fine-tuned engines, where chrome headers gleamed and engine blocks boasted custom paint. He would then lead me to the driver's side window, so I could check out the interior. I did not understand at the time, but the leather seats, all the fancy dials and gauge clusters—most of which looked to my young eyes like controls on a spaceship, the factory-grade paint jobs, and time spent bringing each classic car back to life cost more than my entire house.

One man, whose hands and fingers looked like they were stained black from grease and whose head was clean shaven, opened the door to his 1970 Dodge Charger R/T and said, "Here, son. Have a seat. Imagine what it would be like to speed down the highway in this."

I slipped into the seat and wrapped my fingers around the steering wheel. I could barely see over the dashboard, but even then, my view was blocked by a massive supercharger sticking out of the hood. I closed my eyes and imagined pressing the pedal so hard it touched the floor. The engine roared. The power and torque of this beautiful machine caused the front wheels to lift off the ground as I peeled out in a glorious symphony of screeching tires, firing pistons, and thunderous exhaust. All the people cheered as I raced by, and then as if by magic, I found myself on the open highway stretching between El Paso and Kerrville. It was just me, the car, and miles of empty road in front of me.

I enjoyed reliving those moments with my dad as I followed Chance's Bronco to Hector Chavez's Wrecker Service. The image I brought with me was a treasure. When we arrived and saw Lane's Camaro parked behind the garage, my first thought was, *what a piece of shit.*

Our caravan pulled up to the front of the building. Deputy Figgs brought up the rear and parked his cruiser perpendicular to the parking entrance, creating a barricade. I parked, stepped out of the Explorer, and walked over to Chance. His dark Ray-Ban sunglasses masked his eyes and the brim of his hat kept most of his face shaded.

"What do you think?" I asked.

"At this hour on a Sunday morning, we'll be lucky if we find Hector at all. Even if we do, chances are that he will be too hungover to remember anything that happened last night. Probably doesn't even know Lane's car is here."

Chance walked up to the window and peered inside. Chavez Wrecker Service was painted in bright red and yellow lettering that arched from one side of the glass to the other. Beneath the name was the number twenty-four and a contact number.

If you are as unreachable as Chance says, open twenty-four hours seems misleading, I thought.

"Figured as much. No one's here," Chance said,

backing away from the window. "Let's go around back and have a look at the car."

I caught Deputy Figgs's eye and signaled that we were heading around back. He acknowledged with a two-fingered salute and remained on guard standing next to his cruiser.

Walking up to the Camaro, I saw that it looked just as beaten up as it did from the road. It had noticeable rust eating away at the wheel wells and rocker panels, and the cowling looked as brittle as a dried leaf in fall. The driver's side tires were beginning to bald, and there were dents and scratches from the front paneling to the taillights, and that was just what I could see from where I was standing. It was a base model but still quite a desirable car in its day.

The one thing that made this car stand out most was its coloring—camel metallic. In other words, shitty brown. Sports cars were supposed to have that special look, and their paint was what made it pop. Burt Reynolds drove a black Trans Am with a golden *Screaming Chicken* on the hood. James Garner drove a gold Pontiac Firebird, not as souped up as the Bandit's higher end Trans Am, but cool enough. And Tom Selleck? A red Ferrari 308 GTS. Even the Dukes of Hazzard drove a Dodge Charger painted Hemi Orange topped off with a Confederate flag. Of all the color possibilities and combinations, I had to ask myself, what guy lost his job over ordering camel metallic paint for the Chevrolet Camaro.

Chance walked around the car, stopping next to the passenger side door. He leaned forward and glanced in.

"Locked."

Taking a closer look, I saw the door lock plunger on my side stood tall in the inner door panel.

"Not this side," I said.

Using my shirt to cover my fingers, I cupped them under the door handle and pulled up. With a groan and feeble click, the door unlatched and swung open. I leaned in, being careful not to touch anything, and scanned the interior—the seats were worn and ripping at the seams, a stellate pattern of cracks radiated from multiple points on the dashboard, cigarette butts littered the console ashtray, a black tire iron lay discarded on the passenger floorboard, four fist-crushed Coors Light cans were scattered across the back seat, and sitting in the middle of the snarl of silver bullets was a key chain with a Marvel's Punisher skull and two keys.

"Got something, Chance." My voice sounded muffled as if caught up in the craggy mess of this poorly cared for classic's interior. I stood up and looked over the roof. "Keys tossed onto the back seat. I'd be willing to bet they'd crank this bad boy up if we tried them."

Chance took off his sunglasses and leaned his forearms against the Camaro's roof.

"Charlotte said both boys took off in this car yesterday afternoon. They haven't been seen since, but we find the car here with the keys left behind and only the passenger door is locked? Cass . . ."

"You don't have to say it. Let's work the problem."

I leaned back inside the car so Chance could not see the angst I felt beginning to boil on my face. I squeezed my fists as I fought to relieve the pain of not knowing if Spencer was safe. On any other case I would have already voiced my doubts about the missing persons, but this was my son we were talking about.

Closing my eyes, I whispered to myself, "Come through for me, Flint. Find my boy."

I overheard Chance on his radio calling for Deputy Bostwick to report to us with a forensic fingerprinting kit. Bostwick's attention to detail became apparent to me during the investigation at the cottonwood grove on the CR. Since we already had the CSI team out of Lajitas working Deputy Santos's murder scene, Boss was the next best choice to come dust the car.

I exited the Camaro and closed the door to only a crack. Chance waited for radio confirmation from dispatch.

"Ten-four, Sheriff Gilbert. Deputy Bostwick en route. ETA, seven minutes."

"Thanks, Shirley," he said, then fastened his radio to its shoulder harness.

We stood for a moment. Neither of us said a word. Each of us was diving further into the events and details of the past few hours. Chance pinched his lips to one side of his face, huffing deliberate puffs of air from his nostrils. His mustache hair fluttered with each breath. I rolled my tongue inside my mouth and squinted my eyes as I stared at Lane's Camaro. I shook my head, trying to clear the overloaded slate of questions and evidence in my mind. This was the puzzle from hell. It felt like more and more pieces continued to slip through my fingers. The worst part was that every time I paused or let my guard down, a vision of Spencer pleading for my help appeared before my eyes and each time, just as my vision reached out to him, he would disappear. I forced myself to remain vigilant. As long as I stayed focused on working the problems of which I had control, I could maintain functionality.

"Look," I finally said, breaking the silence between us. "With Boss on the way, I'm going to head over to the jail as we discussed earlier. It shouldn't take too long to compile the lists of guards and their scheduled assignments. As soon as I'm done, I'll report back to you at the office."

Chance nodded his approval, and I was off.

I briefed Deputy Figgs before leaving. Pulling

out of the parking lot, I saw Chance appear from the side of the building. His uniformed figure, dark glasses, and determined gait could have placed him in any number of Hollywood crime thrillers.

I pressed the gas, unleashing the Explorer's power on the empty roads of Brewster. As I sped off toward the jail, I could hear the gong of Sunday morning church bells ring out. Their Gothic clang sent a shiver down my spine as I thought, *let's just hope that this movie doesn't emulate real life.*

CHAPTER 47

A trifecta of rattled nerves, excessive caffeine, and billowing exhaustion plagued Raven, causing her to burst into tears when she saw the faint rise of dust coming from the gravel road as a car approached the CR. There were so many possibilities of who it could be. She prayed with every fiber of her being that it was Flint and that Spencer would be sitting next to him, so when an unfamiliar, small white truck pulled into view, she lost control.

In a wave of tears and a riptide of emotion, Raven sat down on the front porch step and buried her head in her hands. She heard the truck pull to a stop near the house. She heard two doors open and close. But it was not until she heard the voice of her dear friend that she found a way to lift her head.

"Oh, my girl! Raven. Honey, we're here."

Hair stuck in wet strands to Raven's forehead. Her eyes were puffy and red from crying. Mucus clung to her hand when she pulled it away from her face creating a thin thread of sorrow to dangle in front of her.

Cruzita approached. In one motion, she sat down next to Raven and wrapped both arms around her in a loving, safe hug.

"*¿Qué pasó, amiga?*"

Raven sniffed, then pulled away as Cruzita lessened her embrace.

"It's . . . it's . . . Spencer. He's missing."

"*Ay, mi corazón, lo siento mucho que estés pasando por esto.* I'm so sorry, my girl."

Tears continued to flow down Raven's cheeks. "That's not all. One of Cass's deputies was killed last night. Someone . . ." Raven paused to catch her breath, then noticed that Cruzita was not alone. "Oh my. Alma? What are you doing here?"

Alma slowly stepped closer, but Cruzita offered an explanation. "Alma stayed with me last night. When she heard you were in some kind of trouble, she offered to drive me out here when my car would not start. And don't you know I just got it out of the shop, too!"

"Raven," Alma said. "Is there anything I can do?"

The two women locked eyes. Alma's concern sounded real enough, but Raven sensed something disingenuous beneath her comforting words. Maybe it was her disposition, but Raven elected to overlook the awkward feeling and instead, apologized to Alma.

"I'm . . . sorry, Alma. I've just been through so much that I . . . I . . ."

Alma stepped forward and spread her arms out to embrace both women. They sat huddled on the porch in a mix of tears and reassurances as they rocked together in a supportive group hug.

Cruzita gently hushed Raven while Alma patted her on the back. When the surge of emotion began to subside, the three loosened their arms and parted. Alma stood up. Cruzita used the sleeves of her shirt to dry Raven's tears.

"Come. Let me take you inside," Cruzita said. "I'll help you wash up, and we can sit and talk if you want."

"Yes," Alma added. "It will do you some good to freshen up. Things will work out for you."

Raven looked up at Alma. Her eyes glimmered. Raven forced a welcoming, thankful smile. Alma returned a smile, and yet again, Raven had an uncomfortable feel about it. Was it an honest attempt to be a part of her healing or the subtle smirk of a snake eyeing its prey?

"Yes, girl! It will all be all right. We're gonna take good care of you. And then we'll be here to celebrate when Spencer comes home."

Raven continued to look at Alma but answered Cruzita.

"Okay. I'll make some fresh coffee and . . ."

"Raven, you go inside with Cruzita. I've got the best coffee in the world in one of my bags. Colombian. I'll bring it in and brew some for us."

Raven glanced at Cruzita and saw her face light up. Feeling overwhelmed with everything, Raven nodded.

"Let me help you stand up, girl." Cruzita

held hands with Raven as they stood together.

"I'll grab my bag," Alma said.

"Yes! I'm taking her inside," Cruzita replied. She then looked at Raven and spoke in a lower voice. "She can let herself in, no?"

Raven watched Alma walk toward her truck. Turning to Cruzita, she said, "We don't really know her, do we?"

"Girl, I do. She's the best. Not the best like you, but pretty good."

Raven sighed, feeling reluctant but thought maybe she was overreacting after all.

"Okay. I'm sorry. I'm just so frazzled by everything. Of course, she can let herself in."

Cruzita hugged Raven again.

"You won't regret this, girl. We're here for you."

Arm in arm, they entered the house. Raven glanced back and saw Alma rummaging in her truck and fought the urge to lock the door.

CHAPTER 48

Of the few bags that Ana carried in her truck, one held a small pouch, the contents of which originated in Cauca, a department located within the Andean region of Colombia. Inside the pouch were coffee beans that, when properly brewed, create a most unique taste. The beans grown in Cauca are cultivated through a combination of high-altitude, volcanic soil, and traditional farming techniques, the result of which makes them highly sought after. Ana considered this specific blend "one to die for."

Reaching in, she removed the bag of delicious beans, then paused to look at something else. A small black device sat dormant inside the bag. The words, *Artemis OmniLocator*, etched in matte-black lettering were displayed across the top. Ana laid a hand on the device but did nothing to activate it.

"Let's see if you have brought me to the right location," Ana said, smiling. She cinched the bag closed and patted herself on the hip, her smile widening as if she were a proud mother watching her child take their first steps. "If so, we may not have time for coffee after all."

Ana closed the door and walked to the house, one hand holding a bag of special beans, the other begging her not to brew them.

PART 4
Kill Order

CHAPTER 49

The inside of Deputy Warden James's office at the South Brewster County Jail looked like a shrine to the El Paso Chihuahuas, a minor league baseball team affiliated with the San Diego Padres. There was a Chihuahuas team poster on the wall listing their home and away games along with three pennants, each sporting the team's black and red colors—one displaying the team name with a small, snarling chihuahua wearing a spiked collar and a baseball uniform, one celebrating a stretch of Pacific Coast League Southern Division titles spanning from 2015–2017, and one for a 2019 division title. A framed Hunter Renfroe jersey hung behind his desk. Two signed baseballs encased in acrylic cubes sat on one side of a bookshelf and a signed 2023 team photo stood in a wooden picture frame on the other. Even the clock on the wall, albeit the institutionalized version similar to the one in Chance's office, was dressed with a small chihuahua sticker. The whole thing made me want to throw up. *Go Astros,* I thought.

Upon my arrival, I learned that the Deputy Warden was not in his office. I asked a secretary to take me there anyway and asked that she locate him right away. Her raised eyebrow and annoyed look told me she was not one for being told what to do. I had checked my usual professional demeanor at the door in exchange for a directness that demanded quick responses. They might have all the time in the world to spare watching over the dregs of society, but I did not. To quote Flint, "I've got shit ta do."

I picked up the name plate that sat front and center on his desktop and read it aloud to myself while I waited for the Deputy Warden to arrive. "Deputy Warden Mitch James." I gave a nod of approval, then set it back on his desk. "Mitch. Good to know you have a first name." I figured that since he had made me wait for an excessive amount of time, we would now be on a first-name basis. When he did arrive, I stood and took his hand when he offered it, but my pursed lips and agitated expression must have given away my disapproval of having to wait so long.

"Investigator Callahan. What brings you in so early on a Sunday?"

"It's just another day, Mitch." I saw his eyes widen a bit, taken aback by my informal approach. I shifted my body in my seat and continued. "It's been a hell of a night, so I'll be direct. Yesterday seems like playtime compared to what we find ourselves in today. I need a list of every guard on duty during the time Luis López met with his female visitor, Marta Jiménez, as well as what guards led him to solitary following our conversation in the interrogation room."

"Guards? You want a list of guards."

I sat back and crossed my legs watching Deputy Warden James, Mitch, try to determine why I would want guard names and not inmates. I let that ruminate for as long as I could stand it, then took over the conversation.

"Mitch. I don't have much time. I have reason to believe that there is someone on the staff that knows something about the murder committed by Luis López as well as his alleged suicide."

"Alleged? The report states clearly that he removed a shiv from a hidden fold in his sleeve and . . ."

"Horse shit. Have you ever heard of anyone ramming a sharp object into their own eye before? It doesn't seem likely that we have the first ever suicide by self-inflicted brain tapping."

Opening a desk drawer, he removed a yellow folder and tossed it to me. "It's written right here. Read it for yourself."

I opened the folder and scanned the report. Sure enough, the reporting guard attested that *López took his own life by stabbing himself in the eye*. I flipped to the second page of the document and noted the name of the guard who filed the report. Eduardo Terrazas. I closed the folder and held it up next to me.

"You believe everything you read? Why don't

we start compiling a list? While you are doing that, I want to speak with Eduardo."

"I don't believe he is on duty this morning."

"Well, make a call and get him up here."

"Mr. Callahan. I'm getting a little tired of your tone."

"Mitch, I call you Mitch because goddamn, if I were in charge and had a murder and a suicide happen right under my nose on the same day, and I bought the load of crap that had been dished to me, I'd either be an asshole or I'd be canned for not doing my job. Now, let's start listing names and get Guard Eduardo Terrazas up here right away. Wake him up if you have to, but I am willing to bet that he has more he is going to want to add to his report."

CHAPTER 50

It was Sunday morning and churchgoers were too busy filing into the chapel to notice that one of the congregational vans was pulling away from the church. Had they paid better attention, they would have seen a middle-aged Latin-looking man behind the wheel sipping coffee from a Styrofoam cup, driving away as if he had Ms. Daisy herself in the rear of the van. As it were, one young girl did notice. When she locked eyes with the driver, instead of telling someone what she saw, she smiled and waved. Mata took time to smile at the girl and waved back. It was Sunday morning after all.

He drove back to the motel and parked in front of his room. Wasting no time, he loaded his bags in the rear of the van and shut the door.

"Mornin', stranger!"

Mata jumped, startled by the surprise greeting. His hands clenched into fists, and he teetered on the edge of making a swift physical response.

"Whoa there, mister. Didn't mean ta scare ya."

Mata composed himself, inwardly cursing his relaxed awareness. He mustered a smile, which went a long way to ease the growing tension between the two men.

"I am sorry, señor. I did not see you standing there."

"Shoot fire. Old timer like me? Ya must'a been thinkin' 'bout somethin' else." The old man stretched the wrinkles on his face with a gummy smile. He balanced himself with a crooked wooden cane that looked to be hand carved and most likely homemade. He wore blue overalls and a white dress shirt. Strands of white hair curled beneath an old, red hat adorned with a TSCRA (Texas and Southwestern Cattle Raisers Association) patch featuring a blue star and a longhorn steer. "The name's Walter. Walter Weatherford. My friends call me Dubs."

Mata listened to the man while also hearing El Despiadado's whispers. *"Kill this man."*

"You know, on account of the two Ws."

Walter grinned again, his toothless smile bursting with untold stories.

"Oh!" Mata acted surprised to make the connection. "That is clever, Mr. Weatherford."

"Come on. I done told ya my friends call me Dubs. You can, too."

"Very well, Dubs."

"What brings you to town?"

Mata smiled at Dubs, thinking, *you ask too many questions, old man.* "I am just passing through."

"Oh, I figured ya were with the church er somethin'." He knocked the rubber stopper of his cane against the van wall.

"Yes. What I mean to say is, I am with the

Catholic Diocese of El Paso. I have been sent to Santa Teresa de Jesus Catholic Church to oversee the sacraments."

Dubs looked at Mata, then in the direction of the church. "I think ya may be runnin' a little late, friend."

"Kill him."

"Señor Dubs, you are right. I must be going."

"He may be old, but he will remember you. Kill him now."

"I suppose." Dubs paused and scratched his chin. "Never did catch yer name."

"You see. He is not trusting you. Do it. NOW!"

Mata smiled. "Where are my manners? My name is Ignacio Valdez." Maintaining eye contact, he reached for the handle of the sliding van door and pulled. "Let me give you my card."

Dubs chomped his gums.

"If you come by the church later, I can offer you a hot meal."

Dubs leaned to his right and glanced inside the van. Mata followed his gaze, realizing Dubs's curiosity had elevated to a suspicious level.

"Oh, I ain't the church'n type."

"Kill the old man!"

"You do not have to be," Mata said. "There was a time when I walked in your shoes as well."

"That so?"

"Snap his brittle neck."

"Come, let me give you my card, and I will see you at five o'clock for supper."

Mata offered an empty hand.

"It will be easy. It will feel so good."

Dubs inched forward. He reached out his hand to Mata. Mata took ahold. The old man's hand and long fingers were strong, bony, rough with calluses earned from a life of hard work.

This is an honorable man, Mata thought as he released Dubs's hand. He turned and reached into the closest bag to him, rummaged around the inside, then pulled it out again.

"I am sorry, Señor Dubs. It seems I am out of cards at the moment. But please, join me tonight. It will not be any trouble at all."

Dubs gazed at Mata, at El Despiadado. His face softened. He removed his hat and slicked his hair back before replacing it on his head.

"Well, if ya say it won't be no trouble."

"It would be my pleasure."

"Your pleasure to spill his blood."

"All right. I thank you kindly, Ignacio."

"But, of course."

Mata laid a hand on the van door. Dubs shuffled his feet to turn around. The door did not slide closed. Instead, El Despiadado grabbed Dubs around the neck and lifted him off the ground in one powerful thrust. He rotated so Dubs hung facing the open door of the van. El Despiadado felt a surge of guilty pleasure well up from his groin to his neck as he tightened his grip around Dubs's throat. The old man's legs kicked out. He dropped his cane and tried to wedge his aged fingers into El Despiadado's deadly hold. With one violent shake of his arms and twist of his wrists, El Despiadado felt the snap of brittle bones beneath his palms.

Walter Weatherford's arms fell limp to his side. A slow, involuntary gurgle leaked from Dubs's mangled throat as El Despiadado carefully leaned into the van and placed his dead body on the floorboard between the front and first-row rear seats.

Sweat trailed down El Despiadado's cheeks. The thrilling sensation subsided. The power he felt in the strength of his hands dissipated. He opened and closed them, flexing the muscles in his palms and forearms. He took a deep breath while he looked at the old man.

"I am sorry, Señor Dubs. Your meal will have to wait."

A wash of cold filtered down Mata's back and arms. His fingers felt fuzzy, and then, as if each digit could fire a round of relief, the feeling escaped him. Mata stepped back. He heard a snap on the ground. Looking down, he saw the cane that Dubs had carried with him, now cracked in the middle of its crooked curve. It too was as fragile as the old man who wielded it.

Such is life, Mata thought. He bent down and

picked up the damaged cane, then tossed it into the van. With a gentle pull, he slid the van door closed.

"There can be no more distractions," Mata whispered to himself.

In three steps, he was inside his motel room. He double-checked that he had everything loaded and was quickly back in the van. Stepping into the driver's seat, he adjusted the wires beneath the console. The engine spit once, twice, then engaged in a satisfying rumble that settled into a quiet vibration. He closed the door, checked the rearview mirror, and backed out of the parking spot.

Before pulling away, he stopped the van and got out. Leaving the engine running, he walked the few steps back to the parking spot. Kneeling, Mata picked up the red hat with the blue patch. Looking at it, he wondered what life Dubs had left behind. With a sigh, he returned to the van and loaded up. With his foot on the brake, he shifted the gears into drive, then twisted around to look at Dubs sprawled on the floor behind him.

"A man should always have a hat to cover his head. I would hate for you to leave yours behind, my friend."

Leaning back, he placed the hat over Dubs's face, covering the glassy stare from his cold, lifeless eyes.

CHAPTER 51

A thin, stabbing light pierced Spencer's vision as his eyelids fluttered, daring to part ways with the unconscious safety of sleep. The storm had passed leaving the scraps of an overcast sky to fend for itself. Sunlight broke the cloudy barrier like bullet holes in an old beer can, streaming down in radiant yellow beams. The air was cool, but it was early.

As he came to, Spencer's head felt heavy as if he suffered from a string of late-night escapades along North Gate where the music was loud and the girls in boots and short skirts were the main attraction. That, and for most others, the beer. Though he was not yet of age, he found ways to get rowdy with his friends without partaking in their alcoholic romp-arounds. Like the deep bass beat during a throwback version of Los del Rio's "Macarena," Spencer's temples throbbed in rhythm with his injured ankle. The middle finger of his left hand was raw where the nail had been ripped away. He felt achy and stiff from the position in which his body had spent the last few hours, but the good news, if there was any to be recognized, was that his mouth was moist and his skin felt supple—lifesaving side effects of being caught in last night's thunderstorm.

The ground beneath him felt softer, like the grimy cousin of a pig's warm mudhole. The canyon floor was oversaturated by runoff that had nowhere to go. Small pools and larger puddles littered the area like muddy lily pads scattered across the desert.

With considerable strain, Spencer fought through the pain in his head and back and tried to sit up. His clothes were soaked through. Grit had found a way to dig into the cuts and scrapes on his back, causing them to itch and burn. Spencer placed his palms on the ground to help steady his upright position. When they began to press into the sloshy mix of sand and dirt, he recoiled so his raw finger would not be subjected to a sandpaper-like scrubbing.

Between the sunbeams cascading like theater lighting in circles across the canyon floor and the numerous puddles of water, some of which reflected the light making it seem as if the earth itself was shining, the canyon looked to Spencer like something out of a dream.

More like a nightmare, he thought.

He took a deep breath, then slowly let it out again. He repeated the same pattern three more times, feeling a little better after each lungful of fresh air. The thumping ferocity in his head eased, but his ankle screamed at every small twitch he made. Relieved to be alive, Spencer looked at his feet and noticed one foot was bare.

He immediately remembered the reason, then glanced to the right of where he sat and saw his missing shoe and sock.

The shoe sat upright and was filled with gray-looking water. His sock rested just under the water line, balled into a tight fit and shoved under the tongue and laces to help prevent any collected water from escaping. So far, it was doing a good job.

Laughing to himself, Spencer addressed the water in his shoe. "I'll keep you until I need you, so stick around, okay? No leaking or trying to evaporate too soon." Spencer laughed again. "I must be going crazy. I'm talking to a shoe. Maybe I should give in and call it Wilson. That's what Tom Hanks would do."

The jagged ceiling of clouds provided plenty of shade and did not look to be floating off anytime soon. They had rained themselves out, and like Spencer, seemed just too tired to move.

Spencer eased himself back down, lying in the same cast of mud that had formed around his body over the past few hours. He gazed wearily up at the rim of the canyon. *How could freedom be so close, yet so unattainable,* he thought. *I know Mom and Dad are worried, but if I know them, they are already doing everything they can to find me. Still . . .*

He reached into his pocket and pulled out his cell phone. His battery level had dropped to eight percent. The words NO SERVICE stood out like an angry reminder to stop checking to see if there were any bars available. He was not expecting any. He tapped the camera icon, activating the app, then slid his finger along the bottom. Toggling through the many choices of video and photography options, he stopped on video, then pressed the circular arrows that switched the view from the main camera to selfie mode. He held the camera above him so he could see his face on the screen and pressed the large, red record button.

"Mom. Dad. I hate to think that you are watching this right now. If you are, I really screwed up, and I am so sorry. I know making the decision to come out here was a bad one, but you always said, 'learn from your mistakes.' I wish it had come to that. I want you to know that I fought hard and used every last survival skill you taught me in hopes of pulling through. I even tried scaling the side of the cliff behind me in the dark, but you see where that got me."

Spencer bit his bottom lip. His eyes filled with precious moisture he could ill afford to waste, but his emotions took control, and there was nothing he could do but let the tears come.

"I want you to be proud of me. I just hope you don't feel like I let you down. I love you both very much."

Spencer lowered the phone and kissed the screen. He lifted it again and smiled the best he could, then pressed the red button again to end the message. Laying the phone on his chest, Spencer cried. He cried because he was sorry. He cried because he missed his family. He cried because he did not want to die.

Time became irrelevant to Spencer, but his safety was thrust back into the forefront of his mind when he heard the rustling of sliding rocks. He sat up and swiveled his head around trying to see how far off the sound had traveled. Everything at the base of the canyon seemed to echo louder and seemed closer than their sounds truly were. With wide eyes, he scanned the rock wall from rim to floor in both directions. As he looked one direction, more noises filtered around him from behind. Looking back, he caught a glimpse of dust fanning up from the ground from a spot where a larger stone had just landed.

The mountain lion is back, he thought.

Using what little strength he had left, he scooched his body to the cliff and leaned flat against the rock. He had nowhere to hide. No ability to try and escape.

The clouds above him looked like they had ripped apart as sunlight and heat flooded the canyon like the deluge of last night. He reached for his water-filled shoe and slid it near, then bent his good leg at the knee and wrapped his arms around it.

Brighter and brighter, the sun blazed overhead,

spewing its rays down on the canyon. Spencer heard more rocks tumble and hit the ground, but with all the puddles and pool of water scattered about, the glare became immense, as if the floor were made of one giant mirror.

There was nothing left for Spencer to do except pray. He bowed his head, closed his eyes, and buried his face in his arms. The pounding of rock and dirt continued until the padding of heavy steps took its place. Spencer squeezed his eyes shut and flexed his muscles. He rocked back and forth, spent of his resolve, preparing to accept what pain was to come, and felt the presence and shadow grow before him.

CHAPTER 52

The idea of a fresh, tantalizing sip of exotic coffee became quickly overshadowed by the pounding and preparation of the coffee beans. Raven sat at the kitchen table with Cruzita. Alma stood at the counter near the stove holding a wooden mallet in her hand. Spread out before her was a cotton cloth covered in pale brown beans. With gentle, lethal strokes, she crushed the beans with powerful blows, then pressed and rotated the end of the mallet over the coarse remains until a fine ground had formed. Cruzita watched in awe at Alma's skillful handling of the mallet, but Raven's heart thumped harder as each bean was crushed. Alma talked while she worked.

"My *abuela* would use a *pilón y mazo* to make coffee in her village in Colombia. My *abuelo* was good with knives and would carve special things for *abuela* to use for cooking. I watched many times as she crushed the beans in wooden bowls my grandfather made for her. Sometimes, he would play games to try and antagonize *abuela* while I watched. He would smile at me, and I would smile back. When Abuela caught on, she would chase Abuelito out of the kitchen with the pestle and try to hit him on the head yelling, '¡*Vamos, viejo, ya basta*! *Sal de mi cocina en este instante o dile adiós a tu café!*' He would run, and she would never catch him. When Abuela returned to her work, she would look at me and smile, knowing that I was the reason for Abuelito's fun and games. When the coffee was done, she would pour a cup for him anyway, but before handing it over, would playfully threaten him not to tease her again. *Abuelo* would answer with a kiss on her forehead and then would sit beside me and tell me about the next thing he would carve for her, and that if I liked, I could help."

"That is a beautiful story," Cruzita said. "What fond memories you must have."

"It is all I have of them. They were killed by soldiers the following summer."

Cruzita gasped. Raven felt a pang of remorse, but it did not ease the tension in her gut.

"Why? What happened?" Cruzita's voice fluttered.

"It was only to show power in the region. The soldiers came into the village and dragged three families into the streets, then burned their houses. My *abuelos* and I were among them. The soldiers yelled for everyone in the village to watch. They threatened to return if money was not paid. The people were very frightened and gave everything they could give to satisfy the soldiers. It must not have been enough. Before they went away, they shot each person in the head, including my *abuelos*. I was the last to be targeted. When a soldier turned his gun on me, he pulled the trigger, but the gun only clicked. I jumped at the sound, fearing that my life was over, but I did not cry. The soldier looked at me and laughed. Then he said, '¡*Eres muy suertuda*!' I stared back at the soldier, but I did not feel lucky at all."

Cruzita stood up and walked over to Alma. She hugged her from behind, but Alma continued to prepare the beans.

"You must have been very brave," Raven said.

Alma stopped what she was doing and turned around. "I do not think so. I only wished to protect them, but I was too young and too small. How can one be brave if they do not act when danger is near?"

"You were only a little girl. What could you have done but angered the soldiers and then been killed yourself?" Raven added.

"I promised myself that I would not let anyone hurt me or the ones I love again." Alma gripped the mallet hard enough for her knuckles to turn white. Her eyes blazed.

Raven saw, but Cruzita was still buried in a supportive hug from behind. "I'm sorry, Alma. I did not mean to upset you."

Alma relaxed her grip on the mallet and laid it on the counter. She turned back to the beans. Cruzita whispered something into Alma's ear, then released her hug and sat back down at the table.

To Raven, the sounds of water boiling in a pot on the stove and the steam rising resembled the last twelve hours of her life—a slow buildup of heated emotions set to bubble over at any moment.

The aroma from the coffee grounds began to filter throughout the kitchen as Alma scooped and piled, kneaded and pressed them into a fine grain. Alma wrapped the grounds in the cotton cloth, then used two clothespins to hold the pouch of coffee over an empty carafe.

The smells spread in thick, scented waves as Alma slowly poured the boiling water into the top of the pouch. As the hot water filtered into the grounds and settled at the bottom of the cotton cloth, the weight of the mix and the porous nature of the pouch forced drops of rich coffee to seep through. With each drip of coffee, a more enticing flavor filled the carafe, its scent wafting out into the kitchen for all to smell.

Alma wiped the counter, placed the mallet in the sink, and sat down at the table next to Cruzita. There was nothing left to do but wait. Raven glanced at her phone again, hoping for a miracle. Alma reached across and placed her palm on top of Raven's hand.

"Do not worry. It will all be over soon. I just know it."

Raven forced a smile while slowly recoiling her hand and phone from under Alma's grasp. Though she had been busy at the counter, Alma's hand felt cold to Raven. It made her flesh crawl and sent tingles into the hairs on her neck.

On cue, Cruzita broke the ice and said, "So, Alma. Tell Raven why you have come to town. I'm sure that she would like to hear the story."

Alma smiled, her face soft and innocent, but her eyes still burned with fire and foreboding.

"I am searching for something. A lost family artifact."

Cruzita grabbed Raven's hand. "Isn't that wild, girl? It's like she's a modern-day girl version of Indiana Jones. All she needs is a whip, and she's on the hunt to find the treasure."

Alma stood and walked to the counter, returning promptly with the carafe of steeping coffee. She placed it on the table between them. Steam rose and South American tradition filled the kitchen in generous puffs of delicious smells as Alma poured three small helpings of her coffee. Cruzita passed the cups around, and when each woman had their own, she offered a toast.

"To the safe return of Spencer and for good luck for Alma on her hunt."

They lifted their cups and sipped. Cruzita savored the taste with closed eyes, but Alma and Raven had locked onto one another over the rim of their drinks. As she sipped, Raven wondered about the true nature of Alma's visit to Brewster, and how her seemingly fortunate circumstances had led her to the CR. She did not believe in coincidences but was unable to pinpoint exactly what made her feel so uncomfortable around Alma.

They sat in silence. The steam lessened and the carafe slowly emptied as refills were offered and accepted, but the aroma lingered in the air as did the stagnant feeling that festered within Raven. She had learned a bit of Alma's history, but Raven had a history, too.

CHAPTER 53

Brewster was as empty as a ghost town on Sunday mornings. People were either at church praying and asking for forgiveness of one kind or another or sleeping off bad choices from the night before and also asking for the same. This morning was no different, which made it an easy decision for Chance to drop by the jail before making a final stop at the sheriff's office. He left Deputy Bostwick to dust the Camaro and sent Deputy Figgs back out on patrol. It would be a light day for them, too.

Stopped at a red light, Chance took the momentary solitude to gather his thoughts. While the cases at hand were a top priority, he could not help but visualize fishing off the banks of the Rio Grande with the towering peaks of the Sierra del Carmen Range rising across the river in Mexico. He and Cass had planned a late fall trip to Big Bend National Park and were looking forward to getting away, even if only for a short while. It was one of those trips Raven called "a guy's paradise and a girl's worst nightmare." Chance chuckled at the thought.

The empty intersection made running the red light tempting, but Chance's character always opted for wise decisions, even when no one was looking. It was a lesson he picked up in grade school and one he reminds the vagrants and criminals he hauls off to jail of when their carelessness caught up with them. It turned out, as usual, to be the right choice. A church van, empty of passengers, drove through the intersection just before Chance's light turned green. He watched it for a moment, wondering what souls they were off to collect this morning, then turned in the opposite direction and headed the final two miles to the South Brewster County Jail.

CHAPTER 54

Carlos Ruiz-Mata took a long look in the rearview mirror after driving through the intersection where a South Brewster County Sheriff's Bronco waited for the light to change. Though he did not catch sight of the driver as he passed by, he did take note of the vehicle make and model for reference sake. His gaze remained fixed on the Bronco until he saw it turn and drive off in the opposite direction. With his foot on the gas, he smiled and continued toward his final destination for this trip into the United States. If all went well, it would be a brief stop, but then, that would not be up to him.

CHAPTER 55

After waiting for Deputy Warden Mitch James to make two phone calls, one of which was to summon Eduardo Terrazas in to work on his day off and the other to gripe at his secretary to hurry up and print out employee work rosters, I found myself back in the control room rewatching tapes and cross-referencing guards on duty and their respective assignments throughout the day.

"Look who is hard at work in the belly of this proverbial beast." Chance walked into the control room boasting a wide smile that stretched his face and the mustache that rode solo on his upper lip. "I'll say one thing, you're one hell of an investigator."

"Thanks, Chance."

"But you may want to work on your tact."

"Come again?"

"I saw . . ."

I interrupted. "You bumped into Mitch on your way in, huh? That guy is lucky to hold the job he has. If you ask me, he's just as dumb as Joe Sinclair. Please tell me you did not have a hand in securing him the job of Deputy Warden."

"What have you found?" he asked, sitting down next to me.

Letting that last comment go, huh, Sheriff? I

thought. "Filtering through the list isn't the issue. It's connecting which guard was on what assigned duty, then checking that with time-stamped video footage on the monitors. Turns out, guards are covering like mad for one another, so this list is only good for use as a roll sheet as to who was actually on the job on any particular day."

Chance huffed, then shook his head, seeming quite displeased with my initial report. I knew he was not upset with me or the way I was doing my job, but what I had discovered suggested that sloppy personnel management was to blame.

"Have you made any progress at all?"

"That's the good news. As much of a pile of crap as this is, I have narrowed down the list in two places. First, Guard Eduardo Terrazas was the one who led Ms. Marta Jiménez to the isolation bay where she spoke over the phone with Luis López. He also led her out. Watch the video."

I used a remote to rewind the footage showing Guard Terrazas leading Marta Jiménez to bay number six.

"As you'll see in the video, Jiménez sat without addressing Terrazas and waited patiently for Luis López to arrive. As recorded, she spent two minutes and thirty-six seconds on the phone. When she was done speaking with him, or possibly to him, she hung up, stood up, and left bay six without any cause to show emotion or concern for López. Guard Terrazas met her at the door and ushered her out to the waiting room where she promptly exited the jail. Her hair is draped over her face so it is hard to tell if she spoke to Terrazas or not. She would have only had time for a phrase or brief comment, but if Terrazas had anything to do with López's alleged suicide, that may have been all she needed to communicate orders to him."

"You're leaning on Terrazas then?"

"Yes. For the moment anyway. He is on his way in for questioning, and he'll need to answer for even more than what you have already seen."

Chance straightened up and gave me an inquisitive look. "Continue, please."

"Terrazas and a guard named Luther Brown were the two that escorted López from interrogation to solitary."

"So, we need to speak with Brown as well?"

"Not necessarily. When they reached the final security checkpoint, Brown held back to talk with Guard Takisha Sampson. I guess he had other things on his mind and felt that Terrazas could handle López on his own. What's odd is that there was an electrical surge in that wing of the jail just as López was being locked away. It was brief, only three to four seconds, but we lost all video footage for a period of ten seconds as a result. When the power came on the cameras had to reboot, causing the additional delay in coverage. It was during that time that López killed himself."

"And, let me guess, Terrazas was the one reporting the incident."

"Bingo," I said.

"Okay, so we need ta speak with Terrazas, but let's not leave out Brown or Sampson. And who is the facilities manager? The electrical surge seems a little too well timed for my liking. I also want ta have my own one on one with Deputy Warden James. And where has Warden Macias been through all of this?"

"Great points, Chance. As for the facilities manager, his name is . . ." I ruffled through the paperwork in front of me. "Hernando Gomez. He's been here for about five years. Not sure of his prior employment, but his background check would have cleared him for his current position." I paused. "But you're right; the timing of that electrical surge does raise questions."

Chance shifted his stance and looked thoughtful. "I've always said, 'Trust, but verify.' Bring Gomez in for questioning as well. See if he can provide any logs or maintenance records that could explain the surge."

I nodded. "As for Warden Macias, he is out of town visiting family in Richmond, my neck of the woods, sort of. Deputy Warden James claims to have kept him in the loop, but the lack of direct communication is concerning."

Chance raised an eyebrow. "It's a glaring omission, isn't it? If there's a significant incident in my facility, I'd want ta be informed directly. And if he was informed, I find it strange that Macias didn't contact me. Follow up on that angle as well."

"Roger that. My guess is when he does get back, there may be a little reorganization that takes place around here, wouldn't you agree?" I asked.

Chance gave me a *you nailed it* look, then stood up.

"All right," Chance said. "Let's go see if Terrazas has shown up. I've had enough of this office. Maybe I can have that chat with Mitch now."

I tossed the remote onto the table beneath the monitors and stood up. "You're on the 'Mitch' bandwagon, too."

"Damn right. If you have a title, respect it—maybe then others will as well."

We left the control room and headed down a tight corridor to a hallway that led to the Deputy Warden's office, a cluster of clerical desks, and the exit to the waiting room. It was dimly lit. The cement walls did nothing to reflect the light. Instead, they seemed to suck the life out of each bulb, tamping its brightness and absorbing what good there was of it. I had visited many jails and prisons over the years and this one, at least in this section, was akin to the pit of despair—"Don't even think of trying to escape."

When we reached the Deputy Warden's door, Chance reached for the knob and began to let himself in.

"Hold up there, Chance. May want to brace yourself."

"Brace myself? For what?"

I shook my head as if I were evading a sneeze, then said, "Never mind. See for yourself."

We let ourselves in, startling Mitch so that he hung up the phone on whoever he had been speaking with, then gave us an intrusive glare.

"Ever hear of knocking?"

I sensed that his irritation was aimed at me.

"Oh. Yeah," I said, knocking three times on his desktop. "But I don't give a fuck."

Mitch stood up, visibly ruffled. While he glared at me, Chance surveyed the room, taking in all the baseball paraphernalia. "¡Esto está mal!" he said, looking back at me.

I bulged my eyes and flattened my lips in reply.

"Wrong. All of this." Chance motioned to the décor in one sweep of his arm. "Learn some Spanish, amigo." He looked at Mitch and placed his hands on his hips. "You do know you are working in a government facility, no?"

"What?" Mitch replied.

I could tell that his annoyed tone did not sit well with Chance. "Tell you what. I'm going to step outside and wait for Terrazas to arrive. You two have your fun in here without me."

Chance looked at me as if I had just announced I had slept with his sister. I smiled and raised my eyebrows once, then exited the room, leaving the door open behind me.

CHAPTER 56

To Raven, each minute her phone remained quiet felt like the end of the world was closing in. The silence clawed at her, suffocating in its intensity. She was not alone, but at the CR, not everyone was a welcome distraction.

Alma. Who the hell is she? Why does she make me feel so . . . suspicious? So uncomfortable.

Raven looked to the corral, asking herself these questions as if trying to make sense of it all. Cruzita and Alma had strayed away from the house and were leaning on the fence. It seemed to Raven that Cruzita had a full-on crush and ate up everything Alma had to say. Raven knew Cruzita was a single woman, and she did not think that romantic feelings were involved, but the way she hung on every word Alma said made it seem to Raven like there was a bit of idolization in her close friend's eyes.

The sun had risen high and bright. The breeze diminished to a few random tufts of wind puffing by as the storm in the distance had blown itself out. Raven continued to fidget with the touchscreen, activating her phone so she could see the picture of Cass and Spencer, then raising it up as if the few feet of movement would garner a stronger cell signal, just in case the three bars she already was receiving was not enough.

Why won't somebody call?

Raven sighed. She felt heavy. Helpless. At least last night she was on the move, and the possibility of finding Spencer herself did not seem too far out of reach. Sitting and waiting wore her down, and the exhaustion she felt did nothing but strain her thinking and play games with her imagination.

With her eyes stuck to her phone, she did not see the women return from the corral. Their footsteps on the wooden porch caused her to jump. Startled, her grip faltered, sending her phone spiraling through the air to land face-down at Alma's feet.

"You poor thing," Alma said as she bent over to pick up the phone.

Cruzita knelt and embraced Raven's hands in a comforting grasp. "Oh, my girl. I'm so sorry. I bet Spencer is on his way right now."

Alma stepped over and handed Raven her cell phone. "I think it may have cracked."

Of all things, Raven laughed. "Well, shit. Things couldn't get much worse."

"Come," Cruzita said, standing. "Let's go inside and sit where it is more comfortable." The sparkle in Cruzita's gaze was one of genuine compassion, a dutiful desire to help a friend in need. Still holding onto Raven's hands, she gently tugged, coaxing her to stand. "That's my girl."

Cruzita wrapped an arm around Raven's shoulder and led her into the house. Alma followed, pulling the door closed after passing through. Her hand lingered on the knob.

Cruzita and Raven sat on the couch together. Alma walked behind them and put a hand on Cruzita's shoulder. "I am truly sorry, but would you help me gather my things in the kitchen?"

Cruzita looked back at her. "Are you leaving?" Her expression was a blend of confusion and hurt.

Alma smiled at Raven. "I am sure things will work out for your son, but I have a job to do."

Cruzita stood up and turned around. "But . . . it's Sunday, and Raven needs us."

"And I need her, too."

Alma's reply was direct. Her eyelids narrowed, not in concentration but in a subtle display of challenge. Her smile twisted, broadening not from affection but with a hint of derisive amusement as her lips curled upward and outwards. Call it years in an elementary school classroom or a fondness of Dr. Seuss, or both, but for a second, Raven saw a resemblance in Alma's smile to the one of the evil Grinch as he was stealing Christmas.

"What do you mean, 'you need her, too?'" Cruzita became defensive. "She's going through hell right now. What could you possibly need from her? What's gotten into you?"

Raven turned. "Alma, I don't even know you." She pulled Cruzita around to look her in the eyes. "You don't even know her."

From behind them, Alma let a theatrical sigh escape her. "You may be right. But what is there to knowing someone, truly?"

Cruzita stood. "Alma, you're scaring me. Maybe you should go."

Crossing her arms, Alma lowered her head, hiding her eyes.

"You are right. I am mistaken." Alma looked at Raven. "Forgive me. I'll gather my things and be on my way." Without waiting for a reply, she disappeared into the kitchen.

Cruzita turned to Raven, her voice low and cross. "Oh my god. What is happening? One minute she's acting like my new homegirl, the next like a psycho bitch."

Clanks and dings sounded in the kitchen. Raven stood up. She took Cruzita by the shoulders and turned her so that they faced each other.

"I may be paranoid, but we need to get out of the house right now."

"You are not paranoid," Alma said, emerging from the kitchen. "And there is no reason to leave. We have only just begun to become acquainted."

Cruzita's nostrils flared. She pulled away from Raven and walked around to confront Alma.

"Bitch, I don't know who you think you are but . . ."

A solid, wooden thud caused Cruzita to stop mid-sentence. A second thud just as swift as the first resounded, ending this time with a horrific crack.

Cruzita spun toward the couch, doubling over. Blood poured from a gash on her skull. Standing behind her, Alma held the mallet in her hand. Blood dripped down the wooden handle as if it were syrup, running over her grasping fingers.

The room seemed to grow dark and time stood still. Visions of Alma smashing the coffee beans cycled relentlessly like flashes from an ancient movie projector rolling in Raven's mind, each clip Alma growing more sinister, each frame the shattered beans taking on the haunting contours of a human skull.

A fuzzy, terrified surge of electrical stings rippled over Raven's skin as she watched a dominating, evil glare twist the landscape of Alma's face.

Cruzita tried to hold herself up, but a third whack of the mallet on the back of her head sent her crumbling to the floor. Droplets of red spattered Alma's clothing and stained the back of the couch.

Lost of breath and delving back into her mind to the day Guillermo Morales, a.k.a. Gordo, invaded her Houston home threatening to rape her, to kill her, caused Raven's knees to weaken and her heart to gallop within her chest. Her phone slipped from her hand and fell to the floor as shock set in.

"No," she whispered.

She pulled her hands to her face, covering her mouth in disbelief at what she had just witnessed.

"I believe the word you are looking for is *yes*," Alma said as she slithered around the back of the couch toward Raven.

CHAPTER 57

The bells at Santa Teresa de Jesus Catholic Church tolled gracefully, their deep tones wafting on a breeze so crisp and clean it felt almost holy. Its announcement filtered throughout Brewster signaling a day of rest and reflection was at hand. It was a Sunday for picnics or for calling relatives on the phone. To some, a drive south to Big Bend National Park for an outing with the family was in order. For others, it marked the time to lounge in chairs in front of the TV for the first NFL kickoff of the day. To El Despiadado, it meant it was time to go to work.

Dressed in black jeans and custom leather boots, a dark gray button-down dress shirt with a black sport coat over the top, El Despiadado walked with a casual stride to the front doors of the South Brewster County Sheriff's Office. Behind his sunglasses, he noted only three patrol cars in the lot and one red Ford Escort. He had one button secured, holding the flaps of his jacket closed. It wore heavy and concealed much.

Acting as if he were familiar with his surroundings, he wasted no time opening the front door and walked inside. A cool rush of air brushed his face and a buzzing sound briefly tingled in his ears as the door closed behind him. He stopped long enough to remove his sunglasses, gain eye contact from a young woman in civilian clothes sitting behind plexiglass at a receiving counter, and smile.

With Latin swagger, he strolled to the counter and leaned his right elbow on the ledge.

"*Hola, preciosa.* Are you . . ." He glanced at the temporary name plate on the glass. "Sofia de la Cruz?"

The woman pursed her lips, unimpressed and looking rather annoyed.

"I am sorry. When I see a beautiful woman, I must know her name. At least then I will have a memory to remember her by."

El Despiadado saw her eyes dilate before the words came from her mouth.

"How can I help you, sir?"

He knew he had sparked a feeling in her. A few more moments would tell him all he needed to know.

"I came in here prepared to ask if your information technology manager was available, but now that I see you, my request can certainly wait." El Despiadado's lips parted in a thin, seductive smile, then he looked away as if losing interest. Patience was his most trusted ally; he just needed the woman to take the bait.

With eyes focused away from the counter, he noted the cameras perched in each corner of the waiting room, the emergency locking mechanism on the entrance door, the security window adjacent to the entrance, and saw through the glass door into the parking lot as one patrol car pulled away. *Only two patrol cars left.*

"Sir, may I have your name?"

El Despiadado whirled around, his face brewing with excitement. "I thought you would never ask. I will give you my name, and all you have to do is nod if yours is truly Sofia de la Cruz. It is a harmless thing to do, no?"

The woman allowed her annoyance to falter into a passive smile. El Despiadado locked eyes with her, posturing for a deep dive into her being as he stared into her delicious chocolate-colored gaze. Her cheeks accentuated the deep undertones of her olive-colored skin as blood rushed to her face. Had the plexiglass not been between them, El Despiadado would have leaned in to seal the deal. After a moment, Sofia blinked, then looked away before returning her gaze.

"Your name?"

"Ricardo," El Despiadado said, rolling his Rs. "Ricardo Mata."

What difference would it make if he used his last name. The girl would be dead before long.

"I am sorry, Ricardo."

I'm in, he thought.

"Our IT Manager only works the weekends if there is a system update or technological emergency."

"Emergency?" El Despiadado laughed. "Like a

terminator walking through the door? What were the words? I'll return? I'll be right back? I'll be . . ."

"Back," Sofia said, finishing the phrase. She lifted an eyebrow as if amused.

He smiled, then noticed a man in a deputy uniform crossing an open space two desk rows behind her. He lowered his tone. "If I may, is the sheriff here?"

"No, Sheriff Gilbert is out. We had an office tragedy last night."

I know. Why share such things if you were not comfortable with me, eh?

"That is terrible." El Despiadado paused, then let his face sag in disappointment. "I have traveled a long way. Do you suppose you could let me through? My employer has asked me to visit and see if there is anything I could do for you here."

"Oh, I don't think so. I'm not supposed to . . ."

"It would only be for a moment. I could place my card on your sheriff's desk, peek at your servers, and be gone before anyone noticed. Then, tomorrow, I can call with a generous bid and would make sure to give you the credit for the sale."

"Ricardo, that's . . ."

"It could result in a substantial commission for me, of which I would gladly share a portion with you?"

"Mr. Mata, I am in no position to . . ."

"That sounded worse than I had intended. Would you consider dinner as an alternative form of thanks? To be honest, I would be honored if you join me for dinner either way."

Sofia tapped her fingers on her desktop, then looked over her shoulder. The deputy had disappeared from view. She looked back at El Despiadado. A smile lit up her face. She stood and leaned toward the plexiglass.

"Don't tell anybody. I'm only covering for a friend today, but I know we'll both get in trouble if Sheriff Gilbert finds out. You can give me your card at dinner."

Sofia placed two fingers to her lips. El Despiadado pinched his fingers on his lips, pretending to lock them shut.

"So, I can trust you then?"

El Despiadado's lips curled up. With a lustful stare, he squinted his eyes just enough to conceal the raging storms brewing inside him.

"But, of course."

CHAPTER 58

With mallet in hand and freshly stained with blood, Alma poised to strike again, but it was not Raven that stood to be in danger.

"Where are the files, Raven?"

Looking perplexed and terrified, Raven responded. "Files? What the hell are you talking about? Who are you?"

Alma looked at Raven. "I'm Ana, you know that."

"What?"

"Oops . . . I know. I know. So many names. What do you call me now?" Ana paused. "I think maybe it is time I come clean. Tell you the truth. I am La Sombra Negra."

Raven looked puzzled, then spoke out. "Black Shadow? Who are you?"

"Oh, your Spanish is very good, Raven. Congratulations."

It was not beneath Ana, La Sombra Negra, to entertain a game-like attitude when tormenting a helpless victim, but time was an issue, and she did not have any to spare. She stopped her advance at the edge of the couch. From where she stood, she could see Cruzita's body lying listless on the floor. Clicking her tongue in her mouth, she shook her head as if saddened by Cruzita's condition.

"*Pobrecita*. Look Raven, she looks to be in a lot of pain."

"Stay away from her."

La Sombra Negra took a step closer to Cruzita. Raven motioned as if she were going to intervene, but Ana raised the mallet in a threatening display, cocked and ready to strike either Cruzita or Raven should she charge.

"I did not hear you. What was that again?" La Sombra Negra toyed with Raven.

"I said stay away from her, you bitch."

"Let's see what she has to say about you calling me such names, huh?"

La Sombra Negra tossed the mallet into the kitchen, then reached down and hoisted Cruzita onto the back of the couch. Blood continued to flow, though more slowly as her wounds had begun to clot. She moaned. Her arms twitched.

"I will not ask again. Where are the files?"

Ana watched Raven's eyes widen as she looked from her to Cruzita and back again.

La Sombra Negra reached to her belt and depressed a hidden locking mechanism. When activated, the handle of a small knife clicked into her palm. With delicate pleasure, she withdrew the knife, revealing its razor-sharp, double-sided blades. Its steel frame felt natural to La Sombra Negra. The grip, a polished and rounded extension of the blade, warmed in her grasp. She held the knife before her, admiring its beauty as she tilted it one way, then another.

"This is the first knife my grandfather let me handle. It fit perfectly in my small hands. Over time, it has become part of me. Now, since you are not giving what I ask for, it will become part of Cruzita, too."

La Sombra Negra took a handful of Cruzita's hair and slowly lifted her bloody head upward, exposing her neck. Wet trails of blood carved lines on her skin from her scalp and down her neck, disappearing into the front of her shirt.

La Sombra Negra glared at Raven. A cold sensation settled over her, yet the knife remained warm. Hungry. Playtime was over. Through gritted teeth, she gave a final warning.

"This is your last chance to save her."

CHAPTER 59

Raven was drowning in a flood of emotion, but one look at the knife bearing down on Cruzita's throat unleashed a surge of adrenaline that propelled her into action. In one fluid motion, Raven twisted around and grabbed one of the antiquated porcelain cowboy and horse lamps, ripping the cord from the wall, and hurled it at Ana.

The lamp hit her square in the face. As if deciding to forgo their eternal struggle, the cowboy and the horse separated into two razor-sharp chunks of porcelain. The cowboy dug his heels in and the horse kicked one final time, each finding flesh and tasting blood before falling to the floor in a pile of fine, shattered clay.

Ana dropped her knife and staggered back. A guttural scream pierced the room. She wiped her hands across her bloodied face. Whether it was pain or fury building in Ana, Raven did not wait to find out. In two swift steps, she lunged at her over the couch, narrowly missing Cruzita. Like a truck ramming into a brick wall, Raven and Ana collided, tumbling to the floor in a heap.

Hands became fists and flew at an alarming rate. Raven was in an all-out fight for survival, and an inner rage had begun to awaken. Ana took a flurry of punches to the face that further deepened her wounds and pounded the tiny shards of porcelain cowboy and horse that still clung to her skin deeper into her flesh. Blood and sweat and angry tears blended with the screams and racket the two women made as they rolled in a fortified rumble of hate and passion.

Rolling on top of Ana, Raven raised a fist to strike again, but Ana found an opening and took full advantage. Thrusting her knee up, she caught Raven in the ribs. Hearing Raven screech upon impact, Ana moaned like a heroin addict getting a quick fix at the sickening crack that emanated from Raven's chest.

Raven wheezed. Her chest stung, but her will to endure was stronger. Mustering a savage yell, Raven fought back like a cage fighter.

Relaxing her right fist, Raven palm-struck Ana under the chin. Ana's teeth knocked together, cutting through a thin thread of lip, resulting in another fresh flow of red from her face. Raven then used both hands to grab Ana's hair over each ear and prepared to slam the back of her head onto the floor, but Ana was ready.

Using the momentum Raven exerted to pull her head off the ground, Ana surged forward, ramming her forehead into Raven's. A furious flustering of flashes briefly blinded Raven. Her body swayed to one side as she recoiled from the blow.

Ana slipped from beneath Raven and crawled away on her hands and knees.

Dazed, Raven shook her head to clear her vision and saw Ana on all fours, her palms sweeping the ground as if searching for something.
The knife!

CHAPTER 60

The metallic buzz and activated click of the security door disengaging its lock was all El Despiadado wanted to hear. Though industrial in nature, it was a beautiful sound signifying a small victory that was sure to lead to an overwhelming triumph.

He watched as Sofia stood and turned her back to him as she made her way for the door, then he reached into a front coat pocket and retrieved a small electrical device. It looked like a smartwatch without a strap. The face was smooth and sleek, colored matte black while the back panel had a sticky, gelatinous layer covered with a thin protective film. El Despiadado removed the film and stuck the device on the outside of the door before walking through, then touched a finger to its control interface to activate a silent receiver beacon.

"Stay next to me," Sofia whispered.

"No place I'd rather be, *mi amor*."

Sofia was petite. Her shapely figure would be a prize for any man. Her olive skin and flowing black hair were a treasurable bonus, but El Despiadado was drawn to her eyes from the start. He found them to be such an exquisite feature—molten pools of caramel warmth swirled with tiny flecks of darker brown. Had they met under different circumstances, Sofia would be worth fighting for. But circumstances were not to be, and soon those eyes would turn a mix of yellow and gray before crystallizing into a lifeless, sunken stare.

The two passed into the belly of the South Brewster County Sheriff's Office, bypassing a break room.

"Shhh," Sofia said. "Deputy Delgado is waiting in there for Deputy Perez to return with lunch." She turned and looked at El Despiadado with want in her eyes. "Those two don't know it yet, but the chemistry they have is set to explode at any minute."

More than they know.

El Despiadado planted another device near a wall switch while Sofia's back was turned. She led him further, none the wiser.

The server room was located at the rear of the building. Sofia unlocked the door and led El Despiadado inside. She promptly shut the door behind them, ensuring their privacy. It was cold in the room. A loud, steady hum streamed from each working rack while a choppy, electronic ping that sounded more like Morse code *ditted* and *dahhed* inside a centralized mainframe unit. Blinking red and green and amber lights gave an almost hypnotic, astral appearance to the entire data center.

El Despiadado inspected a stack on the far wall. He ran his finger along a string of green lights, then tapped the last one as if expecting it to change color.

"Very impressive." He turned to Sofia. "Did you know that Cisco has recently waged a war against a company in Mexico, one of whom you have probably never heard, claiming that they have unlawfully obtained coding and protocols that have a proprietary feature that will allow for multiple source data processing and global tracking of information shared to external devices within a single hemisphere?"

To El Despiadado, Sofia looked confused. Perfect. He had no idea what he was saying except to state the technical features of his Artemis OmniLocator device and throw in some terms he learned from speaking with a man at Servicios Financieros Cortez y Asociados before setting out on his mission.

"Sounds like corporate espionage." Sofia stepped close to El Despiadado. "Sounds rather . . . exciting."

Now we are getting somewhere.

"It is a very risky thing for sure. To take something that does not belong to you and use it against the very ones from whom it was stolen? Myself . . ." he paused to inhale Sofia's scent. A mix of perfume and sweat ripening from excitement, yearning for pleasure. "I would not be able to do such a thing. But that is not my job."

"What is your job, exactly?" Sofia's voice turned soft. Desirable. The hum in the room and the rhythmic churn of the machines acted as a synthetic siren charged with distraction and deception, while in the same blend of symphonic melody, it set the stage for something irresistible. She stepped closer to El Despiadado, then brushed her fingers against his.

"Let us not discuss such things. This moment has become bigger than either of us could have ever imagined, I think."

El Despiadado placed his left palm on her forearm. With one smooth glide of his hand, he ran his fingers just above her skin to her shoulder, then across the front of her chest.

He watched her close her eyes. He watched her lips parted. As he trailed his fingers between her breasts, a sensual moan rumbled from deep within her.

Her arousal was too much to pass up. In one quick motion, El Despiadado reached his right hand to cup the backside of Sofia's neck and pulled her into an embrace that began a tongue twisting dance of lust. Lips smacked, breaths exhaled, and then, as if disappointed with himself, El Despiadado pulled away.

"Ricardo, why did you stop?" Sofia was out of breath.

El Despiadado gazed at her with stormy eyes,

eyes that held Carlos Ruiz-Mata a prisoner within the beast.

"I am sorry."

He stepped into Sofia, feeling her body against his. The shudders and trembles of ruined ecstasy still fired in uncontrolled ripples within her as she pressed herself against him, coaxing him to reconsider. She was living a fantasy and was not ready for it to end.

"I must do the job for which I have come."

"Is there anything I can do to help?"

"But . . ."

This time, he did not finish what he was saying. Instead, he placed one gentle palm on her shoulder and the other on the side of her neck. Her skin felt soft and warm beneath him. With one rigid thrust, he chopped her neck with the side of his hand, then laced his fingers together around her throat and twisted. The sound of her neck popping was no more noticeable than the *ditts* and *dahhs* or the recognizable hum from the stacks of electronics in the room, all masked beneath the *woosh* of the air conditioner making the room as cold as the lifeless stare of Sofia's chocolate eyes.

CHAPTER 61

On any other day, I would have enjoyed the atmosphere swirling around town. A quiet ambiance built around fairer weather and the coming of fall made the day most enjoyable.

Enjoyable to those not caught up in murder, suicide, and missing persons.

I stood by the Explorer and looked at my reflection in the deep, black tinted windows. The shadow of a man looked back. Though recognizable, my true feelings were conflicted, and with everything that had happened over the past twenty-four hours, who could blame me?

I glanced at my watch.

12:07

I had yet to receive an update from Flint, and it had been too long since I had last spoken with Raven. While I buried myself with distracting work, I knew she was counting each second until Spencer was brought home, and it was eating her alive. I had to get to the CR, if only for a short time.

Eduardo Terrazas had still not shown himself, though I had assurances from Deputy Warden James that he was on the way. My gut told me otherwise.

Vibrations filled the front of my jeans as my

phone alerted me that I had an incoming text. I dove my hand into my pocket, eager to read good news about Spencer. It was Chance telling me he was heading out. My nerves were on edge. Each blip or buzz from my phone sent me on a rollercoaster of hope and fear, and every single one left me feeling stuck upside down at the apex of the track.

I clicked the phone icon and pressed Raven's name on the favorites tab.

I gotta hear her voice, I thought.

Leaning against the grill of the Explorer, I listened as the phone rang once, twice, three times, then was picked up by voicemail—"Hey! This is Raven. Leave a message and I'll call ya back."

Too busy to answer the phone? Maybe that's a good thing.

A long beep sounded out signaling it was time to leave a message.

"Rave. Just checking in. Nothing on my end yet, but I know everything will be okay. Just keep doing whatever it is you are doing, and I'll be home later. Call me back if you need anything. Love you, Little Bird."

I disconnected the call and slid the phone back into my pocket. Looking up, I saw Chance exit the jail. He placed his sunglasses over his eyes and walked up to me.

"Terrazas?"

"Nope. You get anywhere with Mitch?"

"He's about as useful as a saddle on a snake."

We shared a look that spoke of suspicions that led to more than just our mystery woman or Guard Eduardo Terrazas.

"Let's head over to the office. Maybe grab some lunch on the way, and I'll fill you in unless you're wantin' ta head home to check on Raven."

"I do," I said. "Just called, but she didn't answer. I'll join you for a bite and try her again in a bit. She's either asleep or up to her ears in something that is hopefully keeping her mind off our troubles."

CHAPTER 62

"Fly Away" by Lenny Kravitz, a favorite song of Raven's and her current ringtone sounded out, his voice a muffled anthem sang out from somewhere in the room.

"*I want to get away, I want to fly away, Yeah, yeah, yeah.*"

Phone! Where's my phone?

Raven's chest burned with every breath as she struggled to stand. Her ribs stung. She could see Ana on the ground, searching for the knife. Pulling herself to her feet, Raven leaned on the edge of the couch as the room began to spin. She could feel the pressure building in her temples as blood rushed into her throbbing head.

Raven glanced at Cruzita. She was alive, but in bad shape. She needed medical attention soon. The horror of it all was that there was nothing Raven could do for her. She had to get out of the house and call for help.

Where is my damn phone?

Raven took a step and found that every movement caused a surge of sharp pain to shoot across her torso. She grabbed at the source, as if holding it would be a way to keep the agony from growing.

Get out of the house.

"There you are."

Raven froze, her pounding heart adding to her discomfort when she heard Ana's voice. She had found the knife. If only Raven could remember where she had left her gun. Her Purple Demon was the one thing she had bought for herself that could protect her at a time like this, and now, where had she left it?

Think, Raven. Think. You brought it into the house before going to town. Faster! Remember, damn it!

"Raaaa . . . ven." Ana's voice sounded raspy, unnatural. "Be a good girl, and tell me what I want to hear, or when I am done with you, I will wait for Spencer to come home. Oh . . . and I will take my time with him."

What had meant to scare Raven, lit a fire under her. The pain in her body was real and did not go away, but Raven fought past it and lunged for the front door.

Grabbing the knob, she tried to pull it open. It would not turn.

What? she thought, filling with fresh terror.

She jiggled the knob again. Nothing. She could see Ana's reflection in the window grow as she slowly tried to stand. With angry jolts and tugs, Raven fought the doorknob.

Since being attacked in Houston, Raven had drifted away from the church, away from God, and the beliefs that she had held close to her throughout her life. Praying out of necessity or for Divine intervention was never something in which she believed. But, in the height of her struggle, when a small voice from the past whispered to her, Raven listened.

"Sometimes the answer is right in front of you. All you have to do is look to see it."

The voice was hers. The words were hers, spoken as encouragement for her students when she saw them struggle with an assignment in class.

Forcing herself to slow down and breathe, Raven took her own advice and centered her attention on the doorknob. The simplicity of it all would have caused Raven to laugh at herself had she not been in a fight for her life. The knob was locked.

With a quick pinch of the turn button and a twist of the wrist, the door was unlocked. Raven opened the door and escaped onto the porch. For Cruzita's sake, she hoped that Ana would follow her outside.

The barn looked to be a hundred yards away, though in reality, was much closer. There would be places to hide, but more importantly, Raven knew there was a radio stashed somewhere near the workbench. If she could find it, she could call for help on emergency channel 9.

Raven stepped off the porch, moving as fast as her injuries would allow. The sting and burn in her chest waged its own war against her, but keeping the image of Spencer in the front of her mind helped her fight back.

Halfway to the barn, she heard the house door swing open and bang against wood siding.

"Raven!" Ana screamed.

Ignore her. Keep moving. Don't look back.

She was thirty feet from the side of the barn when she heard a truck door open, then slam closed behind her.

"I'll kill you!"

Come on, almost there.

With each painful step, Raven kept moving. Fifteen feet to go. Ten.

BANG!

Raven flinched. Barnwood splintered in front of her as a bullet pierced the outer wall. Her ribs pulsed. Her lungs spasmed causing her to cough.

"That was a warning. The next one will ease your pain, Raven."

Up to now, Raven had been trudging along with slow steady paces. But the edge of the barn was so close, four quick steps could bring her to safety. Without hesitating, Raven dug deeper than ever before and ran. Her body hated her for it, but her mind knew it was the only way.

As if on cue, a second shot cracked through the air just as she rounded the edge of the barn.

CHAPTER 63

El Despiadado placed and activated four explosive devices that were slightly larger than the previous ones he had planted throughout the office and stepped to the server room door. Before pulling it open, he looked back at Sofia. He had propped her body so that it sat in an upright position on the floor. Her head dangled in an inhuman angle to one side as the weight of it had no support from the broken bones beneath. Her throat was swollen and had turned a purplish black where his fingers had crushed the life from her. Sofia's hair fell over her face, covering her once beautiful olive-toned skin as it slowly took on a chilling, waxy pallor.

"*Adios, mi amor.*"

El Despiadado brought his hand to his lips and blew her a kiss. With no remorse, he turned the handle of the door, and peered into the hall. It was empty.

Exiting the room, he closed the door with a delicate touch, then made his way down the hall toward the break room. He heard two distinct voices chattering about food, and what restaurants were the best around.

So, you have returned, deputy. I think this will be a most memorable lunch for you and your woman. But where is the third deputy hiding?

El Despiadado reached into his jacket and pulled one of two handguns discreetly holstered on his waist. The HK USP Compact Tactical was the perfect choice for this occasion. Chambered in 9mm, its bullets had both precision and stopping power, and when paired with a threaded suppressor, each lethal shot would be nothing more than a muted whisper in the wind.

The weight in his hands added to the dark, powerful feeling inside of him. He paused to consider his options.

These two are easy targets, ripe for the killing. But the third? If he is near, he may hear the muffled blasts, and most certainly react to the suspicious sounds from the break room. The dead do not always go as quietly as planned. Still, I have the upper hand. No one knows I am here, so why would he think it any more than his comrades acting foolish. If Sofia knew the deputies' unspoken romantic intentions, it would not be a secret to the rest of the house.

El Despiadado paused, then scolded himself.
You are wasting time!

Like a panther on the prowl, he moved into position outside the entrance to the break room. The door was propped open allowing him to hear every word from within. Listening to their conversation helped him visualize where each deputy was in the room.

"So, you say you like Italian?" a male's voice said.

"Who doesn't?" the female answered.

"Have you tried Casa di Amore?"

"Hmmm. That sounds . . ." Her voice trailed off.

Enough of this.

"I'd say it has a rather romantic appeal. Perfect for the two of you," El Despiadado said as he stepped into the room.

"Who are . . ." the male deputy started to say, but the thwump from El Despiadado's gun halted any further inquisition.

The bullet tore through the air and penetrated the deputy's forehead just above his nose. His eyes popped open as if he had an epiphany, though the final thing to enter his mind was the searing tear of a lead, hollow-point bullet. Upon entering his skull, the bullet fragged apart, cutting through brain and tissue without exploding from the back of his head. He toppled out of his chair and was dead before he hit the floor.

El Despiadado turned his attention to the woman.

"Safe journey, mi amor."

The terrified woman's mouth hung open in disbelief. She still held a fork full of food in her hand when El Despiadado pulled the trigger again.

Rocked by the bullet, her head snapped backward, then rebounded toward the table where she came to slump. Blood rained down on the tabletop from a hole between her eyes as her limp head teetered forward like a discarded ragdoll.

El Despiadado stepped close to her, then reached out and stroked the woman's hair.

"To be a star-crossed lover is romance at its finest."

Move!

Reaching into his jacket pocket, he felt the final two devices waiting to have their chance to shine. He removed one and began to place it on the table, then stopped.

"No, this is how I want to remember you," he said, looking at his two victims.

He turned and leaned into the hall. Squinting his eyes, he focused his senses on sounds around the office. The whir of wind in the air vents, the scratch of a radio, a phone clanging on an empty desk—and then he heard what he was hoping to hear; the shuffling of feet heading in his direction.

He stepped into the hallway, then crouched holding his gun pointed at the intersection of the hall and adjoining office area.

"What's going on back here? You two need to get a room already."

A male voice echoed just out of sight but grew louder with each step taken.

El Despiadado whispered to himself, "Now, it is your turn my friend. But first, I wonder, will you beg for your life?"

A male deputy rounded the corner. Without warning, El Despiadado fired. He was not so merciful with this man. Why would he be? He was El Despiadado, The Merciless, and he would have his day.

The first two bullets took out the deputy's legs. One tore into his right thigh, breaking his femur. The other disintegrated his left knee-cap. Should he chance to survive this attack, he would never walk again. But that is not what El Despiadado had in mind. A third bullet struck the deputy in the shoulder. Split second aiming after locating the deputy's hip holster told El Despiadado on which side he should shoot.

In a matter of two seconds, the deputy was on the floor, writhing in agony. El Despiadado stood and walked over to the man.

"I sensed some jealousy in your voice. Did you not approve of the other deputies' budding relationship?"

The deputy did not answer. He rolled back and forth on the floor.

"Maybe you are in too much pain to answer. So, I will answer for you."

El Despiadado knelt next to the man. He tapped him on the forehead with the suppressor, finally gaining the deputy's attention. The whites of his eyes were bloodshot. His pupils looked glazed over. When the deputy laid eyes on

El Despiadado, the terror remained, but a hint of confusion appeared.

El Despiadado looked at his victim's name badge and smiled. "There you are. Hola, Deputy Riley." He arched his eyebrows and gave a nod, as though genuinely pleased to meet the deputy. "As I was saying, I could not help but hear a bit of resentment in your tone. It makes me wonder if you had feelings for the woman, too?"

In desperation, Deputy Riley struggled to reach for his shoulder-mounted radio. El Despiadado stood up.

"Oh, my friend. If you will not talk to me, you will not talk to anyone."

He aimed and fired in one skillful motion, shooting Deputy Riley in the face. The results were more grotesque than El Despiadado had intended. Stepping over the deputy's corpse, he avoided the massing blood spreading out like spilled Big Red cola and headed for the heart of the sheriff's office.

Halfway to the front desk, he spied a separate room, walled in with windows that were covered in old and fading metal blinds. The office door had an inscription that caught his attention: *Sheriff Chance Gilbert, South Brewster County.*

He tried the door and was pleased to find that it was unlocked. Stepping into Sheriff Gilbert's office, he looked around and admired the décor.

"Wow. This Sheriff Gilbert has a taste of the

old country as well as the new. And this desk? Is that oak? Cherry? Perhaps walnut? Such a grand feature for such a powerful man."

El Despiadado walked behind the desk to look at a map of Texas and Mexico that hung on the wall.

"1912," he mused. "This is an old map." He ran his fingers along the painted topography, stopping where the colors had begun to fade. "Indeed, it is artistic. Worthy of any museum I have encountered."

He turned and placed both palms on the desktop as if he were addressing someone in the empty chair across from him. He smiled at a Mexican flag standing in a small desktop display next to an American flag. He removed both flags. He held the Mexican flag before him, saluted, then placed it in his chest pocket. He then looked at the American flag and smirked.

"You think you know so much."

He tossed the American flag onto the desktop. Glancing around one final time, he noticed a stack of papers and a small USB drive sitting atop the pile.

"Oh, the secrets I bet you have and will be willing to share," he said, picking it up. He slipped the USB drive into his pocket and set one of his last two explosive devices in its place. He smiled as he tapped the activation screen, then left the room.

Minutes felt like hours to El Despiadado, and the memories would last a lifetime. He came to the security door, leaned into Sofia's work area behind the plexiglass, and pushed a release button that disengaged the locking mechanism. An industrial buzz sounded out, and the door opened.

As El Despiadado exited the South Brewster County Sheriff's Office, he glanced at the cameras perched in the corners that overlooked the entrance. He paused to smile and took a courteous bow, then pushed his way out the door and headed for the church van.

Hopping in, his blood was rushing. His hands tingled with excitement. He reached into a bag resting on the seat behind him, and pulled out a small, black device with a transmitter antenna.

El Despiadado crossed the necessary wires beneath the dashboard to start the engine and reversed the van out of its parking spot. Before driving off, he pressed the brakes, rolled down his window, and took in the sight that was the South Brewster County Sheriff's Office.

"Dubs," he called out to the corpse on the floor. "You are not going to want to miss this."

With the push of one button, the Sunday that had been so peaceful, so bright and full of possibilities, turned black as if the devil himself had a hand in crucifying this holy day.

CHAPTER 64

Mass at Santa Teresa de Jesus Catholic Church had ended and parishioners milled about on the sidewalks and in the courtyard, but their joyous day took an immediate turn when a sudden explosion rocked the town. Everyone ran for cover.

A shockwave swept down Main Street like a tidal wave surging ashore. Windows rattled. Car alarms were triggered. The traffic light swayed back and forth, and the ground shook as if we had experienced a small earthquake.

I stepped out of the Explorer to have a clear look around and witnessed a small, black mushroom-shaped cloud of smoke billow into the air from the opposite end of Brewster. I looked to my left and saw Chance standing outside of his vehicle. He tore his sunglasses from his eyes. His jaw dropped in an unbelievable look of shock and awe.

Parents pulled their children inside the church. A few people ran to the street to see what had happened. One ran over to us, his face frightened, his voice full of concern.

"Sheriff! What was that?"

Chance snapped out of his temporary daze and reached for the radio. The man from the church was persistent.

"Sheriff?"

I snapped at the man, "We don't know what that was. For your own safety, get inside the church."

The man did not argue with me. Instead, he turned and ran back to the crowd of people rushing back inside the church. In emergency situations, sometimes all a person needs is to be told what to do.

Chance jumped into the driver's seat and picked up his mic. After a brief pause, he rolled down the passenger window.

"Dispatch lines are down."

"Dispatch is down. That doesn't make any sense. What about tactical channels?"

A crackle from my radio provided the answer.

"Sheriff Gilbert? Are you seeing this?"

It was Deputy Bostwick.

Chance lifted his mic and replied. "From a distance. Not sure the origin of the blast yet."

"It's the house, sir. The sheriff's office is on fire."

Chance and I locked eyes. He spoke into the mic.

"Boss, contact Fire and EMS, then get on the horn with the hospital. Tell 'em we may have casualties coming their way."

I jumped in the Explorer, and we sped off. I had always known Deputy Bostwick to be vigilant and act professionally, but the sound of her voice hinted at a touch of worry. I could not help but feel the same. There were deputies on duty. Friends. Family. We had already lost Deputy Santos today. I just hoped that no one was inside at the time of the explosion. I shook my head, thinking *false hope at best.*

Our sirens blared and our lights flashed as Chance and I raced to the scene. I saw Deputy Figgs's unit in the rearview mirror as he pulled in behind us, leaving his patrol to join our response. The radio burst with chatter. Fire and EMS were en route to the scene.

Chance's voice commanded the radio. *"I need all available deputies to sound off all clear."*

There was a momentary pause, then, one by one, Chance's deputies responded.

"Bostwick, check in, clear."
"Figgs, clear, on your six."
"Diego Leo, check in, clear."
"AC Castillo, check in, clear."

Radio silence followed. That was not a good sign. The airy tone of the empty tac-channel lingered like a bad headache until Chance interrupted the void.

"That's not everyone. Who are we missing?"

Sirens echoed along the streets in every direction. Fire trucks from Station One swerved into view, led by a yellow command vehicle.

As we raced to catch up to the pumpers and tanker trucks, I saw two children standing on a sidewalk. They looked to be no more than ten years old. They jumped up and down waving their hands high above their heads as the fire trucks sped by as if this had been a planned parade, and they had a front row seat. They had no idea the gravity and danger we were set to face, but the excitement of the explosion, the lights and sirens in the streets, and the high speeds of the response cars gave them such delight. They continued to wave as we passed by.

A secondary explosion rocked the air, breached our comms, and shook the Explorer as we drew near to ground zero. Smoke careened skyward. The two children dropped their arms and jumped back, looking startled, then seemed to chant for more.

My heart sank. My memories betrayed me, pulling me back into an explosive front-line battle between insurgents and Dragon Company during my last tour in Iraq. The blare of the sirens and the roar of the engines fell silent to me. I squeezed my eyes shut and popped them open again. I found myself still driving the Explorer but could almost taste the gritty smoke, feel the dusty haze, and smell the putrid stench of the dying country in which I had been stationed so many years ago.

"Do not drift," I told myself.

I shook my head, and the siren's scream and engine's growl returned. Moments later, our caravan pulled in line with the fire station's command vehicle. Deputy Figgs was joined by Deputy Bostwick. They positioned their patrol cars across opposite ends of the facing street to create a makeshift barricade while they rolled out perimeter tape to block anyone from venturing too close to the scene.

I stepped out of the Explorer in disbelief of what I saw. With eyes on the destruction, I joined Chance next to his Bronco. We did not speak.

The South Brewster County Sheriff's Office was completely destroyed. Flames shot into the sky from the middle of the burning rubble. Tiny fires littered the parking lot and the area surrounding the main blaze where pieces of building, splintered wood, insulation, ceiling tiles, paperwork, anything that survived the blasts, burned.

Firefighters set straight to work, but the job was bigger than one company could handle. I saw the fire chief, Desmond Arroyo, lean into his command vehicle and remove a handheld radio. His face contorted as he spoke, then listened. He shouted into the mic, then threw the radio into the cab of the SUV. With hands on his hips, he caught my gaze, then walked over to me and Chance.

"This is bad, Sheriff. I've got calls into Lajitas and Presidio, but their response time is at least forty-five minutes at best. My crew will do what they can, but you're probably looking at a total loss."

Understatement of the year, I thought.

"Do what you can," Chance replied, nodding at Arroyo. He then turned to me. "Come."

I followed Chance away from our cars, walking toward the perimeter where Deputy Bostwick was posted. He grumbled as he walked.

"What's on your mind, Chance?"

Chance turned to face me. Tears welled behind his eyes. He huffed, wiped his face, but took a long time before he said a word.

"This . . . this . . . terrible thing. And on a day where we have already lost a fine young man. Now?" he motioned to the destruction behind us. "More are sure to have died. How do we pick up the pieces and recover from this? I have failed the community."

I looked Chance square in the eyes. "One piece at a time, one day at a time." I stepped closer to him, lowering my voice to a whisper. "You told me once that judgment should never be cast until the whole story has been explained. We don't have the whole story, Chance. Mark my words, when we do, I'll be right beside you the whole way. This is in no way your fault." I paused to let my words sink in. "Now, take a minute to collect yourself. I'm going to go speak with Boss."

I stepped away from Chance. He was a brave, compassionate, fair-minded professional, but even the toughest of men have their breaking point. But, if I knew Chance, he would rebound with a resolve fit to lead a nation. Right now, he just needed to be alone.

CHAPTER 65

Light filtered in through separations in the walls where barn wood had warped and holes where bullets had passed. From outside, Raven heard the menacing demands of Ana continue, followed by a shot at the barn. She needed a place to hide, but first she had to find the radio.

"Raven! No one escapes La Sombra Negra. She is a shadow. She will disappear, and when you think you are safe, you're dead. Raven!"

Bang!

Wood splintered just over her head. A new, small beam of light followed the bullet through the barn wall. Raven dropped to the floor. Immediate pain, as sharp as a knife's blade, sliced across her body. She felt for new wounds. She searched her hands for blood. There was none to be found. Her quick reaction to the shot was to blame.

Relieved, but writhing, she crawled across the dirt floor to Flint's work area. She searched the shelves beneath the workbench first. No radio. Reaching up, she grabbed ahold of the counter and pulled herself up. Her breathing scorched her insides, and she sounded like she was in a losing battle with a handful of COPD conditions, but still, Raven pushed on.

"Where is it . . . where is it?"

She searched the shelves and rummaged through drawers, moving at a frantic pace as she heard Ana draw nearer to the barn door. Using the counter as leverage, she moved her body down one side, then back across to the other. Still nothing. With only moments to spare, she whirled around and leaned on the counter. Tears of frustration and fright slid over her cheeks. She gritted her teeth.

"You are trapped. Where are the files? What do you know, Raven? Tell me, and maybe I'll let you live."

Raven's heart could not have beat faster. She wanted to scream out, *what files are you talking about? I don't have any fucking files!* Exhaustion set in as she had spent what adrenaline she had left. She looked to the barn door, then scanned the barn to look for a place to hide. She looked back across the open space and saw a cabinet on the far wall. It called out to her.

"There. It's got to be in there."

Running on pure will, Raven shuffled across the barn to the cabinet. She undid the latch and swung the door open. A smile cracked its way to the surface, and her eyes widened. With no time to spare, Raven emptied the cabinet and hobbled her way to the first stall in the barn. For the first time since this whole ordeal began, Raven had found hope in Flint's cabinet.

CHAPTER 66

Carlos Ruiz-Mata pulled the church van next to a ramshackle garage that stood deep in the brambles of the West Texas terrain. It was a forgotten building left to rot and one day collapse, yet it still held one vital tool for Mata's return to Mexico.

"Here is where we part ways, old friend," he said, looking at Walter Weatherford. His sunken eyes gave Dubs a ghastly appearance, dreadful to look at and nonetheless peaceful. His skin was pale. His knuckles looked skeletal. His cheek bones stretched his leathery face to the point of casting an evil grin. "May your eternal journey take you to far off places where wine flows freely and the breeze smells as sweet as fresh rain." He patted Dubs on the shoulder, then opened the van door and stepped outside.

Mata felt invigorated. Alive. In just a few short hours and a short boat ride, he would be dining in Jose Falcon's Restaurant in Boquillas, Mexico. There, his courier would deliver the Range Rover he had left behind two days ago.

Walking up to the dilapidated building, Mata peered through a cracked, dust covered window. Inside, hidden under a canvas car cover, was a vehicle gassed and ready for the short drive south.

He rounded the building and stepped through an entryway, only to have the door's rusted hinges pull away from the rotten wood, sending the door crashing inward.

"¡*Ay ay ay*! This place is crumbling beneath my fingers. Before I leave, I will help it on its way."

A large rectangular door remained closed at the opposite end of the building. Given what happened with the door on his way in, Mata opted for a more direct manner to get the car out. He pulled the cover away. Dust swirled as did the tarp when Mata tossed it aside. A 1994 tan Isuzu Rodeo came into view. The car beneath was nothing special. An older model ORV, but certainly a less than desirable make and model. He did not need to draw attention to himself on the road, but preferred a vehicle with four-wheel drive should the need to travel cross country arise.

The driver's door was unlocked. He opened it, taking a moment for the stale air within to escape. Satisfied he would not suffocate once inside, he entered the vehicle and found the keys in the center console. He also found a small, unopened bottle of Casa Dragones Tequila.

"How nice. You know . . ." he said to his reflection in the rearview mirror. "Sometimes it is the little things that make all the difference."

He opened the bottle and took a swig. With one draw, he was transported into old Mexico: the soft, floral notes; a touch of sweetness; the smooth flow down his throat; the warmth that followed judiciously behind. It was a pleasurable ending and welcomed surprise for a successfully completed mission.

He replaced the cork in the bottle, then placed it securely between his thighs. He inserted the key into the ignition and turned. The engine hummed to life. Without hesitation or regard for the ancient structure, Mata shifted the Rodeo into reverse, and stomped on the gas. With a jolt, he plowed his way through the brittle wood door. Splinters flew like tiny spears. Larger chunks of wooden wall caved in, narrowly missing the hood of the ORV. Metal rollers pulled from their tracks and fell to the ground as the back half of the building collapsed.

Mata pressed the brakes and slid to a stop. He raised the bottle again, removed the cork, and took another generous taste. Stepping outside, he toasted the building.

"To the aged ones who stand the test of time, only to be forgotten for the deeds they have accomplished. Rest well."

Mata took a third sip, then tossed the bottle into the middle of the fallen structure.

"Like brittle bones, they cracked and fell, and all of us can go to hell." El Despiadado rested.

Wasting no more time, Mata transferred his bags from the van to the Rodeo. He took the last explosive device from his pocket, removed the protective film, and stuck it to the side of the van just above the gas tank. He tapped the surface to activate the receiver.

"*Gracias* Santa Teresa de Jesus Catholic Church. Your van has served me well."

He patted the van with his palm. Two loud, metal thuds sounded out in reply. With one destination left, and Mexico on his mind, Mata loaded up in the Rodeo and drove away from the fallen garage, away from the church van, and away from Walter Weatherford. Reaching into a bag on the seat next to him, he removed the same transmitter used to activate the explosives at the sheriff's office.

"*Vaya con Dios.*"

He pressed the button. Lights and flame filled the air with a cloud of smoke and a thunderous boom that echoed across the barren terrain of West Texas—a final send-off for the esteemed Carlos Ruiz-Mata, El Despiadado.

CHAPTER 67

Ana's face bled from the horse and cowboy's assault, from Raven's flailing punches, from her own teeth biting into her lip, but to La Sombra Negra, it felt and tasted good. Her lips quivered like a snarling beast preparing to gnash and claw at a helpless victim. Sweat dribbled around the trails of blood on her cheeks. Most dripped to her shoulders or to the ground, but some pooled at the edge of her mouth, creating a white film that made her look even more ravenous. La Sombra Negra was a beast, and she felt unstoppable.

The gun in her hand was a necessity, but the knife she held in the other was like a lover in her grasp. It was with that lust that she wished to plunge the cold steel blade into Raven until she told her everything she wanted to know, or until the spark in her eyes was snuffed out. Like an old typewriter wielding its arms to jab at paper feeding around the platen, La Sombra Negra would leave marks on Raven that would tell a tale of dread and suffering.

"Come out, Raven," she said as she entered the barn. "Is this really where you want to die?"

She took a breath, smelling the mix of odors that lingered in the stale air. To Ana, it reminded her of the old days when she would visit relatives in their villages of Colombia. The open stalls, the roaming chickens, the rank effects of living without any semblance of plumbing; to her, the aromas had meaning. To La Sombra Negra, shit smelled the same regardless of where she was hunting.

"Let me make this easy for you. Maybe you do not understand what you have done. It really does not matter, and it will not change what is going to happen to you, but I will tell you anyway." La Sombra Negra moved with purpose, one foot over the other with soft, padded steps. Her head swiveled from side to side. Her eyes investigated every sound or subtle movement within the shadows of the barn. "The files are what led the police to Joe Sinclair. They were stolen and not meant for your eyes. To my employer, you know too much. That is where I come in. Hand over whatever you used to access the files, and I will make sure that your dying friend inside does not suffer any more than you will."

La Sombra Negra stood in the center of the barn. She saw a workbench in front of her. Tools lay scattered about. An old, tan felt hat hung on a hook on the wall. A shop light with a short pull chain dangled above the work area. To the right was a larger door. Tiny creaks sounded out above her. She looked to the rafters when the scratching of scurrying feet scuttled over the hard wooden beams. A large spider web, masterfully woven, though looking as if it had been abandoned for some time, filled the corner of the barn where the walls met the slant of the roof. She looked back to her left. *There.* Her snarling lips curled into a merciless smile.

"I know where you are hiding. Like an animal, you are cowering right now. I can feel it. Do not think the darkness scares me. I am La Sombra Negra. I live in the shadows. I hunt in the shadows. I know where you are."

La Sombra Negra zeroed in on the walkway that ran adjacent to the interior stalls of the barn. The shutters had all been pulled and the far end of the barn was closed creating a monochromatic mix of threaded sunlight and darkened corners. She slid the pistol between her belt and her waist, then leaned over and pulled her left pant leg up to reveal a sheath strapped to her calf. With eyes engaged on the stalls, she pulled a second knife from its hiding place. It was longer in blade than the other and had been crafted with a slight curve of the steel making this the perfect instrument with which to filet.

La Sombra Negra straightened her stance and took one step forward before stopping to revel in sounds so simple, yet so revealing coming from the first stall in the barn. Was it shifting weight? The involuntary movement to ease a sudden pain? The click of a latch? And then she heard something so distinctive, it caused La Sombra Negra to charge.

Squelch . . . static . . . *"ten eighty-nine, South Brewster Sheriff's Office, Rescue seven, Lajitas, enroute. ETA six minutes . . ."*

CHAPTER 68

With trembling hands, Raven lifted the radio to her mouth, pressed the mic button, and spoke. "Cass!"

CHAPTER 69

Watching the firemen work to extinguish the blaze, I leaned against Deputy Bostwick's patrol car and wondered what the hell happened. Chance stood off to one side speaking on his cell phone. Boss was next to me. Her hands fidgeted, but her face was stone focused.

As we watched the scene unfold, another patrol car pulled up and parked on the opposite side of Boss's rig. Deputy AC Castillo hopped out and joined us.

"Hell of a thing," he said.

Neither Boss nor I answered.

"Any word on what caused it yet?"

"No. Too early to tell," Boss replied.

"Investigator Callahan," Castillo said, addressing me. "I heard you spent time in the military. Toured in the Middle East. Iraq, Afghanistan?"

"I did."

"Sir, I did as well. I was a combat engineer. E Company, 45th Engineer Battalion."

"You were with The Thunderbolts?"

"Yes, sir."

"Heard of you guys. Tough outfit. Dangerous work. What's on your mind Castillo?"

"Sir, may I speak freely?"

I nodded, sensing what he had to say may

add more weight to an already heavy situation.

"Thank you. Sir, have you noticed anything strange about the damage? I heard that there has been some speculation that this was caused by a gas leak, or something of that nature, but I don't think that was the initial cause. The secondary explosion, maybe. But the first . . ." Deputy Castillo paused and shook his head as if in total disagreement of the original assessment.

"What are you getting at?" Boss asked.

Deputy Castillo stepped in front of us and pointed at what remained of the building.

"My first impression . . . This was not caused by a gas leak."

Boss walked over and stood next to him. "How can you tell?"

"Well, even from this distance, I can see some telltale signs. The structure itself is what's really catching my eye. Even with the fire, you can see the roof is gone, and only a portion of the walls are standing. The blast radius doesn't square with a standard gas explosion. Gas would create a more uniform, spherical pattern of damage. Here, it looks more directional.

"Directional, meaning what exactly?" Boss said.

"Meaning the blast was channeled. See how one side of the building is more intact than the other? Classic sign of a shaped charge. Also, look at the fire's pattern. It's not spreading uniformly.

If this were an accidental gas line rupture, I'd expect a more even, widespread fire. But the flames are concentrated on the far side of the building. That's not consistent with a simple gas leak."

Listening to his explanations sparked my interest, while giving me a grave feeling in the pit of my stomach. "So, what are we likely dealing with?"

"I'm suspecting high-explosive material. The extent of the damage, the directional debris, and the spalling on the remaining walls—all point to a high-order detonation. This wasn't amateur hour. We might be dealing with comp B or even C-4. I wouldn't rule out a complex triggering mechanism either, something designed to set off secondary explosions or even tertiary ones."

I looked at the scene, at the firefighters risking their safety, at the flames, and at the points Castillo had pointed out. I glanced at Chance. He had just ended a phone conversation and did not seem so happy with whatever had been said on the call.

"Castillo, go find Fire Chief Arroyo. Tell him what you just told me, and that they need to proceed with extreme caution."

"Yes, sir."

"What should I do?" Boss asked.

"Find me the closest National Guard Armory with an active combat engineer division. We'll need their added expertise if this turns out to be the way Castillo explained."

Chance walked up to us trading his frustration for curiosity.

"What's going on, Cass?"

"We may have a bigger problem on our hands."

"Cass!"

I froze. Chance gave me an odd look.

"Did you hear that?" Boss asked.

"That sounded like . . ."

"Raven," I said, cutting Chance off. "Why is she using this frequency?"

I darted inside Deputy Bostwick's patrol car and grabbed the mic.

"Raven. Raven. Come in. Over."

CHAPTER 70

Hearing Cass's voice over the radio was a relief to Raven, but she knew his voice alone would do nothing to help her now. And if she heard him, Ana could have as well. Raven looked at the stall gate, wishing she were anywhere but here.

With the radio still in hand, she heard Ana rushing across the barn, and she was getting closer every second.

"Raven. Did you hear from . . ."

Raven pressed the mic button to speak, interrupting Cass's transmission. She locked the transmitter in place, then set the radio on the ground.

"Cass!"

Screaming his name was the only word she had time to say before the gate to the stall was kicked in.

With knives raised in both hands, and eyes full of rage, Ana had found her.

"Are you ready to . . ."

With a solid squeeze of her finger, Raven pulled the trigger of the Winchester .308 rifle she had discovered with the radio. The shot erupted with a thunderous boom, knocking Ana off her feet, and sent her tumbling out of the stall and out of Raven's direct line of sight. She knew firing the

422

rifle would cause her more pain, but it was better than the alternative. Raven was right.

The force of the rifle's recoil jostled Raven's body causing her to wince in extreme pain. It felt as if all the air had been sucked from her lungs and that every rib in her body was broken. She collapsed on the ground in a breathless heap of agony. Her chest burned as if a raging fire had been set ablaze inside of her. Spent of energy and overwhelmed by her injury, Raven lay helpless on the dirt floor of the stall.

CHAPTER 71

A moment of sheer terror filled me as I listened helplessly to the action happening on the other side of the radio. Deputy Bostwick's stoic look turned to outright concern. Chance's eyes bulged as if he could not believe what he had just heard.

"Raven!" I yelled.

Driven by fear, I whirled around and sprinted to the Explorer. Jumping in, I pressed the ignition button, and the engine roared to life. Shifting into reverse, I pressed the pedal to the floor. The tires peeled and loose gravel clanked inside the wheel wells as the Explorer shot backward. Switching my foot to the brake, I jammed the pedal to the floor. I surged forward in my seat as the Explorer slid to a sudden stop. Not waiting for the backward motion to subside, I shifted into drive, and slammed the accelerator to the floor. With a burst of speed and anxiety the likes of which I had only felt one time before, I tore away from the scene.

With lights ablaze and sirens piercing the air, I raced toward the CR. The angry churn of the engine propelled me faster and faster out of town and down RR170. I tried to respond over the radio but was unable to hail a response. I reached for my cell phone, swerving and almost flipping the Explorer as I jiggled my leg so that my pocket would release it.

Oblivious to everything except the road in front of me and with the phone in my hand, I pressed the phone icon, then selected the number labeled Little Bird, and activated the call.

One ring. Two rings. Three rings. Voicemail.

"Goddamn it!"

I disconnected the call and tried again, ending with the same result.

"Oh baby, please be okay."

I could feel tears fighting to the surface. I did not have time for tears. With a groan and an angry, fearful, yell I pressed my foot as hard as I could on the accelerator and squeezed the steering wheel tight enough to turn my knuckles white.

The road in front of me closed in. The blacktop painted a dark trail through an ever-tightening tunnel as the world around me became a blur. Minutes of desperate driving passed. When I finally approached the turnoff for the CR, I applied the brakes, making sure to maintain a straight path while decelerating to a speed that would handle a tactical turn. My palms were sweaty. My armpits and neck were soaked. With expert timing, I pulled the steering wheel hard to the right. The Explorer slid into the turn. The rear of the vehicle began to slide too far, but a quick thrust of the front wheels into the skid pulled me out of danger and back on a straight line for the ranch.

Dust blew into the air. Gravel seemed to jump out of the way. I sped on at three times the safe speed, but what safe may have meant to others was irrelevant to me.

A few short moments later, I saw the archway at the entrance to the CR. Slowing to an acceptable speed, I drove the Explorer over the cattle guards. The rails sounded pissed, clanging with objection as I bounded past them with rugged authority.

On approach, the CR looked as it always had except for the small, white pickup parked in front of the house. I skidded to a stop, hopped out of the Explorer, and pulled my gun. Stepping to the house, I saw blood spatters on the porch.

"What the hell?"

I crept to the door, positioning myself along the edge of the outer wall, then reached for the knob and opened the door. I leaned and looked, then dropped back into a covered position again. My quick glance saw no immediate threat, and the lack of a retaliatory or verbal response gave me reason to believe the front of the house was safe to enter.

I opened the door and stepped in.

"Oh, shit!"

I saw a woman lying in a heap on the floor. Her black hair was matted with crusted patches of blood. I checked her vitals. Her heart beat at a slow pace and her breathing was shallow, but she was alive. She needed immediate medical care, but I had to find Raven first. I searched the house, noting the distinct aroma of fresh coffee in the kitchen, but did not find anyone else inside.

Exiting the house, I followed the blood trail. With my Glock 17 leading the way, I scanned the yard, as I headed for the barn. As I closed in, I saw small holes in the barn wall. My anxiety wanted to explode through the roof. I leaned on my training to keep my wits and ensure my own safety while I searched for Raven.

I entered the barn, sweeping my gun across the open space between me and the workbench. No visible threats presented themselves. With slow, deliberate steps, I moved into the heart of the barn. It was eerily quiet. The usual scurry of rodents in the rafters or the playful whinny of our new foal Luna were absent.

I felt alone in the barn, but I could not shake the feeling that Raven was somewhere in here.

"Raven." I called out with a sharp whisper.

No reply. I raised the stakes and spoke louder. If someone were going to attack me, it would have already happened.

"Raven?"

I flinched at the sound of something scratching on wood. It was soft at first but gained in intensity. I stepped with caution toward the walkway that led down the row of stalls.

"C . . . c . . . casss . . ."

My heart sank and filled with joy at the same time causing my chest to pound in what felt like irregular beats. I rushed to the stall and looked over the edge.

"Jesus!"

Raven lay in the far corner, her legs tucked into a fetal position. The radio stood by itself near the far wall as if standing guard over her. Flint's .308 rifle lay by her side. I hurried in and slid on my knees next to her.

"Christ. Raven. What happened?"

Raven opened her eyes and looked at me.

"Cruzita?"

"Is that who was inside? Honey, what is going on?"

Raven strained to sit up. I set the rifle aside and reached for her hands to help her.

"Easy," she whispered. "I think I have some broken ribs."

"What?"

"A woman came out here . . ." Raven wheezed, then cringed in pain. I supported her the best I could as she struggled to sit up, but nothing seemed to ease her suffering.

"What woman?"

"I met her yesterday in town. When you left earlier, I needed company, so I called Cruzita and asked her to come out here. Ana, Alma, shit she had so many names. She showed up with Cruzita.

She pretended to be this nice woman at first, then she turned . . ."

"Turned how?"

"Evil. She attacked Cruzita and threatened me. She said I had files and that she would kill me because I looked at them. I don't understand."

"Come on," I said. We need to get you and Cruzita to the hospital. Where is the woman now?"

Raven gasped. Her eyes had softened as we spoke, but now, they bulged in her sockets.

"I shot her. She was just outside the stall."

I looked at the stall gate. A tingling sensation grew in my fingers.

"Let's get you out of here."

"Cass, what is it?"

I looked at Raven as I helped her to her feet.

"No one is out there."

CHAPTER 72

I grabbed the radio and spoke into the mic. "Ten ninety-nine, Callahan Ranch, in need of backup and immediate medical assistance." I released the transmitter and slid the radio onto my belt. Slinging Flint's .308 over my shoulder, I turned to Raven.

"You ready?" I said, standing up.

Raven nodded. She reached out with both arms like a toddler wanting to be picked. I let her grasp my arms, and together we got her to her feet. With ginger steps and my senses on high alert, I led Raven out of the stall.

"I know I hit her," she said.

"You did. Look."

I motioned to a dark splotch of moistened dirt on the barn floor as we moved past it. Beyond it were smaller stains that looked like miniature Jackson Pollock paintings strewn across the walkway. I saw drag marks leading further down the line of stalls but did not see or hear anything more out of the ordinary than the spilled blood.

"Come on. I'm getting you to the Explorer."

"She has a gun, Cass. And knives."

"I have a gun, too. And a badass wife who will protect me if I need her to."

"Don't make me laugh. It hurts too much."

I felt her squeeze my arm as each foot impacted the ground. Every step must have been brutal for her, but she muscled through like a champ.

With the transmitter deactivated, I heard multiple responses to my call for backup, but Chance's voice was the first.

"En route, Cass. Hold on!"

Deputies Leo and Bostwick sounded next.

"I'm code three, EMS is on the way," Boss announced.

"Roger that," Leo replied. "Unit seven, also en route to Callahan Ranch for ten ninety-nine, ETA six minutes."

We reached the barn door.

"Hear that? Help is on the way."

Raven nodded, holding her breath to combat her pain.

Stepping out of the barn and into fresh air, the sunlight itself seemed to carry a gentleness about it, warming my skin. It also shed light on the extent of some of Raven's injuries. Her forehead had a swollen bump that was red at its base. In the center, there was a white indentation the size of a dime, surrounded by a purplish bruise flowing away from the wound that looked like a volcano preparing to erupt. Her arms were covered in scratches. Her knuckles were red and raw. Seeing her in this condition was gut-wrenching. I took the chance and gently pressed my lips to the side of her head as we walked.

"Almost there. Just a little way further."

Sound carries across the barren West Texas terrain, so the faint sound of sirens in the distance added a degree of comfort to a situation that was still far from over. I could feel Raven growing weaker with each step. Her breathing was strained. I wanted to pick her up but knew it would only cause her more discomfort.

Like a true soldier, Raven endured the distance from the barn to the Explorer. I reached for the door handle to open the door, then noticed a swirl of dust rising from the road. The sirens were still too far off for it to be Chance, an ambulance, or either of the deputies. Raven felt my hesitation and looked up as well.

"What is it?"

"Nothing. Just a car on the road. It's not our backup." I opened the passenger door. "Think you can sit?"

"Yeah, I'll try."

I leaned Flint's rifle against the rear door and positioned myself to be a brace for Raven as needed. Raven turned her body so she could ease into the seat but froze before even trying to sit.

"What's wrong? Too painful?"

Raven's face, already drained of color, looked as if she had just seen a ghost.

"La Sombra Negra," she whispered.

"Huh?"

Raven pointed, then screamed. "It's her!"

I whirled around and saw a Hispanic-looking young woman with black hair stagger from the garage side of the barn. Her face was bloodied. She had gashes on each check and her eyes were swollen. Most noticeable was the large, dark stain on her shirt. She held one hand over a severely bleeding wound to her gut, yet still had the crazed ambition to hold a knife above her head.

"Raven!" she yelled.

I pulled my Glock and aimed it at her. The rumble of tires over gravel grew louder, adding to the mix of yells and commands. Sirens filled the air, but were not yet to the CR.

"Put the knife down!"

"I hunt in the shadows . . . I live where light is afraid to go."

"I repeat, put the knife DOWN!"

She moved toward me, her legs carrying her on a crooked path. Her feet crossed over one another. Her body twitched. The curved blade of the knife gleamed in the light. Blood dripped from her midsection like melting chocolate under the hot sun. She rambled words that seemed to come from some outdated horror movie.

"I will slice your skin and pull you into the dark. I am La Sombra Negra."

With eyes locked on her eyes, and my aim center mass, I warned her again.

"If you come closer, I will shoot. Drop the knife and stop where you are."

The cattle guards rumbled as a vehicle approached from the road.

"The woman must die," she screamed.

As if she drew a surge of reserved strength, she lunged forward. She pulled her hand from her stomach and threw a smaller, concealed knife at me. It was a solid but futile attempt on my life. I fired three quick rounds, hitting her in the chest with each pull of the trigger. She toppled backward, landing with a muffled thud on the ground.

With my gun raised and ready to fire again, I approached her. The rumble of an engine and the squeal of brakes sounded out behind me, but I could not take my eyes off the woman until I knew she was dead. Three paces out, I lowered my weapon. Blood seeped from four holes in the woman's chest. My three shots were precise. Tight. Lethal. All centered around her sternum. The fourth hole was large and ragged, a direct result of Raven's self-defense.

I stood over her feeling angry, afraid, out of breath, but most of all, relieved. This part of my living nightmare was over.

"Dad?"

For an instant, my body froze. The voice echoed in my head as if traveling across space and time, hitting me hard and capturing my heart just as powerfully as the first time I heard its wonderful sound.

CHAPTER 73

Breaking through the emotions, I turned around to see Spencer standing in front of Flint's truck, wrapped in Raven's arms. God, how much that must have hurt, but I knew there was no pain too great that would keep her from it.

What started as a walk turned into a run. I could hear Raven sobbing. I could hear my own heart thumping. I could hear the wail of the sirens entering the ranch, but all I wanted to hear was that one special word again. And then, there it was.

"Dad."

I wrapped my arms around both Spencer and Raven.

"Dad, I am so . . ."

"Don't, Spence." I interrupted. "I'm just so glad to have you home."

The melding of emotions was palpable. Tears flowed. Our family embrace was one of which I never wanted to let go, but beneath my arms, I felt Raven start to wiggle free. I let go and saw her lay a hand around her chest as if her arm was cradled in a sling. I saw her look around until her eyes stopped on their target. She took three steps away from Spencer to stand directly in front of Flint. She looked up at him, eyes draining.

"Flint . . . I."

"Oh, Ms. Raven, you don't have to say a thing. I . . ."

Without warning, and to Flint's surprise, Raven wrapped her arms around him and hugged him. She burst into sobs again. Through the tears, she thanked him over and over again. At first, Flint just stood there, but with a glance from me, an unmistakable understanding settled over the both of us. With respectful reception, Flint returned her hug.

I looked at Spencer and placed a hand on his shoulder.

"You okay?"

"Yeah."

"Seems like you'll have quite the story to share."

I could tell by the look in his eyes how deep his remorse was pitted. Fresh tears formed and flowed.

"We'll get to that later."

Raven released her hug on Flint and returned to Spencer.

"Mom, what happened to you?"

Raven looked at me, then back to Spence.

"It doesn't matter. What matters is our family . . ." she glanced at Flint once more. "Our whole family is back together, safe and sound."

The wail of sirens filled the CR. I stepped into view as Chance pulled onto the ranch, followed by an ambulance from Brewster County Hospital. Boss and Leo followed in line. I acknowledged Chance with a wave, and then directed the ambulance to park near us. Boss and Leo pulled in front of Flint's tiny house. Two EMTs, a man and a woman equipped with medical gear, sprang into action, heading for the dead woman's body.

I gave them a whistle. "In the house. One victim with serious head trauma. My wife needs attention as well. This is a working crime scene. Do not approach the body."

The EMTs about-faced. The male EMT headed to the house to check on Cruzita. The female walked over to Raven. Raven held out a hand to stop her.

"Please, help the woman inside first. Her name is Cruzita Vásquez. She's in worse shape than me."

"Ma'am, I . . ."

"Please," Raven pleaded.

Before the EMT left Raven to assist with Cruzita, she reached into her kit and produced a self-activating cold pack.

"At least apply this to your forehead until I can give you a proper assessment." She looked at Spencer. "Can you help her to the back of the ambulance?"

"I can try," Spencer replied.

The EMT turned around and headed for the house.

"Come on, Mom," Spencer said, holding an arm out for her to hold.

"Better let yer dad handle this one, Spence." Flint then spoke to me. "His ankle is busted up pretty bad. Don't think it's broke, but I ain't a doctor."

I helped Raven to the ambulance. Spencer hobbled behind using Flint as a crutch.

When they were both situated, I walked with Flint to join Chance and the deputies around the body. Halfway there, I stopped and placed my hand on Flint's shoulder. He stopped and turned to me. I tried to speak, but the words I wanted to say became jumbled in my throat. I glanced away, then regained eye contact with him.

"Flint . . ."

"You ain't got ta say a word."

"Yeah, I do." I offered my hand to Flint. "Thank you."

Flint took a hold. To me, our handshake was a turning point for us. I always believed trust was earned, and Flint had struck gold.

He nodded, and we let go. Chance was speaking with Boss and Leo when we joined them. He acknowledged me, and changed his tune to ask the one thing we were all wondering.

"How the hell did Raven get wrapped up in all this?" he asked me.

"Still trying to figure that out myself. She said this woman threatened to kill her because she saw some files. Right before she charged me, she called herself La Sombra Negra."

"Black Shadow? Pretty self servin' if ya ask me," Flint said.

"Raven said she called herself different names. Ana. Alma."

"Marta Jiménez," Chance added. "Look. I'll be damned if that isn't the same woman we saw on the video feed at the jail."

My mind went into overdrive as I started to connect events.

"Listen. If this is the same woman from the jail, I can say with a good deal of certainty that she ordered the hit on Luis Lopéz. Deputy Castillo asserts that what happened to the sheriff's office was no accident. What if she planted some kind of device and activated the explosion with a remote detonator, then made her way out here to the ranch."

"Why would she come to the ranch?" Leo asked.

"Son of a bitch," I said to myself. "The drive. The damn USB drive. I'd bet my life that those are the files she was referring to when she threatened Raven. She called herself La Sombra Negra. That doesn't sound like just a nickname. It's more like a call-sign. If you ask me, and this is the city slicker talking, she was sent to tie up any loose ends, otherwise known as Joe Sinclair, and destroy any information that would lead us back to the Camargo Cartel. Think about it. The only two places that the files were accessed were in Chance's office and here at the CR. Goddamn technology led her right to us."

"With the severity of the explosion, there's no way to know if it was her. All the video feeds will be gone," Deputy Bostwick said.

"Not necessarily." Chance scratched his chin. "If I am not mistaken, surveillance footage of the office was not only stored in-house but was also backed up to a remote server."

"Ah, the cloud. What will Bill Gates think up next," Deputy Leo said with sarcastic glee.

"That's another issue," Boss added.

"We can log in and check the feed to see what happened right up to . . ." Chance paused.

A grim quiet fell over all of us. Flint looked confused but kept any questions he may have had to himself. We all looked at the dead woman with differing levels of disgust.

"As for how she ended up like this?" Chance asked me.

Before I could answer, Flint chimed in.

"Plain an' simple, if ya ask me," he said. "Bitch brought a knife to a gunfight."

CHAPTER 74

The CR became a buzz of official activity, but I did not give two shits about any of it. All I wanted was to tend to my family. Period. Chance knew that. They all did. And at the time, that's what they wanted, too.

Deputies Leo and Bostwick processed the scene. Chance contacted the local meat wagon to come collect our uninvited guest and was on the radio with Deputy Castillo being brought up to speed about the ongoing situation at the sheriff's office. The EMTs tended to Cruzita. And Flint? Now that Raven and Spence were safe, he went back to work.

"I got shit ta do," he said with a tip of his hat and a smile.

"Don't you think you've earned a break?" I asked as he walked away.

He stopped and looked at me over his shoulder. "Maybe, but the horses don't. Cows neither. And that damn fence line has been itchin' ta fall over fer weeks. See ya around, Cass." He gave a two-fingered wave and went on his way.

"Well, I'll be damned," I whispered to myself. "Hardest working man in Texas."

Raven waited in the ambulance for the EMTs to bring Cruzita out of the house. She held the ice pack to her head as instructed but kept peeking out of the back of the rig to see if they were coming. Spencer sat next to her with his foot propped up. Whether she knew it or not, Raven rested her free palm on Spencer's shoulder the entire time. I knew it calmed her. She did the same thing when he was a baby sleeping next to our bed. She said the rhythmic vibrations from his bassinet that comforted him had the same effect on her, but I knew the touch of his tender skin on hers was the real reason. Some things never change.

When the EMTs finally appeared, Spencer had to slide out of the way to make room for Cruzita, the gurney, and the attending EMT. I helped him down and steadied him while Cruzita was loaded in the back of the ambulance. Raven was given the option to stay with her or follow behind. Either way, she needed to go to the hospital, too.

She took hold of Cruzita's hand. "I'll ride along."

"We'll be right behind you, Raven," I said.

I blew a kiss to her as the EMT pulled the rear door shut.

"Come on, Spence, let's get you loaded up."

I wrapped my arm around him and showed him that no matter how big he was, he would always be my little boy. Lifting him off the ground, I carried him the few feet to the Explorer, then set him down while I opened the door. With a few grunts and groans, he was able to get in on his own. I closed the door, then motioned to him to hold tight.

Chance walked over to me, shaking his head. "Fires out. No more explosions, thank god. A few hot spots left but Chief Arroyo says they are close to wrapping things up."

"I suppose that's as good a news as can be expected," I said.

"Yeah. You get the family settled. I'm gonna track down our IT guy and figure out how ta access the recordings remotely. When I have something ta share, I'll call."

"Any further word from Castillo?"

Chance lowered his head.

"Only that the firefighters are in the process of removing four bodies from the building. What's left of it anyway."

"Damn. Do we know who is being recovered?"

"Leticia Delgado, Antonio Perez, and Dixon Riley were on the roster. There is one other person that hasn't yet been identified. I'm hearing it may be a fill-in for Shirley Watson, but we'll have to wait and see. Deputy Figgs has been trying to track her down. In the meantime, Dr. Frannie and her team are on the way. Hopefully she can identify the fourth victim. I'm calling in every available deputy to help out. North Brewster County Sheriff's Department and DPS out of Lajitas are sending out three units each to help fill the gaps. This is about to become a media nightmare, and we'll need all the help we can get." Chance paused as the ambulance chirped its horn and began to roll out. "You better hit the road. Keep me in the loop, *amigo*."

"You bet," I said. "As far as the CR is concerned, *mi casa, su casa*. The door is unlocked."

"Well, what do ya know. Yer finally comin' around."

Chance's face widened beneath his trademark smile, all teeth with a bareback-riding, black mustache curling up right along with it.

"Yeah," I said.

On a day filled with so much tragedy, where emotions rose and fell like elevators in a skyscraper, it felt good to smile.

The rumble of the ambulance over the cattle guard at the entrance to the CR was my cue to get moving. I hopped in the Explorer, pressed the ignition, and looked at Spencer.

"You ready?"

"Hit it, Dad."

CHAPTER 75

The drive to the hospital gave me and Spencer a chance to talk. Just the boys. I felt we had a relationship that differed from the typical father-son dynamic. It was the kind where a mutual respect of the other lent its ways to joking, shit talk, open channels, honesty, and when serious conversations were needed, they came easily. We were buds but could drop the drape of friendship to man up and discuss things that were on our minds. We did not always agree, but that is what helped make things stronger between us. It was a unique relationship, and one for which I will be forever grateful.

Spencer told me everything. Had I not heard it straight from his mouth, I might have thought it had been the plot of another Craig Johnson novel. He started with his initial plans with Charlotte being challenged by Lane to his dumb-ass agreement to prove he was not a chickenshit, his words, not mine, and detailed everything until their run-in with a stranger. That's when his words came slower. Emotion tried to take control, but Spencer fought through, telling me with grotesque detail what the man did to Lane, and how he then chased him. I cringed at the very image, but not as much as when I learned how

Spencer had escaped. I knew he was a tough kid, and even though he should have known better than to put himself in that situation in the first place, my admiration for him grew as he explained the measures he took to stay alive. Tumbling down the cliff, fending off the mountain lion, climbing the slab in the dark, in the rain—the description of all he went through clawed at my soul.

He paused during his story, wiped his eyes, and apologized again and again for being so irresponsible, so stupid, before revealing that he had thought he was going to die. He told me that he had recorded a goodbye message to his mother and me. When he offered to share it, I stopped him.

"Better if you delete that, Spencer. You have no need for it anymore."

"Don't you want to see it?"

"It's not that I don't, it's just that whatever you said, whatever feelings you shared, I already feel them, and I always will. Your mother, too. Playing that for her would be devastating, even though you are safe." I rubbed the back of Spencer's neck. "You'll understand one day."

He finished up by telling me that when he heard what ended up being Flint rappelling down to him, that he closed his eyes and prepared to accept whatever fate had in store for him. Flint's gruff voice and strong hands pressing on his shoulders felt like a living dream and were not what he had expected.

The climb out was not as tough as Spencer thought. Flint ascended first, then devised a pulley system with ropes and knots to pull him up the rock.

"I've never seen anything like it, Dad. It was like Flint was some kind of survival genius or military special forces expert. The way he rigged everything together . . . it was amazing."

When I asked him if he could remember where Lane's body was, he said he could, but that it did not matter. He had already told Flint exactly where to look. He explained that they would have been back earlier, but Flint took some time to search for Lane's body. After an exhaustive search, Flint came up empty. Lane's body was not where Spencer had said and was nowhere to be found. The only things Flint did find were the remnants of a few dead cigarette butts. With all the rain, any evidence of blood or remains had been washed away, if not scavenged upon first. The thought of somebody's son disappearing in such a manner, even if it was Lane Jespers, weighed on my heart.

By the time we arrived at the hospital, Spencer had told me the whole story. The gamut of emotions shared during our drive was more than I would ever like to experience at any one time for the rest of my life, but it was important to hear everything from him, no matter how painful.

The ambulance pulled into the receiving bay at the emergency room. I pulled past it and stopped in the opposite lane. Leaving the motor running, I hopped out to retrieve a wheelchair for Spencer and made sure someone was assisting Raven.

The EMTs unloaded Cruzita. The metallic click of the gurney legs extending and locking in place echoed under the ER driveway overhang. She looked like she was in bad shape. With all the tubes sticking out of her and the dried blood and obvious bruising to her head and face, she looked like an MVA (Motor Vehicle Accident) survivor. She remained unconscious as the EMTs brought her in. A male nurse waited with a wheelchair and helped Raven out of the ambulance. I rolled Spencer next to her.

"Hey, Mom."

Raven smiled at him, then reached over and took his hand. Even as we made our way inside the hospital, she did not let him go.

Cruzita was immediately attended to by doctors and was rolled away behind closed doors. Raven waited only a few minutes before being seen by a doctor that looked like he was only a few years older than Spencer. She rolled her eyes at me as she was pushed away. That subtle look told me she was going to be just fine. I stayed with Spencer. After filling out the necessary insurance and billing paperwork, we waited. And waited. The nurses must have seen Spencer pretending to be Evel Knievel in the waiting area, popping wheelies and spinning in circles with his wheelchair, and decided to expedite his examination.

The nurse who brought him to triage shook her head as he described the other tricks he had planned for his new set of wheels. His cuts and scrapes were cleaned and the finger with the missing nail was bandaged making it look three times as big as normal.

"Check it out," he said, laughing and purposefully flipping me the bird to show me the bandage. I shared his humor. The nurse did not. To her relief, an x-ray technician arrived and took him away for imaging. I could tell they hit it off right away when the tech leaned Spencer back in the chair and hauled him away on two wheels as he mouthed the words to "I Can't Drive 55." I had to admit, the tech had taste.

I was directed to the waiting room and was told I would be called when either Spencer or Raven was able to have visitors. The waiting room had magazines on the tables and NFL football playing on a distant TV. I saw it was the Houston Texans, and though they were technically my hometown team, they were not *my* team. I gave up on Houston football the day the Oilers left town. Luv Ya Blue!

The ER was located near a side entrance to

the hospital, but I could see the main entrance from where I stood. To my surprise, walking out of the main entrance was a man I had been meaning to visit. On quick feet, and ignoring the disapproving looks from a number of would-be Karens peering over their secretarial counter, I hurried through the lobby and out the front of the hospital.

"Hey! They finally sending you home?"

The black hand tattoo came into view as Ramón turned around to face me.

"Callahan," he said. "I've been wondering when I'd see you again. We have a lot to discuss. *El que juega con fuego, se quema*. Remember?"

CHAPTER 76

Monday morning on the CR felt like heaven on earth now that everyone I cared about was safe and resting under the same roof. I rose early to clean up the mess of the disastrous fight and expel any remaining memories from the horrible event.

I started in the kitchen, making sure to open all the windows so fresh air could replace the coffee smell that still lingered when we arrived home from the hospital last night. While I had to admit the leftover aroma did smell good, Raven's new aversion to coffee was well justified. When I finished, I moved my housekeeping efforts to the front room. I threw out the couch cushions and began treating the floor where Cruzita and Ana had bled. I removed the broken pieces of cowboy and horse lamp and swept up the shards of porcelain that I could not remove with my fingers. When Raven felt better, we would look into buying a new couch and would replace the floors. She had wanted to install hardwood for a while. No better time than now to make things fresh and new.

The results of Raven's exam and x-rays were painful to hear, but promising. She suffered two cracked ribs from her fight and had a mild concussion. According to her doctors, she should not have been able to move as well as she did for the amount of time she was alone and fighting for her life. Raven's resolve must be made of grade A solid American steel. I challenge anyone who would say otherwise.

Spencer's cuts and scrapes along his back were all superficial. The doctor assured him that his nail would grow back with time and that the tip of his finger would remain sensitive for a week or so. The best news was that his ankle was not broken. He did have a grade 2 sprain which suggested a partial ligament tear and would need to use crutches for a few weeks. The best part, according to him, was that the doctor insisted that he follow a strict R.I.C.E protocol for at least the next few days. Rest, ice, compression, and elevation. That also meant he would have to be waited on, which I knew he would enjoy. He was given a doctor's note to pass on to his college professors because he would miss his classes for the week.

When my chores were done, I stepped onto the porch and sat down. The morning air felt crisp. It cooled my face and made for a pleasant atmosphere on the CR. Fog settled over the ground in the distance, but the rising sun made it appear like a sea of gold was floating right where the Gateway to Paradise began. I was still tired, and there was much to do, so when my cell phone vibrated in my pocket, I knew it could only be one person at this hour, and I was right.

"Mornin', Chance."

"*Buenos dias, amigo.* How is everyone?"

"Like my buddy used to say from the cockpit of the helicopter he flew over in Iraq, 'We'll probably make it.' "

"Good. That's excellent news."

"What's on tap for us today, Chance?"

"I spoke with our IT guy this morning. He wasn't too happy about taking my call so early, but his comfort is the least of my problems. He sent me an email with a link that will allow us to access the video feeds from the office. How would ya feel about me dropping by so we could have a look. You'll be at home if anyone needs anything, an' we can still get some work done."

"Sounds good, Chance."

"I'll be there in an hour."

I got up, took a look at the golden swath out on the CR one last time, and headed inside to find Spencer sitting at the kitchen table.

"Didn't hear you get up, bud. How you feeling?"

"Stiff. Sore. Glad to sleep in a bed."

"Hungry?"

"As a mountain lion."

I straightened my stance and gave him a look.

"Too soon?" he said.

I made pancakes and bacon, of which he consumed six of each, and offered him a glass of milk or a cup of tea.

"Tea? What about . . ."

"Coffee? No longer on the menu, Spence."

"OK, what about hot chocolate?"

"What? You think this is Cracker Barrel?"

"Yer right, I mean, after everything I've been through and all, I . . ."

His sarcastic pity party was not fooling me. I threw a kitchen towel at him, hitting him square on the face. It flopped over and came to rest on his head.

"Nice," he said.

He pulled the towel off his head and smiled when he saw the can of Swiss Miss in my hands. We shared a laugh as I prepared his drink.

He blew the steam away from his cup the way he did when he was four years old and had to have a drink just like the grownups. The mental image of him sipping his first black, no cream, no sugar coffee was something I would never forget. It would have been a top three pick on *America's Funniest Home Videos* had we been filming him at the time. But in true Spencer fashion, when the cringey nature and twist of his face corrected itself, he went in for another taste. The boy always wanted to grow up too fast. Raven switched his cup for a mug of hot chocolate, and the rest is history.

A short time later, I heard a car pull in front of the house. Spencer heard as well.

"Someone's here."

"Yeah. Chance and I are going over some things at the house today. There's a real shitshow going on in town, and we have work to do. Plus, I'll be around if you or your mom need anything."

"Cool. Maybe I can help?"

If he could, I knew he would, but I suggested he relax in his room or on the porch for a while. Chance and I were going to take over the kitchen.

"All right," he said. "But if you need me, you know where to find me."

With that, Spencer grabbed his crutches and dare-deviled his way out of the kitchen in two long arching strides. I cleared the table, but before I had an opportunity to meet Chance at the door, he was standing in the kitchen.

"Spencer let me in," Chance said. "Does the boy even know he is injured?"

"Doubtful. The kid's a machine."

"*Más fuerte que un toro.*"

I gave Chance a curious look. "Something about a bull?"

"*Ay yi yi.* And here I thought we were getting somewhere. It means he is stronger than a bull. For you, maybe I teach the term dumb as an ox?"

"Careful," I said, shaking a playful fist. "Don't crap where you eat."

"No, no. I never. Let's get to work."

Chance placed a bag on the table and took out a laptop computer. He fired it up, connected to the Wi-Fi, and opened an email, subject line: LINK TO ARCHIVED VIDEO_SBCSO_ SKYSTREAM VAULT. Within the email was a link and instructions explaining how to navigate, review, and download any .mp4 or .mkv clips we needed for our investigation.

"This is the part of the job I hate," I said.

"You and me both, *amigo*."

Chance clicked the link and was directed to a page within SkyStream Vault to the SBCSO account. He logged in and scanned the page until he found the corresponding date for files we needed to view. Placing the cursor over the date 10/01/2023, he clicked the file. A small pop-up box appeared as a video screen that showed multiple views from cameras placed throughout the office. It displayed buttons for play, rewind, fast-forward, pause, and frame-by-frame toggle. There were also other advanced technical options that could enhance or print still frames and activate high-res, slow motion playback.

Chance selected the first camera that covered the main entrance to the sheriff's office. At first, nothing out of the ordinary had been recorded. Chance toggled forward until we noticed activity in the waiting room.

"This could be something," Chance muttered.

A tall man with black hair wearing black jeans and boots and a black sport coat entered the lobby and walked over to the reception desk. The cameras captured every movement. The way he sauntered through the lobby, how he leaned on the counter, crossing his feet, his overall flaunting demeanor suggested he was flirting with the receptionist.

"We ever identify the fourth victim?" I asked.

Chance paused the playback.

"Yes. Her name is Sofia de la Cruz. She's the one our mystery man is speaking to right now. We learned late yesterday that Shirley Watson had asked de la Cruz to cover for her. Turns out former Deputy Watson had more important things to do with someone other than her husband this weekend."

"Former deputy?"

"Hell yes. I fired her on the spot. Watson's poor choices cost the lives of four individuals. No way should that de la Cruz girl have been working the counter without proper training. Watson knew that. She was just looking for an easy way out, and in doing so, betrayed more than just her husband with this debacle. Sofia de la Cruz was just a stand in, and now she is dead."

Frustrated, Chance pressed play, and the video stream continued. Only a few moments passed when we caught a glimpse of the man's face. He looked away from the counter and seemed to glance at the lobby camera. I had hoped we could identify him from that shot, but his brief movement and the distance away from the camera caused his face to look blurry.

We continued to review the footage. I had Chance pause the film again as de la Cruz activated the security door to allow the man through and pointed out he had stuck something to the exterior wall.

"See that? Could that be a small incendiary device?" I said.

We watched Sofia lead him through the office. The man's mannerisms looked calm. Sofia looked nervous, but not uncomfortable, leading me to believe he had turned on a degree of Latin charm. Her subtle smiles added to my suspicion. When they disappeared into the server room, we discovered that there was no camera mounted inside. After a few moments, and the man reappeared alone in the hallway and produced a gun, we discovered something else. Chance stopped the playback.

"All this time I have been waiting to see the woman we hauled off yesterday. Who the hell is this man?"

Seeing the man holding the gun, then adding a suppressor to the barrel made me sick to my stomach. I knew what we would see next. From the look on Chance's face, he knew as well. As much as I did not want to watch, it was our job. I shared a look of angst and anger with Chance.

"Keep going."

He pressed the play button, and we continued to watch, becoming more horrified with each clip. Each silent burst from his weapon, the agonizing looks on the deputy's faces, each moment we watched that man in the building, our house, made me want to do more to him than simply place him in handcuffs. The clips showed a living nightmare, a horror show like I have never seen nor ever want to see again.

As the man returned to the front of the office, I was wrong to feel that I had experienced the worst of what we had seen. We watched as he approached the exit, then paused to stare directly into the camera. He smiled and took a bow before walking out of the building.

"Jesus Christ!"

I stood up and slid my chair back. The screeching sound of its feet dragging along the kitchen floor was as unsettling as the growing mass of angry butterflies in my stomach. My quick movement startled Chance.

"What is it, Cass?"

I leaned over Chance to take over the controls of the video feed and toggled the frames back until we looked the man in black, the killer, in the face, then paused the stream.

"That's the son of a bitch who bought my coffee yesterday morning. I talked to him. I looked him in the eyes, told him my name, thanked him, and even shook his goddamn hand!"

I stood up fuming and walked away from the table.

"Cass, are you sure this is the same man?"

"Hey . . . I've seen that guy."

I turned around to see Spencer balancing on his crutches near the entrance of the kitchen. He was well behind Chance but had a clear view of the laptop screen from where he stood.

"What are you talking about, Spencer?"

"That guy," he said, pointing at the screen. "He's the guy that killed Lane. He's the one that chased me into the canyon."

I walked around the table to Spencer and looked him in the eyes. I know he saw the anger in me, the frustration, but what he did not see was my relief. I wrapped my arms around him and squeezed. Spencer may have known he had been in considerable danger, but up until right now, I had no idea how lucky he was to be alive. The man on the video feed was a professional. He knew how to kill. He had all the right tools, all the right training.

Spencer held on to me, tightening his grip, and asked, "Did he cause the explosion? Did he get away? Are we safe?"

I held onto my boy and whispered into his ear.

"Don't you worry, son. I promise he will never hurt you or anyone we care about again."

Spencer pulled away from me, his eyes wide with concern.

"How do you know that?"

I could feel Chance close in behind me. He knew what I was going to say. I gripped Spencer's biceps and spoke with a calm, serious voice.

"Because Spence. I am going to find that son of a bitch and stop him myself."

CHAPTER 77

The airy hush coming from my phone after being placed on hold was a pleasant contrast to the nasal voice of the switchboard receptionist at the El Paso FBI field office questioning me as to why I felt speaking with FBI Special Agent Thomas Zuñiga was urgent. I sat with Chance at my kitchen table, speaker engaged, and waited to be put through. As we sat, I ran through scenarios in my head that could lead me to find the man who attacked my son and killed my friends.

The phone beeped to life. "Special Investigator Cass Callahan. I might have known you would call."

"Great," I said. I was in no mood for games. "I'm with Sheriff Chance Gilbert. We're sending you a screenshot of a man who attacked the sheriff's office in Brewster yesterday. Also, a photo of a woman. There are no records on the man or the woman, but we are under the assumption that they may have had ties to one of the cartels. We need IDs as soon as possible."

"I heard it on the news last night. It's a terrible thing. My condolences to you and the deceased."

"That's good and all, and we appreciate the sentiment, but what we need is information."

"What makes you think that the cartels are

involved? It would be too risky for any one of them to wage such an attack on American soil," Zuñiga said.

"I don't think you heard me," I said. "It did happen. We have reason to believe that the woman ordered a hit on Joe Sinclair. You remember him. She called herself *La Sombra Negra*. Then, I don't know how, but she knew that the files on the USB drive I found during the Sinclair investigation were accessed at my home. *My home!* She found her way out here and attacked my wife, then threatened to kill her if she didn't hand them over."

I paused. The line remained quiet. I had spoken with a raised, excitable voice. I shifted gears, eased my tone, and continued.

"Special Agent Zuñiga. Thomas. These are bad people. We killed La Sombra Negra in a standoff, but the man got away."

I gave Chance a *what do you think* look while we waited for a reply. He pursed his lips and shrugged. Zuñiga finally responded.

"Send the photos to me. I will run them through our database and see what comes up."

I attached the photos to an email and sent them while we were still on the phone. I had expected more interference from Zuñiga, especially because the files I mentioned were the ones I had yet to send him, and now, never would. Silence ensued, but our call had not been disconnected. I could hear his fingers tapping a keyboard, pause, then continue before pausing again.

"Cass," Zuñiga said. "These two pictures of the man and the woman . . . protocol dictates that I should thank you for the information and make a veiled promise to get back to you."

Chance spoke up. "What are you implying?"

"I am implying that I am looking at the photos right now and already know who they are. But . . ." he let his voice trail off like a storyteller banking reaction of a cliffhanger.

"But???" I said, my voice breeding of impatience.

"Their identities are classified. There are higher level operations in play, and I am unable to tell you more."

I stood up, knocking over my chair in the process. My nostrils flared, and I flexed my fingers to try and alleviate my frustrations.

"Special Agent Zuñiga," Chance began. "You must understand what we are dealing with down here. We have multiple fatalities, a completely destroyed sheriff's office, and a county on edge and already overrun with issues that I will not get into. There must be something you can tell us."

"Sheriff Gilbert, this is bigger than you and me."

"Horse shit!" I said, slamming my hands onto the table. The laptop jostled and my phone flipped over. I straightened the phone and had my say.

"Zuñiga, you once asked me if I would join your team. *Kill Hydra*, I believe you called it. Help you go after the Camargo Cartel. You said, 'it's going to take more than one man to kill the beast.' Hell, I kicked Agent Sharp's ass for accusing me of not doing anything to fight a so-called war going in my backyard, so hear me now when I say this, sign me up. Give me a team, and I will track this murdering bastard and anyone who gave the kill order down."

"What makes you think I haven't changed my mind about you, Cass? More importantly, what changed yours?"

"I could give you a load of bullshit and say that I realized it was my duty, or that after careful consideration I might have made a mistake turning you down in the first place, but I won't. These motherfuckers came after my family. They came onto my property. They invaded my country. You wanted a guy like me fighting the cartels. I'll go after them with you or without you. I was not all in before but believe me when I say I am now."

Silence emanated from the phone, from the kitchen, from the house. I stood up, took a breath, and looked around. Chance sat back in his chair; a somber look swept over him. Spencer balanced on his crutches in the entryway to the kitchen. Raven stood beside him. Both wore looks of concern, but Raven showed more on her face.

I had always promised to protect her, no matter what, and felt that possibly I had let her down over the incident in Houston.

When we locked eyes, I drew a strength from her I never would have expected. In the past, when situations were tense and danger filled my job at every turn, Raven absorbed it all. I could read her worrisome emotions with a clarity that only a soul mate would know, and I carried that worry with me. Now, when she met my gaze, her eyes sharpened into a look of untamed intensity. It was a silent, unspoken permission, a green light to find the man in black and bring the Camargo Cartel to its knees, no matter the cost. Kill Hydra.

ACKNOWLEDGMENTS

First and foremost, I extend my deepest gratitude to the courageous men and women who have devoted their lives to the field of law enforcement. Your commitment to upholding justice and safeguarding the welfare of our communities, schools, counties, and nation is nothing short of heroic. Your sacrifices—both seen and unseen—do not go unnoticed or unappreciated. May providence safeguard you as you continue your noble mission of serving and protecting. Thank you for your extraordinary service.

Many thanks to my friend and Sergeant (Ret), Fort Bend County Sheriff Office, Carlos Castillo. He continues to give insight into a wide range of information about law enforcement, weaponry, gun safety, and situational job procedures that help make the situations within the Cass Callahan novels as realistic as possible within a fictional setting. I would also like to thank Master Chris Martinez for sharing his wisdom both on and off the Taekwondo mat.

My family has played vital roles in my writing as well, and as always, deserve to be recognized. My parents, Jack and Margie, my sister, Julie, my sons, Ryan and Jackson, and my wife, Joellan. Thank you for your daily support as I continue my writing journey. Love you all.

ABOUT THE AUTHOR

Chris Mullen is an accomplished and award-winning author, recognized for his captivating storytelling and literary talent. Hailing from Richmond, Texas, he is a proud graduate of Texas A&M University. With a career spanning twenty-three years in education, Chris has been a dedicated teacher in both Kindergarten and PreK, cultivating his passion for storytelling and nurturing young minds. In 2019, he received the prestigious Connie Wootton Excellence in Teaching Award—a testament to his commitment to education and his profound impact on students' lives, bestowed upon him by the Southwest Association of Episcopal Schools (SAES). It was during this time that the idea for his young adult western adventure series, Rowdy, was born.

The first installment, *Rowdy: Wild and Mean, Sharp and Keen*, was met with critical acclaim and earned the esteemed title of 2023 Independent Press Distinguished Favorite. Notably, the third book, *Rowdy: Dead or Alive*, stands as a 2023 Will Rogers Medallion Finalist. Garnering numerous awards, Chris's Rowdy series continues to captivate readers of all ages, cementing his place as an author in the young adult western genre.

When he's not weaving stories, you can find Chris honing his craft in local coffee shops, pizza places, or even the neighborhood grocery store. Currently, he is hard at work on an adult, contemporary western mystery series for Wolfpack Publishing.

To connect with Chris, visit his website www.chrismullenwrites.com, where you can access updates, behind-the-scenes glimpses, and much more. Additionally, be sure to follow his Amazon Author Page and catch him on various social media platforms—Facebook, Instagram, Threads, and TikTok @chrismullenwrites, as well as on Twitter @cmullenwrites. For any inquiries or heartfelt messages, feel free to reach out directly at chrismullenwrites@gmail.com.

Center Point Large Print
600 Brooks Road / PO Box 1
Thorndike, ME 04986-0001 USA

(207) 568-3717

US & Canada:
1 800 929-9108
www.centerpointlargeprint.com